Canadian Classics

An Anthology of Short Stories

Critical Commentary by
John Metcalf
Ottawa

Bibliographical and Textual Research by
J. R. (Tim) Struthers
Department of English
University of Guelph

McGRAW-HILL RYERSON LIMITED
Toronto Montreal New York Auckland Bogotá Caracas Lisbon
London Madrid Mexico Milan New Delhi Paris San Juan
Singapore Sydney Tokyo

Canadian Classics
An Anthology of Short Stories

ISBN: 0-07-551332-3

1 2 3 4 5 6 7 8 9 0 D 2 1 0 9 8 7 6 5 4 3

Sponsoring Editors: Catherine A. O'Toole and Anne Louise Currie
Production Editor: Kathleen Price
Permissions Editor: Norma Christensen
Cover & Text Design: Dianna Little

Cover: David Milne 1882–1953
Relaxation 1916
Watercolour over pencil on paper
38.5 cm x 46.7 cm
McMichael Canadian Art Collection
Gift of the Founders, Robert and Signe McMichael
1966.16.24
Reproduced under license of The David Milne Estate, © 1993.

Printed and bound in Canada by John Deyell Company Limited.

Canadian Cataloguing in Publication Data

Main entry under title:

Canadian classics
an anthology of short stories

ISBN 0-07-551332-3

1. Short stories, Canadian (English).* 2. Canadian fiction (English) – 20th century.* I. Metcalf, John, 1938– . II. Struthers, J. R. Tim, 1950–

PS8329.C35 1992 C813'.54 C92-094593-7
PR91997.32.C35 1992

Care has been taken to trace ownership of copyright material contained in this text. The publishers will gladly take any information that will enable them to rectify any reference or credit in subsequent editions.

Contents

≈

About the Editors

≈

John Metcalf has won wide acclaim as one of Canada's finest writers, critics, and editors. Co-founder, with Hugh Hood, of The Montreal Story Tellers at the beginning of the 1970s, and a resident of Ottawa since 1981, Metcalf has produced several volumes of fiction, including *The Lady Who Sold Furniture*, *The Teeth of My Father*, his *Selected Stories*, and *Adult Entertainment*. In addition, he has published three books of criticism, *Kicking Against the Pricks*, *What Is A Canadian Literature?*, and, with Sam Solecki and W. J. Keith, *Volleys*. Metcalf has also prepared a large number of ground-breaking anthologies and textbooks — among them, *The Narrative Voice*, *Making It New*, and *The New Story Writers*. Together, John Metcalf and J. R. (Tim) Struthers have prepared the landmark collections *Canadian Classics* and *How Stories Mean*. Through his involvement with various Canadian publishers over the years, and in particular as senior editor for The Porcupine's Quill since 1988, John Metcalf has arranged for publication of many works by his contemporaries, by earlier modern writers, and by talented new writers.

J. R. (Tim) Struthers has won wide recognition for his efforts as a bibliographer, interviewer, critic, editor, and publisher. He completed a Ph.D. in English at The University of Western Ontario with a specialization in Canadian literature, was awarded a Social Sciences and Humanities Research Council of Canada post-doctoral fellowship for study of the works of Hugh Hood, then joined the Department of English at the University of Guelph on July 1, 1985. He is the editor of three critical books: *Before the Flood*, a volume of criticism on Hugh Hood; *The Montreal Story Tellers*, a collection of autobiography and criticism; and *New Directions from Old*, a volume of criticism on Canadian short fiction. He has also prepared the two-volume anthology *The Possibilities of Story* and, with John Metcalf, the collections *Canadian Classics* and *How Stories Mean*. As an editor for The Porcupine's Quill and as the publisher of Red Kite Press, J. R. (Tim) Struthers has arranged for and supervised the publication of a considerable number and variety of books of criticism and literature.

About the Photographers

≈

Paul Orenstein is a photographer working and living in Toronto. His photographs have been used by a wide range of clients in advertising and publishing. He has also exhibited his work in group and solo shows. "Although there is great diversity in the subject matter and uses in the work, I like to feel that there is a connection between my subjects and myself that the viewer can relate to. Almost like recognition."

Photographs of Hugh Hood, Alice Munro, Audrey Thomas, John Metcalf, and Margaret Atwood courtesy of Paul Orenstein.

Sam Tata was born in Shanghai on September 30, 1911, and immigrated to Canada in 1956. He was honoured by CAPIC (The Canadian Association of Photographers and Illustrators in Communication) with the presentation of their Life Achievement Award in 1990. Ryerson Polytechnical Institute's Film and Photography Department invited him to participate as a guest lecturer in the Kodak Chair Lecture Series 1990–1991. In 1992, he was honoured by Montreal's photographic community at the Canadian Centre of Architecture.

Photographs of Mavis Gallant, Norman Levine, Leon Rooke, Clark Blaise, and Ray Smith courtesy of Sam Tata.

Introduction

≈

A literature is a relationship between books and readers. A literature is rather like a conversation. It is a conversation not only with those around us but also with those who have gone before us. Through their books the dead live on with us and are a living part of what we are and do. This is what a tradition means. From the vast family of writers, some will emerge as classics; we hear their voices more clearly than others. Their works provide the standards of comparison we need to discuss and to measure later writing.

Without classics a literature has no foundation. But without readers there can be no classics. Readers must engage constantly in analysis and evaluation. This anthology presents two stories each by ten writers whom we think might in time come to be considered classics. The inclusion of two stories each by ten writers is meant to involve readers in close comparisons between stories by the same writer and between stories by different writers. Without comparison, a real grasp of a writer's achievement is impossible.

Ernest Hemingway's first collection of stories, *In Our Time*, was published in 1925. When I was in secondary school in England in 1955 — that is, only 30 years later — Hemingway was required reading. Some of his best-known stories come from that volume and *Men Without Women* (1927) and *Winner Take Nothing* (1933). As a schoolboy in a foreign country, then, I was reading these stories within 30 and 28 and 22 years of their publication. Lately I've been thinking about these dates and time spans and I've been applying them to our situation in Canada.

The writers in this anthology have been publishing for 25 or 30 years or more yet their stories are not accepted and established in Canada in the way that Hemingway's are in the United States and elsewhere. We have been familiar for years with the stories of such writers as Ernest Hemingway, William Faulkner, and Eudora Welty. Many readers could doubtless identify the authors of "Hills Like White Elephants", "A Rose for Emily", and "Why I Live at the P.O." but how many readers could identify the authors of "Irina", "A Small Piece of Blue", and "Going Out as a Ghost"? Why have the Americans and the British classics while we do not? Canadian writers are producing work just as rich as that produced by writers who are acknowledged as classics. We only need to recognize and to appreciate our own.

We all know what the word 'classic' means but defining a classic is difficult. Obviously a classic must be popular but with how many people? If simple numbers were the key, then our classics could be determined by checking bestseller lists. Nor does acceptance by literary critics and universities and school systems necessarily define a classic; many books which have received the imprimatur of literary and intellectual establishments have come to be seen 30 years later as embarrassingly inadequate. John Steinbeck, for example, once universally admired and awarded the Nobel Prize for literature in 1962, has failed to become a classic. Is it because he was once too popular, too easy to understand? Is it because the politics in his books are too obviously black and white? Is it because the books are sentimental, soft in the centre? Is it because his use of language is undemanding or inadequate?

It also happens that writers who were largely unknown in their lifetimes come to be more widely respected after their deaths; Nathanael West in the United States and Ronald Firbank in England are two examples of that phenomenon.

All this is to suggest, then, that when we are thinking about classics, one of the factors we must pay attention to is time. Although I was reading Hemingway as a 'classic' barely 30 years after publication, I think that Hemingway was rather a special case, a writer of genius who imposed himself uniquely. The one constant in literary history is the way reputations diminish and decline. What seems 'classic' to one generation is for the next unreadable. Consider what time has done to the once mighty reputations of Sir Walter Scott and Robert Louis Stevenson and — far closer to us — H. G. Wells and Aldous Huxley and all those American novelists whose work just 10 years ago was found everywhere and was everywhere discussed... you know who I mean... oh, the names for the moment escape me.

My dictionary defines 'classic' as "a literary or artistic work generally recognized as of the highest excellence"; this definition seems to raise more questions than it answers. What is 'the highest excellence'? How general is 'generally'? Who is doing the recognizing?

I'm not brave enough to attempt a detailed definition of the word 'classic' but I'll try to describe some of a classic's characteristics.

Firstly, it will have lasted for a considerable period of time. As a rule of thumb, I'd say that we need to have known and lived with a writer's work for about 50 years before we can call it classic. The winnowing process seems to fall into two periods of about 25 years each, the second period revising the estimations of the first. The second stage is hard on reputations; Morley Callaghan has scarcely survived it. Most of the writers included here are just finishing the first stage. This anthology offers readers an opportunity to assess these writers as they enter the next stage.

Secondly, a classic will be a book that is actually read, that is actually the property of readers who are neither teachers nor students. A classic will have a life outside the school or university. *Gorboduc, or The Tragedy of Ferrex and Porrex* is a play known to all students of drama but it is not a classic. *Hamlet* is. *Gorboduc* is the necessary stuff of history; *Hamlet* we have made our own.

Thirdly, a classic cannot be exhausted, cannot be used up. We are able to return to it again and again deriving from it new pleasures, new depths of experience, new sustenance.

Fourthly, a classic defies being *used for* non-literary purposes. It is difficult to use a classic to serve some simple social purpose, because classics tend to be rich and complex and to have a mysterious emotional life which defies reduction.

Fifthly, a classic will usually retain some difficulty. It's a truism that we grow into difficult work but classics will always challenge us. Joyce's *Ulysses* has grown easier with time but will never be 'easy'. It is also probable — and in the twentieth century nearly certain — that classics will be formally innovative.

Lastly, a classic will embed itself into the language, thought, and culture of a people. A classic will be quoted from or referred to and it will be valued by other writers as a mine to quarry from or as a touchstone.

I feel quite comfortable with the idea of 'classics'; I've read them, could list dozen upon dozen, know which ones I'd choose as the core of my personal library. The idea of 'classics' is, for me, entirely *practical*; they're a source of continued pleasure. Some literary theorists, however, maintain that because reputations fluctuate and judgements are often problematic, choosing classics is a futile activity. They argue that literary judgements are entirely subjective and that 'classics' are simply those books of which now-dead elites approved because the books mirrored their prejudices of class, power, and gender. As a result, much 'classic' literature is simply dismissed.

Those who say that all matters aesthetic are entirely subjective, that there are no grounds for claiming that one book or art object is better than another, are the sort of people antique dealers *dream* of encountering. I agree entirely with Professor W. J. Keith of the University of Toronto who, in his recent collection of essays *An*

Independent Stance, remarks that "literary criticism and evaluation are ultimately inseparable". Literary criticism is not a science but an art and we are bound to make misjudgements but that should not be an excuse for evading evaluation. To reject evaluation is to abdicate intellectual and emotional responsibility; to reject evaluation — in my view, an impossibility anyway — is to refuse a relationship with the book or painting. Writers and artists themselves have little patience with airy theorizing; they are daily evaluating what they do against whatever vision of greatness they have forged for themselves from their artistic inheritance. Classics are their constant companions.

While literary criticism and evaluation are an art and therefore personal and subjective, is it reasonable to say that one person's opinion is therefore as good as another's? It is easy to decry connoisseurship in a scientific age and to point out how x-rays, carbon-14 dating, and thermoluminescence tests have punctured the pretensions of some of the experts but it is a mistake to denigrate what the connoisseur brings to looking at a painting or a pot. The connoisseur is steeped in the history of art and brings a sharp, trained eye. The connoisseur knows for every artist characteristic patterns of brushwork, how this one handles drapery, how that one typically paints lace. The connoisseur has a deep knowledge of wood, linen, canvas, and pigments. The inferior, fudged, or outright faked rarely escapes the connoisseur's detection.

All this knowledge and experience is not purely subjective; if I were about to buy a Renaissance painting, I'd rather have the opinions of Bernard Berenson or Sir Kenneth Clark than those of my next-door neighbour. Literary critics — good ones, anyway — are connoisseurs of books and bring to their judgements a lifetime of experience. They are not infallible but their evaluations are definitely worth listening to and well worth comparing with our own experience. *Comparing* — and obtaining the knowledge necessary to do so intelligently — is the key to making well-founded evaluations.

What ought we to bring to our evaluations? How would we set about choosing a 'classic' short story when the very word is so difficult to grapple with? What would we need to know to propose a Canadian classic?

We would first need to know the history of the short story as a form. We would have to read the great Russians — Gogol, Turgenev, and Chekhov in particular. Then we would have to read Maupassant and Babel, Mansfield and Joyce. A long line of American writers would await us: Sherwood Anderson, Ring Lardner, Ernest Hemingway, William Faulkner, Scott Fitzgerald, Eudora Welty, Caroline

Gordon, Flannery O'Connor... And then the writers of the succeeding generation — writers like, say, Donald Barthelme — who gave stories new shapes and new life. We would need to read widely among our contemporaries, too, in order to get a feel for who is now doing what with form and language.

But to prepare ourselves to choose a classic demands far more than merely reading in the history of the form. We need a knowledge of the literary contexts of these writers. We need to read widely in other forms, in poetry, novels, and drama. We need to develop some understanding of rhetoric and technique. But above all we need to become fully sensitive to the subtleties and nuances of language; we need to have come to a love of words and their deployment.

When we've qualified ourselves to judge, we have to start making conscious comparisons. We must select a story by, say, Clark Blaise and compare it with other Blaise stories. Which Blaise story is the best from *A North American Education*? Which is the best from *Tribal Justice*? How do these stories compare with the stories in *Resident Alien* and *Man and His World*? Which of the stories can we not exhaust? Which remain mysterious? Which ones *will not go away*?

And then we must make more testing judgements. Can the stories we are proposing stand comparison with acknowledged classics? We must compare a Blaise story with a Joyce story or with a Hemingway story. Is this a *silly* comparison? Does the comparison render the Blaise story inadequate? I think Blaise more than stands the test.

(It may be that a story by, say, Alice Munro, seems improbably better than a story by, say, Katherine Mansfield. In most cases, that would be a judgement I'd agree with. But it is important to understand how deeply original and fresh both Katherine Mansfield and Ernest Hemingway were when they burst upon the scene. They might now appear a little faded simply because we're so familiar with their work and have been for so long. The techniques of Mansfield's "The Daughters of the Late Colonel" may seem old hat today but that is only because the story was so pervasively successful; her fresh innovations in 1920 have become our literary and academic foundations.)

Earlier I asked why the Americans and the British had classics while we did not, why Canadian stories of the first rank have not secured a place for themselves with Canadians in the way that American stories have with Americans. There are probably many reasons. Perhaps Canadian society is not capable of discerning and electing classics; we suffer profoundly from what Professor John Meisel of Queen's University describes as "the thinness of a cultural class in Canada". We seem to have far too few people involved with our literature as readers for classics to evolve.

I would argue that Canadian nationalism has, paradoxically, prevented us from recognizing and embracing genuine classics in our writing. Literature in Canada has been valued for non-literary reasons. We have taken to our bosom only those writings which seem to promote Canada and nationalism. The political aim of boosting 'Canadian-ness' has had some peculiarly distorting effects on our perceptions of our literature. We have approved of realist fiction because it depicts Canada but we've been suspicious of any other mode. We have disapproved of fiction by Canadians which is set in countries other than Canada. We have until very recently ignored Canadian writers who chose to live in other countries. We have until very recently been hostile to immigrant writers. Simply because it was Canadian we have touted work as excellent which was barely competent. Canadian nationalism has prevented us from responding to literature in the untrammelled way we should; our literature has become a duty rather than a joy.

To respond to literature with the intensity and the depth we should is an activity that involves the commitment of our whole hearts and minds. This anthology offers a rich exhibition of twenty major pieces by ten masters of the short story form. It is designed to give readers an opportunity for both concentration and reflection. We hope to involve readers in these stories first as inexhaustible experiences and second as points of entry into a consideration of our writing. In the notes on individual writers that follow, I try to suggest matters that we considered while making our selections along with questions for continued discussion. The introductory notes also suggest a number of possible comparisons between these stories and different works by the same and other authors. Additional references cite important criticism about the writers and interviews with and statements by the writers. Each pair of stories is followed by a brief commentary by the author. The comparisons the authors make, the analogies they draw, and the metaphors they use supply a valuable perspective on the art of writing. Bibliographies of each author have been provided to encourage further reading.

We hope that you will join in discussing and evaluating the achievements of these writers. Canadian literature — past, present, and future — depends on you, on all readers; it depends on your involvement. What Walt Whitman wrote in the nineteenth century about American poetry applies absolutely to us: "To have great poets, there must be great audiences, too."

Canadian Classics

Mavis Gallant

≈

Mavis Gallant is undoubtedly a Canadian classic; until relatively recently, however, many people in this country would have begrudged her recognition even as a Canadian let alone as a classic. Her first collection of stories, *The Other Paris*, was published in the United States in 1956 and in England the next year. But despite her brilliance and international reputation, Canada year after year resolutely ignored Mavis Gallant's achievement. Robert Weaver edited a selection of her stories entitled *The End of the World and Other Stories* for the New Canadian Library in 1974 but general approval was withheld until about 1978 when Geoff Hancock brought out a Mavis Gallant issue of *Canadian Fiction Magazine*.

What can explain this regrettable neglect? Mavis Gallant chose to live in Paris; she chose to write about Europe and Europeans — though she has also written about Quebec and the United States; she published nearly all her stories in *The New Yorker*. None of these facts endeared her to our cultural nationalists. She won the Governor General's Award in 1981 for *Home Truths*, a collection of stories with Canadian settings. I think she should have won it for *From the Fifteenth District*, published two years earlier and not even nominated for the award; but those stories were set in Europe.

The Pegnitz Junction: A Novella and Five Short Stories (1973) and *From the Fifteenth District: A Novella and Eight Short Stories* (1979) are Mavis Gallant's most consistently powerful collections to date. We have represented her here with two compelling stories, "An Autobiography" and "Irina", taken from these two volumes. If length had not been a consideration, we would both have chosen to represent her by a story surely destined for classic status, "Speck's Idea", from her collection *Overhead in a Balloon: Stories of Paris* (1985).

Another possible reason for the tardy acceptance of Mavis Gallant is that her stories make big demands on the reader. They are complex, highly intelligent, wry, and ironic. In remarks quoted in the introduction to *Making It New: Contemporary Canadian Stories* (Toronto: Methuen, 1982), Clark Blaise said of her stories,

"...what, pray tell, is the difference between a Mavis Gallant story when she's working at her richest and fullest and most polyphonic and someone else's novel? It's just that the novel becomes smaller and thinner than her story."

By 'thinner' Blaise means thinner in texture, less rich in detail, less particular, less rooted in the real world. Her rootedness in the real — often a reality that seems 'foreign' to the Canadian consciousness — is another possible reason for the slowness of her acceptance in Canada. She is a writer passionately interested in politics and we have to be able to recognize a wide range of reference and allusion to European history and culture if we are to respond adequately to the experience of her stories. In an interview by Debra Martens, Mavis Gallant says of "The Pegnitz Junction": "I wrote it in high spirits, and it was such fun to write because a great deal of it has some references to German writing — parodies and take-offs and skits and all sorts of things that people didn't get...." Are we sufficiently prepared for writing which makes these demands?

In the *Canadian Fiction Magazine* interview by Geoff Hancock, Mavis Gallant gives some background for her deep interest in politics. She talks of "being twenty-two, being the intensely left-wing political romantic I was, passionately anti-fascist," and seeing the first pictures out of the concentration camps. She was bewildered that Germany could have allowed this to happen. And she thought: "If we wanted to find out how and why this happened it was the Germans we had to question. There was hardly a culture or a civilization I would have placed as high as the German."

Thinking back, Mavis Gallant comments: "I never lost interest in what had happened, the *why* of it, I mean. Nothing I ever read satisfied me. ...I had the feeling that in every day living I would find the origin of the worm — the worm that had destroyed the structure. The stories in *Pegnitz Junction* are, to me, intensely political for that reason. It is not a book about Fascism, but a book about where Fascism comes from. That is why I like it better than anything else. Because I finally answered my own question. Not the historical causes of Fascism — just its small possibilities in people."

Her interest in politics is not in party politics, in advancing a theory or a cause. She is concerned with the emotional lives of individuals and families within social and political structures. In the Debra Martens interview she says: "I would think that everything is political, in a certain sense, in people's lives. They don't always realize it; they're either the victims of it or not aware of it. ...I don't think I could consider people, even in a small domestic entanglement — even if I didn't mention it or write about it — without saying what the structure was that they lived in, and what created it, and what at that particular moment was acting on it...." But always her concern is the individual *within* the structure.

≈

Neil K. Besner in his book *The Light of Imagination: Mavis Gallant's Fiction* (Vancouver: University of British Columbia Press, 1988), Judith Skelton Grant in her monograph *Mavis Gallant and Her Works* (Toronto: ECW Press, 1989), and Janice Kulyk Keefer in her book *Reading Mavis Gallant* (Don Mills, ON: Oxford University Press, 1989) provide insightful discussions of Mavis Gallant's work. *Canadian Fiction Magazine* 28 (1978) is devoted entirely to her work and includes commentaries on it by Robertson Davies, George Woodcock, and Ronald Hatch in addition to an important interview by Geoff Hancock. Another interview with Mavis Gallant, by Debra Martens, appears in *So To Speak: Interviews with Contemporary Canadian Writers* (Montreal: Véhicule Press, 1987). Constance Rooke has written specifically on "Irina" in an essay in *Writers in Aspic* (Montreal: Véhicule Press, 1988). An assortment of studies of Mavis Gallant's work, prepared under the guest-editorship of E. D. Blodgett, can be found in *Essays on Canadian Writing* 42 (1990).

≈ AN AUTOBIOGRAPHY ≈

I

I teach elementary botany to girls in a village half a day's journey by train from Montreux. Season by season our landscape is black on white, or green and blue, or, at the end of summer, olive and brown, with traces of snow on the mountains like scrubbed-out paint. The village is made up of concentric rings: a ring of hotels, a ring of chalets, another of private schools. Through the circles one straight street carries the tearooms and the sawmill and the stuccoed cinema with the minute screen on which they try to show things like *Ben-Hur*. Some of my pupils seem interested in what I have to say, but the most curious and alert are usually showing off.

The dull girls, with their slow but capacious memories, are often a solace, a source of hope. Very often, after I have been on time for children raised to be unpunctual, or have counselled prudence, in vain, to these babies of heedless parents, I remind myself that they have not been sent here to listen to me. I must learn to become the substance their parents have paid for — a component of scenery, like a tree or a patch of grass. I must stop battering at the sand castles their parents have built. I might swear, at certain moments, that all the girls from Western Germany are lulled and spoiled, and all the French calculating, and the Italians insincere, and the English impermeable, and so on, and on; but that would be at the end of a winter's day when they have worn me out.

At the start of the new term, two girls from Frankfurt came to me. They giggled and pushed up the sleeves of their sweaters so that I could see the reddish bruises. "Tomorrow is medical inspection," said Liselotte. "What can we say?" They should have been in tears, but they were biting their lips to keep from laughing too much, wondering what my reaction would be. They said they had been pinching each other to see who could stand the most pain. There are no demerits in our school; if there were, every girl would be removed at once. We are expected to create reserves of memory. The girls must remember their teachers as they remembered hot chocolate and after-skiing, all in the same warm fog. I disguised the bruises with iodine, and said that girls sometimes slipped and fell during my outdoor classes and sometimes scratched their arms. *"Merci, Mademoiselle,"* said the two sillies. They could have said *"Fräulein"* and been both accurate and understood, but they are also here because of the French. Their parents certainly speak English, because it was needed a few years ago in Frankfurt, but the children may not remember. They are ignorant and new. Everything they see and touch at home is new. Home is built on the top layer of Ur. It is no good excavating; the fragments would be without meaning. Everything within the walls was inlaid or woven or cast or put together fifteen years ago at the very earliest. Every house is like the house of newly wed couples who have been disinherited or say they scorn their families' taste. It is easy to put an X over half your life (I am thinking about the parents now) when you have nothing out of the past before your eyes; when the egg spoon is plastic and the coffee cup newly fired porcelain; when the books have been lost and the silver, if salvaged, sold a long time ago. There are no dregs, except perhaps a carefully sorted collection of snapshots. You have survived and the food you eat is new — even that. There are bananas and avocado pears and plenty of butter. Not even an unpleasant taste in the mouth will remind you.

I have light hair, without a trace of gray, and hazel eyes. I am not fat, because, unlike my colleagues, I do not hide pastry and *petits fours* in my room to eat before breakfast. My calves, I think, are overdeveloped from years of walking and climbing in low-heeled shoes. I am a bit sensitive about it, and wear my tweed skirts longer than the fashion. Because I take my gloves off in all weather, my hands are rough; their untended appearance makes the French and Italian parents think I am not gently bred. I use the scents and creams my pupils present me with at Christmas. I have few likes and dislikes, but have lost the habit of eating whatever is put before me. I do not mind accepting gifts.

Everyone's father where I come from was a physician or a professor. You will never hear of a father who rinsed beer glasses in a hotel for his keep, or called at houses with a bottle of shampoo and a portable hair-drying machine. Such fathers may have existed, but we do not know about them. My father was a professor of Medieval German. He was an amateur botanist and taught me the names of flowers before I could write. He went from Munich to the university at Debrecen, in the Protestant part of Hungary, when I was nine. He did not care for contemporary history and took no notice of passing events. His objection to Munich was to its prevailing church, and the amount of noise in the streets. The year was 1937. In Debrecen, on a Protestant islet, he was higher and stonier and more Lutheran than anyone else, or thought so. Among the very few relics I have is *Wild Flowers of Germany: One Hundred Pictures Taken from Nature*. The cover shows a spray of Solomon's-seal — five white bells on a curving stem. It seems to have been taken against the night. Under each of the hundred pictures is the place and time we identified the flower. The plants are common, but I was allowed to think them rare. Beneath a photograph of lady's-slipper my father wrote, "By the large wood on the road going toward the vineyard at Durlach July 11 1936," in the same amount of space I needed to record, under snowdrops, "In the Black Forest last Sunday."

I have often wondered whether tears should rise as I leaf through the book; but no — it has nothing to do with me, or with anyone now. It would be a poor gesture to throw it away, an act of harshness or impiety, but if it were lost or stolen I would not complain.

I recall, in calm woods, my eyes on the ground, searching for poisonous mushrooms. He knocked them out of the soft ground with his walking stick, and I conscientiously trod them to pulp. I teach my pupils to do the same, explaining that they may in this way save countless lives; but while I am still talking the girls have wandered away along the sandy paths, chattering, collecting acorns. "Beware of mushrooms that grow around birch trees," I warn. It is part of the lesson.

I can teach in Hungarian, German, French, English, or Italian. I am grateful to Switzerland, where language is a matter of locality, not an imposition, and existence a question of choice. It is better to avoid dying unless the circumstances are clear. If I fall, by accident, out of the funicular tomorrow, it will only prove once again that the suicide rate is high in a peaceful society. In any case, I will see the shadow of the cable car sliding over trees. In a clearing, a woman sorting apples for cider will not look up, although her children may wave. There I shall be, gazing down in order to frighten my vertigo away (I have been trying this for years), in the cable car of my own will, hoping I shall not open the door without meaning to and fall out and become a reproach to a country that has been more than kind. Imagine gliding — floating down to them! Think of the silence, the turning trees! Sometimes I have thought of adopting a strict religion and living by codes and signs, but as I observe my pupils at their absent-minded rites I find they are all too lax and uncertain. These spoiled girls do not care whether they eat roast veal or fish in parsley sauce on Fridays — it is all the same monotonous meal. Some say they have never been sure what they may eat Fridays, where the limits are. My father was a non-believer, and my mother followed, but without conviction. He led her into the desert. She died of tuberculosis, not daring to speak of God for fear of displeasing her husband. He never carried a house key, because he wanted his wife to answer the door whatever the hour; that is what he was like. My only living relation now is my mother's sister, who has disinherited me because I remind her of my father. She fetched me to Paris to tell me so — that old, fussy, artificial creature in a flat stuffed with showy trifles. "Proust's maternal grandfather lived on this street," she said severely. What of it? What am I supposed to make of that? She gave me a stiff dark photograph of my mother at her confirmation. My mother clasps her Bible to her breast and stares as if the camera were a house on fire.

What I wanted to comment on was children — children in Switzerland. I rent a large room in a chalet seven minutes from my school. Downstairs is the boisterous Canadian who married her ski instructor when she was a pupil here eleven years ago. She has a loud laugh and veined cheeks. He had to resign his post, and now works in the place near the sawmill where they make hand-carved picture frames. The house is full of animals. On rainy days their dining room smells of old clothes and boiled liver. When I am invited to tea (in mugs, without saucers) and sit in one of the armchairs covered with shredded chintz and scraps of blanket, I am obliged to borrow the vacuum cleaner later so as to get the animal hairs out of my skirt. One room is kept free for lodgers — skiers in winter, tourists in summer. In August there were five people in the room — a family of middle-aged parents, two boys, and a baby girl. Because of the rain the boys were restless and the baby screamed with anger and frustration. I took them all to the woods to gather mushrooms.

"If a mushroom has been eaten by a snail, that means it is not poisonous," said the father. Rain dripped through the pine trees. We wore boots and heavy coats. The mother was carrying the bad-tempered baby and could not bend down and search, but now and then she would call, "Here's one that must be safe, because it has been nibbled."

"How do you know the snail is not lying dead somewhere?" I asked.

"You must not make the boys lose confidence in their father," the mother said, trying to laugh, but really a little worried.

"Even if it kills them?" I wanted to say, but it would have spoiled the outing.

My mother said once, "You can tell when mushrooms are safe, because when you stir them the spoon won't tarnish. Poisonous mushrooms turn the spoon black."

"How do you know everyone has a silver spoon?" said my father.

He looked at her seriously, with his light eyes. They were like the eyes of birds when he was putting a question. He was not trying to catch her out; he was simply putting the question. That was what I was trying to do. You can warn until your voice is extinguished, and still these people will pick anything and take it home and put their fingers in their mouths.

In Switzerland parents visit their children sometimes, but are always trying to get away. I would say that all parents of all children here are trying to get away. The baby girl, the screamer, was left for most of a day. The child of aging parents, she had their worried look, as if brooding on the lessons of the past. She was twenty-six months old. My landlady, who offered to keep her amused so that the parents and the two boys could go off on their own for once, had cause to regret it. They tricked the baby cruelly, taking her out to feed melon rinds to Coco, the donkey, in his enclosure at the bottom of the garden. When she came back, clutching the empty basket, her family had disappeared. The baby said something that sounded like "Mama-come-auto" and, writhing like a fish when she was held, slipped away and crawled up the stairs. She called upstairs and down, and the former ski instructor and his wife cried, "Yes, that's it! Mama-come-auto!" She reached overhead to door handles, but the rooms were empty. At noon they tried to make her eat the disgusting purée of carrots and potatoes the mother had left behind. "What if we spanked her?" said the former ski instructor, wiping purée from his sleeve. "Who, you?" shouted his wife. "You wouldn't have nerve enough to brain a mad dog." That shows how tough they thought the baby was. Sometimes during that year-long day, she forgot and let us distract her. We let her turn out our desks and pull our letters to bits. Then she would remember suddenly and look about her with elderly despair, and implore our help, in words no one understood. The weeping grew less frightened and more broken-hearted toward the end of the afternoon. It must have been plain to her then that they would never return. Downstairs they told each other that if she had not been lied to and deceived, then the mother would never have had a day's rest; she had been shut up in the rain in a chalet with this absolute tyrant of a child. The tyrant lay sleeping on the floor. The house was still except for her shuddering breath. Waking, she spoke unintelligible words. They had decided downstairs to pretend not to know; that is, they would not say "Yes, Mama-come-auto" or anything else. We must all three behave as if she had been living here forever and had never known anyone but us. How much memory can be stored in a mind that has not even been developed? What she understood was that we were too deaf to hear her cries and too blind to see her distress. She took the hand of the former ski instructor and dragged it to her face so that he could feel her tears. She was still and slightly feverish when the guilty parents and uneasy boys returned. Her curls were wet through and lay flat on her head. "She was perfect," the landlady said. "Just one little burst of tears after you left. She ate up all her lunch." The mother smiled and nodded, as if giving thanks. "Children are always better away from their parents," she said, with regret. Later, the landlady repeated, to me, as if I had not been there, a strange but believable version of that day, in which the baby cried only once.

That was an exceptional case, where everyone behaved with the best intentions; but what I have wanted to say from the beginning is, do not confide your children to strangers. Watch the way the stranger holds a child by the wrist instead of by the hand, even when a hand has been offered. I am thinking of Véronique, running after the stranger she thought was making off with the imitation-leather bag that held her cardigan, mustard, salt, pepper, a postcard of the Pont-Neuf, a pink handkerchief, a peppermint, and a French centime. This was at the air terminal at Geneva. I thought I might help — interpret between generations, between the mute and the deaf, so to speak — but at that moment the woman rushing away with the bag stopped, shifted it from right hand to left, and grasped Véronique by the wrist.

I had just been disinherited by my aunt, and was extremely sensitive to all forms of injustice. I thought that Véronique's father and mother, because they were not here at the exact moment she feared her bag was being stolen, had lost all claim to her, and had I been dispensing justice, would have said so. It was late in June. My ancient aunt had made me a present of a Geneva-Paris round-trip tourist-class ticket for the purpose of telling me to my face why she had cut me out of her will: I resembled my father, and had somehow disappointed her. I needed a lesson. She did not say what the lesson would be, but spoke in the name of Life, saying that Life would teach me. She was my only relative, that old woman, my mother's eldest sister, who had had the foresight to marry a French officer in 1919 and spend the next forty years and more saying "Fie." She was never obliged to choose between duty and self-preservation, or somehow hope the two would coincide. He was a French officer and she made his sense of honor hers. He doted on her. She was one of the lucky women.

Véronique was brought aboard at Orly Airport after everyone else in the Caravelle had settled down. She was led by a pretty stewardess, who seemed bothered by her charge. "Do you mind having her beside you?" she asked. I at first did not see Véronique, who was behind the stewardess, held by the wrist. I placed her where she could look out, and the stewardess disappeared. This would be of more interest if Véronique were now revealed to be a baby ape or a tamed and lovable bear, but she was a child. The journey is a short one — fifty minutes. Some of the small girls in my school arrive alone from Teheran and Mexico City and are none the worse for the adventure. Mishaps occur when they think that pillows or blankets lent them were really presents, but any firm official can deal with that. The child is tossed from home to school, or from one acrobat parent to the other, and knows where it will land. I am frightened when I imagine the bright arc through space, the trusting flight without wings. Reflect on that slow drop from the cable car down the side of the mountain into the trees. The trees will not necessarily catch you like a net.

I fastened her seat belt, and she looked up at me to see what was going to happen next. She had been dressed for the trip in a blue-and-white cotton frock, white socks, and black shoes with a buttoned strap. Her hair was parted in the middle and contained countless shades of light brown, like a handful of autumn grass. There was a slight cast in one eye, but the gaze was steady. The buckle of the seat belt slid down and rested on one knee. She held on to a large bucket bag — held it tightly by its red handle. In the back of the seat before her, along with a map of the region over which we were to fly, were her return ticket and her luggage tags, and a letter that turned out to be a letter of instructions. She was to be met by Mme. Bataille, who would accompany her to a *colonie de vacances* at Gsteig. I read the letter toward the end of the trip, when I realized that the air hostess had forgotten all about Véronique. I am against prying into children's affairs — even "How do you like your school?" is more inquisitive than one has a right to be. However, the important facts about Mme. Bataille and Gsteig were the only ones Véronique was unable to supply. She talked about herself and her family, in fits and starts, as if unaware of the limits of time — less than an hour, after all — and totally indifferent to the fact that she was unlikely ever to see me again. The place she had come from was "Orly," her destination was called "the mountains," and the person meeting her would be either "Béatrice" or "Catherine" or both. That came later; the first information she sweetly and generously offered was that she had twice been given injections in her right arm. I told her my name, profession, and the name of the village where I taught school. She said she was four but "not yet four and a half." She had been visiting, in Versailles, her mother and a baby brother, whose name she affected not to know — an admirable piece of dignified lying. After a sojourn in the mountains she would be met at Orly Airport by her father and taken to the sea. When would that be? "Tomorrow." On the promise of tomorrow, either he or the mother of the nameless brother had got her aboard the plane. The Ile-de-France receded and spread. She sucked her mint sweet, and accepted mine, wrapped, and was overjoyed when I said she might put it in her bag, as if a puzzle about the bag had now been solved. The stewardess snapped our trays into place and gave us identical meals of cold sausage, Russian salad in glue, savory pastry, canned pears, and tinned mineral water. Véronique gazed onto a plateau of food nearly at shoulder level, and picked up a knife and fork the size of gardening tools. "I can cut my meat," she said, meaning to say she could not. The voice that had welcomed us in Paris and had implored Véronique and me to put out our cigarettes now emerged, preceded by crackling sounds, as if the air were full of invisible fissures: "If you look to your right, you will see the city of Dijon." Véronique quite properly took no notice. "I am cold," she stated, knowing that an announcement of one's condition immediately brings on a change for the better. I opened the plastic bag and found a cardigan — hand-knit, light blue, with pearl buttons. I wondered when the change-over would come, when she would have to stop saying "I am cold" in order to grow up without being the kind of person who lets you know that there is a draft in the room, or the beach is too crowded, or the service in the restaurant has gone off. I have pupils who still cannot find their own cardigans, and my old aunt is something of a complainer, as her sister never was. Despite my disinheritance, I was carrying two relics — a compote spoon whose bowl was in the form of a strawberry leaf, and the confirmation photograph of my mother. They weighed heavily in my hand luggage. The weight of the picture was beyond description. I knew that they would be too heavy, yet I held out my hand greedily for more of the past; but my aunt's ration stopped there.

The well-mannered French girl beside me would not drink the water I had poured into her glass until advised she could. She held the glass in both hands and got it back in its slot without help. Specks of parsley now floated on the water. I said she might leave the remains of the cold sausage, which she was chewing courageously. Giddy with indiscipline, she had some of the salad and all of the pear, and asked, indicating the savory pastry, "Is that something to eat?"

"You can, but it's boring." She had never heard food referred to in that way, and hesitated. As I had left mine, she did not know what the correct attitude ought to be, and after one bite put her spoon down. I think she liked it but, not having understood "boring," was anxious to do the right thing. With her delicate fingers she touched the miniature salt and pepper containers and the doll's tube of mustard, asking what they were for. I remembered that some of the small girls in the school saved them as tokens of travel, and I said, "They are for children to keep."

"Why?"

"I don't know. Some children keep them."

I wondered if this was a mistake, and if she would begin taking things that did not belong to her. She curled her hand around the little mustard tube and said she would keep it for *Maman*. Now that she was wearing the cardigan, her purse was empty save for a mint sweet. I told her that a bag was to put things in, and she said she knew, looking comically worldly. I gave her a centime, a handkerchief, a postcard — searching my own purse to see what could be spared. The stewardess let us descend the ramp from the plane as if she had never seen Véronique before, and no one claimed her. I had great difficulty finding anyone at the terminal who knew anything about Mme. Bataille. When I caught sight of Véronique, later, hurrying desperately after a uniformed woman who did not slow her pace for a second, I feared that *was* Mme. Bataille; but fifteen minutes after that I saw Véronique in the bus that was to take us to the railway station. She was next to a mild, thin, harassed-looking person, who seemed exhausted at the thought of the journey to come.

Now, mark the change in Véronique: she shook out her hair and made it untidy, and stood on the seat and jumped up and down.

"You are a very lucky little girl, going to the mountains *and* the sea," said Mme. Bataille, in something of a whine. Véronique took no more notice of this than she had of Dijon, except to remark that she was going to the seashore tomorrow.

"Not tomorrow. You've only just arrived."

"Tomorrow!" The voice rose and trembled dangerously. "Papa is meeting me at Orly."

"Yes," said the stupid woman soothingly, "but not tomorrow. In August. This is June."

The seats between us were now filled. When I next heard Véronique, the corruption of memory had set in.

"It was the stewardess who cut up your meat," said Mme. Bataille.

"No, a lady."

"A lady in a uniform. The lady you were with when I met you."

"*No.*"

The reason I could hear them was that they were nearly shouting.

Presently, all but giving in, Mme. Bataille said, "Well, she was nice, the lady. I mean, the stewardess."

Two ideas collided: Véronique remembered the woman fairly well, even though the flight no longer existed, but Mme. Bataille knew it was the stewardess.

"I came all alone," said Véronique.

"Who cut your meat, then?"

"I did," said Véronique, and there was no shaking her.

II

Even if Peter Dobay had not instantly recognized me and called my name, my attention would have been drawn by the way he and his wife looked at the station of our village. They got out of the train from Montreux and stood as if dazed. One imagined them blinking behind their sunglasses. At that time of year, we saw only excursion parties — stout women with gray curls, or serious hikers who would stamp from the station through the village and up the slopes. Peter wore a dark suit and black shoes, his wife a black-and-white silk dress, a black silk coat, and fragile open sandals. Her blond hair had been waved that day. I wondered how she would walk in the village streets on her thin high heels.

When we were face to face, Peter and I said together, "What are *you* doing here?"

"I live here — I teach," I said.

"No!" Turning to his wife, he said excitedly, "You know who this is, don't you? It's Erika." Then, back to me, "We've come up to see my wife's twins. They're in a summer school here."

"Better than dragging them round with us," said his wife, in a low-pitched, foggy voice. "They're better off in the fresh air." She touched my arm as if she had always known me and said, "I just can't believe I've finally seen you. Poodlie, it's like a *dream*."

I was faced with two pandas — those glasses! Who was Poodlie? Peter, evidently, yet he called her "Poodlie," too: "Poodlie, it's wonderful," he said, as if she were denying it. His wife? Her voice was twenty years older than his.

He went off to see to their luggage and she stopped seeing me, abruptly, as if now that he was gone nothing was needed. She looked at the village — as much as she could see, which was the central street and the station and the shutters of the station buffet. All I could see was her mouth and the tight pinpoint muscles around it, and the flour dusting of face power.

"Well?" she said when Peter returned.

"I can't believe it," he said to me, and laughed. "*Here!* What are you doing *here?*"

"I teach," I began again.

"No, here at the station, now, on Sunday."

"Oh, that. I was waiting for the train with the Sunday papers."

"I told you," he cried to his wife. "Remember it was one of the things I said. Even if Erika was starving, she'd buy newspapers. I never knew anyone to read so many papers."

"I haven't had to choose between starving and reading," I said, which was a lie. I watched with regret the bale of papers carted off to the kiosk. In half an hour, those I wanted would be gone.

"*We're* starving," he said. "You'll have lunch with us, won't you? Now?"

"It's early," I said, glancing at his wife.

"Call it breakfast, then." He began guiding us both toward the buffet, his arms around our shoulders in a peasant-like bonhomie that was not like anything I remembered of him.

"The luggage, Poodlie," said his wife.

"He'll take it to the hotel."

"What hotel?"

"The biggest."

"Then it's there," I said, and pointed to an Alpine fortified castle, circa 1912, of yellowish stone, propped behind the street as if on a ledge.

"Good," he said. "Now our lunch."

That was how, on a cool bright day, just before the start of term, I saw Peter again.

In the dark buffet, Peter and his wife kept their glasses on. It seemed part of their personal decorum. Although the clock had only just struck twelve, the restaurant was nearly filled, and we were given a table between the serving pantry and the door. I understood that this was Peter, even though he didn't look at all like the man I had known, and that I was sharing his table. I avoided looking at him. Across the room, over an ocean of heads, was an open window, geraniums, the mountains, and the sky.

"You have beautiful eyes," said Peter's wife. Her voice, like a ventriloquist's, seemed to come from the wrong place — from behind her sunglasses. "Poodlie never told me that. They look like topazes or something like that."

"Yes," said Peter. "Semiprecious stones from the snow-capped mountains of South America."

He sounded like a pompous old man. His English was smooth as cream now, and better than mine. I spoke it with too many people who had accents. Answering a question of his wife's, I heard myself making something thick and endless out of the letter "t": "It is crowded because it is Sunday. Tourists come for miles around. The food in the buffet is celebrated."

"We'll see," said Peter, and took the long plastic-covered menu with rather an air.

His wife was attentive to me. Parents of pupils always try to make me eat more than I care to, perhaps thinking that I would be less intractable if I were less thin. "Your daughter is not only a genius but will make a brilliant marriage," I am supposed to say over caramel cake. I let myself be coaxed by Peter's wife into having a speciality of the place — something monstrous, with boiled meat and dumplings that swam in broth. Having arranged this, she settled down to her tea and toast. As for Peter — well, what a performance! First he read the whole menu aloud and grimaced at everything; then he asked for a raw onion and a bunch of radishes and two pots of yoghurt, and cut up the onions and radishes in the yoghurt and ate the whole mess with a spoon. It was like the frantic exhibition of a child who has been made uneasy.

"He isn't well," said his wife, quite as though he weren't there. "He treats it like a joke, but you know, he was in jail after the Budapest uprising, and he was so badly treated that it ruined his stomach. He'll never be the same again."

He did not look up or kick me under the table or in any manner ask me not to betray him. It occurred to me he had forgotten I knew. I felt my face flushing, as if I had been boiled in the same water as the beef and dumplings. I thought I would choke. I looked, this time with real longing, at the mountain peaks. They seem so near in the clear weather that sometimes innocent foot travellers set off thinking they will be there in three-quarters of an hour. The pockets of snow looked as if they could have been scooped up with a coffee spoon. The cows on the lower slopes were the size of thimbles.

"Do you ski at this time of year?" said Peter's wife, without turning to see what I was staring at.

"One can, but I don't go up any more. There's an hour-and-a-half walk to the middle station, and the road isn't pleasant. It's all slush and mud." I thought they would ask what "the middle station" meant, but they didn't, which meant they weren't really listening.

When I refused a pudding, Peter said, with his old teasing, "I told you she was frugal. Her father was a German professor at Debrecen, the Protestant university."

"So was yours," said his wife sharply, as though reminding him of a truth he forgot from time to time.

"It never affected me," said Peter, smiling.

"That's where you met, then," said his wife, taking her eyes from me at last.

"No," said Peter. "We were only children then. We met when we were grown up, at the University of Lausanne. It was a coincidence, like meeting today. Erika and I will probably meet — I don't know where. On the moon."

It is difficult enough to listen to someone lying without looking shocked, but imagine what it might be to be part of the fantasy; his lies were a whirlwind, and I was at the core, trying to recognize something familiar. We met in Lausanne; that was true. We met on a bench in the public gardens. I told him I had lived in Hungary and could speak a few sentences of Hungarian still. He was four years younger than I. I told him about my father in Debrecen, and that we were Germans, and that my father had been shot by a Russian soldier. I said I was grateful for Switzerland. He told me he was a half Jew from Budapest and had been ill-used. His life had been saved in some remarkable way by a neutral embassy. He was grateful, too.

He was the first person to whom I had ever spoken spontaneously and without reserve. We met every day for ten days, and when he wanted to leave Switzerland because he thought it would be better somewhere else and would not go without me, I did not think twice. The evening lamps went on in the park where we were sitting, and I thought that if I did not go with him I would suffer every evening for the rest of my life, every time the lamps were lit. To avoid suffering, I went with him. Yet when I told my father's old friends, the people who had taken me in and welcomed me and kept me from starving, I said it was my duty. I said it was Peter who could not live without me. It is true I would never have gone out of Switzerland, out to the wilderness, but for him. My father had friends at the University of Lausanne, and although after the war some were afraid, because the wind had shifted, others took me in when I was seventeen and homeless and looked after me until I could work. I was afraid of telling about Peter. In the end, I had to. I quoted something my father had once said about duty, and no one could contradict that.

It lasted only a short time, the adventure, and can be briefly and accurately remembered. Quickly, then: he had heard there was a special university for refugees in a city on the Rhine, and thought they might admit him. We lived in a hotel over a café, and discovered we were living in a brothel. The university existed, but its quota was full. We were starving to death. We were so attractive a couple, so sympathetic-looking, that people dulled with eating looked at us fondly. We strolled along the Rhine and looked at excursion boats. "Your duty is always before you, plain as that," my father had said, pointing with his walking stick to some vista or tree or cloud. I do not know what he was pointing at — something in his mind.

Because of Peter I was on a sea without hope of landing anywhere. It grew on me that he had been jealous of my safety and had dragged me beyond my depth. There had been floods — I think in Holland — and money was being collected for the victims. Newspapers spoke of "Rhine solidarity," and I was envious, for I had solidarity with no one now. It took me time to think things out, for I had no illusions about my intelligence, and I wondered finally why I did not feel any solidarity with Peter. I loved him, but together we would starve or drown.

"You can't stay here," said the owner of the hotel one day. "It isn't safe for refugees. We have the police in too often."

"We can't move," said Peter. "My wife is ill." But that did not give me a feeling of solidarity, for I was not his wife, and he was a person who would keep moving from one place to another.

He never told the same story twice, except for some details. He said he was picked up and deported when he was ten or twelve. He was able to describe the Swiss or Swedish consulate where they tried to save him. In his memories, the person who hid him was always different. Sometimes he said it was a peasant, sometimes a fat woman who shut him in a cupboard. The forced march must have been true. Someone — he did not say who — was working on his behalf. He hinted he was illegitimate, and that a person of noble birth, who did not wish to be known, was his protector. It is true that sometimes in the marches from Budapest to the border one person in the column was saved, if the order came through in time. It was often at night. The column stopped by the side of the road, and the torches, hooded because of the air raids, moved from face to face. One night, the light picked out an old man who would have died soon in any case, and Peter. He could not see his deliverers — he saw the light moving from face to face. The light was lowered. He tried to hide, but they spoke his name. He thought the light meant an execution. He was taken away in a car, back to Budapest, and in the car was comforted with chocolates. These were the details he repeated: the light on his face, the voice saying his name, and the chocolates. Sometimes, being boastful, he said he was active in the Arrow Cross Party; but he was a victim, and a child. Once, he said he was poor and had sold papers in the street to pay for his shoes. But he was such a liar. He may have been poor, or he may have been from a solid family who lost him along the way; but it was not a Protestant family, and his father was not a professor at Debrecen. Also, he was not in Budapest during the uprising in 1956. He was in a city on the Rhine, starving, with me.

We stood at the foot of the cathedral in this city one day. We had nothing to eat and nothing to do. I could not understand why Peter had brought me here or what he wanted now. He urged me to write my father's old friends in Lausanne, or to my aunt in Paris, but I was proud, and ashamed that he would ask such a thing. I think he believed I was a magic solution just in myself. He lived in a fantasy of false names, false fortunes, false parents, and here was a reality of expired visas and dry bread he could not explain away.

"Goethe climbed to the top of this cathedral to cure himself of vertigo. You should try it," Peter said.

"Oh, Goethe would," I said, and that was the only thing that autumn that made Peter laugh. We climbed and climbed, and looked down at matchbox cars. I felt vertigo, and was surprised he did not. I held out my arms to receive him if he fainted — I was so sure he would not stand this — but he stood smiling down with no intention of toppling over. Below was the sweet nursery world, nursery-sized, with toy trams and toy people. It smiled back at him; he was its lord, at least from up here. My world was my size, and often bigger. I was afraid of the shrunken world as he saw it; he made me unsteady. I left him that day. He went alone to the post office to see if there were phantom letters from ghost friends, and I made myself as tidy as I could and went to my own consulate with a plausible story. And that was the last Peter saw of me, until Peter, or Poodlie, called my name at the station.

I don't know what he remembered. He had taken my family as his, and expected me to smile. Actually, I did. I made him a present of my family. But by now he must have believed that whatever came into his head was true, for he did not thank me — neither then nor later. I leaned over the table and said, "I see what is making the difference. It is the dark glasses." He immediately took them off, but I saw that I still did not recognize him.

An excursion party now trooped into the buffet. Their accents were, I think, industrial England over, I think, Viennese. One of the women smeared thick white cream on her sunburned arms. "Let's finish and pay and get out of here," said Peter's wife, sharply. I stared at him then, but his face showed nothing. He did not add or contribute. It might have had nothing to do with him. She slipped him folded money so that he could pay the bill. I tried to think, but they had stuffed me with food. I clung to one idea: no one would get me out of Switzerland again, as he once had to a city on the Rhine, as my old aunt had got me to Paris. Each time I returned I was wounded, or had failed. Outside the station, I stopped at the kiosk, but of course my newspapers were gone.

The next afternoon, I sat in the lobby of their hotel. His wife now looked through the windows to the station, as if afraid of missing the train out. She poured tea from a leaky pot, and passed chocolate biscuits, shell-shaped, in a thin coating of sugar. They were Poodlie's favorites; she was sorry he wasn't here. She poured with a tense, strong hand — I admired the long fingers, and the short nails, on which the red was thickly spread. Absently but politely, she asked about my work, as if she were a headmistress interviewing me for a post.

I described flowers next to snow, and plants so perfect and minute, rooted on stone, that they must be like the algae on Mars.

"Oh, yes, edelweiss," she said.

He was a parcel posted without an address, and he had come to her. Now I heard her inviting me to join them. I heard the words "The twins would adore you, and he is a different person when you're there. I've never seen him so gay and happy as he was yesterday at lunch." He had put her up to it, and now he was out, walking around in the village, waiting for the barter to be completed. "He has talked about you such a lot," she said.

"What did he tell you?"

"Why, that you were a wonderful person. He said you had been so kind to him."

That part of it ended there. She explained that Peter was walking, not in the village, as I had supposed, but somewhere up a mountain.

He had gone up in a cable car. "I didn't bring the right clothes," she said. "We could drive somewhere, but we never do." It was the only sign of her discontent. The person she had gone to consult when she contemplated this marriage — a rapid psychotherapy, she explained — had warned her not to take over too many head-of-the-family functions from a young husband. That meant, among other things, that she was never to drive the car. But Poodlie was too wild to drive. She gave him cars, but could not trust him to drive them. I thought of him wandering along a steep, windy slope now, not knowing how to keep a foothold in his slippery shoes. He was up above the village in his dark suit and dark glasses and shoes. How could she let him go that way — as if he were lost or had strayed from the towns? He was alone, shivering (no one had told him how cold it would be), dreaming and inventing things to be remembered.

I did not meet her children, but I saw her with them in a tea-room: two plump girls of about fourteen, in clay-colored tights and long pullovers that covered their sturdy hips. They were not girls I had ever seen before. They looked sullen there in the dark shop, which was suffocating with the smell of chocolate. They were choosing éclairs, pointing, discontented and curt. Their school had not yet taught them manners, and their mother, with a stiff smile on her lips and her sunglasses hiding her opinion, could see only the distance between what they were and what they ought to be. She was not an educator. The girls' clumsiness was a twist of the spirit, a sprain. She watched them choose and eat, and I thought how much time she spent watching people choose and eat their food. She removed the glasses and rubbed the space between her eyes. She saw me, and her glance meeting mine almost begged something. Information? Advice? She had the psychotherapy for advice, and she had Peter to tell her stories. Perhaps she wanted me to change my mind about going with them. He must have asked for me, as he asked for cars she would not let him drive because he broke them.

It would have been easy for her to make me believe my choices were wrong, but it would have been another matter to make me change my mind. Once when she was busy with the twins, he came to me. He looked at the saucer full of moss and Alpine plants; and the shelf with tea and hard biscuits and cereal and powdered milk; and at my bed with its shabby cushions; and my walls decorated with photographs of snow and skiers — searching for something. He twitched a curtain as if it hid a view he liked and said, "It's all dirty green, like a customs inspector's uniform."

But I had travelled nearly as much as Peter, and over some of the same frontiers. He could not impress me. I think (like the remark about semiprecious stones and snow-capped mountains) it was a way of talking he had developed because it amused his wife. He knew it was no good talking about the past, because we were certain to remember it differently. He daren't be nostalgic about anything, because of his inventions. He would never be certain if the memory he was feeling tender about was true.

I watched him at the window — the town lad, hating the quiet. "What is that racket?" he said angrily. It was the stream running outside through the garden. There was also Coco, the donkey, braying in his enclosure. He would have preferred a deafening, continued, city noise. I remembered him on streets full of trams and traffic; I remembered the quick turn of his head. When I remembered the horror of the room over the café, I thought it had been the horror of living on a street.

The view here, after the long garden, was of the roof of the chalet farther down the slope. A crash: my bookshelf, containing *Wild Flowers of Germany*, fell from the wall. The house shook.

He looked at the perpendicular, windless rain that had begun to fall. He turned back to the room; he was still searching. "You used to read," he said, still in pursuit of something. I pointed to the floor. "Didn't you hear them fall?" He made a silly remark — I remember the sense of it, not the words. He could not trust me, because I had once run away, vanished, but as he had long ago fabricated something else, he could not remember why he could not trust me. The room grew dark. I served coffee in cups with *Liberté* and *Patrie* and a green-and-white shield of the Vaud on them. The parents of a pupil had bought them in Montreux for me once. He held his cup close to his eyes and read the words, and put it down without saying anything.

I said to myself that he was only a man about whom I had known a great deal and it was so long ago that much of it might have been told to me by someone else. Nostalgia is a weakness; he would be the one to indulge in it, if he dared. I had not gone to him out of duty and had not left him out of self-preservation. It was not that simple. I would have talked, for I knew he was waiting for me to scrape away the dreams and begin again with the truth, but I thought, I shall write him a letter. That will be easier. I shall write about everything, all of the truth.

They came up by train and they left by train — the little red train that has its start among the hotels and swimming pools along the lake. As neither of them could drive the other, they had to take the train. They were leaving the twins behind. The twins were happy, and the fresh air was doing them good. They were enrolled for the autumn term.

The first-class carriages of those trains look as if they had been built for miniature royal tours. There are oval satin-wood panels and Art Nouveau iron roses. Some of the roses had iron worms eating their hearts. I imagine the artist meant something beautiful and did not know it was hideous. As you can imagine, the trains are beautifully polished. The panels gleam, and dust is not allowed to accumulate in the rose petals. The windows are clear for a view of cows and valleys, the ashtrays are emptied and polished, and the floors are swept. I like best the deep-rose velvet, with its pattern of brown leaves and ferns, that covers the seats. It wears slowly; in some very worn places the color is light apricot and the palest lemon, and the pattern can scarcely be seen. Somewhere in storage, preserved from dust and the weather, are bales of the same velvet, and when a seat becomes too worn they simply patch it up again.

He would have stayed if I had wanted. Yes, Poodlie would have left Poodlie. He knew *I* would never go with them. I might have been for sale, but not to her. At a word of truth he would have stayed, if only to hear the rest. He would have made furious plans, and left such an imprint on this place that after his departure I could not have lived here any more. Or perhaps this time one of us would have stayed forever. These are the indecisions that rot the fabric, if you let them. The shutter slams to in the wind and sways back; the rain begins to slant as the wind increases. This is the season for mountain storms. The wind rises, the season turns; no autumn is quite like another. The autumn children pour out of the train, and the clouds descend the mountain slopes, and there we are with walls and a ceiling to the village. Here is the pattern on the carpet where he walked, and the cup he drank from. I have learned to be provident. I do not waste a sheet of writing paper, or a postage stamp, or a tear. The stream outside the window, deep with rain, receives rolled in a pellet the letter to Peter. Actually, it is a blank sheet on which I intended to write a long letter about everything — about Véronique. I have wasted the sheet of paper. There has been such a waste of everything; such a waste.

≈ IRINA ≈

One of Irina's grandsons, nicknamed Riri, was sent to her at Christmas. His mother was going into hospital, but nobody told him that. The real cause of his visit was that since Irina had become a widow her children worried about her being alone. The children, as Irina would call them forever, were married and in their thirties and forties. They did not think they were like other people, because their father had been a powerful old man. He was a Swiss writer, Richard Notte. They carried his reputation and the memory of his puritan equity like an immense jar filled with water of which they had been told not to spill a drop. They loved their mother, but they had never needed to think about her until now. They had never fretted about which way her shadow might fall, and whether to stay in the shade or get out by being eccentric and bold. There were two sons and three daughters, with fourteen children among them. Only Riri was an only child. The girls had married an industrial designer, a Lutheran minister (perhaps an insolent move, after all, for the daughter of a militant atheist), and an art historian in Paris. One boy had become a banker and the other a lecturer on Germanic musical tradition. These were the crushed sons and loyal daughters to whom Irina had been faithful, whose pictures had travelled with her and lived beside her bed.

Few of Notte's obituaries had even mentioned a family. Some of his literary acquaintances were surprised to learn there had been any children at all, though everyone paid homage to the soft, quiet wife to whom he had dedicated his books, the subject of his first rapturous poems. These poems, conventional verse for the most part, seldom translated out of German except by unpoetical research scholars, were thought to be the work of his youth. Actually, Notte was forty when he finally married, and Irina barely nineteen. The obituaries called Notte the last of a breed, the end of a Tolstoyan line of moral lightning rods — an extinction which was probably hard on those writers who came after him, and still harder on his children. However, even to his family the old man had appeared to be the very archetype of a respected European novelist — prophet, dissuader, despairingly opposed to evil, crack-voiced after having made so many pronouncements. Otherwise, he was not all that typical as a Swiss or as a Western, liberal, Protestant European, for he neither saved, nor invested, nor hid, nor disguised his material returns.

"What good is money, except to give away?" he often said. He had a wife, five children, and an old secretary who had turned into a dependent. It was true that he claimed next to nothing for himself. He rented shabby, ramshackle houses impossible to heat or even to clean. Owning was against his convictions, and he did not want to be tied to a gate called home. His room was furnished with a cot, a lamp, a desk, two chairs, a map of the world, a small bookshelf — no more, not even carpets or curtains. Like his family, he wore thick sweaters indoors as out, and crouched over inadequate electric fires. He seldom ate meat — though he did not deprive his children — and drank water with his meals. He had married once — once and for all. He could on occasion enjoy wine and praise and restaurants and good-looking women, but these festive outbreaks were on the rim of his real life, as remote from his children — as strange and as distorted to them — as some other country's colonial wars. He grew old early, as if he expected old age to suit him. By sixty, his eyes were sunk in pockets of lizard skin. His hair became bleached and lustrous, like the scrap of wedding dress Irina kept in a jeweller's box. He was photographed wearing a dark suit and a woman's plaid shawl — he was always cold by then, even in summer — and with a rakish felt hat shading half his face. His wife still let a few photographers in, at the end — but not many. Her murmured "He is working" had for decades been a double lock. He was as strong as Rasputin, his enemies said; he went on writing and talking and travelling until he positively could not focus his eyes or be helped aboard a train. Nearly to the last, he and Irina swung off on their seasonal cycle of journeys to Venice, to Rome, to cities where their married children lived, to Liège and Oxford for awards and honors. His place in a hotel dining room was recognizable from the door because of the pills, drops, and powders lined up to the width of a dinner plate. Notte's hypochondria had been known and gently caricatured for years. His sons, between them, had now bought up most of the original drawings: Notte, in infant's clothing, downing his medicine like a man (he had missed the Nobel); Notte quarrelling with Aragon and throwing up Surrealism; a grim female figure called "Existentialism" taking his pulse; Notte catching Asian flu on a cultural trip to Peking. During the final months of his life his children noticed that their mother had begun acquiring medicines of her own, as if hoping by means of mirror-magic to draw his ailments into herself.

If illness became him, it was only because he was fond of ritual, the children thought — even the hideous ceremonial of pain. But

Irina had not been intended for sickness and suffering; she was meant to be burned dry and consumed by the ritual of him. The children believed that the end of his life would surely be the death of their mother. They did not really expect Irina to turn her face to the wall and die, but an exclusive, even a selfish, alliance with Notte had seemed her reason for being. As their father grew old, then truly old, then old in mind, and querulous, and unjust, they observed the patient tenderness with which she heeded his sulks and caprices, his almost insane commands. They supposed this ardent submission of hers had to do with love, but it was not a sort of love they had ever experienced or tried to provoke. One of his sons saw Notte crying because Irina had buttered toast for him when he wanted it dry. She stroked the old man's silky hair, smiling. The son hated this. Irina was diminishing a strong, proud man, making a senile child of him, just as Notte was enslaving and debasing her. At the same time the son felt a secret between the two, a mystery. He wondered then, but at no other time, if the secret might not be Irina's invention and property.

Notte left a careful will for such an unworldly person. His wife was to be secure in her lifetime. Upon her death the residue of income from his work would be shared among the sons and daughters. There were no gifts or bequests. The will was accompanied by a testament which the children had photocopied for the beauty of the handwriting and the charm of the text. Irina, it began, belonged to a generation of women shielded from decisions, allowed to grow in the sun and shade of male protection. This flower, his flower, he wrote, was to be cherished now as if she were her children's child.

"In plain words," said Irina, at the first reading, in a Zurich lawyer's office, "I am the heir." She was wearing dark glasses because her eyes were tired, and a tight hat. She looked tense and foreign.

Well, yes, that was it, although Notte had put it more gracefully. His favorite daughter was his literary executor, entrusted with the unfinished manuscripts and the journals he had kept for sixty-five years. But it soon became evident that Irina had no intention of giving these up. The children adored their mother, but even without love as a factor would not have made a case of it; Notte's lawyer had already told them about disputes ending in mazelike litigation, families sundered, contents of a desk sequestered, diaries rotting in bank vaults while the inheritors thrashed it out. Besides, editing Notte's papers would keep Irina busy and an occupation was essential now. In loving and unloving families alike, the same problem arises after a death: What to do about the widow?

Irina settled some of it by purchasing an apartment in a small Alpine town. She chose a tall, glassy, urban-looking building of the kind that made conservationist groups send round-robin letters, accompanied by incriminating photographs, to newspapers in Lausanne. The apartment had a hall, an up-to-date kitchen, a bedroom for Irina, a spare room with a narrow bed in it, one bathroom, and a living room containing a couch. There was a glassed-in cube of a balcony where in a pinch an extra cot might have fitted, but Irina used the space for a table and chairs. She ordered red lampshades and thick curtains and the pale furniture that is usually sold to young couples. She seemed to come into her own in that tight, neutral flat, the children thought. They read some of the interviews she gave, and approved: she said, in English and Italian, in German and French, that she would not be a literary widow, detested by critics, resented by Notte's readers. Her firm diffidence made the children smile, and they were proud to read about her dignified beauty. But as for her intelligence — well, they supposed that the interviewers had confused fluency with wit. Irina's views and her way of expressing them were all camouflage, simply part of a ladylike undereducation, long on languages and bearing, short on history and arithmetic. Her origins were Russian and Swiss and probably pious; the children had not been drawn to that side of the family. Their father's legendary peasant childhood, his isolated valley-village had filled their imaginations and their collective past. There was a sudden April lightness in her letters now that relieved and yet troubled them. They knew it was a sham happiness, Nature's way of protecting the survivor from immediate grief. The crisis would come later, when her most secret instincts had built a seawall. They took turns invading her at Easter and in the summer, one couple at a time, bringing a child apiece — there was no room for more. Winter was a problem, however, for the skiing was not good just there, and none of them liked to break up their families at Christmastime. Not only was Irina's apartment lacking in beds but there was absolutely no space for a tree. Finally, she offered to visit them, in regular order. That was how they settled it. She went to Bern, to Munich, to Zurich, and then came the inevitable Christmas when it was not that no one wanted her but just that they were all doing different things.

She had written in November of that year that a friend, whom she described, with some quaintness, as "a person," had come for a long stay. They liked that. A visit meant winter company, lamps on at four, China tea, conversation, the peppery smell of carnations (her favorite flower) in a warm room. For a week or two of the visit her letters were blithe, but presently they noticed that "the person" seemed to be having a depressing effect on their mother. She wrote that she had been working on Notte's journals for three years now. Who would want to read them except old men and women? His moral and political patterns were fossils of liberalism. He had seen the cracks in the Weimar Republic. He had understood from the beginning what Hitler meant. If at first he had been wrong about Mussolini, he had changed his mind even before Croce changed his, and had been safely back on the side of democracy in time to denounce Pirandello. He had given all he could, short of his life, to the Spanish Republicans. His measure of Stalin had been so wise and unshakably just that he had never been put on the Communist index — something rare for a Western Socialist. No one could say, ever, that Notte had hedged or retreated or kept silent when a voice was needed. Well, said Irina, what of it? He had written, pledged, warned, signed, declared. And what had he changed, diverted, or stopped? She suddenly sent the same letter to all five children: "This Christmas I don't want to go anywhere. I intend to stay here, in my own home."

They knew this was the crisis and that they must not leave her to face it alone, but that was the very winter when all their plans ran down, when one daughter was going into hospital, another moving to a different city, the third probably divorcing. The elder son was committed to a Christmas with his wife's parents, the younger lecturing in South Africa — a country where Irina, as Notte's constant reflection, would certainly not wish to set foot. They wrote and called and cabled one another: What shall we do? Can you? Will you? I can't.

Irina had no favorites among her children, except possibly one son who had been ill with rheumatic fever as a child and required long nursing. To him she now confided that she longed for her own childhood sometimes, in order to avoid having to judge herself. She was homesick for a time when nothing had crystallized and mistakes were allowed. Now, in old age, she had no excuse for errors. Every thought had a long meaning; every motive had angles and corners, and could be measured. And yet whatever she saw and thought and attempted was still fluid and vague. The shape of a table against afternoon light still held a mystery, awaited a final explanation. You looked for clarity, she wrote, and the answer you had was paleness, the flat white cast that a snowy sky throws across a room.

Part of this son knew about death and dying, but the rest of him was a banker and thoroughly active. He believed that, given an ideal situation, one should be able to walk through a table, which would save time and roundabout decisions. However, like all of Notte's children he had been raised with every awareness of solid matter too. His mother's youthful, yearning, and probably religious letter made him feel bland and old. He told his wife what he thought it contained, and she told a sister-in-law what she thought he had said. Irina was tired. Her eyesight was poor, perhaps as a result of prolonged work on those diaries. Irina did not need adult company, which might lead to morbid conversation; what she craved now was a symbol of innocent, continuing life. An animal might do it. Better still, a child.

Riri did not know that his mother would be in hospital the minute his back was turned. Balanced against a tame Christmas with a grandmother was a midterm holiday, later, of high-altitude skiing with his father. There was also some further blackmail involving his holiday homework, and then the vague state of behavior called "being reasonable" — that was all anyone asked. They celebrated a token Christmas on the twenty-third, and the next day he packed his presents (a watch and a tape recorder) and was put on a plane at Orly West. He flew from Paris to Geneva, where he spent the real Christmas Eve in a strange, bare apartment into which an aunt and a large family of cousins had just moved. In the morning he was wakened when it was dark and taken to a six-o'clock train. He said goodbye to his aunt at the station, and added, "If you ask the conductor or anyone to look after me, I'll — " Whatever threat was in his mind he seemed ready to carry out. He wore an R.A.F. badge on his jacket and carried a Waffen-S.S. emblem in his pocket. He knew better than to keep it in sight. At home they had already taken one away but he had acquired another at school. He had Astérix comic books for reading, chocolate-covered hazelnuts for support, and his personal belongings in a fairly large knapsack. He made a second train on his own and got down at the right station.

He had been told that he knew this place, but his memory, if it was a memory, had to do with fields and a picnic. No one met him. He shared a taxi through soft snow with two women, and paid his share — actually more than his share, which annoyed the women; they could not give less than a child in the way of a tip. The taxi let him off at a dark, shiny tower on stilts with granite steps. In the lobby a marble panel, looking like the list of names of war dead in his school, gave him his grandmother on the eighth floor. The lift, like the façade of the building, was made of dark mirrors into which he gazed seriously. A dense, thoughtful person looked back. He took off his glasses and the blurred face became even more remarkable. His grandmother had both a bell and a knocker at her door. He tried both. For quite a long time nothing happened. He knocked and rang again. It was not nervousness that he felt but a new sensation that had to do with a shut, foreign door.

His grandmother opened the door a crack. She had short white hair and a pale face and blue eyes. She held a dressing gown gripped at the collar. She flung the door back and cried, "Darling Richard, I thought you were arriving much later. Oh," she said, "I must look dreadful to you. Imagine finding me like this, in my dressing gown!" She tipped her head away and talked between her fingers, as he had been told never to do, because only liars cover their mouths. He saw a dark hall and a bright kitchen that was in some disorder, and a large dark, curtained room opposite the kitchen. This room smelled stuffy, of old cigarettes and of adults. But then his grandmother pushed the draperies apart and wound up the slatted shutters, and what had been dark, moundlike objects turned into a couch and a bamboo screen and a round table and a number of chairs. On a bookshelf stood a painting of three tulips that must have fallen out of their vase. Behind them was a sky that was all black except for a rainbow. He unpacked a portion of the things in his knapsack — wrapped presents for his grandmother, his new tape recorder, two school textbooks, a notebook, a Bic pen. The start of this Christmas lay hours behind him and his breakfast had died long ago.

"Are you hungry?" said his grandmother. He heard a telephone ringing as she brought him a cup of hot milk with a little coffee in it and two fresh croissants on a plate. She was obviously someone who never rushed to answer any bell. "My friend, who is an early riser, even on Christmas Day, went out and got these croissants. Very bravely, I thought." He ate his new breakfast, dipping the croissants in the milk, and heard his grandmother saying, "Well, I must have misunderstood. But he managed. …He didn't bring his skis. Why not? …I see." By the time she came back he had a book open. She watched him for a second and said, "Do you read at meals at home?"

"Sometimes."

"That's not the way I brought up your mother."

He put his nose nearer the page without replying. He read aloud from the page in a soft schoolroom plain-chant: " 'Go, went, gone. Stand, stood, stood. Take, took, taken.' "

"Richard," said his grandmother. When he did not look up at

once, she said, "I know what they call you at home, but what are you called in school?"

"Riri."

"I have three Richard grandsons," she said, "and not one is called Richard exactly."

"I have an Uncle Richard," he said.

"Yes, well, he happens to be a son of mine. I never allowed nicknames. Have you finished your breakfast?"

"Yes."

"Yes who? Yes what? What is your best language, by the way?"

"I am French," he said, with a sharp, sudden, hard hostility, the first tense bud of it, that made her murmur, "So soon?" She was about to tell him that he was not French — at least, not really — when an old man came into the room. He was thin and walked with a cane.

"Alec, this is my grandson," she said. "Riri, say how do you do to Mr. Aiken, who was kind enough to go out in this morning's snow to buy croissants for us all."

"I knew he would be here early," said the old man, in a stiff French that sounded extremely comical to the boy. "Irina has an odd ear for times and trains." He sat down next to Riri and clasped his hands on his cane; his hands at once began to tremble violently. "What does that interesting-looking book tell you?" he asked.

" 'The swallow flew away,' " answered Irina, reading over the child's head. " 'The swallow flew away with my hopes.' "

"Good God, let me look at that!" said the old man in his funny French. Sure enough, those were the words, and there was a swallow of a very strange blue, or at least a sapphire-and-turquoise creature with a swallow's tail. Riri's grandmother took her spectacles out of her dressing-gown pocket and brought the book up close and said in a loud, solemn way, " 'The swallows will have flown away.' " Then she picked up the tape recorder, which was the size of a glasses case, and after snapping the wrong button on and off, causing agonizing confusion and wastage, she said with her mouth against it, " 'When shall the swallows have flown away?' "

"No," said Riri, reaching, snatching almost. As if she had always given in to men, even to male children, she put the book down and the recorder too, saying, "Mr. Aiken can help with your English. He has the best possible accent. When he says 'the girl' you will think he is saying 'de Gaulle.' "

"Irina has an odd ear for English," said the old man calmly. He got up slowly and went to the kitchen, and she did too, and Riri could hear them whispering and laughing at something. Mr. Aiken came back alone carrying a small glass of clear liquid. "The morning heart-starter," he said. "Try it." Riri took a sip. It lay in his stomach like a warm stone. "No more effect on you than a gulp of milk," said the old man, marvelling, sitting down close to Riri again. "You could probably do with pints of this stuff. I can tell by looking at you you'll be a drinking man." His hands on the walking stick began to tremble anew. "I am not the man I was," he said. "Not by any means." Because he did not speak English with a French or any foreign accent, Riri could not really understand him. He went on, "Fell down the staircase at the Trouville casino. Trouville, or that other place. Shock gave me amnesia. Hole in the stair carpet — must have been. I went there for years," he said. "Never saw a damned hole in anything. Now my hands shake."

"When you lift your glass to drink they don't shake," called Riri's grandmother from the kitchen. She repeated this in French, for good measure.

"She's got an ear like a radar unit," said Mr. Aiken.

Riri took up his tape recorder. In a measured chant, as if demonstrating to his grandmother how these things should be done, he said, " 'The swallows would not fly away if the season is fine.' "

"Do you know what any of it means?" said Mr. Aiken.

"He doesn't need to know what it means," Riri's grandmother answered for him. "He just needs to know it by heart."

They were glassed in on the balcony. The only sound they could hear was of their own voices. The sun on them was so hot that Riri wanted to take off his sweater. Looking down, he saw a chalet crushed in the shadows of two white blocks, not so tall as their own. A large, spared spruce tree suddenly seemed to retract its branches and allow a great weight of snow to slip off. Cars went by, dogs barked, children called — all in total silence. His grandmother talked English to the old man. Riri, when he was not actually eating, read *Astérix in Brittany* without attracting her disapproval.

"If people can be given numbers, like marks in school," she said, "then children are zero." She was enveloped in a fur cloak, out of which her hands and arms emerged as if the fur had dissolved in certain places. She was pink with wine and sun. The old man's blue eyes were paler then hers. "Zero." She held up thumb and forefinger in an O. "I was there with my five darling zeros while he… You are probably wondering if I was *ever* happy. At the beginning, in the first days, when I thought he would give me interesting books to read, books that would change all my life. Riri," she said, shading her eyes, "the cake and the ice cream were, I am afraid, the end of things for the moment. Could I ask you to clear the table for me?"

"I don't at home." Nevertheless he made a wobbly pile of dishes and took them away and did not come back. They heard him, indoors, starting all over: " 'Go, went, gone.' "

"I have only half a memory for dates," she said. "I forget my children's birthdays until the last minute and have to send them telegrams. But I know *that* day...."

"The twenty-sixth of May," he said. "What I forget is the year."

"I know that I felt young."

"You were. You *are* young," he said.

"Except that I was forty if a day." She glanced at the hands and wrists emerging from her cloak as if pleased at their whiteness. "The river was so sluggish, I remember. And the willows trailed in the river."

"Actually, there was a swift current after the spring rains."

"But no wind. The clouds were heavy."

"It was late in the afternoon," he said. "We sat on the grass."

"On a raincoat. You had thought in the morning those clouds meant rain."

"A young man drowned," he said. "Fell out of a boat. Funny, he didn't try to swim. So people kept saying."

"We saw three firemen in gleaming metal helmets. They fished for him so languidly — the whole day was like that. They had a grappling hook. None of them knew what to do with it. They kept pulling it up and taking the rope from each other."

"They might have been after water lilies, from the look of them."

"One of them bailed out the boat with a blue saucepan. I remember that. They'd got that saucepan from the restaurant."

"Where we had lunch," he said. "Trout, and a coffee cream pudding. You left yours."

"It was soggy cake. But the trout was perfection. So was the wine. The bridge over the river filled up slowly with holiday people. The three firemen rowed to shore."

"Yes, and one of them went off on a shaky bicycle and came back with a coil of frayed rope on his shoulders."

"The railway station was just behind us. All those people on the bridge were waiting for a train. When the firemen's boat slipped off down the river, they moved without speaking from one side of the bridge to the other, just to watch the boat. The silence of it."

"Like the silence here."

"This is planned silence," she said.

Riri played back his own voice. A tinny, squeaky Riri said, " 'Go, went, gone. Eat, ate, eaten. See, saw, sen.' "

" 'Seen'!" called his grandmother from the balcony. " 'Seen,' not 'sen.' His mother made exactly that mistake," she said to the old man. "Oh, stop that," she said. He was crying. "Please, please stop that. How could I have left five children?"

"Three were grown," he gasped, wiping his eyes.

"But they didn't know it. They didn't know they were grown. They still don't know it. And it made six children, counting him."

"The secretary mothered him," he said. "All he needed."

"I know, but you see she wasn't his wife, and he liked saying to strangers 'my wife,' 'my wife this,' 'my wife that.' What is it, Riri? Have you come to finish doing the thing I asked?"

He moved close to the table. His round glasses made him look desperate and stern. He said, "Which room is mine!" Darkness had gathered round him in spite of the sparkling sky and a row of icicles gleaming and melting in the most dazzling possible light. Outrage, a feeling that consideration had been wanting — that was how homesickness had overtaken him. She held his hand (he did not resist — another sign of his misery) and together they explored the apartment. He saw it all — every picture and cupboard and doorway — and in the end it was he who decided that Mr. Aiken must keep the spare room and he, Riri, would be happy on the living-room couch.

The old man passed them in the hall; he was obviously about to rest on the very bed he had just been within an inch of losing. He carried a plastic bottle of Evian. "Do you like the bland taste of water?" he said.

Riri looked boldly at his grandmother and said, "Yes," bursting into unexplained and endless-seeming laughter. He seemed to feel a relief at this substitute for impertinence. The old man laughed too, but broke off, coughing.

At half past four, when the windows were as black as the sky in the painting of tulips and began to reflect the lamps in a disturbing sort of way, they drew the curtains and had tea around the table. They pushed Riri's books and belongings to one side and spread a cross-stitched tablecloth. Riri had hot chocolate, a croissant left from breakfast and warmed in the oven, which made it deliciously greasy and soft, a slice of lemon sponge cake, and a banana. This time he helped clear away and even remained in the kitchen, talking, while his grandmother rinsed the cups and plates and stacked them in the machine.

The old man sat on a chair in the hall struggling with snow boots. He was going out alone in the dark to post some letters and to buy a newspaper and to bring back whatever provisions he thought were required for the evening meal.

"Riri, do you want to go with Mr. Aiken? Perhaps you should have a walk."

"At home I don't have to."

His grandmother looked cross; no, she looked worried. She was biting something back. The old man had finished the contention with his boots and now he put on a scarf, a fur-lined coat, a fur hat with earflaps, woollen gloves, and he took a list and a shopping bag and a different walking stick, which looked something like a ski pole. His grandmother still, as if dreaming, and then (addressing Riri) decided to wash all her amber necklaces. She fetched a wicker basket from her bedroom. It was lined with orange silk and filled with strings of beads. Riri followed her to the bathroom and sat on the end of the tub. She rolled up her soft sleeves and scrubbed the amber with laundry soap and a stiff brush. She scrubbed and rinsed and then began all over again.

"I am good at things like this," she said. "Now, unless you hate to discuss it, tell me something about your school."

At first he had nothing to say, but then he told her how stupid the younger boys were and what they were allowed to get away with.

"The younger boys would be seven, eight?" Yes, about that. "A hopeless generation?"

He wasn't sure; he knew that his class had been better.

She reached down and fetched a bottle of something from behind the bathtub and they went back to the sitting room together. They put a lamp between them, and Irina began to polish the amber with cotton soaked in turpentine. After a time the amber began to shine. The smell made him homesick, but not unpleasantly. He carefully selected a necklace when she told him he might take one for his mother, and he rubbed it with a soft cloth. She showed him how to make the beads magnetic by rolling them in his palms.

"You can do that even with plastic," he said.

"Can you? How very sad. It is dead matter."

"Amber is too," he said politely.

"What do you want to be later on? A scientist?"

"A ski instructor." He looked all around the room, at the shelves and curtains and at the bamboo folding screen, and said, "If you didn't live here, who would?"

She replied, "If you see anything that pleases you, you may keep it. I want you to choose your own present. If you don't see anything, we'll go out tomorrow and look in the shops. Does that suit you?" He did not reply. She held the necklace he had picked and said, "Your mother will remember seeing this as I bent down to kiss her good night. Do you like old coins? One of my sons was a collector." In the wicker basket was a lacquered box that contained his uncle's coin collection. He took a coin but it meant nothing to him; he let it fall. It clinked, and he said, "We have a dog now." The dog wore a metal tag that rang when the dog drank out of a china bowl. Through a sudden rainy blur of new homesickness he saw that she had something else, another lacquered box, full of old cancelled stamps. She showed him a stamp with Hitler and one with an Italian king. "I've kept funny things," she said. "Like this beautiful Russian box. It belonged to my grandmother, but after I have died I expect it will be thrown out. I gave whatever jewelry I had left to my daughters. We never had furniture, so I became attached to strange little baskets and boxes of useless things. My poor daughters — I had precious little to give. But they won't be able to wear rings any more than I could. We all come into our inherited arthritis, these knotted-up hands. Our true heritage. When I was your age, about, my mother was dying of…I wasn't told. She took a ring from under her pillow and folded my hand on it. She said that I could always sell it if I had to, and no one need know. You see, in those days women had nothing of their own. They were like brown paper parcels tied with string. They were handed like parcels from their fathers to their husbands. To make the parcel look attractive it was decked with curls and piano lessons, and rings and gold coins and banknotes and shares. After appraising all the decoration, the new owner would undo the knots."

"Where is that ring?" he said. The blur of tears was forgotten.

"I tried to sell it when I needed money. The decoration on the brown paper parcel was disposed of by then. Everything thrown, given away. Not by me. My pearl necklace was sold for Spanish refugees. Victims, flotsam, the injured, the weak — they were important. I wasn't. The children weren't. I had my ring. I took it to a municipal pawnshop. It is a place were you take things and they give you money. I wore dark glasses and turned up my coat collar, like a spy." He looked as though he understood that. "The man behind the counter said that I was a married woman and I needed my husband's written consent. I said the ring was mine. He said nothing could be mine, or something to that effect. Then he said he might have given me something for the gold in the band of the ring but the stones were worthless. He said this happened in the finest of families. Someone had pried the real stones out of their setting."

"Who did that?"

"A husband. Who else would? Someone's husband — mine, or my mother's, or my mother's mother's, when it comes to that."

"With a knife?" said Riri. He said, "The man might have been pretending. Maybe he took out the stones and put in glass."

"There wasn't time. And they were perfect imitations — the right shapes and sizes."

"He might have had glass stones all different sizes."

"The women in the family never wondered if men were lying," she said. "They never questioned being dispossessed. They were taught to think that lies were a joke on the liar. That was why they lost out. He gave me the price of the gold in the band, as a favor, and I left the ring there. I never went back."

He put the lid on the box of stamps, and it fitted; he removed it, put it back, and said, "What time do you turn on your TV?"

"Sometimes never. Why?"

"At home I have it from six o'clock."

The old man came in with a pink-and-white face, bearing about him a smell of cold and of snow. He put down his shopping bag and took things out — chocolate and bottles and newspapers. He said, "I had to go all the way to the station for the papers. There is only one shop open, and even then I had to go round to the back door."

"I warned you that today was Christmas," Irina said.

Mr. Aiken said to Riri, "When I was still a drinking man this was the best hour of the day. If I had a glass now, I could put ice in it. Then I might add water. Then if I had water I could add whiskey. I know it is all the wrong way around, but at least I've started with a glass."

"You had wine with your lunch and gin instead of tea and I believe you had straight gin before lunch," she said, gathering up the beads and coins and the turpentine and making the table Riri's domain again.

"Riri drank that," he said. It was so obviously a joke that she turned her head and put the basket down and covered her laugh with her fingers, as she had when she'd opened the door to him — oh, a long time ago now.

"I haven't a drop of anything left in the house," she said. That didn't matter, the old man said, for he had found what he needed. Riri watched and saw that when he lifted his glass his hand did not tremble at all. What his grandmother had said about that was true.

They had early supper and then Riri, after a courageous try at keeping awake, gave up even on television and let her make his bed of scented sheets, deep pillows, a feather quilt. The two others sat for a long time at the table, with just one lamp, talking in low voices. She had a pile of notebooks from which she read aloud and sometimes she showed Mr. Aiken things. He could see them through the chinks in the bamboo screen. He watched the lamp shadows for a while and then it was as if the lamp had gone out and he slept deeply.

The room was full of mound shapes, as it had been that morning when he arrived. He had not heard them leave the room. His Christmas watch had hands that glowed in the dark. He put on his glasses. It was half past ten. His grandmother was being just a bit loud at the telephone; that was what had woken him up. He rose, put on his slippers, and stumbled out to the bathroom.

"Just answer yes or no," she was saying. "No, he can't. He has been asleep for an hour, two hours, at least. ...Don't lie to me — I am bound to find the truth out. Was it a tumor? An extrauterine pregnancy? ...Well, look. ...Was she or was she not pregnant? What can you mean by 'not exactly'? If you don't know, who will?" She happened to turn her head, and saw him and said without a change of tone, "Your son is here, in his pajamas; he wants to say good night to you."

She gave up the telephone and immediately went away so that the child could talk privately. She heard him say, "I drank some kind of alcohol."

So that was the important part of the day: not the journey, not the necklace, not even the strange old guest with the comic accent. She could tell from the sound of the child's voice that he was smiling. She picked up his bathrobe, went back to the hall, and put it over his shoulders. He scarcely saw her: he was concentrated on the distant voice. He said, in a matter-of-fact way, "All right, goodbye," and hung up.

"What a lot of things you have pulled out of that knapsack," she said.

"It's a large one. My father had it for military service."

Now, why should that make him suddenly homesick when his father's voice had not? "You are good at looking after yourself," she said. "Independent. No one has to tell you what to do. Of course, your mother had sound training. Once when I was looking for a nurse for your mother and her sisters, a great peasant woman came to see me, wearing a black apron and black buttoned boots. I said,

'What can you teach children?' And she said, 'To be clean and polite.' Your grandfather said, 'Hire her,' and stamped out of the room."

His mother interested, his grandfather bored him. He had the Christian name of a dead old man.

"You will sleep well," his grandmother promised, pulling the feather quilt over him. "You will dream short dreams at first, and by morning they will be longer and longer. The last one of all just before you wake up will be like a film. You will wake up wondering where you are, and then you will hear Mr. Aiken. First he will go round shutting all the windows, then you will hear his bath. He will start the coffee in an electric machine that makes a noise like a door rattling. He will pull on his snow boots with a lot of cursing and swearing and go out to fetch our croissants and the morning papers. Do you know what day it will be? The day after Christmas." He was almost asleep. Next to his watch and his glasses on a table close to the couch was an Astérix book and Irina's Russian box with old stamps in it. "Have you decided you want the stamps?"

"The box. Not the stamps."

He had taken, by instinct, the only object she wanted to keep. "For a special reason?" she said. "Of course, the box is yours. I am only wondering."

"The cover fits," he said.

She knew that the next morning he would have been here forever and that at parting time, four days later, she would have to remind him that leaving was the other half of arriving. She smiled, knowing how sorry he would be to go and how soon he would leave her behind. "This time yesterday…" he might say, but no more than once. He was asleep. His mouth opened slightly and the hair on his forehead became dark and damp. A doubled-up arm looked uncomfortable but Irina did not interfere; his sunken mind, his unconscious movements, had to be independent, of her or anyone, particularly of her. She did not love him more or less than any of her grandchildren. You see, it all worked out, she was telling him. You, and your mother, and the children being so worried, and my old friend. Anything can be settled for a few days at a time, though not for longer. She put out the light, for which his body was grateful. His mind, at that moment, in a sunny icicle brightness, was not only skiing but flying.

Commentary by
Mavis Gallant

≈

Mavis Gallant is renowned for the richness and ironic force of her prose. The following commentary is taken from "What Is Style?", first published in the anthology Making It New: Contemporary Canadian Stories *(Toronto: Methuen, 1982), and republished in Gallant's* Paris Notebooks: Essays & Reviews *(Toronto: Macmillan, 1986). Here Gallant uses an example from modern painting to make the point that in practice — as distinguished from theory — the vitality of any work of art depends on the integrity of style, the genius, of the individual artist.*

There are rules of style. By applying them doggedly any literate, ambitious and determined person should be able to write like Somerset Maugham. Maugham was conscious of his limitations and deserves appreciation on that account: "I knew that I had no lyrical quality, I had a small vocabulary.... I had little gift for metaphors; the original or striking simile seldom occurred to me. Poetic flights and the great imaginative sweep were beyond my powers." He decided, sensibly, to write "as well as my natural defects allowed" and to aim at "lucidity, simplicity and euphony". The chance that some other indispensable quality had been overlooked must have been blanketed by a lifetime of celebrity. Now, of course, first principles are there to be heeded or, at the least, considered with care; but no guided tour of literature, no commitment to the right formula or to good taste (which is changeable anyway) can provide, let alone supplant, the inborn vitality and tension of living prose.

Like every other form of art, literature is no more and nothing less than a matter of life and death. The only question worth asking about a story — or a poem, or a piece of sculpture, or a new concert hall — is, "Is it dead or alive?" If a work of the imagination needs to be coaxed into life, it is better scrapped and forgotten. Working to rule, trying to make a barely breathing work of fiction simpler and more lucid and more euphonious merely injects into the desperate author's voice a tone of suppressed hysteria, the result of what E. M. Forster called "confusing order with orders". And then, how reliable are the rules? Listen to Pablo Picasso's rejection of a fellow-artist: "He looks up at the sky and says, 'Ah, the sky is blue', and he paints a blue sky. Then he takes another look and says, 'The sky is mauve, too', and he adds some mauve. The next time he looks he notices a trace of pink, and he adds a little pink." It sounds a proper mess, but Picasso was talking about Pierre Bonnard. As soon as we learn the name, the blues, mauves and pinks acquire a meaning, a reason to be. Picasso was right, but only in theory. In the end, everything depends on the artist himself.

SELECTED WORKS BY MAVIS GALLANT

The Other Paris: Stories. Cambridge, MA: Houghton Mifflin, 1956. Rpt. as *The Other Paris*. Toronto: Macmillan, 1986.

My Heart Is Broken: Eight Stories and a Short Novel. New York: Random House, 1964. New Press Canadian Classics. Toronto: General Publishing, 1982.

The Pegnitz Junction: A Novella and Five Short Stories. New York: Random House, 1973. Macmillan Paperbacks 36. Toronto: Macmillan, 1988.

The End of the World and Other Stories. Introd. Robert Weaver. New Canadian Library 91. Toronto: McClelland and Stewart, 1974.

From the Fifteenth District: A Novella and Eight Short Stories. New York: Random House, 1979. Toronto: Macmillan, 1979. Macmillan Paperbacks 11. Toronto: Macmillan, 1986.

Home Truths: Selected Canadian Stories. Introd. Mavis Gallant. Toronto: Macmillan, 1981. Macmillan Paperbacks 20. Toronto: Macmillan, 1987.

Overhead in a Balloon: Stories of Paris. Toronto: Macmillan, 1985. Macmillan Paperbacks 48. Toronto: Macmillan, 1990.

In Transit. Markham, ON: Viking/Penguin Books, 1988. [Paperback ed.] Markham, ON: Penguin Books, 1989.

Norman Levine

≈

Norman Levine's reputation in Canada is rising. In England and in Europe he has been highly regarded for years but in Canada recognition has come slowly. Even though most of his stories had Canadian settings, the fact that he had chosen to live in England was not kindly received here. His early and unflattering travel book, *Canada Made Me* (1958), which no Canadian publisher would touch at the time, also contributed to his exclusion.

Levine's first collection of stories, *One Way Ticket*, was issued in England in 1961. Not until 1971 was a collection — his second, entitled *I Don't Want To Know Anyone Too Well and Other Stories* — published in Canada. I consider "A Small Piece of Blue", reprinted here from that 1971 collection, to be one of Levine's finest stories. It was chosen as the title story of a Levine collection published in Germany and translated by Heinrich and Annemarie Böll. It was, however, excluded by Canadian editors from *Champagne Barn* (1984), a volume which claims to be "a retrospective of Norman Levine's finest work". Also excluded from *Champagne Barn* is another superb story from that 1971 collection, "My Karsh Picture".

Many of the stories Levine wrote in England during the 1970s, starting with "We All Begin in a Little Magazine", were commissioned by Robert Weaver for the CBC radio programme *Anthology*. As Levine was living in straitened circumstances, these commissions were vital to him and he fell into the habit of structuring his stories to fit the time limits of the programme, writing stories which would take fifteen to twenty minutes to read aloud. In the 1980s, when he returned to Canada and was freed from those restrictions, his writing began to change. The stories grew longer, more complex, more layered. The other story selected for this book, the title story from Levine's collection *Something Happened Here* (1991), is a good example of this increasing complexity. If this book were without constraints of length, we could have chosen "Soap Opera", also from *Something Happened Here*, as an example of his evolving work.

Levine's writing always seems clear and simple but nearly always turns out to be much more complicated than at first thought. The emotional force of his stories nearly always inheres in images and dialogue whose significance we must perceive for ourselves. Nor will Levine point up for us the relationships *between* the images. It is up to us to edge into a story's emotional flow. In brief, he's working as a poet works. It's not surprising that his first two books were collections of poetry: *Myssium* (1948) and *The Tight-Rope Walker* (1950).

The beat and the still
And the beat, caught, lift,
Of the rook and the gull
Over sea, roof, hill,
Disturb this place from sleep.

Of these lines he wrote: "it was the first line — describing the way the bird flew — that made me realize that the leaner the language the more ambiguous it becomes, and the more suggestive."

This observation appears in an essay by Levine entitled "Sometimes It Works", published in the anthology *How Stories Mean* (Erin, ON: The Porcupine's Quill, 1993). In the same essay he explains: "The more you tell — the more you are keeping the reader out from bringing his or her experience in. So if you can reduce a thing to a minimum like 'The beat and the still' — then the reader brings his or her associations to that. So contrary to what people think: the more cryptic you are the more resonance there is. Think what makes a good title. Just a couple of words: *Adult Entertainment... Thin Ice...* (of course you have to get the right words)..."

"Something Happened Here" is emotionally a very complicated story. We can only compose it for ourselves by giving ourselves up to its flow of images and to its strange conversations. Put crudely and reductively, it is concerned with the fact that life goes on despite all the ills that flesh is heir to, despite past tragedy — a feeling that Levine vividly embodies in the description of the dead shrew being eaten by the living. But notice how this paragraph is followed by an equally emblematic paragraph describing the quotidian activities of the people on the beach, the mother feeding the child, the repetitive little journeys of the wind-surfer, the continual backwards and forwards of the surf over the pebbles, a dailiness the narrator implicitly embraces when, instead of musing on the Dieppe dead, he joins the people waiting in line to buy duty-free goods. It is in the connecting or juxtaposing of two such paragraphs as these that the life of Levine's writing lies; his stories are as simple or as subtle as the people reading them.

≈

Two literary critics, T. D. MacLulich and Lawrence Mathews, contributed fascinating essays on "A Small Piece of Blue" to *Writers in Aspic* (Montreal: Véhicule Press, 1988); they are completely at loggerheads over this story and the essays offer readers a marvellous opportunity to join in the continuing debate. Lawrence Mathews has also written an important monograph, *Norman Levine and His Works* (Toronto: ECW Press, 1990). Other studies include Frederick Sweet's "Norman Levine" in *Profiles in Canadian Literature*, vol. 4 (Toronto: Dundurn Press, 1983) and Simone Vauthier's "Portrait of the Artist as a (no longer) Young Man: Norman Levine's 'We All Begin in a Little Magazine'" in *New Directions from Old* (Guelph, ON: Red Kite Press, 1991). For additional discussions of Levine's background and his work, see the interviews by John D. Cox, David McDonald, Wayne Grady, and Cary Fagan which appear, respectively, in *Canadian Literature* 45 (1970), *Queen's Quarterly* 83 (1976), *Books in Canada* Feb. 1980, and *Descant* 40 (1983).

≈ A SMALL PIECE OF BLUE ≈

On Thursday morning the train arrived at Sault Ste. Marie. Leaving my bag in the left luggage I asked the way to the office of the Algoma Ore Properties. The man in the company's office was tall and wore a loose-fitting summer suit. He had the appearance of an athlete turned salesman. Straight blond hair combed back without a parting, a well-fed face. But there was something deceptive about the way he talked. For his mouth when open seemed unnatural in that position as in those films where animals are made to speak like human beings. I showed him my letter from the Mine Manager. He read it, said I was lucky, for I would be able to get a train out tomorrow.

"There are only two trains that go up a week, Tuesdays and Fridays."

He walked to a large map on the wall. It hung there framed. The bottom had a large blue area marked Lake Superior. Smaller pieces of blue were scattered all over the map.

"The only other way is by seaplane." He tapped a spot in the far right-hand corner. "There won't be a plane till Saturday and if the weather's bad there won't be a plane."

He enjoyed what he had said for he walked away from the map to his desk and offered me a cigarette.

"It'll cost you twenty more dollars to fly in."

It was the way he mentioned money that brought back those classes in salesmanship we had at high school where we had to stand in front of the class and pretend we were selling something while the teacher criticised our technique.

"Besides it's a job," the tall man said, "finding the right lake. There are thousands like them. And the bush pilots are just as likely to put you down on the wrong one."

I said I would take the company's train.

Sault Ste. Marie was the kind of place that I had been in before. The quick stay in a small town where I knew that after a few years I would remember very little of it, in this case a zoo. Away from the main street I walked in a residential area. The houses were set back from the sidewalk by lawns; grass, trees, but no flowers. One wooden house with a large veranda had a cardboard sign, *Room To Let*, nailed to a veranda post. Above the bell-button was a metal plate, *L. M. Kalma. Music Teacher. Qualified*. I rang the bell. I could hear the bell ringing inside. But the tall, grey door remained closed. I rang and knocked and waited. A window on the top opened but no one looked out. Then I heard steps.

The woman who opened the door was small. She had a dressing-gown on over a nightdress. Her hair was grey, fuzzy, and held in place by a net. Though it was early afternoon the fact that she had obviously just come out of bed did not seem as startling as her face. The eyes were there. So was the mouth. But where her nose should have been there was a flat surface of scarred flesh with two small holes.

"You caught me undressed."

I told her I wanted a room for one night. She led me upstairs to a bedroom. A square room with a window and a large four-poster bed. "It's a feather bed," she said. "They are much better than spring or rubber. The feathers they sleep with you like another person."

My first impulse was to make some excuse, leave, and find another place.

"The clever doctors, to them I ought to be dead."

She said this without sadness or humour. Then she showed me the bathroom, the light switch, asked me if I liked music, if $1.50 was not too much for the room, and placed on the kitchen table some cold chicken with sliced cucumber that she had taken from the ice-box. She insisted that I sit down and eat. I ate the food and she talked. She talked as if we had known each other for a long time. Like boat-passengers who have been forced into each other's company only for a particular journey and are safe with the knowledge that no matter how much one says or does there is no consequence to be faced. I now found a strong physical attraction to her face.

Later in the evening when I returned with my bag from the station it was difficult to recognise her as the same woman who opened the door. She had on a dark dress instead of a dressing-gown, but her face was different. She wore a false nose attached to a false piece of skin that stretched from one ear to the other and by wearing glasses held it in place. Face powder and rouge generously put on only helped to show the falseness. I preferred the scarred face with the two air holes to this manufactured monstrosity. In her attempt to look normal she looked ugly.

Next morning the train did not begin from the railway station but from a private siding by the Algoma Ore Properties' office. In the coach, besides myself, were four middle-aged Americans dressed in bright lumberjack shirts with fishing gear piled around them. The only other person was the ticket collector who, I discovered later, was also our cook.

The coach was old and of a type I had not seen on either the Canadian National or the Canadian Pacific. The inside was like a worn-out billiard table with large patches eaten out of the green.

The seats were hard and uncomfortable. Gas brackets hung from the ceiling. In the centre of the ceiling a light-bulb did not give much light. But we did not go through many tunnels. Travelling into the bush we continually crossed trestle-bridges, curved by small lakes, and moved slowly through miles of pine and soft-wood. By noon the journey had gone on much too long. The total distance was less than a hundred miles north and we had travelled half of it when the ticket collector came and asked me if I wanted some grub. I followed him into his compartment at the head of the coach. One side had deep shelves from the ceiling to the floor and the shelves had tinned goods in them. The ticket collector took a tin from a shelf. He showed me the tin. *Grade A. Specially Selected Ready To Serve Chicken*. "Want this?" he asked. "Go to your seat and I'll call you when she's ready. Here. Have a funny. It's on the house." He went over to the loose papers on top of a bundle. "What do you want? Annie. Tarzan. The Katzenjammer Kids."

A dog barked. In the corner opposite to where we were a cocker spaniel was kept in a large wicker cage.

"She's going the same place as you're going," he said.

I looked out from the small observation window. The train was going through a narrow valley. The earth was banked along the track. We were travelling so slow that it was possible to see the cracks in the soil. The ticket collector put down the chicken tin and filled a bowl with water from a kettle.

"You don't mind if I give her water. Trains give them this thirst."

He made a clucking noise with his tongue and walked over to the wicker basket and put the bowl down so that the dog could reach it.

"She belongs to an engineer at the Mine. He sends her to the Soo whenever she's in heat."

He knelt to the dog and fell over as the coach jolted. Instead of getting up he lay sprawled on the floor and talked to the dog.

"Was it good girl? Eh, my beauty. C'mon tell me —"

I left the ticket collector talking to the dog and returned to my seat with The Katzenjammer Kids and looked out of the window. The first excitement of seeing so much green and trees had passed. The trees were monotonous and I wanted the journey to end. I wondered why I was going to the Mine. Part of it was for the money and the experience. But I felt convinced that there was something else. Four years of lectures and campus enthusiasms had given me an overdose of books and words and examinations. I felt as if I was on a see-saw, stuck to the one side that was raised, where my head was the only part involved in "the goings on". Not that those four years were unpleasant. They only seem a waste of time, looking back.

I did not see the Mine until sundown. From the train it looked like an old ruin on top of a hill where the hills around were without trees or grass. The station was at the bottom of the hill and we stopped by a long wooden platform. The train picked up water. Parcels and crates were moved from the train to the waiting trucks. Then the spaniel, free from the wicker cage, was given to someone in a car. A cream-coloured bus was also by the side of the platform. Some men were inside. I went to the bus. The driver sat like a sparrow over the wheel, a jockey cap on his head. He wore an orange sweater with a large H in green across the front.

"Your name Tree?"

When I said it was he said, "hop in."

The men by the station were watching the re-union of the spaniel with her owner. There were some guttural jokes made at the spaniel's friskiness, for they knew where she had been. Then the bus backed, turned, and drove off.

We came to a lake with wooden houses on one side. The bus stopped by a General Store. Several men with black lunch-pails climbed in. They called the driver Jack in various accents. He punched small cards that the men held up as they entered the bus. We drove around the lake and up a hill. Above us a steel cable carried large buckets of iron ore from the Mine to the Sinter Plant. We stopped at the top of the hill, beside a wooden building. I asked the driver where the office was. He said to follow him. He carried a mailsack over his shoulder.

"Where you from?"

"Montreal."

"Play ball?"

"A bit."

"What position?"

"I pitch."

He remained silent as we went through a wooden gate and into a frame building partitioned off for several offices. The bus driver dropped the mailsack on the floor and a girl came out of one of the partitions.

"Hi, Glorie. Someone from Montreal." And he went out.

She came to the counter, unsmiling, and took some paper, spread it flat.

"When did you come?"

A skirt and sweater and on her sweater at the neck she wore a black cross.

She took my name, age, and home address. Her eyes moved nervously. Her other features were coarse. When my card was filled out she told me to go to the cookhouse, a building some twenty yards away, and ask for the cook.

I crossed the bare hard-packed ground and saw a man with glasses, stripped to the waist, holding a white apron. He stood by the cookhouse near several large barrels filled with garbage and looked towards the horizon. I asked him if he could tell me where I could find the cook.

"Where you from?" he said with a Scottish accent.

"Montreal."

"Montreal," he said the word slowly, "it's seven years since I've been there. How are *The Canadiens* doing?" Not waiting for a reply he became excited and talked quickly. "The last time I was there I did a food crawl. I started at Pauze's with a dozen oysters then I went to the Bucharest for a steak, Ben's for a smoked-meat sandwich, Chicken Charlie's on St. Catherine for spare-ribs, and ended with spaghetti and meat balls at FDR's and before I caught the midnight train I took a taxi to a place called *Au Lutin qui Bouffe* where somebody blind played a piano while I had frog's legs and my picture taken giving a baby's bottle of milk to a little pig." As spontaneously as he started, he stopped. To cover up his embarrassment he became silent, then formal, as he led me to his cookhouse office.

In his office he issued me a new black lunchpail and I signed a slip for it. He told me to scratch my name on the lunchpail with a nail and that supper was at seven-thirty, so that I still had half an hour to get a place to sleep. We walked outside, through the dining-hall. Unpainted large wooden tables. Benches on both sides. The first table near the door had chairs, and a sign, *Staff Only*.

He showed me a building about fifty yards down the hill.

"Go to room nine, Laddie, and ask for Willie Hare."

The cable stretched over the cookhouse and I could hear it creak as the buckets kept passing overhead. Where the cable crossed between cookhouse and office a steel net was suspended above the ground.

I found number nine in a building smelling of paint. Outside the door a bundle of dirty laundry was tied together by a shirt. Some time passed between my knock and the door being opened. At first I thought he was a boy, then he switched the room light on and I could see that he was old, unshaven, and sleepy. He could not be much more than five feet, a thin frame covered by a dirty white shirt buttoned tight at the neck, collar crumpled, and grey trousers that were too small. He wore no shoes but heavy woollen socks. His fly-buttons were undone.

"My name is Tree. The cook told me that you would let me know where I sleep."

He hesitated, then turned back to the room leaving the door open. He went to a cupboard and pulled out a large piece of cardboard. Then he sat down on his bed and began to examine the large writing on one side of the board.

I looked around the room. It stank of old age. Shelves covered an entire wall. In these shelves: toothpaste, soap, razor blades, shoe laces, and chocolate bars were propped up in open boxes. Above his bed, pasted to the wall, was a map similar to the one hanging in the company's office in Sault Ste. Marie. Covering most of the map were pictures of boxers, hockey players, movie stars, old Christmas cards, pin-up girls, and an old calendar advertising Life Insurance.

"Yours will be number forty-two."

He spoke with difficulty for he had no teeth. They were sunk in a glass of water on the floor by his bed.

"You'll have another student in with you later. Tree."

And he laughed. "That's an easy one to spell." He licked the end of the pencil and printed my name large on the cardboard. "You can get most things from me." He showed me the cupboard built into the wall where he returned the piece of cardboard. Inside sprawled hundreds of paper-backed books. "Mystery, cowboy, sex stories, no need to pay. It'll come off of your cheque." He gave me the key to my room and returned to his bed entering between the sheets fully dressed.

"By the way Tree, where you from?"

"Montreal."

I waited. There was no reply.

As I walked out he called back. "Shut the light."

Number 42 was a square room freshly painted white, with one window directly opposite the door. Two beds. Two dressers. A naked light hung from the ceiling. I tried to raise the window but was able to move it only a few inches. I could see the side of a hill, the sky, and trees. The outside air tasted cold in my throat.

I unpacked and had put on a sweater and old flannels when I head a bell tolling. There was nothing urgent about the sound.

Silence. Then the sound again. I went out of the room and looked out of the window in the passage. Men were pressed tight to the door of the cookhouse. Others were running towards it. Suddenly the door opened and those that were there disappeared inside. By the time I reached the cookhouse the tables were crowded with men eating. Late-comers, like myself, were running from one table to another until we found a place on a bench.

At my table they were speaking German. The only one not speaking was deformed. He sat opposite me. Stubbles for fingers on a wrist which was raw. A large red handkerchief, tied around his head, went underneath his chin. He used this handkerchief to hold his jaw together. To eat he would loosen the knot above his head and with one stubbled hand he would slide the food from the table to his mouth while the other worked the jaw up and down.

"You a Canadian?"

He had bad teeth.

"Yes," I said.

"Look at the monkeys eat."

As a platter of food was placed on the table, often before it reached the table, bodies pushed, hands snatched whatever they could get. In less than ten minutes it was all over.

Outside the tramline continued to creak. The men stood waiting by the side of the cookhouse where, on to the main wall, a wooden booth was built. It stuck out like an ear. Steps without handrails led to a door. Someone shouted. "Here he comes." I saw Willie Hare coming from the office towards the cookhouse, his hands full of letters and newspapers. He gave the letters to the first man then went up the ladder to the booth and threw the papers inside. "Shout them out." Another man took the envelopes away from the first man and began to call out names. Letters passed from hand to hand. After all the names had been read out several times the DP's went through them again.

I woke next morning to the sound of blasting followed later by the steady tolling bell. Breakfast was a repetition of the supper last night, except that different faces were at the table. After breakfast I walked over to the office. The manager had not yet arrived. Glorie suggested that I go and see the doctor as I had to have a medical before I could begin work.

The doctor's office (a wooden building as were all the buildings on top of the hill) was a few minutes' walk from the cookhouse. His hours according to a sign were 10-12. I arrived after ten and it was now 11:32 and still no one had arrived. A man with a crew-cut, wearing white shorts and an open shirt, approached. I asked him if he was the doctor.

"I'm not that lucky," he said, and walked on.

The doctor arrived at noon. He was the palest person I had so far seen at the Mine. A long head on a tall thin body. His face reminded me of a goat. Straight black hair parted on the side. A thin mouth. It was difficult to guess his age. He could as easily have been in his thirties as in his forties. He opened the door and indicated that I enter.

"They said in the office to come and see you about a medical."

He remained silent, took off his jacket and flung it on to the leather couch that was near his desk. The room was small and stifling. All the windows were closed. Papers were on the floor. A file, like a broken accordion, lay on the floor with papers sticking out from the bellow pockets. A telephone was on the desk. Beside it, piled high on top of each other, were old telephone directories. On the desk a dish had dried apples, over-ripe pears, and an onion sprouting. A green filing cabinet stood against the wall by the window. On top of it several parcels, tied crudely together, had holes in the brown paper as if the rats had been there. A picture of Mickey Mouse was the only bright spot in the room and it hung as a target on a piece of cardboard underneath the eye-chart. There were three chairs and a leather couch to sit on.

"You another student?"

I said I was.

He began to listen to my chest.

"Where you from?"

"McGill."

He looked up, surprised.

"And how is the dear place. Are they still after you asking to give money for some building or drive, writing you letters, telling you how important you are to them — "

"I just graduated," I said.

"You'll get them soon enough."

He did not bother to examine me further but went over to his filing cabinet, unlocked it, and from the back he brought out two large glasses and a half-full bottle of brandy.

"It's all right, Tree. I was there myself. Good time. Best time I ever had."

He poured the glasses nearly full and we drank.

"We must have a re-union. You know you are the first McGill man who has hit this God-forsaken hole. The others at the staff table are a bunch of hicks from all the hick colleges across the country." Then, as if he remembered something, he came and shook my hand.

"My name is Crepeau."

We continued drinking. I told him who on the faculty had died, who had left, and he appeared to be interested when I said a name he knew. The conversation jumped from the campus, to Montreal, to sport, to the different places we had seen. "Look at yourself," he suddenly interrupted. "You talk. You can talk like I can talk. We both can make talk. Talk on anything. They have seen to that. But what good does it do you, or anybody else? They've sandpapered all your rough edges, your instincts, your intuitions, then turned you out with a fake smartness like a car on the assembly line. You happen to be the 1950 model. I was the 1933. The funny thing is we like it."

He stood up.

So did I.

"You'd better sit. You're only here for this summer so you'd better listen. I was like yourself twenty years back, perhaps better. I had first-class honours, won prizes, had an offer to continue research in a San Francisco hospital. But I said to hell with them —"

He opened his arms indicating the untidy room.

" — they don't make it easy for you to be a failure."

Suddenly he seemed to lose interest in what he was saying for he walked to the filing cabinet and from behind it took out an air rifle and a candle. He lit the candle and stood it up on top of the filing cabinet, in front of the crudely wrapped parcels. He broke his rifle and inserted a slug.

"Let's see what kind of shot you are. Go against the far wall and put the flame out."

The distance was about ten yards. I aimed. I missed. He made me try again. This time I hit the candle, knocking it down, but the wick still burned. He tried. His first shot either went through the flame, or very near it, for it flickered. The next one put it out. He returned the rifle to its place and offered me a cigarette.

"I know I'm tight, but it does not matter. What does any one person matter. They come into your world for a while then leave it just as quickly as they entered."

He finished what was in his glass, poured more in and drank it down.

"Don't expect the men to like you. When they find out that you've been to university and have come here it's like telling them that what they believe in is rotten. They work hard to save money so that their kids can go to university, get a degree, and not have to come to places like this. Then they see you here — "

The room was stuffy yet all the windows were shut. I was glad that he stopped talking for I found the atmosphere in the room and the brandy had made me sleepy and I wondered how much longer he would go on before I could excuse myself and leave.

"Use your eyes and you can see a lot," he said. "Everyone else who is here has not come by choice. The DP's are counting the days, marking them off on their calendars until they can get away to Toronto, Montreal, or Winnipeg. Those who work underground stay as long as the bonus makes it worthwhile, then they drift to some other place. A few scarecrows like Willie Hare and Old Harold hang on because the company ruined them as human beings. For fun the men play crap, smuggle hootch, and pin black lace panties on their walls that they get from the Soo."

He stopped talking to drink and fill the glasses again.

"I suppose you'll return to Montreal," he burped and excused himself.

"I don't want any of that kind of civilisation. I've contracted out from all of them. I drink, and I write poetry."

He tried to get more brandy out of the bottle but it was empty.

"Sometimes I go to the Soo. The last time I took a case of Scotch, found myself a hotel room, locked the door, and I didn't get out of bed as long as the Scotch lasted."

He went over to his desk, unlocked a drawer, and brought out a leather folder. From it he took a piece of paper.

"I wrote this on my last blow."

All your experiences:
Those bits.
Those pieces you carried away with you.
How long will they last?

At the undertaker she showed me the coffin.
'Oak the best wooden one
Won't last you more than twenty-five years.
It falls away like paper.'

Those bits and pieces you carried away.
How long will they?

He stopped. For some reason he looked embarrassed. He went to his desk and returned the piece of paper to the leather folder.

"I've got a couple of hundred poems. Some day I'll get them put into a nice book and send it to the dear old place with my compliments."

The effort of reading seemed to sober him up for he threw the empty bottle into a large sack by his desk that had something soft in it for there was no sound of the bottle hitting. He picked up his jacket.

"There's no point staying in here."

We went out and walked along the slope of the hill. The bell began to toll for lunch. Grass was burnt. And scattered were small patches of blueberry bushes. We walked on a narrow path sunk in the hard ground following the contour of the hill. I could see the tramline going down but we were too far away to hear the buckets creak although the sound of the bell still reached us. The doctor walked in front.

"Fly in?"

"No. I took the train."

"It only takes an hour to fly in."

"The manager at the Soo told me pilots can't find this lake easy."

"There's only one lake in the bush shaped like ours."

We walked on. The sun was still hot. The bell tolled behind us. And I could now see a gull flying alongside the hill and a small piece of blue locked in the surrounding earth and rock growing larger below. The slope of the land entered the water and split the top quarter in two.

"What does she look like to you," the doctor said.

I stood on a flat rock looking at the lake that I had come by on the bus yesterday.

"To me it's more like a heart."

He said this without waiting to hear what I might say.

≈ SOMETHING HAPPENED HERE ≈

I felt at home soon as I got out of the Paris train and waited for a taxi outside the railway station. I could hear the gulls but I couldn't see them because of the mist. But I could smell the sea. The driver brought me to a hotel along the front. It was a residential hotel beside other residential hotels with the menu in a glass case by the sidewalk. It had four storeys. Its front tall windows, with wooden shutters and small iron balconies, faced the sea. On the ground level was the hotel's dining-room. The front wall was all glass. And there was a man sitting alone by a table.

It looked a comfortable family hotel. The large wooden staircase belonged to an earlier time when it had been a family house. The woman who now owned and ran it liked porcelain. She had cups and saucers on large sideboards, on every landing, as well as grandfather clocks and old clocks without hands. They struck the hour at different times. There were fresh and not so fresh flowers in porcelain vases. There were large mirrors, in wooden frames, tilted against the wall, like paintings. There were china plates, china cups, and china teapots on top of anything that could hold them.

My room on the third floor didn't face the sea but a courtyard. I watched a short man in a chef's hat cutting vegetables into a pot. The room was spacious enough but it seemed over-furnished. It had a large double bed with a carving of two birds on the headboard. A tall wooden closet, a heavy wooden sideboard, a solid table, several chairs, a colour television, and a small fridge fully stocked with wine, brandy, champagne, mineral water and fruit juices. On the fridge was a pad and pencil to mark what one drank.

After I partly unpacked and washed I went down to the dining-room and was shown to a table by the glass wall next to the man sitting alone. He was smoking a cigarette and drinking coffee. He had on a fawn shirt with an open collar and a carefully tied black and white cravat at the neck. He also had fawn coloured trousers. He looked like Erich von Stroheim.

The proprietress came to take my order. She wobbled, coquettishly, on high heels. Medium height, a little plump, in her late forties or early fifties perhaps. She had a sense of style. She wore a different tailored dress every day I was there. A striking person. She had a white complexion and black hair. And looked in fine health. Her teeth were very good. There was a liveliness in her dark eyes. Every time I walked by the desk and the lounge she never seemed far away: doing accounts, dealing with the staff, talking to guests.

I gave her my order in English. I ordered a salad, an omelette, and a glass of *vin rosé*.

When she had gone the man at the next table said in a loud voice, "Are you English or American?"

"Canadian."

He began to talk in French.

Although I understood some of what he said I replied, "I can't speak French very well. I'm *English* Canadian."

"I speak English," he said. "I had lessons in Paris at the Berlitz school. My English teacher, she was a pretty woman, said I was very good because I could use the word barbed-wire in a sentence. My name is Georges."

I told him mine. But for some reason he called me Roman.

"Roman, what do you do?"

"I am a writer."

"Come, join me," he said. "I like very much the work of Somerset Muffin and Heavelin Woof. Are you staying in this hotel?"

"Yes. I arrived a half-hour ago."

"I live in the country. Since my wife is dead I come here once a week to eat. What do you write?"

"Short stories," I said, "novels."

"I read many books — but not novels. I read books of ideas. The conclusion I have come is that you can divide the people of the world. There are the sedentary. There are the nomads. The sedentary — they are registered. We know about them. The nomads — they leave no record."

A young waiter, in a white double-breasted jacket, poured more coffee.

"Do you know Dieppe?"

"No, this is my first time here."

"I will show you."

And he did. When I finished eating he took me along the promenade. A brisk breeze was blowing but the sea remained hidden by mist. He brought me to narrow side-streets, main streets, and squares. He walked with a sense of urgency. A short, stocky man, very compact and dapper, with lively brown eyes and a determined looking head. He had a bit of a belly and his trousers were hitched high-up. He carried his valuables in a brown shoulder bag.

In a street for pedestrians only we were caught up in a crowd. It was market day. There were shops on both sides and stalls in the middle.

"Look, Roman, at the *wonderful* colours," Georges said loudly of the gladioli, the asters, lilies, roses, geraniums. Then he admired the peaches, apricots, butter, tomatoes, carrots, the heaped stands of garlic and onions. He led me to a stand that had assorted cheese and large brown eggs, melons, leeks, and plums. And to another that had different sausages and salamis. On one side he showed me live brown and white rabbits in hutches. And laughed when, directly opposite, brown and white rabbit skins were for sale. The street fascinated him. He stopped often and talked loudly to anyone whose face happened to interest him.

We had a Pernod at a table outside a café that had a mustard and orange façade. He lit a French cigarette. I, a Canadian cigarillo. The pleasure of the first puffs made us both silent. Nearly all the tables were occupied, shoppers were passing, and music came loudly from a record store.

I asked Georges, "What do you think of Madame who runs the hotel?"

"*Très intelligente*," he said and moved his hands slowly to indicate a large bosom. "*Et distinguée.*" He moved his hands to his backside to indicate large buttocks. And smiled.

He had a way of talking English which was a lot better, and more amusing, than my French.

He brought me inside an old church. He was relaxed until he faced the altar. He stiffened to attention, slid his left leg forward, as if he was a fencer, and solemnly made the sign of the cross. He remained in that position for several seconds looking like the figurehead at the prow of a ship. When he moved away he relaxed again. And pointed to a small statue of the Virgin with her arms open.

"Roman, the Virgin has opened her legs in welcome."

I was feeling tired when we came out of the church. The train journey, the sightseeing, the conversation…but Georges walked on. He was heading for the docks. I said I would go back to the hotel as I had some letters to write.

"Of course," he said, "forgive me. You must be exhausted. Tomorrow, would you like to see where I live in the country? I will come for you after breakfast."

And he was there, as I came out of the hotel, at eight-thirty, sitting in a light blue Citroen, dressed in the same clothes.

"Did you sleep, Roman?"

"For eight hours."

I could not see the sun because of the mist. But the surf, breaking on the pebbles, glistened. As he drove inland it began to brighten up. He drove fast and well. And he talked continually. Perhaps because he needed someone he could talk English to.

He said he had been an officer in the French navy. That in the last war he had been a naval architect in charge of submarines at their trials.

"I was at Brest, Cherbourg, Toulon, Marseille. My daughter was born when I was stuck in submarine in the mud. My wife told me the nurse came to say, 'The baby she is lovely. But the father — it is dead.' " And he laughed.

On a low hill, ahead, a large institution-like building with many windows and fire escapes.

"Lunatic asylum," Georges said, "full of patriots."

The government, he said, had a publicity campaign for the French to drink more of their wine and appealed to their patriotism. After this whenever he mentioned anyone who liked to drink, Georges called him "a patriot." And if anyone looked more than that, "*Very* patriotic."

The asylum was beside us. A cross on top. And all the top windows barred.

"When I was a boy…this place made big impression. Before a storm…the wind is blowing…and the people in lunatic asylum scream. I will never forget."

He drove through empty villages, small towns. He stopped, walked me around, and did some shopping. I noticed that the elaborate war memorials, by the churches, were for the 1914-1918 war. The only acknowledgement of the Second World War was the occasional stone, suddenly appearing in the countryside, at the side of the road, that said three or four members of the Resistance had been shot at this spot.

"I have been to America," Georges said. "I like the Americans. But sometimes they are infantile. Nixon — dustbin. Carter — dustbin."

He drove up a turning road by a small, broken, stone bridge that had rocks and uprooted trees on either side. "There is a plateau," he said, "high up. It has many meadows. The water gathers there for many rivers. Once in a hundred years the water very quickly goes down from the plateau to the valley and turns over houses, bridges, trees. Last September a priest on the plateau telephone the Mayor and say the water looks dangerous. But the Mayor, a young man, say it is only an old man talking. Half-hour later the water come down and drown thirty people and took many houses. It was Sunday so many people were away from the houses otherwise more drown. All happen last September. In a half-hour. But it will not happen for another hundred years. And no one will be here who knows it. The young won't listen. They will, after some years, build houses in the same place. And it will happen all over again."

In one of the large towns he stopped and showed me the cemetery where his family is buried. It was a vault, all stone, no grass around. Nor did any of the others have grass anywhere. On the stone was a vertical tablet with two rows of de Rostaings. The first was born in 1799. "He was town architect." A few names down. "He had lace factory. ...He build roads. ...See how the names become larger as we come nearer today."

"Will you be buried here?"

"No. My wife is Parisian. She is buried in Paris. I will lie with her."

He continued on the main road, then turned off and drove on a dirt road. Then went slowly up a rough slope until he stopped, on the level, by the side of a converted farmhouse.

"We are here," he said.

We were on a height. Below were trees and small fields — different shades of green, yellow and brown. Instead of fences or hedgerows, the fields had their borders in trees. And from this height the trees gave the landscape a 3-D look.

Georges introduced me to Marie-Jo, a fifteen-year-old schoolgirl from the next farm who did the cooking and cleaning during the summer. Short blonde hair, blue eyes, an easy smile. She was shy and tall for her age and walked with a slightly rounded back. While Marie-Joe barbecued salmon steaks at the far end of the porch, under an overhanging chimney, Georges walked me around. In front of the house, under a large elm, was a white table and white chairs. It was quiet. A light wind on the small leaves of the two near poplars. "They say it will rain," he said. And beside them a border of roses, geraniums, and lobelia.

We ate outside on a white tablecloth. I could hear people talking from the farm below. Further away someone was burning wood. The white smoke rose and thinned as it drifted slowly up. On top of the house was a small stone cross. A larger metal cross was embedded in the concrete of the front fence.

"I am Catholic," Georges said. "There are Protestants here too. My sister married a Jew. A Pole. From Bialystok."

Marie-Jo brought a round wooden board with cow and goat cheeses on it. And Georges filled my glass with more red wine.

"When I was young boy of seven we had great distilleries in my country. We hear the Russians are coming. We wait in the street. It is beginning to snow. But I do not want to go home. Many people wait for the Russians.

"Then they come. They look giants with fur hats and big boots and long overcoats. *Very* impressive.

"After a while — what happens? First the women. They say to Russian soldiers — you want drink? They give them drink. A little later, in the street, you see the women wearing the Russian furs for — "

Georges indicated with his hands.

"Muffs," I said.

"Yes, muffs, muffs. The women all have muffs.

"Then the French men give drink. Later, the French men you see in the street — they are wearing the Russian boots.

"The peasants — they *drowned* the Russians."

Marie-Jo brought ripe peaches, large peaches, lovely colours, dark and light, red to crimson. They were juicy and delicious.

"How did your sister meet her husband?"

"At the Sorbonne. My sister always joking. He serious. I did not think they would stay together. When she go to Poland to meet his family we are worried. We Catholic. They Jew. They have two children. Then the war. The Nazis. He is taken away. My mother, a tough woman, get priest and doctor to make fake certificate — say the two boys baptized. But my mother did not think that was enough. She tell me to take the boys to a farmer she know in the Auvergne. I take them. When I meet the farmer I begin to tell story. But the farmer just shake my hand. Say nothing. The children stay with him for the war."

"What happened to the Polish Jew?"

"He died."

We went to have coffee in the barn. The main room of the house. High ceiling with large windows and the original beams. To get to it from the inside you would go up some stairs. But you could walk to it from the garden by going up a grass slope. "All farmers have this for the cattle to go up and down," Georges said.

It was also his studio. On the walls were oil paintings by his uncle who was dead. Impressionist paintings of the landscape around here. "They sell for 40,000 francs," Georges said. "I have about thirty good ones. Some in the flat in Paris, some in the flat in Cannes. A few here." He also had his own paintings — on the wall, and one on an easel — like his uncle's but not as good.

Marie-Jo appeared with a jug full of coffee.

"I am working on book," he said. "I have contract with Paris publisher. Eleven years — I am not finished. It will be traveller's dictionary of every place in world that someone has written."

We had coffee. He lit a cigarette and went over to his record player.

"Roman — have you heard the Japanese Noh?"

I answered no with a movement of my face.

"Very strange. Sounds like a cat…and a chain with bucket…and a man flogging his wife. I was twenty, a midshipman on cruiser. We visit Japan. Suddenly I was put there, for six hours, listening to this."

He put a record on. "This is the cat…" a single note vibrated… "looking for another cat…" Georges was standing, talking with gestures. "Now, the long chain with a bucket going down well…it needs oil. …This is a man flogging his wife…."

He stopped the record.

"The Japanese they are different from the French. They believe the dead are with us all the time."

He showed me a photograph of his wife, Colette.

She looked a determined woman, in her late forties. A strong jaw, thin lips, blonde hair pulled back on her head, light eyes.

"She had beautiful voice," Georges said. "One of the things I like in people is the voice. If they have bad voice it is difficult for me to stay long with them."

"How long is it since she died?"

"Three years."

He must have thought of something else for he said abruptly, "If you do not come into the world — then you cannot go."

He took me for a walk through the countryside. There were all kinds of wild flowers I didn't know and butterflies and some, like the small black and white, I had not seen before either. But it was the trees that dominated. And I like trees. Probably because I have lived so long in Cornwall facing stone streets and stone terraces.

I wondered why Georges was not curious about my past. He appeared not interested in my personal life. Though I did give him bits of information.

"How long will you be in Dieppe?"

"Two, maybe three days more," I said. "I want to go to England, to a flat I have in Cornwall, and do some work."

It was after nine, but still light, when we got back to Dieppe. "I know a small place but good," Georges said. And brought me to a restaurant opposite the docks called L'Espérance.

We were both tired and for a while didn't talk. I ordered marinated mackerel, a salad, and some chicken. And Georges ordered a half-melon, veal, and cheese. Also coffee and a bottle of red wine.

Two tables away a man and a woman, both plump, in their late fifties or early sixties, were eating with relish. The woman had a large whole tongue on her plate to start with, the man a tureen of soup. He tucked his napkin into his open-neck shirt. Then they both had fish, then meat with potatoes, then cheese, then a large dessert with whipped cream on top. ...And all the time they were eating they didn't speak.

Beside them, going away towards the centre of the restaurant, were two young men. They were deaf and dumb. They were talking with their hands. They also mimed. When they saw us looking they included us in their conversation. One of the men looked Moroccan, with a black moustache on the top lip and down the side of his face. He was lean. And he mimed very quickly and well. He pointed at Georges' cigarette and at my cigarillo. And shook his head. He touched his chest and pretended he was coughing. And shook his head. He then showed himself swimming, the breast stroke. He was smiling. He showed us that he was also a long distance walker, getting up and staying in one place, he moved heel and toe, heel and toe, and that curious rotation of the hips.

"Roman," Georges said loudly. "The woman you see is fat. Her husband is fat. Look how they eat. Beside them two men, slim, young. They have to talk with their hands. They look happy — all the time the food comes — they are talking. But the two beside them — they do not talk at all — they concentrate on next bite. If I had movie camera — that is all you need. No words. No explanation. If I was young man, Roman, I would make films."

As he drove me to the hotel, Georges could not forget the scene in the restaurant. On the hotel's front door there was a sign saying it was full.

"Tomorrow," Georges said, "I no see you."

As tomorrow was Sunday I asked him if he was going to church.

"No, I do not like the clergy. The elm tree need spray. They get disease. I know a young man. He will do it. But I have to get him. And I go to see an old friend. He was officer with me. He now alone in Rouen. We eat lunch on Sunday when I am here. Two old men. I see you the day after."

And we shook hands.

Next morning, I opened the large window of the room. The sun was out. It was warm. A blue sky. After breakfast I decided to go for a walk. I crossed the harbour by an iron bridge. And went up a steep narrow street of close-packed terraced houses. It looked working class. The houses were small, drab, unpainted. And the sidewalks were narrow and in need of repair. They had red and pink geranium petals that had fallen from the window boxes on the small balconies.

I passed an upright concrete church with a rounded top. It stood by itself, stark, against the skyline. I went through tall undergrowth and, when clear of it, I saw I was on top of cliffs. They were an impressive sight: white-grey, sheer, and at the bottom pebbles with the sea coming in.

I walked along for about an hour, on top of the cliffs, when I noticed the path becoming wider as it started to slope down. The cliffs here went back from the sea and left a small pebbled beach. People were on it.

I was looking at the dirt path, as I walked down, because it was uneven and steep when I saw a shrew, about two inches long, over another shrew lying on its side. The one on its side was flattened as if a roller had gone over it. I watched the head of the live shrew over the belly of the dead one — there didn't seem to be any movement. Then, for no reason, I whistled. The live shrew darted into the grass. And I saw the open half-eaten belly of the one on its side, a brilliant crimson. The colour was brighter than any meat I had seen at the butchers.

The small beach wasn't crowded. The surf gentle…the water sparkled…a family was playing boules. Someone was wind surfing across the length of the beach…going one way then turning the sail to go the other, and often falling in. A man in a T-shirt brought a dog, a terrier, on a leash. Then he let him go into the shallows. Under an umbrella a young woman was breast-feeding a baby. Nearer to the water a tall woman with white skin and red hair was lying on her back, topless. People were changing using large coloured towels...while the continual sound of the low surf as it came in breaking over the pebbles and sliding back.

I had brought a picnic: bread, a hard-boiled egg, cheese, tomatoes, a pear. And a can of cider to wash it down. After I had eaten I took off my shirt, shoes, socks, and lay down on the stones.

A loud noise woke me. It was two boys running over the stones between my head and the cliffs. I sat up. I didn't know how long I had been asleep. The surface of the water sparkled. The click of the boules was still going. From somewhere a dog was barking. The cliffs, a few yards behind me and on both sides, had light green streaks in the massive white grey. And high up, on the very top, a thin layer of grass.

The tide was coming in. I put on shirt, socks, and shoes, and walked over the pebbles to a paved slope that led from the beach to the road. I could now see a narrow opening between the cliffs. And as I walked up the slope the opening fanned out to show a suburb of houses with gardens, green lawns, and trees. As I came to the top of the paved slope I saw, across the road, on a stone, in French and English.

On this beach
Officers and Men of the
Royal Regiment of Canada
Died at Dawn 19 August 1942
Striving to Reach the Heights Beyond

You who are alive on this beach
remember that these men died far from home
that others here and everywhere might freely
enjoy life in God's mercy.

When I got back to the hotel the "full" sign had been taken down. Madame greeted me with a smile.

"You have caught the sun. I have surprise for you."

She soon re-appeared with a thin blonde girl of about twelve or thirteen.

"This is Jean. She is from Canada," Madame said proudly. "From Alberta."

"Where from in Alberta?" I asked.

"Edmonton," the girl replied in a quiet voice.

"How long will you be in Dieppe?"

"I live here. I go to school."

"When were you in Edmonton?"

"Three weeks ago."

"Is your father there?"

"No, he is somewhere else. He travels. I'm with my mother."

"Can you speak French as well as you can English?"

"I can speak it better," she said.

And she was glad to go off with Madame's only daughter, who was older and not as pretty, to roller-skate on the promenade.

"She is charming," Madame said as we watched both girls run to get out.

"I went for a walk today, Madame," I said, "and came to the beach where in the war the Canadians — "

"*Ah.*" She interrupted and shook her head, then raised an arm, in distress or disbelief. She tried to find words — but couldn't.

"I have read many books about it," she said quickly. "Do you want to see the cemetery?"

"No," I said.

That evening, while in the dining-room, I decided to leave tomorrow. For over three weeks I had been travelling in France. All inland, until Dieppe. It had been a fine holiday. I had not been to France before. But now I wanted to get back to the familiar. I was also impatient to get back to work. I had brought with me a large notebook but I had written nothing in it.

I said to Madame at the desk, "I will be leaving tomorrow. Could you have my bill ready?"

"Of course," she said, "you will have it when you come down for breakfast."

"It is a very comfortable hotel. Are you open all year?"

"In December we close."

"Has it been a good season?"

"I think I go bankrupt," she said loudly. "Oil — up three times in two months. It is impossible to go on — " She held up a sheaf of bills.

"I will tell my friends," I said.

"Is kind of you," she said quietly. And gave me several brochures that said the hotel would be running a weekly cookery course in January and February of next year.

Late next morning, with my two cases in the lounge, I was having a coffee and smoking a cigarillo, when Georges appeared. He saw the cases.

"Yes," I said. "I'm going today."

"What time is your boat?"

"It goes in an hour."

"I will take you."

He insisted on carrying the cases to his car. Madame came hurrying away from people at the desk to shake my hand vigorously and hoped she would see me again.

While Georges was driving he gave me a card with his address in the country, in Cannes, and in Paris. And the dates he would be there. Then he gave me a large brown envelope. I took out what was in it — a small watercolour of Dieppe that he had painted. It showed the mustard and orange café with people sitting at the outside tables and others walking by. On the back he had written, "For Roman, my new friend, Georges."

"When I get to England," I said, "I will send you one of my books."

"Thank you. I should like to improve my English. Perhaps I find in it something for my traveller's dictionary."

At the ferry I persuaded Georges not to wait.

"Roman, I do not kiss the men."

We shook hands.

I sat in a seat on deck, at the stern, facing Dieppe. The ferry turned slowly and I saw Dieppe turn as well. The vertical church with the rounded top, the cathedral, the square, the houses with the tall windows, and wooden shutters, and small iron balconies.

Then the ferry straightened out and we were in the open sea. After a while it altered course. And there were the cliffs where I had walked yesterday and the narrow opening. I kept watching the cliffs and the opening. And thought how scared they must have been coming in from the sea and seeing this.

The sun was warm, the sea calm. And when I next looked at the cliffs the opening had disappeared. All that was there was the white-grey stone sticking up. I thought of gravestones...close together on a slope. ...You could see nothing else. Just gravestones. And they were gravestones with nothing on them...they were all blank.

On the loudspeaker the captain's voice said that coming up on the left was one of the world's largest tankers. People hurried to the rails with their cameras.

I went down to a lower deck and stood in the queue for the duty free.

Commentary by *Norman Levine*

≈

Norman Levine's sharply sketched stories trigger great depths of emotion. The following commentary is taken from an essay, "Sometimes It Works", published in the anthology How Stories Mean *(Erin, ON: The Porcupine's Quill, 1993). In it Levine discusses how writing, like painting, works on us in ways that are distinct, immediate, unexpected, and lasting.*

Another thing I got from the painters was the need for immediacy. When they finished a painting they wanted me to see it in their studio. And there it was. At a glance. Through the eyes. Onto the nervous system. I remember thinking: how could I get this immediacy in writing? And I remember Peter Lanyon telling me, in his studio, that all that mattered was the work.

"You take something from life. Make something from it. Then you give it back into life."

Also from the painters was their enthusiasm for writing and for books. They were well-read. They talked well. And, from their conversations, they made me want to work more. They also had a good critical sense. And I soon realized that the better the painter the sharper the critical sense.

The one from whom I learned the most, in these conversations, was Francis Bacon. He would talk about the technical difficulties that he encountered in painting. But he would also go off in all kinds of directions, and be very direct. And I remember, after we had talked for hours, that the essence of good conversation was the same as for writing. He talked about so-called ordinary things then, unexpectedly, said something that was memorable. And then went on to talk about ordinary things.

One of the things that he said early on — in November 1959 — was that seeing a painting (we were talking about Rembrandt's late self-portraits) was an emotional experience. "It unlocks the valves of feeling" was the way he put it. And another painting "suggested an opening-up into another area of feeling altogether". I had not thought of painting in that way before. Nor writing — where I felt it even stronger. Until he clarified it.

SELECTED WORKS BY NORMAN LEVINE

One Way Ticket: Stories. London: Martin Secker & Warburg, 1961. London: McClelland and Stewart, 1961.

I Don't Want To Know Anyone Too Well and Other Stories. London: Macmillan, 1971. Toronto: Macmillan, 1971. [Paperback ed.] Ottawa: Deneau, [1982].

Selected Stories. Ottawa: Oberon Press, 1975.

Thin Ice. Ottawa: Deneau and Greenberg, 1979. [Paperback ed.] Ottawa: Deneau and Greenberg, [1980].

Why Do You Live So Far Away? Ottawa: Deneau, 1984.

Champagne Barn. Markham, ON: Penguin Books, 1984.

Something Happened Here. Toronto: Viking/Penguin Books, 1991. [Paperback ed.] Toronto: Penguin Books, 1991.

expos

Hugh Hood

≈

I've been getting the regrettable impression in the last five years or so that Hugh Hood's reputation is in decline. Paradoxically, this may be because he is becoming a classic. It may be that we are so familiar with his accomplishment that we are beginning to take him for granted. Certainly if anyone can lay claim to 'classic' status, it is Hugh Hood. His first volume of stories, *Flying a Red Kite* (1962), has been followed by eight other collections. That brilliant first book is one of the foundation stones in a tradition which is building.

We might well have selected from that volume for inclusion here "Flying a Red Kite", "Silver Bugles, Cymbals, Golden Silks", "Three Halves of a House", or "Where the Myth Touches Us". In the case of Hugh Hood who has written over one hundred stories, the anthologist faces an embarrassment of riches.

Hood's second collection, *Around the Mountain: Scenes from Montreal Life* (1967), is an almost perfect achievement but remains largely and inexplicably unappreciated. Hood derived the book from Turgenev's *A Sportsman's Sketches* and Dickens' *Sketches by Boz* and he intended the sketches to be exactly that — seemingly unworked impressions, narratives in which the topography and the geography of Montreal play essential parts. It is interesting to listen in this book to the evolution of Hood's very distinctive tone, that informal formality, that heightened vernacular which seems so easy but is so singular. I can't think of another voice quite like it.

I could have made a good case for representing Hood's talent in this anthology by choosing from *Around the Mountain* that quiet, luminous little masterpiece "The Village Inside".

The stories we have selected, "Getting to Williamstown" and "Going Out as a Ghost", are taken from Hood's third and fourth collections, *The Fruit Man, The Meat Man & The Manager* (1971) and *Dark Glasses* (1976). We felt it necessary that the stories we did choose reflected Hood's mastery of modernist technique and his devout Catholicism. Compare Hood's stories with those of Morley Callaghan, another Catholic writer and an early and personal influence on Hood. In an essay entitled "The Curate's Egg" which appeared in *Essays on Canadian Writing* 30 (1984-85), I wrote: "Callaghan certainly knew the *shape* of what is now the classic 'modern' story but his sensibilities were not characteristic of 'modern' short-story writing; the story tends to be tentative, exploratory, tremulous even; it tends to be intensely visual and sensuous; it tends — in brief — towards lyric poetry. Callaghan's major impulse was moralistic and didactic, and these qualities are constantly at war within his work with what artistry he had. Which wasn't much." Hood is much too sophisticated a story writer to fall into the same trap. Hood from his earliest stories demonstrated a complete grasp of modernist technique, using language vividly and exactly to elicit our emotional responses. At the same time, he tended to use modernist technique to reflect his religious beliefs. If we do not share his beliefs, are these stories then alien to us? Do they exclude us? Certainly many of Callaghan's stories alienate me, but that is because I find them either mawkish or didactic. Hood's stories are far more subtle, more deeply imagined, and less 'closed' than Callaghan's and therefore ought to be of continuing appeal. One does not have to be a Catholic to see-saw with the narrator at the end of "Going Out as a Ghost".

From this perspective, it is instructive to compare "Getting to Williamstown" and "Going Out as a Ghost" with, say, Callaghan's "A Cap for Steve" and "All the Years of Her Life". Callaghan *presides over* his stories, interpreting, explaining, enforcing, pointing the moral in a way that Hood is far too delicate a writer to do. It would also be interesting to compare some of Hood's stories with those of internationally renowned Catholic writer Flannery O'Connor to see how both writers fare in embodying their beliefs without becoming didactic. Can a deeply religious writer become a classic in a largely secular society?

≈

A lengthy and important interview with Hood by J. R. (Tim) Struthers appears in *Before the Flood: Our Exagmination round His Factification for Incamination of Hugh Hood's Work in Progress* (Downsview, ON: ECW Press, 1979). An illuminating close reading of Hood can be found in Robert Lecker's *On the Line: Readings in the Short Fiction of Clark Blaise John Metcalf and Hugh Hood* (Downsview, ON: ECW Press, 1982). Keith Garebian has written a book, *Hugh Hood* (Boston: Twayne, 1983), and a monograph, *Hugh Hood and His Works* (Toronto: ECW Press, 1985); and Susan Copoloff-Mechanic has written a book, *Pilgrim's Progress: A Study of the Short Stories of Hugh Hood* (Toronto: ECW Press, 1988). Also recommended as ways into the pleasures of Hood's prose are Kent Thompson's articles "Hugh Hood and His Expanding Universe" in *Journal of Canadian Fiction* 3.1 (1974) and "Formal Coherence in the Art of Hugh Hood" in *Studies in Canadian Literature* 2 (1977), John Mills's "Hugh Hood and the Anagogical Method" and Lawrence Mathews' "The Secular and the Sacral: Notes on *A New Athens* and Three Stories by Hugh Hood" in *Before the Flood,* J. R. (Tim) Struthers' "Hugh Hood" in *Profiles in Canadian Literature,* vol. 2 (Toronto: Dundurn Press, 1980), Lawrence Mathews' "Hood and Evil" in *The Montreal Story Tellers: Memoirs, Photographs, Critical Essays* (Montreal: Véhicule Press, 1985), and J. R. (Tim) Struthers' "A Secular Liturgy: Hugh Hood's Aesthetics and *Around the Mountain*" in *Studies in Canadian Literature* 10 (1985). W. J. Keith has written specifically on "Going Out as a Ghost" in *Writers in Aspic* (Montreal: Véhicule Press, 1988) and has included two other essays on Hood in *An Independent Stance: Essays on English-Canadian Criticism and Fiction* (Erin, ON: The Porcupine's Quill, 1991).

≈ GETTING TO WILLIAMSTOWN ≈

Many a green isle needs must be
In the deep wide sea of misery.

Driving out of Montreal in the old days, it used to take me a couple of hours to get off the island — they do it in forty-five minutes now — and by the time I was up around the Ontario line I would decide to by-pass Cornwall, "smelly Cornwall," the kids called it, rightly. How it stank, that town, of sulphur and God knows what else! We got off the highway at Lancaster, jog right a hundred yards, jog left onto County Road 19, and away.

Mr. Fessenden...Mr. Fessenden?

There was a creek we followed upstream for miles, Raisin Creek, was it? More than a creek, almost a river in places, but shallow. Broad but shallow, like a lot of things, with trees bending over in the summer so they almost formed an arch over the water. We always meant to stop and wade; we could have done it easily. The children would have loved it but we had to get on. Raisin Creek there, with the little bridges and culverts, and from time to time in the distance to the south a view of the main line, and beyond the glitter of the river. It seemed to be always sunny back then.

The road wound back and forth, not a modern highway, badly engineered on the curves so that you couldn't go over forty without braking suddenly at every new curve. I taught the children what the highway signs meant, a cross, a curved line to right or left, railroad tracks, intersections at various angles. We were surrounded by rolling, beautifully cultivated fields with the only interruption a few lines of maples bordering the farms, the road and the river. The fields were expansive and rich, peaceful, ah, God!

I see it now, projected on my walls as though real. Five miles west of Lancaster, about two-fifteen in the afternoon, we pass a gas-pump and a refreshment stand, abandoned for the last few seasons. The pump has a globe of opaque white glass for a head, with three red stars on it. Underneath there is a transparent glass cylinder with gallonage calibrated from zero to twenty, and below that the pump, with a long handle at the side. As the attendant gives you gas, the level drops in the glass cylinder and the clean brilliant red fluid splashes and foams while the children watch fascinated. I pay him, and stand for a moment as he pumps gas back into his apparatus, until at last the cylinder is that beautiful red clear to the top, no nonsense about premium quality or tetraethyl.

Beside the abandoned gas-pump there's this old refreshment stand. In the late twenties somebody used it to sell pop and ice cream in the summer, and farm produce around harvest time. The shingled walls were green and the roof red; but now in 1934 the paint has flaked and peeled and I can just barely make out the colour. We made up stories about it; it was a little house or an enchanted castle. In truth the stand and pump sat there in overgrown grass, amid wildflowers, lonely and haunted.

Now we are coming to Williamstown; the trees are growing plentiful and the children need, they say, to stop. Deep, deep in the countryside. They can wet in the ditch at the roadside if they must, for there's no-one to see or mind very much. But they hope for ice cream at the general store, so we don't stop by the side of the road. The trees thicken; bright sunlight glances on the green. I see it on these white walls.

The town lies tranquilly in a tiny valley beside the creek, in an island of green under the sun. We dip down in our Chrysler Airflow — there weren't big enough windows in that car; it was too experimental! Down we sail as the highway narrows and becomes King William Street, steep as we come into town, swooping toward a dangerously narrow bridge at the foot of the hill. As we descend, the foliage obscures the sun. We pass fields on our left, and on our right I have the sense, through the narrow windows of my Airflow, of a white building standing the width of a field from the edge of town, a building in a field that I have never really seen, but shining, always freshly painted, in the last sun before the shade trees crowd in on King William Street.

Careful turning onto the bridge. Cars cannot pass here but in twenty years I never had to dispute the passage with anyone, certainly not with a citizen of Williamstown. Once I recall, I came to the bridge, going west into town, just as a farmer arrived, going east and homewards. He had a Model-T truck with a load of crated chickens; the crank stuck out of the face of the Model-T like a pipe. We smiled at one another and I backed off. When he drove past, he waved and nodded politely. Across the bridge we take a right, passing the few houses this side of the stores. This is where my heart stopped, every trip for fifteen years.

Just this side of the stores stands an old house that's for sale, has been ever since I've been driving through. It's yellow, or would be if the paint were restored; the porch sags somewhat. The windows are comprised of sixteen small leaded panes apiece; some are broken. It is a heavenly place. The backyard opens on fields, as do all the backyards in town, and the house will be maybe a hundred and thirty years old. There is a small lawn in front which someone cares for, perhaps the long-dead realtor whose bald sign penetrates the turf. Going by, I sigh and yearn. But for some reason, we never stopped just there. We proceeded to the general store, grocery store, variety store, butcher shop, what would you call it?

Outside Williamstown the highway is paved, but in front of the cluster of stores, for whatever reason, the street is always dusty with a light haze hanging in the air. BUSTIN'S DRUGS: pharmacist's globes dim in the window. DEVLIN'S HARDWARE: a display of C.C.M. bikes and a cream separator. In the window of the grocery store appear the name of the proprietor and the words SALADA TEA arranged in an arc, in white tin letters appliquéd to the glass in some mysterious way. Here we stop, taking no special care to park in this or that direction.

The kids have used the toilet here so often, at least six times a year, that the proprietor believes he knows us. He gives them extra large scoops of ice cream, dipping it from a cooler with big round holes in the top, and thick lids like gladiators' shields. Then he sprinkles orange and red and chocolate flakes of candy on top of the double-dips; this costs a nickel. He has a glittering and lethal meat slicer with which he cuts boiled ham and pork for picnic lunches, and a superb coffee grinder, and the place smells of spice and coffee. The showcases are bound in a beautiful walnut. I can't smell that smell. I can think of it but I can't recreate it. Later, perhaps.

"That's quite a car, Mister."

"Yes, that's what they call streamlining. It came in this year."

Into the dark hot car, then, and down King William Street westwards past the District Catholic School, just where the sidewalks end. It's three o'clock and we'll have to make up time if we're going to be in Maitland for dinner. The highway straightens and we get up to fifty, going straight west away from heaven.

Time for Mr. Fessenden's injections.

But you couldn't get in and you couldn't get out, in those days. It took half a day to get to Williamstown and another three hours to Maitland, in all a seven-hour drive, a hundred and thirty miles, what with lunch in the car, stops for the toilet, occasional car-sickness. I dreamed of commuting, for it can't have been more than sixty-five miles from the city.

"I could go in by the day."

"No you couldn't, Henry, you'd be exhausted. No, don't begin to explain it to me; there can't be any question of driving in and out of Montreal every day. Think of it! Your heart would never stand it."

"But I'm a young man, Irma, and there's nothing wrong with my heart. I've just had my checkup and I'm fine, just fine. And only think of the peace in the winter, alone, a couple of feet of snow. Black dark and little lights in the parlour windows; there's a school, a good one I'm sure, and later on we could send them into Lancaster on a bus, or they could come with me."

"And you seriously propose to bury me in that place with the children? Who would they play with?"

"I imagine there are children living there; there must be five hundred people in the place."

"And what about me? What would I do for amusement, with the car gone all day? I'd go mad in a place like that."

"It might be good for you, Irma."

"What are you insinuating?"

"Oh, nothing, nothing. I love you, Irma."

She would have a lightning switch of mood.

"I don't know how you put up with me, Henry, I'm such a mess."

"Well, we all have faults, dear."

"Yes, but think, Henry. No movies, no friends, no theatre."

"We don't go to the theatre."

"But we might sometime, and we *can* if we're desperate. No concerts, no public transit."

"You don't need streetcars in a town that size; you can walk to church and the store. And I want to live there. It wouldn't be like this."

"There's nothing wrong with this. You're doing splendidly. You have all your friends in the office and inside of two years you'll be a trust officer. You'd have to get up at five to drive into Montreal, and you wouldn't get home till nine, which exactly reverses your present hours. It would kill you."

"I could make better time than that."

"We don't have enough money to fix up that ruin."

"Now that's not fair. You've never even been inside it."

"Have you?"

"No. I've never been there but with you, driving through on the way to your mother's."

"Henry, you have no idea what it costs to fix up a place in the country; that house looks good to you, seeing it for the first time from the outside; but it'll be full of dry rot and structural faults; there's no plumbing."

"How do you know?"

"There's a little house in the backyard."

"I didn't notice."

"No, you wouldn't! I'm the one who'd have to nurse the children through typhoid."

"I'll bet there isn't any more typhoid, per capita, in Williamstown than here."

"We'll wait till they're a little older before we run the risk!"

She always closed a discussion by tabling the children's needs; we moved from the condition of my health to the children's needs and back. They were the poles of her dialectic. And about most points in the argument, she had fact and reason on her side. I *did* have friends in the office and almost nowhere else, and I *did* become a trust officer in charge of important portfolios, and I didn't have to go to war on account of the family and my public responsibilities as a trust officer. In Montreal, the public responsibilities of a financial officer are taken to be great and pressing.

"Mother, how can my friends come to an upstairs duplex? It was all right when I was small; I didn't understand. But look at the difference between us and the Lewises. It makes me so ashamed. Why can't we have a house like everybody else?"

"Sssshhh! Mustn't disturb your father, Frances. He's lying down before dinner."

"He's always having his rest. What does he have to lie down for?"

"It's better, dear, when a man is middle-aged, for him to conserve his energy. Come into the dining-room." Their steps recede.

"I want to have a skating party with coffee after."

"Aren't some of the children young for coffee?"

"Oh, mother!"

"We can call it a coffee party anyway and no harm done. What sort of house do you think we should have, dear?"

"Mother, I want to live in the Town of Mount Royal!"

"So do I, dear!"

Oh thickening trees, oh shady sunlight, leaded panes and quiet dusty street.

There are no trees in the Town of Mount Royal; this is a fact. Here and there one finds a stunted shrub or two; but when they laid out the developments during, and just after, the war, they bulldozed down all the trees, a bad mistake that nobody seems to regret. Without noticing it, the citizens live on an arid plain where the grass yellows in May. If the land were clear prairie they would see this; but amidst the ranch houses the desert effect is half-obliterated.

That you can't sit in your own backyard in July because of the glare seems to be taken for granted by all but me. It takes me an hour and a half to drive two miles to work, because of a bottleneck at a level crossing. In wintertime, it takes much longer.

"Everybody else has a television aerial."

"Some people put them up without a set," says Bunker.

"Oh, your father would never do that, would you, darling?"

"What is it, darling?"

"Frances and Bunker think we should have television."

"Everybody on the street has it but us."

"Then I'll order one today. I hadn't noticed. Are there good programs?"

"I believe it depends on your aerial, dear."

"Ah, like the radio. I'll see about it this afternoon."

At this, the children — and wonderfully they aren't children any more — are silently pleased, as they should be. I've never denied them anything. Irma hugs me, and they observe us indulgently, gratified.

Yes, comatose, a terminal case, I'm afraid.

Terminal, that's what they said when Irma went and the house was empty, Frances married and living in Toronto, and Bunker in Maitland. He's a real grandmother's boy, that one, looking after the store and the farm properties, and seeing about Irma's flowers now and then, something I couldn't do myself from Montreal.

"That's quite a car, Mister."

"Yes, that's a French car, a Citroen. Most comfortable car on the road, you ought to try it sometime."

I can go back and forth to Maitland in under three hours now, with 401 connected to the Metropolitan Highway and only one traffic light between the Town of Mount Royal and Toronto. I don't have to have a fast car; the Citroen isn't what you'd call a fast car. I just average a comfortable sixty miles an hour and I'm there in no time. Why, Bunker might just as well have been living with me, we've seen so much of each other, and he's been in to see me…to see me here.

401 follows the river pretty much, about half a mile inland. You pick it up at the Ontario border; you don't go into Lancaster, and naturally you don't go anywhere near Williamstown. I haven't been through Williamstown since before Irma died, I don't believe. Maybe I'll go, one of these days. But I've been going out on 401, and for a while it's pretty country down by the locks and the islands; every few minutes you can see the sunlight on the water. But soon, northwest

of Cornwall, the geography changes; you can't see the river and the land is swamp. Scrub timber, marsh, cattails, and the occasional concession road running north into the scrub. There are probably plenty of flies in there; but I've never stopped to see. Coming back down at night, it's black as a yard up a stovepipe along 401; there isn't the traffic to justify a superhighway through there but it had to go in because of Montreal and Toronto. There are only the two gas stations between the border and Maitland, and the province has to subsidize them, and the food is bad, especially the coffee.

Going along in my Citroen between the railroad tracks and the river, I can always tell when we're passing Williamstown because I can see the steeple of some church peeking up out of a clump of trees a few miles to my right, a rectangular white tower with a pointed lead steeple on top; the town must be five or six miles off the highway and one of the county roads connects. One of these days I'll take the ramp, turn off north in my Citroen and astonish the grocer, though the children won't be with me.

"You'd be better off to come and live in Maitland, Dad, where you'd be near Mother."

"Well, but Bunker, she's dead. I mean, I can't see that it matters where I am, relative to where she is."

"Haven't you got any feelings on the subject? After all, the DeVebers have been established in Maitland almost a hundred and fifty years. Grandmother used to tell me, and she showed me pictures."

"I'm not a DeVeber. And I'm a Town of Mount Royal man, if there is such a thing."

"You don't like it in the Town, do you Dad? Think what that big house is costing to keep up, now we're all out of it. And maybe you'd enjoy helping me with the business; there's talk of a shopping plaza out by the 401 cloverleaf and I'm considering putting a store in there. Naturally there would have to be additional capital."

"DeVeber capital, I hope."

"Oh now, Dad, it would be a good investment. You could put in what you get for the house without liquidating any of your other holdings; that might be enough. What do you suppose the house is worth?"

How does he seem today, nurse?

Bunker has been in to see me right along; he drives down afternoons and has his supper in the city. Then he goes back after nine o'clock. He's attentive all right, and it's cheerful to have somebody here, although I can't work up the strength to discuss the house with him. Perhaps we'll sell. I never liked it, and it looks as if I may be here some time. No use having it standing empty and a tax charge. But I don't feel up to talking now. It wouldn't be good for me. I mean, I'm not well.

"Bunker, if you've brought me all this way on a false alarm, I'll kill you. You think you're the only one in the world with business to look after. Thursday night is Debbie's school play, and I haven't finished her costume. Tomorrow night Butler has tickets for the O'Keefe Centre, and you drag me to Montreal on a wild goose chase. Look at him, he's as comfortable as he could possibly be. They're doing everything they can *for* him, not that there's much they can do, in his condition."

"He'll hear you!"

"No, he won't. They've got him sedated. They have to because it's very painful at the end if they don't. I don't suppose he's felt a thing for days, poor Dad, but at least he isn't in any pain."

"It's wonderful what they can do with drugs, these days."

"Sometimes they don't help though. When I had Debbie, they had me doped right up and it still hurt like mad. I screamed my head off. But with this, it seems to work."

"He's quiet enough, all right, poor old man. He was never the same, you know, after he lost Mother. He went right downhill, just as if he'd lost part of himself, and it isn't as if he were that old, either."

"He's sixty-five, isn't he?"

"Sixty-six. He quit the Trust on his sixty-fifth birthday."

"I remember. I guess they'll look after…uh…things, won't they?"

"Yes, they're the executors, with me."

"With you?"

"If we're going to discuss this, let's whisper, Frances."

"Why you, Mister Smartie, why not me? I'm older."

"I'm a man."

"I don't see it makes much difference. Anyway you're not that much of a man."

"Frances!"

"Ah, I'm sorry, Bunker, I'll take that back. Who named the executors?"

"Dad."

"Why did he leave me off?"

"I have no idea; he probably thought it didn't matter. When you're making a will, you likely think all will be harmony and concord afterwards."

"Just you try any tricks, Bunker Fessenden, and I'll harmony and concord you!"

"There'll be no tricks; the whole testament is as plain as day. The office wrote it up for us, and as far as succession duties go, it's a masterpiece. We get everything and the government gets nothing."

"Nothing?"

"Practically. The minimum, and you can't do any better than that. The estate is divided equally between us. That's fair, isn't it?"

"I'm older. And I have Debbie."

"But you've got a husband to look after you."

"Hah!"

"Butler supports you, in spite of everything. Nobody supports me, and I've been thinking of getting married."

"You?"

"Yes, me. That's a big house you know, and with grandmaw gone I'm all alone."

Alone in a big house. Our house was the first California-redwood ranch in the Town of Mount Royal, with the refrigerator hung on the kitchen wall — too high to reach comfortably but very stylish. There's much glass, too much. When I wander through the house alone nights, with all the lights on, I'm always exposing myself accidentally to the curious stares of passers-by. It's a house where you have to be careful how you quit bathroom or bedroom; there's always somebody looking at you from out on the sidewalk. The recreation room gives on the main street; it's the shape of a small bowling alley, with a tiled floor which gives your steps a curious dead ring. Walking back and forth in there at night, with a vast expanse of plate glass on one side of me, and the television and bar on the other, I'm unutterably solitary, like some aquatic creature in a tank, going purposelessly round and round. Now and then I throw darts at the wall; it must look very strange from outside, the brightness, the solitude, the aimless activity. It's a good thing we had that window in the recreation room, because that's how they found me.

Banging on the window, rap, rap, rap, reverberations in the sash.

Feet upstairs, then coming down.

Indistinct shapes beside me.

"You were right, Mary, it's Mr. Fessenden, and he's sick."

"Should we get mixed up in this?"

"We can't leave him here."

"We can call the police and wait till they come."

"I'll call them."

"Don't touch anything, and be sure to get a release."

Feet going away and then, later, being carried gently.

"What's his trouble?"

"*Sais-pas*. Some kind of a deep coma."

"No fractures, no hemorrhaging? Careful how we handle him; it might be anything."

"What do you think?"

"Heart or malignancy."

"Yes."

"The tests will show."

"Yes."

"Off we go."

What is this, this heavenly feeling of being carried, this lightness never felt before, lie back and float into the white room and the level bed, and afterwards the pictures flashed on the walls and now and then a voice or voices. Being carried, ah, ah.

Bunker lives in a stone house; they'll never find him when comes time; he'd better get married, start the whole thing off again in Maitland; but I won't come to the wedding. I'm going to take the ramp when I see that white rectangle, that leaden tower, in the sun above the trees five miles to the north. I see the sun on the walls now, and now coming through the walls. The trees bend over as we glide along beside the river; the walls open and fade and give on the country road and the rich cornfields, a line of trees in the distance and coming closer, lustrous in the sun.

Look after the Fessenden business, orderly!

Being carried along at the top of the hill and we swoop downwards as trees thicken, a green island, around us and here at the edge of town I see the white building gleaming in the sun under the soft sheen of the tower, one narrow field from town. Being carried gently in by men in white to the porch of the white building in the bright sun. Blaze of glory on leaves moving in the windows as these six bear me kindly up the aisle.

≈ GOING OUT AS A GHOST ≈

The children were preparing for Halloween, a festival they preferred to Christmas. The sombre mysterious end of October, when it grows colder and nobody yet knows how cold it may become, had always seemed more inviting to them than the steady weather of the solstice. They set great store by their costumes — had in different years presented themselves as Laurel and Hardy, four Marx brothers, knights in armour and hairy serfs, the two ends of a horse. They were a quartet agreeably near in age inclined to form pairs, liking to complement one another: master and slave, fat man and thin.

Their father, a confused man, joked with them about the reach and complication of these conceptions. "Going to go out this year?" he would inquire as they grew older. "What are you going out as?" The boys would argue between themselves, the girls exchange secret smiles, giving nothing away.

"I'll throw a sheet over my head and cut holes in it," their father would say at the very last minute. "I'm going out as a ghost." And the entire family would laugh uproariously, for this struck them as the lowest deep of impoverished fantasy. "Going out as a ghost," they all sang together, laughing, but inwardly troubled by the concept of dressing up as a clown or a cowboy. Such children could — probably did — miss altogether the intense, absorbed September and October during which the dress-up box was emptied, filled, emptied: old organdy and silk from costumes of years past held to the light. They had also a property box filled with daggers, stilettos, swords, false noses, wigs, grotesque false ears. Theatrical make-up was available, nose putty, crêpe hair. A family half sunk in show-business. All this began in late summer with vacation still in progress.

"If you're going into town, bring back my gorilla mask," said the older of the boys to his father on a Wednesday in late August. "I want to compare the fur."

"Where is it in the house? In your closet?"

"It's hanging on the light fixture in our room," said the younger boy. "I hung it there to make it look like a head sticking out of the wall."

"There should be a gorilla's hind-end sticking out of the wall in the next bedroom," said the father. He chatted amusingly with the children, but the image of the gorilla mask stayed with him disagreeably as he drove into the city. One of those rubber, over-the-head, monster disguises which can be found at theatrical costumers, it had been a birthday gift to his son, who had a collection of them: Dracula, Frankenstein's monster, the Wolf-Man, the Gorilla. In a poor light the thing was genuinely horrific and might prove shocking to householders on that dreary night nine weeks in the future. He was troubled by the human cast of the bestial shape. The coarse red of the cheeks, upturned snout, matted dangling hair, the powdery texture of the pliant rubbery skin. The boys played up certain simian characteristics in their movements; they liked to lower their hands around their knees by flexing the knee-joints. They would gibber in simulated ape-language. The younger boy often hung head downward in trees. With the gorilla mask over either head, full disguise was at once effected, a whole transformation of behaviour threatened. "Now I'm going to tear you limb from limb," they would say.

He had further worries, minor repairs impending on his automobile, which gave trouble as he drove along; the radiator leaked, spreading the odour of coolant through the passenger compartment, the smell of ethylene glycol, and some sweetish, doubtless wholly poisonous, additive — radiator cleanser or sealer; there might be holes in the hoses. Late in the day he arrived in his city neighbourhood and left the auto with a local service man who at once, before his eyes, dismantled it, rendering it inoperative. "Tomorrow, one o'clock," said the mechanic, a highly trustworthy man.

"Going back to the country in the afternoon."

"You can have it by one. Not before."

He was glad to leave his car sitting on the lot, always felt better about it at such times, as one does about the seriously-ill member of the family who is at last "in good hands." As he walked the short distance to his empty house, it began to rain, then in the next hour settled into a steady downpour. He let himself in, stepped over the pile of mail lying on the floor below the letter slot, into the quiet hall. He had always liked the look of this house in the late afternoon with no electric light on; what light there was entered freely through large windows front and rear, then diffused itself into the corners of dark halls. He mounted to the second floor and standing in the doorway of his sons' bedroom he saw the gorilla mask hanging over the light socket, from which the bulb had been removed. Outside the rain continued to fall; it was now very dark for this time of year. The house was shut tight and stuffy, yet the mask moved and lifted slightly in some faint air current. He stared. He decided to have his evening meal delivered, Chinese, or barbecued chicken, no need to go out again. He might call a friend, see if he wanted to watch a late movie. What else had the kids asked for, was it masking tape?

Later he shuffled through the mail, discarded almost all, phoned for chicken, phoned David, who agreed to drive round at 9:30. Unmarried, self-employed, chronically at loose ends at night, David seemed pleased to be asked. "There are two good films on tonight," he said. "I hope my car starts." He came a little early, barely past nine, surprising his host, who was ensconced before the TV in the basement, picking chicken from the spaces between his teeth, listening to the rain, not making much sense of the program he watched, which was loud. The doorbell rang several times before he grasped that it was not part of the soundtrack, which might well have had bells in it.

He switched on the porch light and peered out at the rain. Might as well be Halloween, he thought, and opened the door for David. "You're early."

"You said any time. You're alone, right? How much do you charge to haunt a house anyway?"

"What makes you say that?"

"I just thought of it. Your house is always a little haunted, you know." This seemed a disobliging comment which he could only ignore; they descended to the TV which they watched with pleasure for over an hour, until the telephone rang. This bell, different in tone from the doorbell, could not be assimilated to the sound of TV, had to be answered at once or attention would stray. He climbed unwillingly to the ground floor and went to the telephone in the studio at the very back of the house, where he fondled the clamorous instrument, gazing through the huge window at shining wetness. He put the receiver to his ear.

"Bet you don't know who this is," said a melodious voice. The line clicked and crackled strangely; the voice echoed, seemed familiar, then wholly unrecognizable. He had heard it, he knew, but how very long ago. "Bet you don't know who this is…this is…is…who?"

"We were in school together," he said firmly, shutting off the unsteady echoes.

The voice cooed, "You're getting close."

He listened harder; he had heard the voice somewhere in the past. There was a *castrato* music to it, high, sexually elastic though certainly male. "It's Philly White."

"Who?"

"Philly White. We went to parish school together, don't you remember the Whites, my brother Bob, my sister Pauline? We made our First Holy Communion together."

"So we did. So we did. Of course I remember. You had smallpox when we were in, the third grade?"

He could remember the effects of the disease vividly, the spoiled face, the depth of indentation of the small round scars, about the size of a flake of confetti. His complexion had been like his name, white, the holes in his face changing colour as embarrassment or exposure moved the boy. He had often been in trouble with the teachers, hadn't been heard from in forty years. The voice was irrefutable testimony, when linked to a past and a name.

"I'm here at the Prevention Centre on Parthenais Street." The voice in the receiver pronounced the name wrong, as an Ontarian would, and translated the name of the institution too literally. *Centre de Prévention* doesn't mean "prevention centre," it means "detention centre," a quasi-jail where persons are held to await trial or, in certain cases, sentencing after conviction. Until now he had never heard of the place or seen it, knew nothing about it, couldn't have identified it from glimpses at a distance. It is a deceptive building. It is the embodiment of a lie. It doesn't look like what it is; suicide is routine inside. Men have spent fifteen months there awaiting trial, the presumed innocent often treated far worse than the proven guilty — because the innocence is purely formal and presumptive. Most inmates are habitual offenders. None of this was familiar to him. "What are they holding you for?" he asked.

"Some trouble about a cheque. Well, actually two cheques. Three. You knew my family, you knew Bob was ordained, you knew...I was married there for a while; then I moved out west. I had a car business in Vancouver and then came back east. Two little girls. We're separated now of course...you're the only one here in the city...I don't want my wife to know yet. I was hoping for a reconciliation. I want to get straightened out and start again."

"What's the charge?" He felt proud of the way he phrased the question; he had no contact with police, courts, criminals, or even people who were being held, detained, prevented. "Have they got anything to go on?"

"Actually..." indecision floated into the quavering voice. "I can't talk any more; they're taking me back. They might let you see me. Could you try to see me?"

"The charge?"

"Matter of two years...I've been sentenced..." He never found out whether the term of the sentence was two years, or whether a longer term might be reduced to two for good conduct. "They're deciding whether to send me to a dry-out clinic. There's a problem of alcoholism. And they're waiting for information from Vancouver."

"What sort of information?" He felt damp; the studio was damp.

"...conviction for fraud...not serious."

"What else?"

"Hotel bills in Dorval. They brought me in from Dorval. I was there a month. I have to go now." It sounded as if the call had been cut off at the main switchboard. He put the receiver into its cradle and took several deep breaths, then called downstairs. In a few moments, David appeared from the depths. "You're missing some good takeoffs," he said.

"Will you do me a favour?"

"Yes."

"My car's in for repair and I have to go out unexpectedly. Would you do me a great kindness and drive me across town? I'm not sure exactly where to go. Do you know where Parthenais is?"

They had to unearth David's street-guide in the glove compartment, then consult its small print as they drove along Sherbrooke in the persistent rain; the windows kept fogging over; it was difficult to see. Parthenais was well out toward the east end, past De Lorimier almost at D'Iberville. They turned south when they came to it, down the steep hill toward De Maisonneuve. In a few minutes a massive dark shape stood up indistinctly before them, an ultra-modern office building fourteen stories high, in glassy black plastic siding, standing on a small plot of land surrounded by chain-link fence topped with multiple strands of shining barbed wire. It reminded him of a shiny polished dark monolith seen in some science-fiction film. Some sort of object of perverse worship. Close up, the building looked like most others built around 1969. They parked across the narrow street and approached the main entrance which opened into a spacious glassed-in hall two stories high, with an elevator bank to the right and a reception desk nearby. One or two guards idled in corners, paying no attention to them. He asked at the desk if he would be able to see Philly White, and the receptionist — perfectly agreeable and forthcoming — laughed jovially.

"Tomorrow, 1:30. Come back then."

"He seemed in pain or frightened. Could he be afraid of something?"

"Tomorrow, 1:30. Come back then."

One of the guards moved indecisively.

Time to get out of here while we still can, he thought. He felt great waves of imaginary fugitive guilt washing over him. Hundreds of movies lodged in his memory now rose up to frighten, to accuse. He thought of the fearful ending of *I Am a Fugitive from a Chain Gang* and hastened away. "What do you do, how do you live?" "I steal."

Driving homeward, David said, "I didn't care much for the atmosphere…"

He had to force himself to return the next afternoon. Just before he left the house, he got a call from a police sergeant in Dorval. "...heard from Philly White this morning — he's not a bad fellow, Philly, he wouldn't hurt anybody. He has no violence on his record."

"Record? What record?"

"Oh a long, long record. Four convictions in BC. Fraudulent auto sales with forgery. Fraudulent roofing contracts. But no violence, I was glad when he told me he found a friend to help him out. If I come by your house, can I give you his radio? He left it in the cells here and I know he'll miss it. That Parthenais...it isn't like the Dorval Jail. It's no picnic, you bet." He recited a series of calamitous occurrences which had taken place at the detention centre. Group suicides, self-mutilations. "So you see if old Philly has a friend to help, I'll be glad. His family won't do nothing."

"His family aren't here. His mother is dead and they all live in Toronto."

"Did he tell you that? His mother lives in Montreal with one of his sisters and one brother. They don't go to see him. His wife and kids are here too."

"Does his wife know he's awaiting sentence?"

"No, she doesn't know a thing...nobody knows anything about Philly White for sure. Can I drop off his radio?"

"I'm not sure I'm going to be here. I have to go to the country. I have to pick up my car. I don't believe I can make it; the family's expecting me back. I have to go and..."

"He'll be disappointed. He said you were coming down."

"He seems to say whatever he likes."

"That's right."

"Mail him the radio. I'll be away."

"No. No. I think I'll deliver it by hand."

The car was ready when he went over to get it. "It's ready; it's ready. You said it would be," he said happily; the garageman looked at him in surprise.

"It always is."

"A pleasure...a pleasure."

The building on Parthenais looked more horrible in bright sunshine than in rainy darkness. Huge, slab-sided, far too glassy. Your gaze went right through it and out the other side. He went in, explained his errand to the man on the desk — the same man as the night before; didn't he ever sleep? And ascended to the tenth floor in an ordinary elevator. At the third, fifth and eighth floors it stopped automatically; he peered out without ostentation. Each floor seemed perfectly normal; you could see across the hall and out the windows. Ordinary office space. The view grew progressively more distant and spread-out as the car rose in the shaft. He was prepared for a handsome prospect as he stepped out on ten, and was chilled and repelled by the barred, electrically-locked gate, the approaches beyond it to heavy steel doors. The four top floors of the building form a maximum security jail. There is no exercise yard. There is no sports program. Prisoners may use one of three small recreation areas for periods of up to one hour, every second day, if they aren't receiving special discipline.

"...you are not permitted to see him. What gave you the idea you could see him? Are you a relative?"

"No, he told me on the phone that..."

"I'm sorry, sir. His case is awaiting disposition. Only relatives."

"He told me he had no relatives nearer than Toronto."

"He told you a lie."

"Does his wife come to see him? How long has he been in here? I want to try to help."

"You aren't an officer of the John Howard Society?"

"No, nothing like that."

"Not a lawyer conferring with a judge about the sentence?"

"No, no."

The walls of this dreadful bullpen — a long counter or booth like that in a government liquor store or customs house — were painted a very pale grey-blue which did nothing to conceal their metallic chill. He began to look around wildly.

"What is your name, sir? Why did you come here?"

"This man called me on the telephone last night and told me he was in trouble; he didn't say how serious it was, but I gathered that he felt pretty desperate..."

"...they'll all tell you that."

"Yes, I'm sure they will. I would myself, I think, if I had to stay here. Can't you tell me anything at all?"

"I've never seen the man."

"How do you know so much about him?"

"I'm simply following general regulations, sir."

"And he has no right to a visitor, like he claimed?"

"Certain relatives, his lawyer of record, officially authorized prison visitors."

"All right, then, a sergeant from Dorval is bringing in his radio. He left it there. Would you see that he gets it?"

"I don't know anything about that at all."

He left the bullpen and walked quickly through the massive doors. He felt very glad that they opened for him, that the elevator came, some time after he pressed the DOWN button. All the way out to the street and into the driver's seat of his car, he felt as if a hand might descend on his shoulder. There was a parking ticket under the left windshield wiper. The rubberized gorilla mask smiled up at him from where he had dropped it on the front seat. He felt intensely happy to see it there, happy that he'd remembered it, that his children enjoyed having it. He made the best of his way out of town.

The mask alone was not enough, naturally. Four imaginative new costumes were required. The boys decided to go out as soldiers of the American Civil War, one in blue uniform, one in grey; design and fitting of these intricate costumes occupied much of September and early October.

"What are you going out as?"

"Soldiers of the War Between the States, as they would have been dressed at Gettysburg." The younger son was a student of Civil War history and a bitter partisan of the North, an admirer of Lincoln and Grant.

"But don't you think Lee was the greatest general of that war?"

"He lost, didn't he?"

Not much to be said to that.

And of course, he reflected, on the essential issue of slavery the North had been in the right. He was certain of that; what could possibly be urged in favour of slavery, of imprisonment, detention, referral to clinic? He felt mixed up, his head crowded with civilized misgiving. He started to get letters addressed to Philly White, in his care. He wouldn't open them and couldn't decide what to do with them. Some were postmarked Vancouver. One looked like an Income Tax refund cheque. A month after the first phone call, there came another. "Yes, it's me. I want to thank you for everything you've done for me. Sergeant Bastien told me how you helped him."

"The man from Dorval with your radio."

"He said how kind you were."

"Were you actually talking to Sergeant Bastien?" It had become important to extract some unambiguous, verifiable statement.

"Not actually talking to him in so many words…exactly."

"How then?"

"Well, he got through to me all right. These veteran police officers have ways of dealing with things that you and I wouldn't think of."

"I didn't do anything for you. White. I have no intention of doing anything for you." He at least could be unambiguous, or hoped he could.

"But you came down to the Prevention Centre to see me, didn't you?"

"I did. Anybody would have done that."

"But you came twice, didn't you?"

"How do you know?"

"I know." There was a noxious appeal to this way of talking. He felt himself being drawn into the position of co-conspirator and even accomplice. He had enough free-floating fear of having done something criminal in his imagination without this.

"Just handle my mail for me," begged White.

"Why can't it go directly to jail?" He felt dreadfully like laughing. He thought, "Go directly to Jail; do not pass GO; do not collect $200"; he remembered the cards in the pile marked "Get out of Jail free."

"Would you like your wife to have to send her letters to such a place?"

"No."

"Do this for me then, for the sake of the old days."

"What old days? Do you know, I can barely remember you. That's 40 years ago. I don't have any responsibility for you."

"We are all responsible for one another," said White.

"Then why did you…never mind."

"I can use your address?"

"I'll forward anything that arrives."

The call was abruptly ended by that strange echoing click suggestive of constant switchboard surveillance. He wondered who was listening, and thought of making misleading and ambiguous remarks the next time White telephoned, just to give the listeners something to think about, realizing at the same moment that such an action would cause them to set up a dossier on him, which would then have the assured and interminable existence of an official file.

A flood of correspondence ensued, much of it from distant provinces, all addressed to his quiet Montreal street, all for Philly White. He would wait for three or four days till he had a dozen or so items, then bundle them together in a single large envelope and forward it to Parthenais Street. Certain letters obviously got through to White, who discussed them in later phone calls. Some were perhaps suppressed by the authorities or censored by them, but on the whole White seemed well abreast of his outside affairs; he had now been at the *Centre de Prévention* for August, September, most of

October — almost thirteen weeks; this was nothing compared to the detention of other unfortunates. The top floors were designed to hold 250 inmates, all in one way or another of special status. Either they could not be brought to trial because the prosecutor's case was incomplete, or the dockets were overburdened, or their lawyers were evading the event for tactical reasons: those in this last category might wait forever without their process coming on. Many died on Parthenais Street without receiving either condemnation or justification. And there were always more than 300 crowded into the cells.

There were many like White whose guilt had been legally established. Convicted, criminals in the eyes of the law, sentenced, as yet undisposed of, they could not be conveniently put away and forgotten in this or that prison because a humane penology wished to "cure" them — in White's case apparently to dry the liquor out of him and begin treatment for alcoholism. A cured alcoholic, he might no longer be a fraud-artist and con-man, but this was doubtful. The alcoholism and the pathological addiction to lying might be elements of deeper ruin, probably were.

Nobody knows what is truly criminal, who are culpable. There are legal definitions, always abstract, inexact. There is observably bad — at least socially unacceptable — behaviour: what is called the "psychopathic personality" where social responsibility is rejected together with the possibility of truthfulness. What oppressed the listener to Philly White's phone calls was that he never, even by accident, said the plain truth.

Disguise abounded; cold came on. Toward the end of the month the boys completed their Civil War costumes and began to parade around the house in them, looking from a short distance wonderfully authentic. The younger lad had constructed one of those flat, forward-slanting Confederate caps with a badge of crossed rifles over the peak, and the letters C.S.A. sewn into it irregularly. The effect was truly persuasive. He had a cardboard musket and a water bottle. He kept saying, "Pickett's charge represented the high-water mark of the Confederacy," and his father never managed to establish what that meant. The older boy had decided to approach the northern infantryman's dress with less historical correctness and more freedom of interpretation. He carried a powder-horn — more appropriate for the Revolutionary War — and wore a shaggy false beard made of stuff chopped from an old Borghana coat of their mother's, which gave him an unexpectedly Russian air.

The girls hovered over alternatives. Then in a late fury of artistic creation they evolved two superb and original designs. For the younger girl, the baby of the family, they made a horse's body from a painted and draped cardboard carton fitted around her waist like an Eskimo's kayak. This was completed by floppy artificial legs hanging from a painted saddle — a caricature of a circus equestrienne. Her sister had then simply to dress herself as a ringmaster: red coat, tall hat, white breeches, riding whip, and the illusion was perfect and striking.

Mixed images of strangely-caparisoned, smallish persons capering around him wound their way into their father's worried judgment. All day on the 31st of the month he lazed around the house among orange and black festoons, expecting some sort of resolution of the affair of White the bunco steerer. The weekend before, all clocks had been put back. It was full dark by six pm. The children departed for their exciting annual night walk, gangs of neighbourhood kids beginning to press the doorbell. The phone rang in the midst of other urgent pealings, as he raised his coffee cup to his lips. Of course it was his old friend on Parthenais Street, with his first concrete demand for money. "If you'll just make the one payment for me, $184.80, we can retain ownership, they won't repossess. It's in the wife's name. I'll tell you where to send your cheque, and thanks for what you're trying to do. I really mean it."

He felt great anger squeezing his throat. "You don't mean it at all," he said, "you're just trying it on. I knew it would get to this point. A hundred and eighty from the poor sucker for openers, eh? It's finished, White, you get me? That's it. Don't call again and don't have any more mail sent here. I thought you needed me. I thought you meant it. All just a big con. You're still at it even though they've locked you up. You've been sentenced. How come they don't put you where you belong?"

"*They're* trying to help me."

"Let them! Whoever *they* are."

"I'm only trying to make contact."

"Good-bye White. Don't call again."

He hoped the listeners got it all; there wouldn't be any more calls. The doorbell rang and he walked through the house, opened the door and confronted a small visitant dressed as a ghost. He handed this person many sugary treats, then shut the door. I did right, he told himself, I did right (wrong), I did right, right (wrong), I did right…

Commentary by *Hugh Hood*

≈

Hugh Hood's writing strikes a balance between observation and contemplation. The following commentary is taken from an essay, "Sober Colouring: The Ontology of Super-Realism", first published in Canadian Literature *49 (1971) and republished in Hood's* The Governor's Bridge is Closed *(Ottawa: Oberon Press, 1973). In it Hood discusses how his fiction — like other arts, or philosophy, or religious practice — relies on very particular and highly formal elements to illuminate transcendental truths.*

My interest in the sound of sentences, in the use of colour words and of the names of places, in practical stylistics, showed me that prose fiction might have an abstract element, a purely formal element, even though it continued to be strictly, morally, realistic. It might be possible to think of prose fiction the way one thinks of abstract elements in representational painting, or of highly formal music. I now began to see affinities between the art I was willy-nilly practising and the other arts, first poetry, then painting and music. I have always been passionately attached to music and painting — I have gone so far as to marry a painter on mixed grounds — and have written many stories about the arts: film-making, painting, music less often because it is on the surface such a non-narrative art. I find that it is hard to speak about music.

I have also written some stories about a kind of experience close to that of the artist: metaphysical thought. My stories "A Season of Calm Weather" (with its consciously Wordsworthian title) and "The Hole" are about metaphysicians. The second of the two tries to show a philosopher's intelligence actually at work, a hard thing to do. Like musical thought, metaphysical thought seems to take place in a non-verbal region of consciousness, if there is such a thing, and it is therefore hard to write about, but to me an irresistible challenge.

My novels *White Figure, White Ground* and *The Camera Always Lies* dealt respectively with the problems of a painter and a group of film-makers. It is the seeing-into-things, the capacity for meditative abstraction, that interests me about philosophy, the arts and religious practice. I love most in painting an art which exhibits the transcendental element dwelling in living things. I think of this as true *super-realism*. And I think of Vermeer, or among American artists of Edward Hopper, whose paintings of ordinary places, seaside cottages, a roadside snack bar and gasoline station, have touched some level of my own imagination which I can only express in fictional images. In my story "Getting to Williamstown" there is a description of a roadside refreshment stand beside an abandoned gas pump, which is pretty directly imitated from a painting of Hopper's. I see this now, though I didn't when I wrote the story. That is what I mean by the unconscious elements in my work which co-operate with my deliberate intentions.

SELECTED WORKS BY HUGH HOOD

Flying a Red Kite: Stories. Toronto: The Ryerson Press, 1962. Ryerson Paperbacks. Toronto: The Ryerson Press, 1967. Rpt. as *Flying a Red Kite*. Introd. Hugh Hood. *The Collected Stories: I.* Erin, ON: The Porcupine's Quill, 1987.

Around the Mountain: Scenes from Montreal Life. Toronto: Peter Martin Associates, 1967. [Paperback ed.] Toronto: Peter Martin Associates, 1976.

The Fruit Man, The Meat Man & The Manager: Stories. Ottawa: Oberon Press, 1971.

Dark Glasses. Ottawa: Oberon Press, 1976.

Selected Stories. Ottawa: Oberon Press, 1978.

None Genuine Without This Signature. Downsview, ON: ECW Press, 1980. [Text ed.] Introd. Keith Garebian. Downsview, ON: ECW Press, 1980.

August Nights. Toronto: Stoddart Publishing, 1985.

A Short Walk in the Rain. Introd. Hugh Hood. *The Collected Stories: II.* Erin, ON: The Porcupine's Quill, 1989.

The Isolation Booth. Introd. Hugh Hood. *The Collected Stories: III.* Erin, ON: The Porcupine's Quill, 1991.

You'll Catch Your Death: New Stories. Erin, ON: The Porcupine's Quill, 1992.

Alice Munro

≈

Over a period of 25 or 30 years — a figure that keeps cropping up in this book — a writer's work will inevitably change. The work of some writers will mature, growing deeper and more complex; the work of others will not so much mature as seek new directions. Hugh Hood's more recent stories, for example, have become shorter and have moved into an ironic relationship with mass media. Norman Levine's stories have grown longer, more episodic, more intensely poetic in construction.

Alice Munro's stories have grown away from the more conventional stories she published in her first book, *Dance of the Happy Shades* (1968). Her stories in more recent years — including the two we've selected here, "Royal Beatings" from *Who Do You Think You Are?* (1978) and "Meneseteung" from *Friend of My Youth* (1990) — often challenge the very notion of boundaries between 'fact' and 'fiction', between 'autobiographical' elements and 'invention'. This searching concern with the relationship between autobiography and fiction links her work with mine and with that of Clark Blaise, Norman Levine, and Audrey Thomas. Comparisons among this body of work would probably be fruitful.

The naïve interest of some readers in what is 'true' or 'real' in a story is mildly deplored in Alice Munro's essay "What Is Real?", which she wrote to accompany "Royal Beatings" and the title story of *Who Do You Think You Are?* in the anthology *Making It New: Contemporary Canadian Stories* (Toronto: Methuen, 1982): "Writers answer such questions patiently or crossly according to temperament and the mood they're in. They say, no, you must understand, my characters are composites; no, those things didn't happen the way I wrote about them; no, of course not, that isn't Wingham (or whatever other place it may be that has had the queer unsought-after distinction of hatching a writer). Or the writer may, riskily, ask the questioners what is real, anyway?" For a writer, the nature of fictional reality is much more complex, subtle, and mysterious than such readers might at first assume.

Both Tim Struthers and I have a fascination with and a huge regard for Alice Munro's story "Walker Brothers Cowboy" from *Dance of the Happy Shades* and were tempted to include it here.

But splendid as that story is, Alice Munro's work has grown beyond it; she often writes stories now which have the intensity of dreams and something of the same mysteriousness. Some of these stories resist logical or interpretive approaches; we must give ourselves up to their imagery and event, enter into them as into a dream. The section of "Meneseteung", for example, where Almeda Roth discovers the 'dead' body has an intensity which, if we are to experience the story fully, must not simply 'mean' but must oppress us like that nightmare from which we cannot wake.

But if Alice Munro's work has changed over the years, two things have remained constant — her love of the details of the visible world and her ability to capture them in ravishingly accurate prose. Del Jordan, the narrator of Alice Munro's episodic novel *Lives of Girls and Women* (1971), says of her hometown, Jubilee: "It did not occur to me that one day I would be so greedy for Jubilee.... I would try to make lists. A list of all the stores and businesses going up and down the main street and who owned them, a list of family names, names on the tombstones in the Cemetery and any inscriptions underneath.... And no list could hold what I wanted, for what I wanted was every last thing, every layer of speech and thought, stroke of light on bark or walls, every smell, pothole, pain, crack, delusion, held still and held together—radiant, everlasting."

Twenty years later, the narrator of "Meneseteung" shows much the same impulse searching for the grave of fictional poetess Almeda Roth: "I thought that there wasn't anybody alive in the world but me who would know this, who would make the connection. And I would be the last person to do so. But perhaps this isn't so. People are curious. A few people are. They will be driven to find things out, even trivial things. They will put things together. You see them going around with notebooks, scraping the dirt off gravestones, reading microfilm, just in the hope of seeing this trickle in time, making a connection, rescuing one thing from the rubbish." As an introduction to Alice Munro's work, or to the art of writing, I think readers can do no better than to *immerse* themselves in passages such as these.

≈

A variety of critical approaches to Alice Munro's work, as well as interviews with her by J. R. (Tim) Struthers and Harold Horwood, can be found in the following collections: *Probable Fictions: Alice Munro's Narrative Acts,* edited by Louis K. MacKendrick (Downsview, ON: ECW Press, 1983), and *The Art of Alice Munro: Saying the Unsayable,* edited by Judith Miller (Waterloo, ON: University of Waterloo Press, 1984). Additional studies of Munro include: Hallvard Dahlie's *Alice Munro and Her Works* (Toronto: ECW Press, 1984), W. R. Martin's *Alice Munro: Paradox and Parallel* (Edmonton: University of Alberta Press, 1987), E. D. Blodgett's *Alice Munro* (Boston: Twayne, 1988), Ildikó de Papp Carrington's *Controlling the Uncontrollable: The Fiction of Alice Munro* (DeKalb: Northern Illinois University Press, 1989), Beverly J. Rasporich's *Dance of the Sexes: Art and Gender in the Fiction of Alice Munro* (Edmonton: University of Alberta Press, 1990), and Neil K. Besner's *Introducing Alice Munro's* Lives of Girls and Women (1990). Robert Thacker presents a thorough commentary on criticism of Alice Munro's work in his essay "Go Ask Alice: The Progress of Munro Criticism" in *Journal of Canadian Studies* 26.2 (1991). Also recommended is Catherine Sheldrick Ross's biography *Alice Munro: A Double Life* (Toronto: ECW Press, 1992).

≈ ROYAL BEATINGS ≈

Royal Beating. That was Flo's promise. You are going to get one Royal Beating.

The word Royal lolled on Flo's tongue, took on trappings. Rose had a need to picture things, to pursue absurdities, that was stronger than the need to stay out of trouble, and instead of taking this threat to heart she pondered: how is a beating royal? She came up with a tree-lined avenue, a crowd of formal spectators, some white horses and black slaves. Someone knelt, and the blood came leaping out like banners. An occasion both savage and splendid. In real life they didn't approach such dignity, and it was only Flo who tried to supply the event with some high air of necessity and regret. Rose and her father soon got beyond anything presentable.

Her father was king of the royal beatings. Those Flo gave never amounted to much; they were quick cuffs and slaps dashed off while her attention remained elsewhere. You get out of my road, she would say. You mind your own business. You take that look off your face.

They lived behind a store in Hanratty, Ontario. There were four of them: Rose, her father, Flo, Rose's young half brother Brian. The store was really a house, bought by Rose's father and mother when they married and set up here in the furniture and upholstery repair business. Her mother could do upholstery. From both parents Rose should have inherited clever hands, a quick sympathy with materials, an eye for the nicest turns of mending, but she hadn't. She was clumsy, and when something broke she couldn't wait to sweep it up and throw it away.

Her mother had died. She said to Rose's father during the afternoon, "I have a feeling that is so hard to describe. It's like a boiled egg in my chest, with the shell left on." She died before night, she had a blood clot on her lung. Rose was a baby in a basket at the time, so of course could not remember any of this. She heard it from Flo, who must have heard it from her father. Flo came along soon afterwards, to take over Rose in the basket, marry her father, open up the front room to make a grocery store. Rose, who had known the house only as a store, who had known only Flo for a mother, looked back on the sixteen or so months her parents spent here as an orderly, far gentler and more ceremonious time, with little touches of affluence. She had nothing to go on but some egg cups her mother had bought, with a pattern of vines and birds on them, delicately drawn as if with red ink; the pattern was beginning to wear away. No books or clothes or pictures of her mother remained. Her father must have got rid of them or else Flo would. Flo's only story about her mother, the one about her death, was oddly grudging. Flo liked the details of a death: the things people said, the way they protested or tried to get out of bed or swore or laughed (some did those things), but when she said that Rose's mother mentioned a hard-boiled egg in her chest she made the comparison sound slightly foolish, as if her mother really was the kind of person who might think you could swallow an egg whole.

Her father had a shed out behind the store, where he worked at his furniture repairing and restoring. He caned chair seats and backs, mended wickerwork, filled cracks, put legs back on, all most admirably and skillfully and cheaply. That was his pride: to startle people with such fine work, such moderate, even ridiculous charges. During the Depression people could not afford to pay more, perhaps, but he continued the practice through the war, through the years of prosperity after the war, until he died. He never discussed with Flo what he charged or what was owing. After he died she had to go out and unlock the shed and take all sorts of scraps of paper and torn envelopes from the big wicked-looking hooks that were his files. Many of these she found were not accounts or receipts at all but records of the weather, bits of information about the garden, things he had been moved to write down.

> *Ate new potatoes 25th June. Record.*
> *Dark Day, 1880's, nothing supernatural. Clouds of ash from forest fires.*
> *Aug 16, 1938. Giant thunderstorm in evng. Lightning str. Pres. Church, Turberry Twp. Will of God?*
> *Scald strawberries to remove acid.*
> *All things are alive. Spinoza.*

Flo thought Spinoza must be some new vegetable he planned to grow, like broccoli or eggplant. He would often try some new thing. She showed the scrap of paper to Rose and asked, did she know what Spinoza was? Rose did know, or had an idea — she was in her teens by that time — but she replied that she did not. She had reached an age where she thought she could not stand to know any more, about her father, or about Flo; she pushed any discovery aside with embarrassment and dread.

There was a stove in the shed, and many rough shelves covered with cans of paint and varnish, shellac and turpentine, jars of soaking brushes and also some dark sticky bottles of cough medicine.

Why should a man who coughed constantly, whose lungs took in a whiff of gas in the War (called, in Rose's earliest childhood, not the First, but the Last, War) spend all his days breathing fumes of paint and turpentine? At the time, such questions were not asked as often as they are now. On the bench outside Flo's store several old men from the neighborhood sat gossiping, drowsing, in the warm weather, and some of these old men coughed all the time too. The fact is they were dying, slowly and discreetly, of what was called, without any particular sense of grievance, "the foundry disease." They had worked all their lives at the foundry in town, and now they sat still, with their wasted yellow faces, coughing, chuckling, drifting into aimless obscenity on the subject of women walking by, or any young girl on a bicycle.

From the shed came not only coughing, but speech, a continual muttering, reproachful or encouraging, usually just below the level at which separate words could be made out. Slowing down when her father was at a tricky piece of work, taking on a cheerful speed when he was doing something less demanding, sandpapering or painting. Now and then some words would break through and hang clear and nonsensical on the air. When he realized they were out, there would be a quick bit of cover-up coughing, a swallowing, an alert, unusual silence.

"Macaroni, pepperoni, Botticelli, beans — "

What could that mean? Rose used to repeat such things to herself. She could never ask him. The person who spoke these words and the person who spoke to her as her father were not the same, though they seemed to occupy the same space. It would be the worst sort of taste to acknowledge the person who was not supposed to be there; it would not be forgiven. Just the same, she loitered and listened.

The cloud-capped towers, she heard him say once.

"The cloud-capped towers, the gorgeous palaces."

That was like a hand clapped against Rose's chest, not to hurt, but astonish her, to take her breath away. She had to run then, she had to get away. She knew that was enough to hear, and besides, what if he caught her? It would be terrible.

This was something the same as bathroom noises. Flo had saved up, and had a bathroom put in, but there was no place to put it except in a corner of the kitchen. The door did not fit, the walls were only beaverboard. The result was that even the tearing of a piece of toilet paper, the shifting of a haunch, was audible to those working or talking or eating in the kitchen. They were all familiar with each other's nether voices, not only in their more explosive moments but in their intimate sighs and growls and pleas and statements. And they were all most prudish people. So no one ever seemed to hear, or be listening, and no reference was made. The person creating the noises in the bathroom was not connected with the person who walked out.

They lived in a poor part of town. There was Hanratty and West Hanratty, with the river flowing between them. This was West Hanratty. In Hanratty the social structure ran from doctors and dentists and lawyers down to foundry workers and factory workers and draymen; in West Hanratty it ran from factory workers and foundry workers down to large improvident families of casual bootleggers and prostitutes and unsuccessful thieves. Rose thought of her own family as straddling the river, belonging nowhere, but that was not true. West Hanratty was where the store was and they were, on the straggling tail end of the main street. Across the road from them was a blacksmith shop, boarded up about the time the war started, and a house that had been another store at one time. The Salada Tea sign had never been taken out of the front window; it remained as a proud and interesting decoration though there was no Salada Tea for sale inside. There was just a bit of sidewalk, too cracked and tilted for roller-skating, though Rose longed for roller skates and often pictured herself whizzing along in a plaid skirt, agile and fashionable. There was one street light, a tin flower; then the amenities gave up and there were dirt roads and boggy places, front-yard dumps and strange-looking houses. What made the houses strange-looking were the attempts to keep them from going completely to ruin. With some the attempt had never been made. These were gray and rotted and leaning over, falling into a landscape of scrub hollows, frog ponds, cattails and nettles. Most houses, however, had been patched up with tarpaper, a few fresh shingles, sheets of tin, hammered-out stovepipes, even cardboard. This was, of course, in the days before the war, days of what would later be legendary poverty, from which Rose would remember mostly low-down things — serious-looking anthills and wooden steps, and a cloudy, interesting, problematical light on the world.

There was a long truce between Flo and Rose in the beginning. Rose's nature was growing like a prickly pineapple, but slowly, and secretly, hard pride and skepticism overlapping, to make something surprising even to herself. Before she was old enough to go to school, and while Brian was still in the baby carriage, Rose stayed in the store with both of them — Flo sitting on the high stool behind the counter, Brian asleep by the window; Rose knelt or lay on the wide creaky floorboards working with crayons on pieces of brown paper too torn or irregular to be used for wrapping.

People who came to the store were mostly from the houses around. Some country people came too, on their way home from town, and a few people from Hanratty, who walked across the bridge. Some people were always on the main street, in and out of stores, as if it was their duty to be always on display and their right to be welcomed. For instance, Becky Tyde.

Becky Tyde climbed up on Flo's counter, made room for herself beside an open tin of crumbly jam-filled cookies.

"Are these any good?" she said to Flo, and boldly began to eat one. "When are you going to give us a job, Flo?"

"You could go and work in the butcher shop," said Flo innocently. "You could go and work for your brother."

"Roberta?" said Becky with a stagey sort of contempt. "You think I'd work for him?" Her brother who ran the butcher shop was named Robert but often called Roberta, because of his meek and nervous ways. Becky Tyde laughed. Her laugh was loud and noisy like an engine bearing down on you.

She was a big-headed loud-voiced dwarf, with a mascot's sexless swagger, a red velvet tam, a twisted neck that forced her to hold her head on one side, always looking up and sideways. She wore little polished high-heeled shoes, real lady's shoes. Rose watched her shoes, being scared of the rest of her, of her laugh and her neck. She knew from Flo that Becky Tyde had been sick with polio as a child, that was why her neck was twisted and why she had not grown any taller. It was hard to believe that she had started out differently, that she had ever been normal. Flo said she was not cracked, she had as much brains as anybody, but she knew she could get away with anything.

"You know I used to live out here?" Becky said, noticing Rose. "Hey! What's-your-name! Didn't I used to live out here, Flo?"

"If you did it was before my time," said Flo, as if she didn't know anything.

"That was before the neighborhood got so downhill. Excuse me saying so. My father built his house out here and he built his slaughterhouse and we had half an acre of orchard."

"Is that so?" said Flo, using her humoring voice, full of false geniality, humility even. "Then why did you ever move away?"

"I told you, it got to be such a downhill neighborhood," said Becky. She would put a whole cookie in her mouth if she felt like it, let her cheeks puff out like a frog's. She never told any more.

Flo knew anyway, as who didn't. Everyone knew the house, red brick with the veranda pulled off and the orchard, what was left of it, full of the usual outflow — car seats and washing machines and bedsprings and junk. The house would never look sinister, in spite of what had happened in it, because there was so much wreckage and confusion all around.

Becky's old father was a different kind of butcher from her brother according to Flo. A bad-tempered Englishman. And different from Becky in the matter of mouthiness. His was never open. A skinflint, a family tyrant. After Becky had polio he wouldn't let her go back to school. She was seldom seen outside the house, never outside the yard. He didn't want people gloating. That was what Becky said, at the trial. Her mother was dead by that time and her sisters married. Just Becky and Robert at home. People would stop Robert on the road and ask him, "How about your sister, Robert? Is she altogether better now?"

"Yes."

"Does she do the housework? Does she get your supper?"

"Yes."

"And is your father good to her, Robert?"

The story being that the father beat them, had beaten all his children and beaten his wife as well, beat Becky more now because of her deformity, which some people believed he had caused (they did not understand about polio). The stories persisted and got added to. The reason that Becky was kept out of sight was now supposed to be her pregnancy, and the father of the child was supposed to be her own father. Then people said it had been born, and disposed of.

"What?"

"Disposed of," Flo said. "They used to say go and get your lamb chops at Tyde's, get them nice and tender! It was all lies in all probability," she said regretfully.

Rose could be drawn back — from watching the wind shiver along the old torn awning, catch in the tear — by this tone of regret, caution, in Flo's voice. Flo telling a story — and this was not the only one, or even the most lurid one, she knew — would incline her head and let her face go soft and thoughtful, tantalizing, warning.

"I shouldn't even be telling you this stuff."

More was to follow.

Three useless young men, who hung around the livery stable, got together — or were got together, by more influential and respectful men in town — and prepared to give old man Tyde a horsewhipping, in the interests of public morality. They blacked their faces. They were provided with whips and a quart of whiskey apiece, for courage. They were: Jelly Smith, a horse-racer and a drinker; Bob Temple, a ball-player and strongman; and Hat Nettleton, who worked on the town dray, and had his nickname from a bowler hat he wore, out of vanity as much as for the comic effect. (He still worked on the dray, in fact; he had kept the name if not the hat, and could often be seen in public — almost as often as Becky Tyde — delivering sacks of coal, which blackened his face and arms. That should have brought to mind his story, but didn't. Present time and past, the shady melodramatic past of Flo's stories, were quite separate, at least for Rose. Present people could not be fitted into the past. Becky herself, town oddity and public pet, harmless and malicious, could never match the butcher's prisoner, the cripple daughter, a white streak at the window: mute, beaten, impregnated. As with the house, only a formal connection could be made.

The young men primed to do the horsewhipping showed up late, outside Tyde's house, after everybody had gone to bed. They had a gun, but they used up their ammunition firing it off in the yard. They yelled for the butcher and beat on the door; finally they broke it down. Tyde concluded they were after his money, so he put some bills in a handkerchief and sent Becky down with them, maybe thinking those men would be touched or scared by the sight of a little wry-necked girl, a dwarf. But that didn't content them. They came upstairs and dragged the butcher out from under his bed, in his nightgown. They dragged him outside and stood him in the snow. The temperature was four below zero, a fact noted later in court. They meant to hold a mock trial but they could not remember how it was done. So they began to beat him and kept beating him until he fell. They yelled at him, *Butcher's meat!* and continued beating him while his nightgown and the snow he was lying in turned red. His son Robert said in court that he had not watched the beating. Becky said that Robert had watched at first but had run away and hid. She herself had watched all the way through. She watched the men leave at last and her father make his delayed bloody progress through the snow and up the steps of the veranda. She did not go out to help him, or open the door until he got to it. Why not? she was asked in court, and she said she did not go out because she just had her nightgown on, and she did not open the door because she did not want to let the cold into the house.

Old man Tyde then appeared to have recovered his strength. He sent Robert to harness the horse, and made Becky heat water so that he could wash. He dressed and took all the money and with no explanation to his children got into the cutter and drove to Belgrave where he left the horse tied in the cold and took the early morning train to Toronto. On the train he behaved oddly, groaning and cursing as if he was drunk. He was picked up on the streets of Toronto a day later, out of his mind with fever, and was taken to a hospital, where he died. He still had all the money. The cause of death was given as pneumonia.

But the authorities got wind, Flo said. The case came to trial. The three men who did it all received long prison sentences. A farce, said Flo. Within a year they were all free, had all been pardoned, had jobs waiting for them. And why was that? It was because too many higher-ups were in on it. And it seemed as if Becky and Robert had no interest in seeing justice done. They were left well-off. They bought a house in Hanratty. Robert went into the store. Becky after her long seclusion started on a career of public sociability and display.

That was all. Flo put the lid down on the story as if she was sick of it. It reflected no good on anybody.

"Imagine," Flo said.

Flo at this time must have been in her early thirties. A young woman. She wore exactly the same clothes that a woman of fifty, or sixty, or seventy, might wear: print housedresses loose at the neck and sleeves as well as the waist; bib aprons, also of print, which she took off when she came from the kitchen into the store. This was a common costume at the time, for a poor though not absolutely poverty-stricken woman; it was also, in a way, a scornful deliberate choice. Flo scorned slacks, she scorned the outfits of people trying to be in style, she scorned lipstick and permanents. She wore her own black hair cut straight across, just long enough to push behind her ears. She was tall but fine-boned, with narrow wrists and shoulders, a small head, a pale, freckled, mobile, monkeyish face. If she had thought it worthwhile, and had the resources, she might have had a black-and-pale, fragile, nurtured sort of prettiness; Rose realized that later. But she would have to have been a different person altogether; she would have to have learned to resist making faces, at herself and others.

Rose's earliest memories of Flo were of extraordinary softness and hardness. The soft hair, the long, soft, pale cheeks, soft almost invisible fuzz in front of her ears and above her mouth. The sharpness of her knees, hardness of her lap, flatness of her front.

When Flo sang:

Oh the buzzin' of the bees in the cigarette trees
And the soda-water fountain…

Rose thought of Flo's old life before she married her father, when she worked as a waitress in the coffee shop in Union Station, and went with her girl friends Mavis and Irene to Centre Island, and was followed by men on dark streets and knew how pay-phones and elevators worked. Rose heard in her voice the reckless dangerous life of cities, the gum-chewing sharp answers.

And when she sang:

Then slowly, slowly, she got up
And slowly she came nigh him
And all she said, that she ever did say,
Was young man, I think you're dyin'!

Rose thought of a life Flo seemed to have had beyond that, earlier than that, crowded and legendary, with Barbara Allen and Becky Tyde's father and all kinds of old outrages and sorrows jumbled up together in it.

The royal beatings. What got them started?

Suppose a Saturday, in spring. Leaves not out yet but the doors open to the sunlight. Crows. Ditches full of running water. Hopeful weather. Often on Saturdays Flo left Rose in charge of the store — it's a few years now, these are the years when Rose was nine, ten, eleven, twelve — while she herself went across the bridge to Hanratty (going uptown they called it) to shop and see people, and listen to them. Among the people she listened to were Mrs. Lawyer Davies, Mrs. Anglican Rector Henley-Smith, and Mrs. Horse-Doctor McKay. She came home and imitated them at supper: their high-flown remarks, their flibberty voices. Monsters, she made them seem; of foolishness, and showiness, and self-approbation.

When she finished shopping she went into the coffee shop of the Queen's Hotel and had a sundae. What kind? Rose and Brian wanted to know when she got home, and they would be disappointed if it was only pineapple or butterscotch, pleased if it was a Tin Roof, or Black and White. Then she smoked a cigarette. She had some ready-rolled, that she carried with her, so that she wouldn't have to roll one in public. Smoking was the one thing she did that she would have called showing off in anybody else. It was a habit left over from her working days, from Toronto. She knew it was asking for trouble. Once the Catholic priest came over to her right in the Queen's Hotel, and flashed his lighter at her before she could get her matches out. She thanked him but did not enter into conversation, lest he should try to convert her.

Another time, on the way home, she saw at the town end of the bridge a boy in a blue jacket, apparently looking at the water. Eighteen, nineteen years old. Nobody she knew. Skinny, weakly looking, something the matter with him, she saw at once. Was he thinking of jumping? Just as she came up even with him, what does he do but turn and display, holding his jacket open, also his pants. What he must have suffered from the cold, on a day that had Flo holding her coat collar tight around her throat.

When she first saw what he had in his hand, Flo said, all she could think of was, what is he doing out here with a baloney sausage?

She could say that. It was offered as truth; no joke. She maintained that she despised dirty talk. She would go out and yell at the old men sitting in front of her store.

"If you want to stay where you are you better clean your mouths out!"

Saturday, then. For some reason Flo is not going uptown, has decided to stay home and scrub the kitchen floor. Perhaps this has put her in a bad mood. Perhaps she was in a bad mood anyway, due to people not paying their bills, or the stirring-up of feelings in spring. The wrangle with Rose has already commenced, has been going on forever, like a dream that goes back and back into other dreams, over hills and through doorways, maddeningly dim and populous and familiar and elusive. They are carting all the chairs out of the kitchen preparatory to the scrubbing, and they have also got to move some extra provisions for the store, some cartons of canned goods, tins of maple syrup, coal-oil cans, jars of vinegar. They take these things out to the woodshed. Brian who is five or six by this time is helping drag the tins.

"Yes," says Flo, carrying on from our lost starting-point. "Yes, and that filth you taught to Brian."

"What filth?"

"And he doesn't know any better."

There is one step down from the kitchen to the woodshed, a bit of carpet on it so worn Rose can't ever remember seeing the pattern. Brian loosens it, dragging a tin.

"Two Vancouvers," she says softly.

Flo is back in the kitchen. Brian looks from Flo to Rose and Rose says again in a slightly louder voice, an encouraging sing-song, "Two Vancouvers — "

"Fried in snot!" finishes Brian, not able to control himself any longer.

"Two pickled arseholes — "

"Tied in a knot!"

There it is. The filth.

Two Vancouvers fried in snot!
Two pickled arseholes tied in a knot!

Rose has known that for years, learned it when she first went to school. She came home and asked Flo, what is a Vancouver?

"It's a city. It's a long ways away."

"What else besides a city?"

Flo said, what did she mean, what else? How could it be fried, Rose said, approaching the dangerous moment, the delightful moment, when she would have to come out with the whole thing.

"Two Vancouvers fried in snot!/Two pickled arseholes tied in a knot!"

"You're going to get it!" cried Flo in a predictable rage. "Say that again and you'll get a good clout!"

Rose couldn't stop herself. She hummed it tenderly, tried saying the innocent words aloud, humming through the others. It was not just the words snot and arsehole that gave her pleasure, though of course they did. It was the pickling and tying and the unimaginable Vancouvers. She saw them in her mind shaped rather like octopuses, twitching in the pan. The tumble of reason; the spark and spit of craziness.

Lately she has remembered it again and taught it to Brian, to see if it has the same effect on him, and of course it has.

"Oh, I heard you!" says Flo. "I heard that! And I'm warning you!"

So she is. Brian takes the warning. He runs away, out the woodshed door, to do as he likes. Being a boy, free to help or not, involve himself or not. Not committed to the household struggle. They don't need him anyway, except to use against each other, they hardly notice his going. They continue, can't help continuing, can't leave each other alone. When they seem to have given up they were really just waiting and building up steam.

Flo gets out the scrub pail and the brush and the rag and the pad for her knees, a dirty red rubber pad. She starts to work on the floor. Rose sits on the kitchen table, the only place left to sit, swinging her legs. She can feel the cool oilcloth, because she is wearing shorts, last summer's tight faded shorts dug out of the summer-clothes bag. They smell a bit moldy from winter storage.

Flo crawls around underneath, scrubbing with the brush, wiping with the rag. Her legs are long, white and muscular, marked all over with blue veins as if somebody had been drawing rivers on them with an indelible pencil. An abnormal energy, a violent disgust, is expressed in the chewing of the brush at the linoleum, the swish of the rag.

What do they have to say to each other? It doesn't really matter. Flo speaks of Rose's smart-aleck behavior, rudeness and sloppiness and conceit. Her willingness to make work for others, her lack of gratitude. She mentions Brian's innocence, Rose's corruption. Oh, don't you think you're somebody, says Flo, and a moment later, Who do you think you are? Rose contradicts and objects with such poisonous reasonableness and mildness, displays theatrical unconcern. Flo goes beyond her ordinary scorn and self-possession and becomes amazingly theatrical herself, saying it was for Rose that she sacrificed her life. She saw her father saddled with a baby daughter and she thought, what is that man going to do? So she married him, and here she is, on her knees.

At that moment the bell rings, to announce a customer in the store. Because the fight is on, Rose is not permitted to go into the store and wait on whoever it is. Flo gets up and throws off her apron, groaning — but not communicatively, it is not a groan whose exasperation Rose is allowed to share — and goes in and serves. Rose hears her using her normal voice.

"About time! Sure is!"

She comes back and ties on her apron and is ready to resume.

"You never have a thought for anybody but your ownself! You never have a thought for what I'm doing."

"I never asked you to do anything. I wished you never had. I would have been a lot better off."

Rose says this smiling directly at Flo, who has not yet gone down on her knees. Flo sees the smile, grabs the scrub rag that is hanging on the side of the pail, and throws it at her. It may be meant to hit her in the face but instead it falls against Rose's leg and she raises her foot and catches it, swinging it negligently against her ankle.

"All right," says Flo. "You've done it this time. All right."

Rose watches her go to the woodshed door, hears her tramp through the woodshed, pause in the doorway, where the screen door hasn't yet been hung, and the storm door is standing open, propped with a brick. She calls Rose's father. She calls him in a warning, summoning voice, as if against her will preparing him for bad news. He will know what this is about.

The kitchen floor has five or six different patterns of linoleum on it. Ends, which Flo got for nothing and ingeniously trimmed and fitted together, bordering them with tin strips and tacks. While Rose sits on the table waiting, she looks at the floor, at this satisfying arrangement of rectangles, triangles, some other shape whose name she is trying to remember. She hears Flo coming back through the woodshed, on the creaky plank walk laid over the dirt floor. She is loitering, waiting, too. She and Rose can carry this no further, by themselves.

Rose hears her father come in. She stiffens, a tremor runs through her legs, she feels them shiver on the oilcloth. Called away from some peaceful, absorbing task, away from the words running in his head, called out of himself, her father has to say something. He says, "Well? What's wrong?"

Now comes another voice of Flo's. Enriched, hurt, apologetic, it seems to have been manufactured on the spot. She is sorry to have called him from his work. Would never have done it, if Rose was not driving her to distraction. How to distraction? With her back-talk and impudence and her terrible tongue. The things Rose has said to Flo are such that, if Flo had said them to her mother, she knows her father would have thrashed her into the ground.

Rose tries to butt in, to say this isn't true.

What isn't true?

Her father raises a hand, doesn't look at her, says, "Be quiet."

When she says it isn't true, Rose means that she herself didn't start this, only responded, that she was goaded by Flo, who is now, she believes, telling the grossest sort of lies, twisting everything to suit herself. Rose puts aside her other knowledge that whatever Flo has said or done, whatever she herself has said or done, does not really matter at all. It is the struggle itself that counts, and that can't be stopped, can never be stopped, short of where it has got to, now.

Flo's knees are dirty, in spite of the pad. The scrub rag is still hanging over Rose's foot.

Her father wipes his hands, listening to Flo. He takes his time. He is slow at getting into the spirit of things, tired in advance, maybe, on the verge of rejecting the role he has to play. He won't look at Rose, but at any sound or stirring from Rose, he holds up his hand.

"Well we don't need the public in on this, that's for sure," Flo says, and she goes to lock the door of the store, putting in the store window the sign that says "Back Soon," a sign Rose made for her with a great deal of fancy curving and shading of letters in black and red crayon. When she comes back she shuts the door to the store, then the door to the stairs, then the door to the woodshed.

Her shoes have left marks on the clean wet part of the floor.

"Oh, I don't know," she says now, in a voice worn down from its emotional peak. "I don't know what to do about her." She looks down and sees her dirty knees (following Rose's eyes) and rubs at them viciously with her bare hands, smearing the dirt around.

"She humiliates me," she says, straightening up. There it is, the explanation. "She humiliates me," she repeats with satisfaction. "She has no respect."

"I do not!"

"Quiet, you!" says her father.

"If I hadn't called your father you'd still be sitting there with that grin on your face! What other way is there to manage you?"

Rose detects in her father some objections to Flo's rhetoric, some embarrassment and reluctance. She is wrong, and ought to know she is wrong, in thinking that she can count on this. The fact that she knows about it, and he knows she knows, will not make things any better. He is beginning to warm up. He gives her a look. This look is at first cold and challenging. It informs her of his judgment, of the hopelessness of her position. Then it clears, it begins to fill up with something else, the way a spring fills up when you clear the leaves away. It fills with hatred and pleasure. Rose sees that and knows it. Is that just a description of anger, should she see his eyes filling up with anger? No. Hatred is right. Pleasure is right. His face loosens and changes and grows younger, and he holds up his hand this time to silence Flo.

"All right," he says, meaning that's enough, more than enough, this part is over, things can proceed. He starts to loosen his belt.

Flo has stopped anyway. She has the same difficulty Rose does, a difficulty in believing that what you know must happen really will happen, that there comes a time when you can't draw back.

"Oh, I don't know, don't be too hard on her." She is moving around nervously as if she has thoughts of opening some escape route. "Oh, you don't have to use the belt on her. Do you have to use the belt?"

He doesn't answer. The belt is coming off, not hastily. It is being grasped at the necessary point. *All right you*. He is coming over to Rose. He pushes her off the table. His face, like his voice, is quite out of character. He is like a bad actor, who turns a part grotesque. As if he must savor and insist on just what is shameful and terrible about this. That is not to say he is pretending, that he is acting, and does not mean it. He is acting, and he means it. Rose knows that, she knows everything about him.

She has since wondered about murders, and murderers. Does the thing have to be carried through, in the end, partly for the effect, to prove to the audience of one — who won't be able to report, only register, the lesson — that such a thing can happen, that there is nothing that can't happen, that the most dreadful antic is justified, feelings can be found to match it?

She tries again looking at the kitchen floor, that clever and comforting geometrical arrangement, instead of looking at him or his belt. How can this go on in front of such daily witnesses — the linoleum, the calendar with the mill and creek and autumn trees, the old accommodating pots and pans?

Hold out your hand!

Those things aren't going to help her, none of them can rescue her. They turn bland and useless, even unfriendly. Pots can show malice, the patterns of linoleum can leer up at you, treachery is the other side of dailiness.

At the first, or maybe the second, crack of pain, she draws back. She will not accept it. She runs around the room, she tries to get to the doors. Her father blocks her off. Not an ounce of courage or of stoicism in her, it would seem. She runs, she screams, she implores. Her father is after her, cracking the belt at her when he can, then abandoning it and using his hands. Bang over the ear, then bang over the other ear. Back and forth, her head ringing. Bang in the face. Up against the wall and bang in the face again. He shakes her and hits her against the wall, he kicks her legs. She is incoherent, insane, shrieking. *Forgive me! Oh please, forgive me!*

Flo is shrieking too. *Stop, stop!*

Not yet. He throws Rose down. Or perhaps she throws herself down. He kicks her legs again. She has given up on words but is letting out a noise, the sort of noise that makes Flo cry, *Oh, what if people can hear her?* The very last-ditch willing sound of humiliation and defeat it is, for it seems Rose must play her part in this with the same grossness, the same exaggeration, that her father displays, playing his. She plays his victim with a self-indulgence that arouses, and maybe hopes to arouse, his final, sickened contempt.

They will give this anything that is necessary, it seems, they will go to any lengths.

Not quite. He has never managed to really injure her, though there are times, of course, when she prays that he will. He hits her with an open hand, there is some restraint in his kicks.

Now he stops, he is out of breath. He allows Flo to move in, he grabs Rose up and gives her a push in Flo's direction, making a sound of disgust. Flo retrieves her, opens the stair door, shoves her up the stairs.

"Go on up to your room now! Hurry!"

Rose goes up the stairs, stumbling, letting herself stumble, letting herself fall against the steps. She doesn't bang her door because a gesture like that could still bring him after her, and anyway, she is weak. She lies on the bed. She can hear through the stovepipe hole Flo snuffling and remonstrating, her father saying angrily that Flo should have kept quiet then, if she did not want Rose punished she should not have recommended it. Flo says she never recommended a hiding like that.

They argue back and forth on this. Flo's frightened voice is growing stronger, getting its confidence back. By stages, by arguing, they are being drawn back into themselves. Soon it's only Flo talking; he will not talk any more. Rose has had to fight down her noisy sobbing, so as to listen to them, and when she loses interest in listening, and wants to sob some more, she finds she can't work herself up to it. She has passed into a state of calm, in which outrage is perceived as complete and final. In this state events and possibilities take on a lovely simplicity. Choices are mercifully clear. The words that come to mind are not the quibbling, seldom the conditional. Never is a word to which the right is suddenly established. She will never speak to them, she will never look at them with anything but loathing, she will never forgive them. She will punish them; she will finish them. Encased in these finalities, and in her bodily pain, she floats in curious comfort, beyond herself, beyond responsibility.

Suppose she dies now? Suppose she commits suicide? Suppose she runs away? Any of these things would be appropriate. It is only a matter of choosing, of figuring out the way. She floats in her pure superior state as if kindly drugged.

And just as there is a moment, when you are drugged, in which you feel perfectly safe, sure, unreachable, and then without warning and right next to it a moment in which you know the whole protection has fatally cracked, though it is still pretending to hold soundly together, so there is a moment now — the moment, in fact, when Rose hears Flo step on the stairs — that contains for her both present peace and freedom and a sure knowledge of the whole down-spiraling course of events from now on.

Flo comes into the room without knocking, but with a hesitation that shows it might have occurred to her. She brings a jar of cold cream. Rose is hanging on to advantage as long as she can, lying face down on the bed, refusing to acknowledge or answer.

"Oh come on," Flo says uneasily. "You aren't so bad off, are you? You put some of this on and you'll feel better."

She is bluffing. She doesn't know for sure what damage has been done. She has the lid off the cold cream. Rose can smell it. The intimate, babyish, humiliating smell. She won't allow it near her. But in order to avoid it, the big ready clot of it in Flo's hand, she has to move. She scuffles, resists, loses dignity, and lets Flo see there is not really much the matter.

"All right," Flo says. "You win. I'll leave it here and you can put it on when you like."

Later still a tray will appear. Flo will put it down without a word and go away. A large glass of chocolate milk on it, made with Vita-Malt from the store. Some rich streaks of Vita-Malt around the bottom of the glass. Little sandwiches, neat and appetizing. Canned salmon of the first quality and reddest color, plenty of mayonnaise. A couple of butter tarts from a bakery package, chocolate biscuits with a peppermint filling. Rose's favorites, in the sandwich, tart and cookie line. She will turn away, refuse to look, but left alone with these eatables will be miserably tempted, roused and troubled and drawn back from thoughts of suicide or flight by the smell of salmon, the anticipation of crisp chocolate, she will reach out a finger, just to run it around the edge of one of the sandwiches (crusts cut off!) to get the overflow, get a taste. Then she will decide to eat one, for strength to refuse the rest. One will not be noticed. Soon, in helpless corruption, she will eat them all. She will drink the chocolate milk, eat the tarts, eat the cookies. She will get the malty syrup out of the bottom of the glass with her finger, though she sniffles with shame. Too late.

Flo will come up and get the tray. She may say, "I see you got your appetite still," or, "Did you like the chocolate milk, was it enough syrup in it?" Depending on how chastened she is feeling, herself. At any rate, all advantage will be lost. Rose will understand that life has started up again, that they will all sit around the table eating again, listening to the radio news. Tomorrow morning, maybe even tonight. Unseemly and unlikely as that may be. They will be embarrassed, but rather less than you might expect considering how they have behaved. They will feel a queer lassitude, a convalescent indolence, not far off satisfaction.

One night after a scene like this they were all in the kitchen. It must have been summer, or at least warm weather, because her father spoke of the old men who sat on the bench in front of the store.

"Do you know what they're talking about now?" he said, and nodded his head towards the store to show who he meant, though of course they were not there now, they went home at dark.

"Those old coots," said Flo. "What?"

There was about them both a geniality not exactly false but a bit more emphatic than was normal, without company.

Rose's father told them then that the old men had picked up the idea somewhere that what looked like a star in the western sky, the first star that came out after sunset, the evening star, was in reality an airship hovering over Bay City, Michigan, on the other side of Lake Huron. An American invention, sent up to rival the heavenly bodies. They were all in agreement about this, the idea was congenial to them. They believed it to be lit by ten thousand electric light bulbs. Her father had ruthlessly disagreed with them, pointing out that it was the planet Venus they saw, which had appeared in the sky long before the invention of an electric light bulb. They had never heard of the planet Venus.

"Ignoramuses," said Flo. At which Rose knew, and knew her father knew, that Flo had never heard of the planet Venus either. To distract them from this, or even apologize for it, Flo put down her teacup, stretched out with her head resting on the chair she had been sitting on and her feet on another chair (somehow she managed to tuck her dress modestly between her legs at the same time), and lay stiff as a board, so that Brian cried out in delight, "Do that! Do that!"

Flo was double-jointed and very strong. In moments of celebration or emergency she would do tricks.

They were silent while she turned herself around, not using her arms at all but just her strong legs and feet. Then they all cried out in triumph, though they had seen it before.

Just as Flo turned herself Rose got a picture in her mind of that airship, an elongated transparent bubble, with its strings of diamond lights, floating in the miraculous American sky.

"The planet Venus!" her father said, applauding Flo. "Ten thousand electric lights!"

There was a feeling of permission, relaxation, even a current of happiness, in the room.

Years later, many years later, on a Sunday morning, Rose turned on the radio. This was when she was living by herself in Toronto.

Well sir.

It was a different kind of a place in our day. Yes it was.

It was all horses then. Horses and buggies. Buggy races up and down the main street on the Saturday nights.

"Just like the chariot races," says the announcer's, or interviewer's, smooth encouraging voice.

I never seen a one of them.

"No sir, that was the old Roman chariot races I was referring to. That was before your time."

Musta been before my time. I'm a hunerd and two years old.

"That's a wonderful age, sir."

It is so.

She left it on, as she went around the apartment kitchen, making coffee for herself. It seemed to her that this must be a staged interview, a scene from some play, and she wanted to find out what it was. The old man's voice was so vain and belligerent, the interviewer's quite hopeless and alarmed, under its practiced gentleness and ease. You were surely meant to see him holding the microphone up to some toothless, reckless, preening centenarian, wondering what in God's name he was doing here, and what would he say next?

"They must have been fairly dangerous."

What was dangerous?

"Those buggy races."

They was. Dangerous. Used to be the runaway horses. Used to be a-plenty of accidents. Fellows was dragged along on the gravel and cut their face open. Wouldna matter so much if they was dead. Heh.

Some of them horses was the high-steppers. Some, they had to have the mustard under their tail. Some wouldn step out for nothin. That's the thing it is with the horses. Some'll work and pull till they drop down dead and some wouldn pull your cock out of a pail of lard. Heh.

It must be a real interview after all. Otherwise they wouldn't have put that in, wouldn't have risked it. It's all right if the old man says it. Local color. Anything rendered harmless and delightful by his hundred years.

Accidents all the time then. In the mill. Foundry. Wasn't the precautions.

"You didn't have so many strikes then, I don't suppose? You didn't have so many unions?"

Everybody taking it easy nowadays. We worked and we was glad to get it. Worked and was glad to get it.

"You didn't have television."

Didn't have no T.V. Didn't have no radio. No picture show.

"You made your own entertainment."

That's the way we did.

"You had a lot of experiences young men growing up today will never have."

Experiences.

"Can you recall any of them for us?"

I eaten groundhog meat one time. One winter. You wouldna cared for it. Heh.

There was a pause, of appreciation, it would seem, then the announcer's voice saying that the foregoing had been an interview with Mr. Wilfred Nettleton of Hanratty, Ontario, made on his hundred and second birthday, two weeks before his death, last spring. A living link with our past. Mr. Nettleton had been interviewed in the Wawanash County Home for the Aged.

Hat Nettleton.

Horsewhipper into centenarian. Photographed on his birthday, fussed over by nurses, kissed no doubt by a girl reporter. Flash bulbs popping at him. Tape recorder drinking in the sound of his voice. Oldest resident. Oldest horsewhipper. Living link with our past.

Looking out from her kitchen window at the cold lake, Rose was longing to tell somebody. It was Flo who would enjoy hearing. She thought of her saying *Imagine!* in a way that meant she was having her worst suspicions gorgeously confirmed. But Flo was in the same place Hat Nettleton had died in, and there wasn't any way Rose could reach her. She had been there even when the interview was recorded, though she would not have heard it, would not have known about it. After Rose put her in the Home, a couple of years earlier, she had stopped talking. She had removed herself, and spent most of her time sitting in a corner of her crib, looking crafty and disagreeable, not answering anybody, though she occasionally showed her feelings by biting a nurse.

≈ MENESETEUNG ≈

I

Columbine, bloodroot,
And wild bergamot,
Gathering armfuls,
Giddily we go.

Offerings the book is called. Gold lettering on a dull-blue cover. The author's full name underneath: Almeda Joynt Roth. The local paper, the *Vidette*, referred to her as "our poetess." There seems to be a mixture of respect and contempt, both for her calling and for her sex — or for their predictable conjuncture. In the front of the book is a photograph, with the photographer's name in one corner, and the date: 1865. The book was published later, in 1873.

The poetess has a long face; a rather long nose; full, sombre dark eyes, which seem ready to roll down her cheeks like giant tears; a lot of dark hair gathered around her face in droopy rolls and curtains. A streak of gray hair plain to see, although she is, in this picture, only twenty-five. Not a pretty girl but the sort of woman who may age well, who probably won't get fat. She wears a tucked and braid-trimmed dark dress or jacket, with a lacy, floppy arrangement of white material — frills or a bow — filling the deep V at the neck. She also wears a hat, which might be made of velvet, in a dark color to match the dress. It's the untrimmed, shapeless hat, something like a soft beret, that makes me see artistic intentions, or at least a shy and stubborn eccentricity, in this young woman, whose long neck and forward-inclining head indicate as well that she is tall and slender and somewhat awkward. From the waist up, she looks like a young nobleman of another century. But perhaps it was the fashion.

"In 1854," she writes in the preface to her book, "my father brought us — my mother, my sister Catherine, my brother William, and me — to the wilds of Canada West (as it then was). My father was a harness-maker by trade, but a cultivated man who could quote by heart from the Bible, Shakespeare, and the writings of Edmund Burke. He prospered in this newly opened land and was able to set up a harness and leather-goods store, and after a year to build the comfortable house in which I live (alone) today. I was fourteen years old, the eldest of the children, when we came into this country from

Kingston, a town whose handsome streets I have not seen again but often remember. My sister was eleven and my brother nine. The third summer that we lived here, my brother and sister were taken ill of a prevalent fever and died within a few days of each other. My dear mother did not regain her spirits after this blow to our family. Her health declined, and after another three years she died. I then became housekeeper to my father and was happy to make his home for twelve years, until he died suddenly one morning at his shop.

"From my earliest years I have delighted in verse and I have occupied myself — and sometimes allayed my griefs, which have been no more, I know, than any sojourner on earth must encounter — with many floundering efforts at its composition. My fingers, indeed, were always too clumsy for crochetwork, and those dazzling productions of embroidery which one sees often today — the overflowing fruit and flower baskets, the little Dutch boys, the bonneted maidens with their watering cans — have likewise proved to be beyond my skill. So I offer instead, as the product of my leisure hours, these rude posies, these ballads, couplets, reflections."

Titles of some of the poems: "Children at Their Games," "The Gypsy Fair," "A Visit to My Family," "Angels in the Snow," "Champlain at the Mouth of the Meneseteung," "The Passing of the Old Forest," and "A Garden Medley." There are other, shorter poems, about birds and wildflowers and snowstorms. There is some comically intentioned doggerel about what people are thinking about as they listen to the sermon in church.

"Children at Their Games": The writer, a child, is playing with her brother and sister — one of those games in which children on different sides try to entice and catch each other. She plays on in the deepening twilight, until she realizes that she is alone, and much older. Still she hears the (ghostly) voices of her brother and sister calling. *Come over, come over, let Meda come over.* (Perhaps Almeda was called Meda in the family, or perhaps she shortened her name to fit the poem.)

"The Gypsy Fair": The Gypsies have an encampment near the town, a "fair," where they sell cloth and trinkets, and the writer as a child is afraid that she may be stolen by them, taken away from her family. Instead, her family has been taken away from her, stolen by Gypsies she can't locate or bargain with.

"A Visit to My Family": A visit to the cemetery, a one-sided conversation.

"Angels in the Snow": The writer once taught her brother and sister to make "angels" by lying down in the snow and moving their arms to create wing shapes. Her brother always jumped up carelessly, leaving an angel with a crippled wing. Will this be made perfect in Heaven, or will he be flying with his own makeshift, in circles?

"Champlain at the Mouth of the Meneseteung": This poem celebrates the popular, untrue belief that the explorer sailed down the eastern shore of Lake Huron and landed at the mouth of the major river.

"The Passing of the Old Forest": A list of all the trees — their names, appearance, and uses — that were cut down in the original forest, with a general description of the bears, wolves, eagles, deer, waterfowl.

"A Garden Medley": Perhaps planned as a companion to the forest poem. Catalogue of plants brought from European countries, with bits of history and legend attached, and final Canadianness resulting from this mixture.

The poems are written in quatrains or couplets. There are a couple of attempts at sonnets, but mostly the rhyme scheme is simple — *a b a b* or *a b c b*. The rhyme used is what was once called "masculine" ("shore"/"before"), although once in a while it is "feminine" ("quiver"/"river"). Are those terms familiar anymore? No poem is unrhymed.

II

White roses cold as snow
Bloom where those "angels" lie.
Do they but rest below
Or, in God's wonder, fly?

In 1879, Almeda Roth was still living in the house at the corner of Pearl and Dufferin streets, the house her father had built for his family. The house is there today; the manager of the liquor store lives in it. It's covered with aluminum siding; a closed-in porch has replaced the veranda. The woodshed, the fence, the gates, the privy, the barn — all these are gone. A photograph taken in the eighteen-eighties shows them all in place. The house and fence look a little shabby, in need of paint, but perhaps that is just because of the bleached-out look of the brownish photograph. The lace-curtained windows look like white eyes. No big shade tree is in sight, and, in fact, the tall elms that overshadowed the town until the nineteen-fifties, as well as the maples that shade it now, are skinny young trees with rough fences around them to protect them from the cows. Without the shelter of those trees, there is a great exposure — back yards, clotheslines, woodpiles, patchy sheds and barns and privies — all bare, exposed, provisional-looking. Few houses would have anything like a lawn, just a patch of plantains and anthills and raked dirt. Perhaps petunias growing on top of a stump, in a round box. Only the main street is gravelled; the other streets are dirt roads, muddy or dusty according to season. Yards must be fenced to keep animals out. Cows are tethered in vacant lots or pastured in back yards, but sometimes they get loose. Pigs get loose, too, and dogs roam free or nap in a lordly way on the boardwalks. The town has taken root, it's not going to vanish, yet it still has some of the look of an encampment. And, like an encampment, it's busy all the time — full of people, who, within the town, usually walk wherever they're going; full of animals, which leave horse buns, cow pats, dog turds that ladies have to hitch up their skirts for; full of the noise of building and of drivers shouting at their horses and of the trains that come in several times a day.

I read about that life in the *Vidette*.

The population is younger than it is now, than it will ever be again. People past fifty usually don't come to a raw, new place. There are quite a few people in the cemetery already, but most of them died young, in accidents or childbirth or epidemics. It's youth that's in evidence in town. Children — boys — rove through the streets in gangs. School is compulsory for only four months a year, and there are lots of occasional jobs that even a child of eight or nine can do — pulling flax, holding horses, delivering groceries, sweeping the boardwalk in front of stores. A good deal of time they spend looking for adventures. One day they follow an old woman, a drunk nicknamed Queen Aggie. They get her into a wheelbarrow and trundle her all over town, then dump her into a ditch to sober her up. They also spend a lot of time around the railway station. They jump on shunting cars and dart between them and dare each other to take chances, which once in a while result in their getting maimed or killed. And they keep an eye out for any strangers coming into town. They follow them, offer to carry their bags, and direct them (for a five-cent piece) to a hotel. Strangers who don't look so prosperous are taunted and tormented. Speculation surrounds all of them — it's like a cloud of flies. Are they coming to town to start up a new business, to persuade people to invest in some scheme, to sell cures or gimmicks, to preach on the street corners? All these things are possible any day of the week. Be on your guard, the *Vidette* tells people.

These are times of opportunity and danger. Tramps, confidence men, hucksters, shysters, plain thieves are travelling the roads, and particularly the railroads. Thefts are announced: money invested and never seen again, a pair of trousers taken from the clothesline, wood from the woodpile, eggs from the henhouse. Such incidents increase in the hot weather.

Hot weather brings accidents, too. More horses run wild then, upsetting buggies. Hands caught in the wringer while doing the washing, a man lopped in two at the sawmill, a leaping boy killed in a fall of lumber at the lumberyard. Nobody sleeps well. Babies wither with summer complaint, and fat people can't catch their breath. Bodies must be buried in a hurry. One day a man goes through the streets ringing a cowbell and calling, "Repent! Repent!" It's not a stranger this time, it's a young man who works at the butcher shop. Take him home, wrap him in cold wet cloths, give him some nerve medicine, keep him in bed, pray for his wits. If he doesn't recover, he must go to the asylum.

Almeda Roth's house faces on Dufferin Street, which is a street of considerable respectability. On this street, merchants, a mill owner, an operator of salt wells have their houses. But Pearl Street, which her back windows overlook and her back gate opens onto, is another story. Workmen's houses are adjacent to hers. Small but decent row houses — that is all right. Things deteriorate toward the end of the block, and the next, last one becomes dismal. Nobody but the poorest people, the unrespectable and undeserving poor, would live there at the edge of a boghole (drained since then), called the Pearl Street Swamp. Bushy and luxuriant weeds grow there, makeshift shacks have been put up, there are piles of refuse and debris and crowds of runty children, slops are flung from doorways. The town tries to compel these people to build privies, but they would just as soon go in the bushes. If a gang of boys goes down there in search of adventure, it's likely they'll get more than they bargained for. It is said that even the town constable won't go down Pearl Street on a Saturday night. Almeda Roth has never walked past the row housing. In one of those houses lives the young girl Annie, who helps her with her housecleaning. That young girl herself, being a decent girl, has never walked down to the last block or the swamp. No decent woman ever would.

But that same swamp, lying to the east of Almeda Roth's house, presents a fine sight at dawn. Almeda sleeps at the back of the house. She keeps to the same bedroom she once shared with her sister Catherine — she would not think of moving to the large front bedroom, where her mother used to lie in bed all day, and which was later the solitary domain of her father. From her window she can see the sun rising, the swamp mist filling with light, the bulky, nearest trees floating against that mist and the trees behind turning transparent. Swamp oaks, soft maples, tamarack, bitternut.

III

Here where the river meets the
inland sea,
Spreading her blue skirts from the
solemn wood,
I think of birds and beasts and
vanished men,
Whose pointed dwellings on these
pale sands stood.

One of the strangers who arrived at the railway station a few years ago was Jarvis Poulter, who now occupies the next house to Almeda Roth's — separated from hers by a vacant lot, which he has bought, on Dufferin Street. The house is plainer than the Roth house and has no fruit trees or flowers planted around it. It is understood that this is a natural result of Jarvis Poulter's being a widower and living alone. A man may keep his house decent, but he will never — if he is a proper man — do much to decorate it. Marriage forces him to live with more ornament as well as sentiment, and it protects him, also, from the extremities of his own nature — from a frigid parsimony or a luxuriant sloth, from squalor, and from excessive sleeping or reading, drinking, smoking, or freethinking.

In the interests of economy, it is believed, a certain estimable gentleman of our town persists in fetching water from the public tap and supplementing his fuel supply by picking up the loose coal along the railway track. Does he think to repay the town or the railway company with a supply of free salt?

This is the *Vidette*, full of shy jokes, innuendo, plain accusation that no newspaper would get away with today. It's Jarvis Poulter they're talking about — though in other passages he is spoken of with great respect, as a civil magistrate, an employer, a churchman. He is close, that's all. An eccentric, to a degree. All of which may be a result of his single condition, his widower's life. Even carrying his water from the town tap and filling his coal pail along the railway track. This is a decent citizen, prosperous: a tall — slightly paunchy? — man in a dark suit with polished boots. A beard? Black hair streaked with gray. A severe and self-possessed air, and a large pale wart among the bushy hairs of one eyebrow? People talk about a young, pretty, beloved wife, dead in childbirth or some horrible accident, like a house fire or a railway disaster. There is no ground for this, but it adds interest. All he told them is that his wife is dead.

He came to this part of the country looking for oil. The first oil well in the world was sunk in Lambton County, south of here, in the eighteen-fifties. Drilling for oil, Jarvis Poulter discovered salt. He set to work to make the most of that. When he walks home from church with Almeda Roth, he tells her about his salt wells. They are twelve hundred feet deep. Heated water is pumped down into them, and that dissolves the salt. Then the brine is pumped to the surface. It is poured into great evaporator pans over slow, steady fires, so that the water is steamed off and the pure, excellent salt remains. A commodity for which the demand will never fail.

"The salt of the earth," Almeda says.

"Yes," he says, frowning. He may think this disrespectful. She did not intend it so. He speaks of competitors in other towns who are following his lead and trying to hog the market. Fortunately, their wells are not drilled so deep, or their evaporating is not done so efficiently. There is salt everywhere under this land, but it is not so easy to come by as some people think.

Does this not mean, Almeda says, that there was once a great sea?

Very likely, Jarvis Poulter says. Very likely. He goes on to tell her about other enterprises of his — a brickyard, a limekiln. And he explains to her how this operates, and where the good clay is found. He also owns two farms, whose woodlots supply the fuel for his operations.

Among the couples strolling home from church on a recent, sunny Sabbath morning we noted a certain salty gentleman and literary lady, not perhaps in their first youth but by no means blighted by the frosts of age. May we surmise?

This kind of thing pops up in the *Vidette* all the time.

May they surmise, and is this courting? Almeda Roth has a bit of money, which her father left her, and she has her house. She is not too old to have a couple of children. She is a good enough housekeeper, with the tendency toward fancy iced cakes and decorated tarts that is seen fairly often in old maids. (Honorable mention at the Fall Fair.) There is nothing wrong with her looks, and naturally she is in better shape than most married women of her age, not having been loaded down with work and children. But why was she passed over in her earlier, more marriageable years, in a place that needs women to be partnered and fruitful? She was a rather gloomy girl — that may have been the trouble. The deaths of her brother and sister, and then of her mother, who lost her reason, in fact, a year before she died, and lay in her bed talking nonsense — those weighed on her, so she was not lively company. And all that reading and poetry — it seemed more of a drawback, a barrier, an obsession, in the young girl than in the middle-aged woman, who needed something, after all, to fill her time. Anyway, it's five years since her book was published, so perhaps she has got over that. Perhaps it was the proud, bookish father encouraging her?

Everyone takes it for granted that Almeda Roth is thinking of Jarvis Poulter as a husband and would say yes if he asked her. And she is thinking of him. She doesn't want to get her hopes up too much, she doesn't want to make a fool of herself. She would like a signal. If he attended church on Sunday evenings, there would be a chance, during some months of the year, to walk home after dark. He would carry a lantern. (There is as yet no street lighting in town.) He would swing the lantern to light the way in front of the lady's feet and observe their narrow and delicate shape. He might catch her arm as they step off the boardwalk. But he does not go to church at night.

Nor does he call for her, and walk with her *to* church on Sunday mornings. That would be a declaration. He walks her home, past his gate as far as hers; he lifts his hat then and leaves her. She does not invite him to come in — a woman living alone could never do such a thing. As soon as a man and woman of almost any age are alone together within four walls, it is assumed that anything may happen. Spontaneous combustion, instant fornication, an attack of passion. Brute instinct, triumph of the senses. What possibilities men and women must see in each other to infer such dangers. Or, believing in the dangers, how often they must think about the possibilities.

When they walk side by side, she can smell his shaving soap, the barber's oil, his pipe tobacco, the wool and linen and leather smell of his manly clothes. The correct, orderly, heavy clothes are like those she used to brush and starch and iron for her father. She misses that job — her father's appreciation, his dark, kind authority. Jarvis Poulter's garments, his smell, his movements all cause the skin on the side of her body next to him to tingle hopefully, and a meek shiver raises the hairs on her arms. Is this to be taken as a sign of love? She thinks of him coming into her — *their* — bedroom in his long underwear and his hat. She knows this outfit is ridiculous, but in her mind he does not look so; he has the solemn effrontery of a figure in a dream. He comes into the room and lies down on the bed beside her, preparing to take her in his arms. Surely he removes his hat? She doesn't know, for at this point a fit of welcome and submission overtakes her, a buried gasp. He would be her husband.

One thing she has noticed about married women, and that is how many of them have to go about creating their husbands. They have to start ascribing preferences, opinions, dictatorial ways. Oh, yes, they say, my husband is very particular. He won't touch turnips. He won't eat fried meat. (Or he will only eat fried meat.) He likes me to wear blue (brown) all the time. He can't stand organ music. He hates to see a woman go out bareheaded. He would kill me if I took one puff of tobacco. This way, bewildered, sidelong-looking men are made over, made into husbands, heads of households. Almeda Roth cannot imagine herself doing that. She wants a man who doesn't have to be made, who is firm already and determined and mysterious to her. She does not look for companionship. Men — except for her father — seem to her deprived in some way, incurious. No doubt that is necessary, so that they will do what they have to do. Would she herself, knowing that there was salt in the earth, discover how to get it out and sell it? Not likely. She would be thinking about the ancient sea. That kind of speculation is what Jarvis Poulter has, quite properly, no time for.

Instead of calling for her and walking her to church, Jarvis Poulter might make another, more venturesome declaration. He could hire a horse and take her for a drive out to the country. If he did this, she would be both glad and sorry. Glad to be beside him, driven by him, receiving this attention from him in front of the world. And sorry to have the countryside removed for her — filmed over, in a way, by his talk and preoccupations. The countryside that she has written about in her poems actually takes diligence and determination to see. Some things must be disregarded. Manure piles, of course, and boggy fields full of high, charred stumps, and great heaps of brush waiting for a good day for burning. The meandering creeks have been straightened, turned into ditches with high, muddy banks. Some of the crop fields and pasture fields are fenced with big, clumsy uprooted stumps; others are held in a crude stitchery of rail fences. The trees have all been cleared back to the woodlots. And the woodlots are all second growth. No trees along the roads or lanes or around the farmhouses, except a few that are newly planted, young and weedy-looking. Clusters of log barns — the grand barns that are to dominate the countryside for the next hundred years are just beginning to be built — and mean-looking log houses, and every four or five miles a ragged little settlement with a church and school and store and a blacksmith shop. A raw countryside just wrenched from the forest, but swarming with people. Every hundred acres is a farm, every farm has a family, most families have ten or twelve children. (This is the country that will send out wave after wave of settlers — it's already starting to send them — to northern Ontario and the West.) It's true that you can gather wildflowers in spring in the woodlots, but you'd have to walk through herds of horned cows to get to them.

IV

The Gypsies have departed.
Their camping-ground is bare.
Oh, boldly would I bargain now
At the Gypsy Fair.

Almeda suffers a good deal from sleeplessness, and the doctor has given her bromides and nerve medicine. She takes the bromides, but the drops gave her dreams that were too vivid and disturbing, so she has put the bottle by for an emergency. She told the doctor her eyeballs felt dry, like hot glass, and her joints ached. Don't read so much, he said, don't study; get yourself good and tired out with housework, take exercise. He believes that her troubles would clear up if she got married. He believes this in spite of the fact that most of his nerve medicine is prescribed for married women.

So Almeda cleans house and helps clean the church, she lends a hand to friends who are wallpapering or getting ready for a wedding, she bakes one of her famous cakes for the Sunday-school picnic. On a hot Saturday in August, she decides to make some grape jelly. Little jars of grape jelly will make fine Christmas presents, or offerings to the sick. But she started late in the day and the jelly is not made by nightfall. In fact, the hot pulp has just been dumped into the cheesecloth bag to strain out the juice. Almeda drinks some tea and eats a slice of cake with butter (a childish indulgence of hers), and that's all she wants for supper. She washes her hair at the sink and sponges off her body to be clean for Sunday. She doesn't light a lamp. She lies down on the bed with the window wide open and a sheet just up to her waist, and she does feel wonderfully tired. She can even feel a little breeze.

When she wakes up, the night seems fiery hot and full of threats. She lies sweating on her bed, and she has the impression that the noises she hears are knives and saws and axes — all angry implements chopping and jabbing and boring within her head. But it isn't true. As she comes further awake, she recognizes the sounds that she has heard sometimes before — the fracas of a summer Saturday night on Pearl Street. Usually the noise centers on a fight. People are drunk, there is a lot of protest and encouragement concerning the fight, somebody will scream, "Murder!" Once, there was a murder. But it didn't happen in a fight. An old man was stabbed to death in his shack, perhaps for a few dollars he kept in the mattress.

She gets out of bed and goes to the window. The night sky is clear, with no moon and with bright stars. Pegasus hangs straight ahead, over the swamp. Her father taught her that constellation — automatically, she counts its stars. Now she can make out distinct voices, individual contributions to the row. Some people, like herself, have evidently been wakened from sleep. "Shut up!" they are yelling. "Shut up that caterwauling or I'm going to come down and tan the arse off yez!"

But nobody shuts up. It's as if there were a ball of fire rolling up Pearl Street, shooting off sparks — only the fire is noise; it's yells and laughter and shrieks and curses, and the sparks are voices that shoot off alone. Two voices gradually distinguish themselves — a rising and falling howling cry and a steady throbbing, low-pitched stream of abuse that contains all those words which Almeda associates with danger and depravity and foul smells and disgusting sights. Someone — the person crying out, "Kill me! Kill me now!" — is being beaten. A woman is being beaten. She keeps crying, "Kill me! Kill me!" and sometimes her mouth seems choked with blood. Yet there is something taunting and triumphant about her cry. There is something theatrical about it. And the people around are calling out, "Stop it! Stop that!" or "Kill her! Kill her!" in a frenzy, as if at the theatre or a sporting match or a prizefight. Yes, thinks Almeda, she has noticed that before — it is always partly a charade with these people; there is a clumsy sort of parody, an exaggeration, a missed connection. As if anything they did — even a murder — might be something they didn't quite believe but were powerless to stop.

Now there is the sound of something thrown — a chair, a plank? — and of a woodpile or part of a fence giving way. A lot of newly surprised cries, the sound of running, people getting out of the way, and the commotion has come much closer. Almeda can see a figure in a light dress, bent over and running. That will be the woman. She has got hold of something like a stick of wood or a shingle, and she turns and flings it at the darker figure running after her.

"Ah, go get her!" the voices cry. "Go baste her one!"

Many fall back now; just the two figures come on and grapple, and break loose again, and finally fall down against Almeda's fence. The sound they make becomes very confused — gagging, vomiting, grunting, pounding. Then a long, vibrating, choking sound of pain and self-abasement, self-abandonment, which could come from either or both of them.

Almeda has backed away from the window and sat down on the bed. Is that the sound of murder she has heard? What is to be done, what is she to do? She must light a lantern, she must go downstairs and light a lantern — she must go out into the yard, she must go downstairs. Into the yard. The lantern. She falls over on her bed and pulls the pillow to her face. In a minute. The stairs, the lantern. She sees herself already down there, in the back hall, drawing the bolt of the back door. She falls asleep.

She wakes, startled, in the early light. She thinks there is a big crow sitting on her windowsill, talking in a disapproving but unsurprised way about the events of the night before. "Wake up and move the wheelbarrow!" it says to her, scolding, and she understands that it means something else by "wheelbarrow" — something foul and sorrowful. Then she is awake and sees that there is no such bird. She gets up at once and looks out the window.

Down against her fence there is a pale lump pressed — a body.

Wheelbarrow.

She puts a wrapper over her nightdress and goes downstairs. The front rooms are still shadowy, the blinds down in the kitchen. Something goes *plop, plup*, in a leisurely, censorious way, reminding her of the conversation of the crow. It's just the grape juice, straining overnight. She pulls the bolt and goes out the back door. Spiders have draped their webs over the doorway in the night, and the hollyhocks are drooping, heavy with dew. By the fence, she parts the sticky hollyhocks and looks down and she can see.

A woman's body heaped up there, turned on her side with her face squashed down into the earth. Almeda can't see her face. But there is a bare breast let loose, brown nipple pulled long like a cow's teat, and a bare haunch and leg, the haunch showing a bruise as big as a sunflower. The unbruised skin is grayish, like a plucked, raw drumstick. Some kind of nightgown or all-purpose dress she has on.

Smelling of vomit. Urine, drink, vomit.

Barefoot, in her nightgown and flimsy wrapper, Almeda runs away. She runs around the side of her house between the apple trees and the veranda; she opens the front gate and flees down Dufferin Street to Jarvis Poulter's house, which is the nearest to hers. She slaps the flat of her hand many times against the door.

"There is the body of a woman," she says when Jarvis Poulter appears at last. He is in his dark trousers, held up with braces, and his shirt is half unbuttoned, his face unshaven, his hair standing up on his head. "Mr. Poulter, excuse me. A body of a woman. At my back gate."

He looks at her fiercely. "Is she dead?"

His breath is dank, his face creased, his eyes bloodshot.

"Yes. I think murdered," says Almeda. She can see a little of his cheerless front hall. His hat on a chair. "In the night I woke up. I heard a racket down on Pearl Street," she says, struggling to keep her voice low and sensible. "I could hear this — pair. I could hear a man and a woman fighting."

He picks up his hat and puts it on his head. He closes and locks the front door, and puts the key in his pocket. They walk along the boardwalk and she sees that she is in her bare feet. She holds back what she feels a need to say next — that she is responsible, she could have run out with a lantern, she could have screamed (but who needed more screams?), she could have beat the man off. She could have run for help then, not now.

They turn down Pearl Street, instead of entering the Roth yard. Of course the body is still there. Hunched up, half bare, the same as before.

Jarvis Poulter doesn't hurry or halt. He walks straight over to the body and looks down at it, nudges the leg with the toe of his boot, just as you'd nudge a dog or a sow.

"You," he says, not too loudly but firmly, and nudges again.

Almeda tastes bile at the back of her throat.

"Alive," says Jarvis Poulter, and the woman confirms this. She stirs, she grunts weakly.

Almeda says, "I will get the doctor." If she had touched the woman, if she had forced herself to touch her, she would not have made such a mistake.

"Wait," says Jarvis Poulter. "Wait. Let's see if she can get up."

"Get up, now," he says to the woman. "Come on. Up, now. Up."

Now a startling thing happens. The body heaves itself onto all fours, the head is lifted — the hair all matted with blood and vomit

— and the woman begins to bang this head, hard and rhythmically, against Almeda Roth's picket fence. As she bangs her head, she finds her voice and lets out an openmouthed yowl, full of strength and what sounds like an anguished pleasure.

"Far from dead," says Jarvis Poulter. "And I wouldn't bother the doctor.

"There's blood," says Almeda as the woman turns her smeared face.

"From her nose," he says. "Not fresh." He bends down and catches the horrid hair close to the scalp to stop the head-banging.

"You stop that, now," he says. "Stop it. Gwan home, now. Gwan home, where you belong." The sound coming out of the woman's mouth has stopped. He shakes her head slightly, warning her, before he lets go of her hair. "Gwan home!"

Released, the woman lunges forward, pulls herself to her feet. She can walk. She weaves and stumbles down the street, making intermittent, cautious noises of protest. Jarvis Poulter watches her for a moment to make sure that she's on her way. Then he finds a large burdock leaf, on which he wipes his hand. He says, "There goes your dead body!"

The back gate being locked, they walk around to the front. The front gate stands open. Almeda still feels sick. Her abdomen is bloated; she is hot and dizzy.

"The front door is locked," she says faintly. "I came out by the kitchen." If only he would leave her, she could go straight to the privy. But he follows. He follows her as far as the back door and into the back hall. He speaks to her in a tone of harsh joviality that she has never before heard from him. "No need for alarm," he says. "It's only the consequences of drink. A lady oughtn't to be living alone so close to a bad neighborhood." He takes hold of her arm just above the elbow. She can't open her mouth to speak to him, to say thank you. If she opened her mouth, she would retch.

What Jarvis Poulter feels for Almeda Roth at this moment is just what he has not felt during all those circumspect walks and all his own solitary calculations of her probable worth, undoubted respectability, adequate comeliness. He has not been able to imagine her as a wife. Now that is possible. He is sufficiently stirred by her loosened hair — prematurely gray but thick and soft — her flushed face, her light clothing, which nobody but a husband should see. And by her indiscretion, her agitation, her foolishness, her need?

"I will call on you later," he says to her. "I will walk with you to church."

At the corner of Pearl and Dufferin streets last Sunday morning there was discovered, by a lady resident there, the body of a certain woman of Pearl Street, thought to be dead but only, as it turned out, dead drunk. She was roused from her heavenly — or otherwise — stupor by the firm persuasion of Mr. Poulter, a neighbour and a Civil Magistrate, who had been summoned by the lady resident. Incidents of this sort, unseemly, troublesome, and disgraceful to our town, have of late become all too common.

V

I sit at the bottom of sleep,
As on the floor of the sea.
And fanciful Citizens of the Deep
Are graciously greeting me.

As soon as Jarvis Poulter has gone and she has heard her front gate close, Almeda rushes to the privy. Her relief is not complete, however, and she realizes that the pain and fullness in her lower body come from an accumulation of menstrual blood that has not yet started to flow. She closes and locks the back door. Then, remembering Jarvis Poulter's words about church, she writes on a piece of paper, "I am not well, and wish to rest today." She sticks this firmly into the outside frame of the little window in the front door. She locks that door, too. She is trembling, as if from a great shock or danger. But she builds a fire, so that she can make tea. She boils water, measures the tea leaves, makes a large pot of tea, whose steam and smell sicken her further. She pours out a cup while the tea is still quite weak and adds to it several dark drops of nerve medicine. She sits to drink it without raising the kitchen blind. There, in the middle of the floor, is the cheesecloth bag hanging on its broom handle between the two chairbacks. The grape pulp and juice has stained the swollen cloth a dark purple. *Plop, plup*, into the basin beneath. She can't sit and look at such a thing. She takes her cup, the teapot, and the bottle of medicine into the dining room.

She is still sitting there when the horses start to go by on the way to church, stirring up clouds of dust. The roads will be getting hot as ashes. She is there when the gate is opened and a man's confident steps sound on her veranda. Her hearing is so sharp she seems to hear the paper taken out of the frame and unfolded — she can almost hear him reading it, hear the words in his mind. Then the footsteps go the other way, down the steps. The gate closes. An image comes to her of tombstones — it makes her laugh. Tombstones are marching down the street on their little booted feet, their long bodies inclined forward, their expressions preoccupied and severe. The church bells are ringing.

Then the clock in the hall strikes twelve and an hour has passed.

The house is getting hot. She drinks more tea and adds more medicine. She knows that the medicine is affecting her. It is responsible for her extraordinary languor, her perfect immobility, her unresisting surrender to her surroundings. That is all right. It seems necessary.

Her surroundings — some of her surroundings — in the dining room are these: walls covered with dark-green garlanded wallpaper, lace curtains and mulberry velvet curtains on the windows, a table with a crocheted cloth and a bowl of wax fruit, a pinkish-gray carpet with nosegays of blue and pink roses, a sideboard spread with embroidered runners and holding various patterned plates and jugs and the silver tea things. A lot of things to watch. For every one of these patterns, decorations seems charged with life, ready to move and flow and alter. Or possibly to explode. Almeda Roth's occupation throughout the day is to keep an eye on them. Not to prevent their alteration so much as to catch them at it — to understand it, to be a part of it. So much is going on in this room that there is no need to leave it. There is not even the thought of leaving it.

Of course, Almeda in her observations cannot escape words. She may think she can, but she can't. Soon this glowing and swelling begins to suggest words — not specific words but a flow of words somewhere, just about ready to make themselves known to her. Poems, even. Yes, again, poems. Or one poem. Isn't that the idea — one very great poem that will contain everything and, oh, that will make all the other poems, the poems she has written, inconsequential, mere trial and error, mere rags? Stars and flowers and birds and trees and angels in the snow and dead children at twilight — that is not the half of it. You have to get in the obscene racket on Pearl Street and the polished toe of Jarvis Poulter's boot and the plucked-chicken haunch with its blue-black flower. Almeda is a long way now from human sympathies or fears or cozy household considerations. She doesn't think about what could be done for that woman or about keeping Jarvis Poulter's dinner warm and hanging his long underwear on the line. The basin of grape juice has overflowed and is running over her kitchen floor, staining the boards of the floor, and the stain will never come out.

She has to think of so many things at once — Champlain and the naked Indians and the salt deep in the earth, but as well as the salt the money, the money-making intent brewing forever in heads like Jarvis Poulter's. Also the brutal storms of winter and the clumsy and benighted deeds on Pearl Street. The changes of climate are often violent, and if you think about it there is no peace even in the stars. All this can be borne only if it is channelled into a poem, and the word "channelled" is appropriate, because the name of the poem will be — it *is* — "The Meneseteung." The name of the poem is the name of the river. No, in fact it is the river, the Meneseteung, that is the poem — with its deep holes and rapids and blissful pools under the summer trees and its grinding blocks of ice thrown up at the end of winter and its desolating spring floods. Almeda looks deep, deep into the river of her mind and into the tablecloth, and she sees the crocheted roses floating. They look bunchy and foolish, her mother's crocheted roses — they don't look much like real flowers. But their effort, their floating independence, their pleasure in their silly selves do seem to her so admirable. A hopeful sign. *Meneseteung.*

She doesn't leave the room until dusk, when she goes out to the privy again and discovers that she is bleeding, her flow has started. She will have to get a towel, strap it on, bandage herself up. Never before, in health, has she passed a whole day in her nightdress. She doesn't feel any particular anxiety about this. On her way through the kitchen, she walks through the pool of grape juice. She knows that she will have to mop it up, but not yet, and she walks upstairs leaving purple footprints and smelling her escaping blood and the sweat of her body that has sat all day in the closed hot room.

No need for alarm.

For she hasn't thought that crocheted roses could float away or that tombstones could hurry down the street. She doesn't mistake that for reality, and neither does she mistake anything else for reality, and that is how she knows that she is sane.

VI

I dream of you by night,
I visit you by day.
Father, Mother,
Sister, Brother,
Have you no word to say?

April 22, 1903. At her residence, on Tuesday last, between three and four o'clock in the afternoon, there passed away a lady of talent and refinement whose pen, in days gone by, enriched our local literature with a volume of sensitive, eloquent verse. It is a sad misfortune that in later years the mind of this fine person had become somewhat clouded and her behaviour, in consequence, somewhat rash and unusual. Her attention to decorum and to the care and adornment of her person had suffered, to the degree that she had become, in the eyes of those unmindful of her former pride and daintiness, a familiar eccentric, or even, sadly, a figure of fun. But now all such lapses pass from memory and what is recalled is her excellent published verse, her labours in former days in the Sunday school, her dutiful care of her parents, her noble womanly nature, charitable concerns, and unfailing religious faith. Her last illness was of mercifully short duration. She caught cold, after having become thoroughly wet from a ramble in the Pearl Street bog. (It has been said that some urchins chased her into the water, and such is the boldness and cruelty of some of our youth, and their observed persecution of this lady, that the tale cannot be entirely discounted.) The cold developed into pneumonia, and she died, attended at last by a former neighbour, Mrs. Bert (Annie) Friels, who witnessed her calm and faithful end.

January, 1904. One of the founders of our community, an early maker and shaker of this town, was abruptly removed from our midst on Monday morning last, whilst attending to his correspondence in the office of his company. Mr. Jarvis Poulter possessed a keen and lively commercial spirit, which was instrumental in the creation of not one but several local enterprises, bringing the benefits of industry, productivity, and employment to our town.

So the *Vidette* runs on, copious and assured. Hardly a death goes undescribed, or a life unevaluated.

I looked for Almeda Roth in the graveyard. I found the family stone. There was just one name on it — Roth. Then I noticed two fat stones in the ground, a distance of a few feet — six feet? — from the upright stone. One of these said “Papa,” the other “Mama.” Further out from these I found two other flat stones, with the names William and Catherine on them. I had to clear away some overgrowing grass and dirt to see the full name of Catherine. No birth or death dates for anybody, nothing about being dearly beloved. It was a private sort of memorializing, not for the world. There were no roses, either — no sign of a rosebush. But perhaps it was taken out. The grounds keeper doesn’t like such things; they are a nuisance to the lawnmower, and if there is nobody left to object he will pull them out.

I thought that Almeda must have been buried somewhere else. When this plot was bought — at the time of the two children's deaths — she would still have been expected to marry, and to lie finally beside her husband. They might not have left room for her here. Then I saw that the stones in the ground fanned out from the upright stone. First the two for the parents, then the two for the children, but these were placed in such a way that there was room for a third, to complete the fan. I paced out from "Catherine" the same number of steps that it took to get from "Catherine" to "William," and at this spot I began pulling grass and scrabbling in the dirt with my bare hands. Soon I felt the stone and knew that I was right. I worked away and got the whole stone clear and I read the name "Meda." There it was with the others, staring at the sky.

I made sure I had got to the edge of the stone. That was all the name there was — Meda. So it was true that she was called by that name in the family. Not just in the poem. Or perhaps she chose her name from the poem, to be written on her stone.

I thought that there wasn't anybody alive in the world but me who would know this, who would make the connection. And I would be the last person to do so. But perhaps this isn't so. People are curious. A few people are. They will be driven to find things out, even trivial things. They will put things together. You see them going around with notebooks, scraping the dirt off gravestones, reading microfilm, just in the hope of seeing this trickle in time, making a connection, rescuing one thing from the rubbish.

And they may get it wrong, after all. I may have got it wrong. I don't know if she ever took laudanum. Many ladies did. I don't know if she ever made grape jelly.

Commentary by *Alice Munro*

≈

Alice Munro's stories possess a bold and commanding energy. The following commentary is taken from "What is Real?", published in the anthology Making It New: Contemporary Canadian Stories *(Toronto: Methuen, 1982). Using an analogy between a story and a house, Munro stresses that if works of literature are to have artistic integrity, writers must pursue their own visions of reality to the deepest — and possibly the darkest — places in their imaginations.*

I did promise to talk about using reality. "Why, if Jubilee isn't Wingham, has it got a Shuter Street in it?" people want to know. Why have I described somebody's real ceramic elephant sitting on the mantelpiece? I could say I get momentum from doing things like this. The fictional room, town, world, needs a bit of starter dough from the real world. It's a device to help the writer — at least it helps me — but it arouses a certain baulked fury in the people who really do live on Shuter Street and the lady who owns the ceramic elephant. "Why do you put in something true and then go and tell lies?" they say, and anybody who has been on the receiving end of this kind of thing knows how they feel.

"I do it for the sake of my art and to make this structure which encloses the soul of my story, that I've been telling you about", says the writer. "That is more important than anything."

Not to everybody it isn't.

So I can see there might be a case, once you've written the story and got the momentum, for going back and changing the elephant to a camel (though there's always a chance the lady might complain that you made a nasty camel out of a beautiful elephant), and changing Shuter Street to Blank Street. But what about the big chunks of reality, without which your story can't exist? In the story "Royal Beatings", I use a big chunk of reality: the story of the butcher, and of the young men who may have been egged on to "get" him. This is a story out of an old newspaper; it really did happen in a town I know. There is no legal difficulty about using it because it has been printed in a newspaper, and besides, the people who figure in it are all long dead. But there is a difficulty about offending people in that town who would feel that use of this story is a deliberate exposure, taunt and insult. Other people who have no connection with the real happening would say "Why write about anything so hideous?" And lest you think that such an objection could only be raised by simple folk who read nothing but Harlequin Romances, let me tell you that one of the questions most frequently asked at universities is, "Why do you write about things that are so depressing?" People can accept almost any amount of ugliness if it is contained in a familiar formula, as it is on television, but when they come closer to their own place, their own lives, they are much offended by lack of editing.

There are ways I can defend myself against such objections. I can say, "I do it in the interests of historical reality. That is what the old days were really like." Or, "I do it to show the dark side of human nature, the beast let loose, the evil we can run up against in communities and families." In certain countries I could say, "I do it to show how bad things were under the old system when there were prosperous butchers and young fellows hanging around livery stables and nobody thought about building a new society." But the fact is, the minute I say *to show* I am telling a lie. I don't do it to show anything. I put this story at the heart of my story because I need it there and it belongs there. It is the black room at the centre of the house with all other rooms leading to and away from it. That is all. A strange defence. Who told me to write this story? Who feels any need of it before it is written? I do. I do, so that I might grab off this piece of horrid reality and install it where I see fit, even if Hat Nettleton and his friends were still around to make me sorry.

SELECTED WORKS BY ALICE MUNRO

Dance of the Happy Shades: Stories. Foreword by Hugh Garner. Toronto: The Ryerson Press, 1968. [Paperback ed.] Foreword by Hugh Garner. Toronto: McGraw-Hill Ryerson, [1971]. Rpt. as *Dance of the Happy Shades*. 2nd Canadian ed. Toronto: McGraw-Hill Ryerson, 1988.

Lives of Girls and Women: A Novel. Toronto: McGraw-Hill Ryerson, 1971. Rpt. as *Lives of Girls and Women*. Markham, ON: Penguin Books, 1990.

Something I've Been Meaning To Tell You...: Thirteen Stories. Toronto: McGraw-Hill Ryerson, 1974. Rpt. as *Something I've Been Meaning To Tell You: Thirteen Stories*. Markham, ON: Penguin Books, 1990.

Who Do You Think You Are?: Stories. Toronto: Macmillan, 1978. Rpt. as *The Beggar Maid: Stories of Flo and Rose*. New York: Alfred A. Knopf, 1979. Rpt. as *Who Do You Think You Are?* Toronto: Penguin Books, 1991.

The Moons of Jupiter: Stories. Toronto: Macmillan, 1982. Rpt. as *The Moons of Jupiter*. Harmondsworth, Eng.: Penguin Books, 1983. Introd. Alice Munro. Markham, ON: Penguin Books, 1986.

The Progress of Love: Stories. A Douglas Gibson Book. Toronto: McClelland and Stewart, 1986. Rpt. as *The Progress of Love*. Markham, ON: Penguin Books, 1987.

Friend of My Youth: Stories. A Douglas Gibson Book. Toronto: McClelland & Stewart, 1990. [Revised ed.] Toronto: Penguin Books, 1991.

Leon Rooke

≈

If you stand in front of an abstract painting and demand to know what it *means*, you're asking the wrong question and asking it precludes an answer. Some readers approach Rooke's work in this spirit. His stories aren't constructed in traditional ways and although they offer traditional rewards they need to be approached creatively. Rooke's stories are essentially *performances*. He's an improviser, a jazz musician in prose whose stories are improvisations on a word, a phrase, or a simple theme. Try reading the first four or five pages of "The Deacon's Tale" — reprinted here from his collection *Cry Evil* (1980) — with this idea in mind. Listen to the process in the story "Sixteen-Year-Old Susan March Confesses to the Innocent Murder of All the Devious Strangers Who Would Drag Her Down" from *Death Suite* (1981). Read the story "Hitting the Charts" from his collection *The Birth Control King of the Upper Volta* (1982) and listen to the riffs on "*Oh frail is thy hand in mine, oh frail is your touch, my darling Caithleene*".

To appreciate Rooke fully a reader has to hear his stories much as they would be performed. Rooke is a southern preacher, the Rev. Jesse Jackson or Martin Luther King of stories. If you think of the way those preachers would edge into a sermon finding a phrase on which to play, a phrase that elicits a response, a phrase that can be built higher and higher, then this too offers a way of looking at Rooke's fiction. We might well have included here one of his 'preaching' stories, most probably "Mama Tuddi Done Over" from *Death Suite*.

Rooke has a background in acting and in theatre and has written several plays. His public readings are sizzling, flamboyant performances during which he has been known to climb surrounding furniture as he works into the particular voice that's talking. If his glasses slip or if he loses his place in the text, he simply improvises. On one occasion when I was reading with him he abandoned the text completely and constructed a shouted conversation of simple, repeated sentences between a mother and son that was rather like the call and response of a sermon. I've heard the story "Some People Will Tell You the Situation at Henny Penny Nursery Is Getting Intolerable" — from *Sing Me*

No Love Songs I'll Say You No Prayers (1984) — performed in a variety of lengths and with the narrator either sober or increasingly drunk. It depends on Rooke's mood and the reaction of the audience.

He rarely leaves his stories alone. He's always revising and rewriting. Between Canadian publication and subsequent American publication, stories and novels get longer. There's a sense in which a Rooke story is never *finished*. We could consider a printed Rooke story in much the way we might consider a transcribed solo by jazz musician Charlie Parker; perhaps both are best served by a recording of a live performance.

There are dangers, of course, with this approach to fiction. Improvisation is not always inspired; it is not always coherent either. Some might say that Rooke is a captive of language and rhetoric, that too many of the stories are, in Horatio's words to Hamlet, "wild and whirling words". It does sometimes seem that Rooke has sacrificed meaning to energy. How well will his work stand up over time *as writing*? Might we be forced to say ruefully years from now, "Well I guess you had to be there"? Or can we train ourselves well enough to hear the music that is on Rooke's pages?

As he goes on, Rooke seems to be drawn more and more to structures that tend toward the parable or exemplum. Consider the title story of his collection *A Bolt of White Cloth* (1984) and his novel *A Good Baby* (1989). One blurb described his stories as "uplifting songs for humanity"; Time might well level the criticism that some of these "uplifting" stories are sentimental if not downright Pollyannaish.

But Rooke's best stories, including the virtuoso title story of *The Birth Control King of the Upper Volta* which we've included here, drive home with a fierce energy. He erupted into Canadian story writing with a much-needed verbal exuberance and stretched the possibilities of the form.

≈

Keith Garebian has written a useful monograph, *Leon Rooke and His Works* (Toronto: ECW Press, 1989). *Canadian Fiction Magazine* 38 (1981) is devoted entirely to Rooke's work and includes an important interview by Geoff Hancock. Russell Brown's article "Rooke's Move" in *Essays on Canadian Writing*

30 (1984-85) can be recommended. Another interview with Rooke, by Peter O'Brien, appears in *So To Speak: Interviews with Contemporary Canadian Writers* (Montreal: Véhicule Press, 1987). Simone Vauthier has contributed the essay "'Entering Other Skins': — or, Leon Rooke's 'The End of the Revolution'" to *Writers in Aspic* (Montreal: Véhicule Press, 1988). An entertaining defence by Rooke of his own work, entitled "A Coherent Fictional *Oeuvre*", is contained in *New Directions from Old* (Guelph, ON: Red Kite Press, 1991).

≈ THE DEACON'S TALE ≈

Here's a story.

Although it has been going on for years, the crucial facts are fresh in my mind so I will have no trouble confining myself strictly to what's essential. Nothing made up, have no worry about that. I live in this world too: when my wife, lovely woman, tells me that people are tired of hearing *stories*, they want facts, gossip, trivia, how-to about real life, I'm first to take the hint. So this is plain fact: yesterday my foot was hurting. The pain was unbearable. I was in mortal anguish and convinced I'd been maimed for life.

My wife, naturally enough, was concerned. Now and then she would look in on me: "How's the foot?" she'd ask. I'd grit my teeth and do what I could to keep from screaming. I hate sympathy, faked or otherwise. Had she come in with a sharp axe to ask whether she could chop it off, I would have felt better. But she was all politeness, you see: "Is it better? No? Shall I bring you a magazine? Fluff your pillows? Comb your moustache?" Her comments are precious and I want to leave out none of them. According to her, the people in my stories are never polite and nice the way people really are. In my stories it's always hocus-pocus, slam-bang, and someone has a knife at your throat. Turns people off, she claims. I'm influenced too much by TV and radio and by what I read in the papers; in real life people are not nearly so anxious and unhappy as I make out. Put in a little comedy, she says. After all, you live in a pleasant house, you've got liquor in the cabinet, a beautiful wife, and most of our *urgent* bills are paid. Why be morbid? It gives people the wrong impression.

All right, I can see I've already gone astray. All this past history is irrelevant in a story meant to be about my foot. I'm getting too subjective, too interpretive, that's another of my flaws. You sound bitter, she'd say. Just stupidly sarcastic. Never mind that she's scowling in the doorway, grumpy and embittered herself because the bedroom is such a mess. When she's in *her* sick-bed, you understand, she likes everything immaculate: tables dusted, all knick-knacks pointing in the proper direction, flowers smiling from every ledge. Anything less is apt to depress her and I grant you her view is not unreasonable. It just happens that I don't like to be surrounded by that kind of false cheer. If I'm on my death-bed, I want two or three undertakers standing by and if a hearse is out in the garden, so much the better. So:

"Are you in pain?" she asks. "Do you think you can eat now?"

I groan. I can't help myself. Lovely and generous women like my wife think that all the ills of the world can be cured by a small wedge of cucumber sandwich or a nice salad with a little lemon dripped over the top. My mother is exactly the same and she is still going strong at ninety-five.

"Speak!" she shouts. "You're the big word-man around here."

The fact is, although I was starving, I wasn't talking to her just then. We'd had a tiff earlier in the week about my alleged promiscuous behaviour at a party but that's not why I wasn't talking to her. I simply *felt* like keeping my silence. It had nothing to do with my outrage over having been falsely accused. I'm accustomed to that. No, all my compassion, all my sympathy and love and concern, was invested in this wretched foot. I was in agony, I tell you. I was worn out. All night I had been in the grip of a fever — fever and chills — and hadn't slept a wink. None of my medicines helped. Penicillin, codeine, morphine, a bottle of eighty-year-old Scotch — nothing had offered any relief. Meanwhile, she had slept like a princess. Her story would be different, of course. She'd have you think she was up every minute putting hot or cold compresses on my brow. She'd tell you that when she finally did doze off she couldn't get any peace because my hands were all over her. That's not true. It is true that about four in the morning she jumped out of bed shouting, "Why don't you go and feel *her* up!" — and went running off to another bed. "What *her*?" I shout. "That bitch Gladys!" she screams back. Then the door slams and I don't see any more of her until breakfast.

Okay. I see I've fallen into my old trap. My stories don't *move*, she says. That is, they move but they don't go forward. I'm always botching them up with too much extraneous material. *"Who cares?"* she'd say. *"You throw in your mealy-mouthed references to Gladys and expect us to interpret them any way we wish. We're supposed to predict all sorts of dire consequences for these people, for their marriage, because you've invoked some slut's name. Well, it won't wash! Get on with it or shut up."* That, of course, is what she'd say after first denying that she'd said anything remotely similar to *Why don't you go and feel her up!* I put that part in, she'd claim, only to get the aroma of sex in my story.

"You get into this trouble only because you have nothing to say."

All right, I've made it clear I had a restless, terrible night. Now she comes in with my lunch on a tray. I'm supposed to comment on how heavenly it looks. She's even brought a little daisy in a vase and has dug out one of the bright yellow napkins she picked up in

Mexico. I'm supposed to be touched. She's had to pick this flower from the garden and she's had to wash this napkin by hand and slave over it with a hot iron. I'm not supposed to remember that she's got a trunkful of these faded things or how she came by them. In Mexico, I mean to say, while on a decadent trip with her beloved Arnold, in the days before she met me. I'm supposed to think she's still a lady when in actual fact she's toured three continents with that jerk! Arnold, I should add, is a first-rate storyteller. If you ask her to, she will put one of his platters on the stereo to prove it: "The Ballad of Johnny Cool," which hit the Top Forty and became a great movie by the same name. But do me a favour and don't take your children to see it.

He's successful, she sometimes tells me, because he knows when to employ dialogue. *"So you've decided to tell us a story about a man with a bum foot. You're smart enough to give him a beautiful, sophisticated and intelligent wife. But right away you impose an impossible burden on yourself. You have him so mad and stupid he can't talk to her. Result, no dialogue. All we get are his lame-brain buckshot musings. It's Dullsville. And I for one couldn't care less about him or his foot. Chop it off indeed. How did he hurt it in the first place? You always deliberately avoid revealing what most people would regard as a most essential part."*

He got it caught in a crankshaft.

"There you go being cute. You ruin every story you tell with these touches that you think are so cute. Nobody believes for a minute that this character's foot got caught in a crankshaft. Most of us don't even know what a crankshaft is. You will go to any extreme to avoid rooting your story in a basic, common, SHARED experience."

It got caught in an elevator door.

"Not believable."

A rhino stepped on it?

"Oh yes, any old lie will do. Anyway, by this time it's too late. Who cares? We're not dunces. If I didn't know any better, if I hadn't had to put up with it, I'd never believe your foot hurt at all."

Forced to, I will tell you what happened to my foot. It was nothing very dramatic. A week ago I was pouring concrete for this absurd gazebo she wanted built on the rocky cliff beside the house. *"Up there, honey,"* she says, *"so we can see for miles!"* Somehow my feet got tangled between bucket, hoe and wheelbarrow. I lost my balance and fell forty feet on this foot which I'd already sprained when I tried kicking a fire hydrant. Then I had to hobble two miles to the hospital because naturally she had the car, out to one of those treasured lunches with friends whom I never see. After treatment I collared a kind Ladies' Auxiliary person and for ten dollars she agreed to help me get home. I'm in bed, half passed-out, when my wife finally comes in. *"So this is how you build my gazebo!"* she exclaims, and tears out in a huff to see whether I've even started it yet. I can hear her up there stomping about, cursing, kicking rocks down the hill, telling neighbours, *"I knew it! I knew it! He's a lazy sod, he's done nothing and I rue the day I ever met him."* Meantime, I have revived somewhat and am trying with my bleary sight to find the front door. I'm going out there to strangle her, to push *her* off the cliff. My crutches slip, I topple over, and damned if the same foot isn't banged again. They sweep up my blood and guts and somehow return me to my bed of pain. Naturally she is all remorseful now, and solicitous, and for the next thirty-six hours baby-talk bubbles out of her: "Does my poor diddums forgive me? Won't my pretty diddums give me his pretty poo-doo smile?" She is so warm and contrite she could cook me in this syrup. Finally, one frostbitten night, I relent and go to put my arms around her in matrimonial harmony: I get her knee in my stomach, a slam of insults, and the next second she's scrambling for another bed. Even if I have chased Gladys, which I deny, it seems to me that our crimes ought to balance out.

Right, so onward, she's now brought the lunch tray in. Ham on rye, a big pickle, a glass of milk, and fresh strawberries under a blanket of homespun cream.

"Eat it," she says. "You know what will happen if you lie about drinking whisky all day."

"What will happen? Let my dark secret out."

"You'll get blotto."

"Ho-ho as my Daddy would say. Big deal."

"Is your foot still throbbing?"

"I don't know. Hit it with a hammer, then I can tell."

That's enough dialogue for a while. She's got her eyes on my strawberries and has already eaten half the bowl. I'm not supposed to notice that and certainly should not remark on it: she's on a diet. It occurs to me that the reason my foot's in such pain is because the bandage is too tight. No circulation. My foot is puffy and red outside the wrapping, my five toes like shrivelled apple peels. It's one of those surgical bandages, the kind that stretches. I try to reach it, but can't. Every time I move, a thunderbolt rips through my leg and a spike bangs into my skull. My wife takes an interest in my contortions. She's quite bedazzled. Her eyes enlarge. My agony sends the blood rushing to her face. I have her sympathy but I certainly can't expect any help with the bandage from her. She won't touch it. It hasn't been washed in seven days. Nor has my foot. That's just what I don't need: to get trapped in a tub with a hundred-pound foot.

"What can I do?" she asks.

"Nothing," I say. "Go away." Howling pain makes a person rude. I lie still, exhausted; the pain diminishes somewhat. My wife's feelings are hurt, but she insists on feeding me. Each time I turn my head there's another spoonful sliding between my lips. "Eat, eat!" she says. "Your mother tells me she had to feed you this way until you were nineteen years old." Oh, she knows how to get at a man. She knows how to humiliate him. "I'm sorry," she next says, "about last night." She knows how to make old hatreds live — to make repulsion for one's swollen foot embrace other swollen members too. I must pay for the sins of every man who has ever clawed at her when she wasn't in the mood. "It's just that I wasn't in the mood." I raise my head to look at her. What I see are her wet eyes. Luscious, trembling lips. Hair trained by Mister Divine to shroud her face like a tent. *Déjà vu*. I have been here before. And the thought I have now is the same I had then. Better, old sport, that you had married a hag. Staked out the most vile neighbourhood witch and mated with her. One glance at this woman's proud, suffering face and I am hit with instant self-doubt and loathing, I am awash in sentimentality. Old True Love is hooking its claws into me. She's the one who's miserable and misunderstood. *I'm* the brute. We don't need God to remind us of our evil deeds; all we need is another person.

I find myself reviewing this most recent encounter with Gladys. A snaky wink through my bifocals. A tawdry giggle under the tree. And yes, three years ago, a single scuffy kiss in the pantry where a fuse had blown. Crimes microscopic in size but all the same I ask myself: am I not better than this? Would I tarnish reputations, cheapen myself in the eyes of the community, betray this fine woman for the sake of such a pale and fleeting lust as poor Gladys can engender? I tell you the experience gives me pause. I grip the neck of my Scotch bottle tighter and that's a fact.

I got gloomy and distressed. Oh, I plunged into a deep foul mood, no doubt of that. Down there where only mole eyes perceive. Me with stubby legs and no visible neck, chomping on earth worms, aware that my path must take me through solid rock. The same thing happens to her. She sulks, she moans, she sweats: you'd think my flaming foot had been transferred to one of her long limbs. As usual, she combats her depression by lashing out.

"Stop complaining about your foot," she cries. "If you mention that goddamned foot to me again I'll scream!"

"But it hurts."

"Shut up! You didn't appear to have any trouble tracking that bitch Gladys! Or Hilda! What a barge pole *she* was! No, your foot didn't hurt then, you were a four-minute miler so long as you had their buttocks shimmying in front of you!"

Hilda? Hilda *Who? Barge poles!* What on earth can this hysterical woman mean?

"Yes, *you*, you twit! You stump-toed turd!"

Hold on a minute. I can't go on without inserting one tiny aside. My spouse is constantly criticizing me for what she calls my dirty mouth. I can't say a word to friends but that she doesn't first have to chase about the room with her pine-scent spray and cotton for the children's ears. *Reduce the filth*, that's what she's always saying. I get it from bartenders too. *Muzzle it, Deacon, or it's out you go*. I go to a movie, for instance, with naked bodies wallowing all over the screen and language that would drive killer bees to suicide, and if I mutter *Pee on this*, right away I've got six ushers driving me to the door. Fellini can have a hundred bodies copulating in a Roman bath but if I have a couple holding hands in a snowstorm I'm accused of being degenerate. *Yes*, she will say, *but your material has no redeeming quality*. Her friends will nod and grandmothers may come back into the room. So hold on. I'm not to be blamed for *her* filthy mouth. The accusation isn't true in the first place. I learned a long time ago to clean up my act. They used to say about my Daddy, that rascal, that he had a mouth like a cat's rear end. You can bet your money I wasn't going to model myself after him.

My wife has no ear for this or any other criticism. Not for nothing has she attended the best schools, known the best people, committed her entire being to this marriage. Her efforts are to be recorded in the Guinness *Book of Records* (under section-heading TOOK MOST CRAP); even now, angels are at work on scrolls to be hung at the Gates of Heaven. I, too, in my dreams, when they are not of dinosaurs and other amiable and extinct creatures, compose encyclopaedic encomiums to this woman:

> Mama Fournose — WIFE. *Married to erstwhile stonemason and oral traditionalist known as* Foot. *At great personal sacrifice she fed & preserved this oaf's soul, nurtured his body, saw to it that his house was not overrun with tramps, drunkards, rogues, deadbeats, Hedonists, etc. All this sweet woman wanted out of life was a marriage that*

would go down in history (dinner by candlelight each evening of the year — Famous Quote: "Isn't this romantic!"), *and loyalty. Got neither of above.*

Betroth me, O serpent, to my fate
Let my bones lie still.

A ludicrous sadness overwhelms us both at times. It charges at us with a banshee zeal, routing us from the careful defences we have laid. We pick up the pieces and limp for higher, more neutral ground. Reach for Rule No. 1 of the *Survivor's Guide to Home Warfare*: after any skirmish, win or lose, effect a quick retreat. Tend to your wounds. Keep a fresh whisky close to your left elbow. I must forget what I know of this woman. A college fraternity, in her tender eighteenth year, voted her Most Impressionable Girl; a year later the same group named her Most Desired; competition faltered and within the season a new crown had been bestowed: A Woman Too Good To Be True. What has happened to my beautiful princess to warrant this impossible title? How many dreary days she must have sat, swilling sherry, staring out of windows in makeshift rooms, paced cities like a loaned-out cat, knocked limbs with phantom shapes, yearning every moment for the day when her heart would truly crack and love's childhood dream of her perfect knight could at last draw to its deadly close. *Look, Father, I am a stranger to you now! Look, Mother, at the woman I have become! Oh, lover, I have survived the best and worst you could do to me! Oh, world, send me a man out of your darkness! I have toyed with prince and rabble and am prepared now to wed whatever stranger next steps into my light.*

"This can't go on," laments my wife.

Most Fashionable now. Her clothes, no less than her black moods, put her at the vanguard of her age. Tomorrow *Chatelaine, Vogue, The Woman's Own Daily* no doubt will call: *We're in a real quandary, honey: this season is it to be mauve or green?*

My rancid foot is killing me.

"Think of something pleasant," she advises. "Try remembering your first wife."

I remember a story that a fellow down at the Motherlode used to tell me. It seems there was this woman down on her luck who one day sat down by a pool thinking she'd throw herself in when this frog suddenly hopped into her lap saying *Kiss me* and she got out her hatchet and chopped off its legs and immediately fried them up on her hibachi and ate them and decided on reflection that she hadn't had such a fine day in years.

All right, forget that story. I can see it's not relevant, what a guy in a beer-hall told ten years ago.

My first wife *was* demented; ever in study of her L. Ron Hubbard; I hardly see how I'm to be blamed for that.

"Or how you wet your bed until you were twenty-one."

Feeble. Such weak humour will not provoke my ire. Anyway, I have more serious matters to ponder. I've had a suspicion now for several days: my foot is only a symptom of the deeper trouble I'm in. I have some dreaded disease of the blood. That's why my doctor has been so guarded in his report. It's why a simple X-ray was not sufficient. Numerous tests were required: my blood was drained, my urine analysed, my body strapped to numerous unidentifiable machines while four hefty nurses held me down. I am either sick in a most complex way or another patient has been confused with me. I suffer weird discolourations of skin: black here, blue there, a purplish tinge all over. The doctor tells me, *Well. Sir, you drink too much. And you had a wicked fall.* He means to keep the news from me. To let the poor soul have a few happy days.

I'm a normal man, I worry about problems such as this. Yesterday I called a friend of mine, Fromm, a practising psychiatrist. Can you help me, Doc? I asked. Am I in trouble or is this delusion? He refused my case. You're terminated, he said. Deacon, I have bigger fish to fry. *I am at work on a case that could change the entire face of Europe.*

A good man but a dope, what does he know?

My wife is, of course, in on the secret. That explains why twice in the past week she has raised the subject of our financial affairs. *It's absurd, darling, but do you by chance have a secret bank account? I ask because I simply can't figure out where all the money goes.* She wanted me to believe her inquiry could be routinely explained: she had seen a hot item in a dress shop and wanted my enthusiasm before spending what amounted to a small fortune. I might have been deceived. But the next day she brought up the question of wills: *everyone writes a will these days. Don't you think we should?*

It explains too why, on the whole, she's been so nice to me lately.

Nothing she can say, however, will induce me to reveal the presence of my secret account. It's there as a buffer against hard times, and because when my first wife left she cleaned me out. The furniture, my dog, my neckties, my thousand-franc Swiss note, and a Maytag appliance repairman all went away with her. *You deserve it,* she told me. *Say any more and I'll take away that silly toupée you wear.*

Ignore the above. I've read the Book of Job and know when I'm well off.

Her successor is now fluffing my pillows and straightening bedclothes, polishing the bureau — ploughing like a moose through the trash of seven days. Into her "White Tornado" housewifery act.

"In case anyone calls," she says.

Because that is how she is. Although I can go six months in this house without seeing another living soul, and often do, in her mind the front steps are forever packed with visitors queueing to get in. I sink my teeth into my arm, and watch. Women are mad. *All* women are demented. That's what makes them women in the first place. But how else are we to be saved? Who else would go to the trouble?

"Lift your foot," she instructs. "You can't rest with the sheets in this untidy state."

"You expect me to be concerned about sheets when I have only a few hours left to live?"

She laughs. Oh, she has a fine old howl at this. Then she becomes reflective, her cheeks puff, her mouth goes tight, eyebrows leap into her scalp: "Ah," she says, "I've got it. You've been trying to think up a story to tell those deadbeats down at the Motherlode! Haven't you? Is it about your foot? But now you've realized that not even those idiots would be interested in a yarn about a foot, so you've thought to deepen your tale by inserting some nonsense about your approaching death. Or about your first wife running off with your neckties. That's it, isn't it?"

"What is wrong with a story about a foot?"

"The average person cannot relate to it."

I remind her that everyone has feet. I even laugh because I know the remark is funny. But she does not crack a smile. I can scent the malice of more criticism in the very way she breathes. My wife the acid-thrower.

"Yes, but their feet don't ache. How many of your average listeners have recently been so drunk at ten o'clock in the morning that they've fallen off a cliff? Your stories are merely extended jokes. No meat. No heart. No humour. They are of no consequence."

I know what she has in mind. She has this theory, for instance, about sex. My stories ought to have more sex. "But don't make it goofy," she will say, "and for God's sake avoid your nasty specifics.

"Or about money. They should be about money. Everyone wants or needs a certain amount of money. You'd have people around you all the time if you ever talked about money. But for God's sake don't make it too intelligent. You always want to appear so smart. It puts people off. You can't stand people knowing you were born a hick and didn't wear shoes until you were twenty years old."

Well, that's what she says. Actually, I was born in a porter's closet in the Louvre, Paris, France, and didn't go country until I was four, after my parents were killed in a tornado in the Aleutians.

"And don't tell it in that twisty language. Or with that hound-dog face. As for that, you'd be a lot better at it if you stayed sober."

She pauses there. She doesn't want to go too far, she knows I have feelings. She knows I can be hurt. She sits on the bed now massaging my poor, hot, throbbing foot. Her hands are deliciously cool. Or perhaps it is the other way around. Perhaps her hands are hot and my foot is cold. I can't be sure. That illustrates another of my faults. I have too many *perhapses* and far too many *can't be sures.* "I like," she has told me a thousand times, "the simple declarative statement." Not a busload of adjectives. Although she does not call them adjectives. She calls them "extra words." That's understandable, after all I'm the one around here who considers himself the professional. "I'm the amateur," she will say. "Just a darned good Eaton's buyer, just cook, maid and sex object. But that doesn't mean I'm ignorant. If I say your stories stink, they stink."

She's saying nothing at the moment. In a half-trance she strokes my foot. Her face catches the sunlight and I can't deny she's lovely. She's lovely, she's nice, she's employed. The truth is, my foot may be either hot *or* cold but, more important, the ache is absent. It may be there but I can't feel it. She stares out the window. Placidly strokes my foot. Probably she is thinking about dinner. Or about the new suit she didn't buy after all. I lie there luxuriating, so to speak, in the touch of her hands. They tickle. I like it, I mean to say. Now and then she runs a hand up my leg. Fingers fold lightly over my knee. There is a soft glide along my thigh. Now back to my foot again. Again. Again. Then once more the somnolent climb up my leg. I dare not move. I'd like to, though. I am definitely getting interested. Her hand strokes and my body of its own accord sinks down, trying to urge the hand ever higher. I dare not speak. One wrong word and this moment is lost forever. I'd like to hire a violinist, Isaac Stern perhaps, and give him permanent residence in the attic. For times such as this. I wonder what will happen when she stops looking out the window. What will happen if *she* gets interested? I close my eyes and think: stroke!...stroke!...now higher! Higher! *Ahhhhh!* That's the ticket! Nice! Nice...

That's where the sex comes into this story. I thought I'd try it. I wouldn't want it said of me that I'm not open to criticism. My idea, moreover, is that by including it I can kill two birds with one stone. I see it as a nice, positive moment in the lives of these two people.

That's another criticism she makes of me. "You're too negative. People are tired of all the negative crap. Who wants to hear a story about another loser? What's the point?" As proof, she usually drags in that story someone told about two guys buried up to their necks in sand. Or the one I like to tell about four shoe-salesmen who fall into a cave and argue for hours about which of them wears a true size ten. "Big deal!" she says. Not that I exactly disagree with her on this score. "People are not a bunch of sows," she will say, "wanting to wallow or root in another's misery. Or in their own, for that matter. Leave us a little hope, will you? A little dignity!"

She ought to know what she's talking about. She gets out much more than I do, she has her lunches three or four times a week, she's in and out of people's houses and gets to know what they are thinking. When she tells me people want realistic, happy stories, I believe it. I know her remarks are meant to be helpful; I realize some of mine are getting a bit ripe. "I've heard that," she will sometimes say. "You told me that one last week." And I can imagine her final assessment of this hurt foot piece: *just another sleazy monologue! It's the same old story, sugar, we practically know it by heart.* She will admit too, if pressed, that she didn't appreciate that part about her stroking my leg. It was insulting, it questioned her natural sensuality, and what about her privacy? "Keep it up, sonnyboy, and roses will grow out of your ears before I stroke you again!"

Don't I honour anything? Is nothing sacred?

That is what she will be saying next. "But do go on. Don't let me hold up your precious story. Your audience is breathless!" How would you react to such ridicule? Do you think you might momentarily flounder? I'm a professional but that's how it affects me. I get red in the face and can't sit still — the thread is lost, you see. I laugh and try to put a light face on it but everyone can see she's stopped me in my tracks. "Where was I," I will lamely persist, "before I was so rudely interrupted?" She will smile knowingly: "You were talking about how I know more about what people are thinking than you do."

I plough stubbornly ahead. Sometimes people *will* drop over. They do. They ring up and ask whether they can shoot over — because they've heard I've been ill or depressed or they haven't seen us lately down at the Motherlode — that sort of thing, all perfectly natural. So we will be sitting down to a drink, eating roasted almonds or cheese or a pizza, say, with these people, and it happens that it is not altogether unheard of for one of them to ask outright for a story. "Tell us a story," they will say. "Let's hear what's been going on with you two." *Long time no see, Deacon, lay one on me, we're all ears!* That sort of thing. I am, naturally enough, happy to oblige, since I have come to think of myself in those terms. As a storyteller. It's what my mother tells her friends: "Deacon doesn't do anything, he just tells stories. That's all he does. He could have had a good trade as a stonemason but it seems he's content to let his wife support him." So I, as I say, am happy to respond to these requests. I get right down to it. *There was once,* I might tell them, *in darkest wintertime, in this most foul time of the year, a man who went about our country with his feet bound in rags, with horrible leaking eyes, and with a great hump on his back in which you would think he carried all the troubles of the world. Now one day, on that very day in which this poor rogue was to breathe his last, on that day a young girl innocent as the dew came dancing along his path.*

As a rule I am interrupted at about this point in the narrative. *She* wants to tell the story. Or *they* do. For her part she doesn't trust me with it. I have, she will claim, already got it wrong. "You are flogging a dead horse and no one in this company wants to hear it." What is wrong with it? "It is pseudo-literary trash," she informs me. "A hump, indeed. If we want Dumas we can go to the library. And your young innocent tra-la-la, what garbage!" She will go on to tell me how my plot is to develop: the stupid old bugger bleeding to death in an alley somewhere, our young innocent then walking up and kicking the corpse — because it's symbolic, you see. Both of them rotten and dirty and disagreeable creatures and somehow all of society having to accept the blame. "Either that," she informs our group, "or he will have no plot, he will simply have the old fart walking down the street thinking his own vile accusatory thoughts while the girl hovers innocently, symbolically, in the background waiting to be redeemed through true love. Nothing ever happening, not even any description except the odd streetcorner lamp now and then and maybe dog feces in the gutter. So don't tell it. It won't make any of us feel any better. It won't make anyone want to rejoice that they are alive. So what if people like your ugly hero do exist, you think that's any excuse? What percentage of people in the world do you think your old bastard represents, him with his filthy psychology and his dog crud in the streets? He's probably out hunting Nazis, right? Why don't you tell a story about an average person for a change, one with average wants and needs? I know too that before you're another minute into this oral beauty you'll start trying to make it sound deep, you'll drop vague hints, the situation will get so tangled up and messy we won't know where we are. It's just another of your hateful disgusting creations and we will want to go and take a bath and regret we ever asked you to open your mouth. Gloom, gloom, gloom, that's all you preach."

The truth is she is better at storymaking than I am. At least if our friends are any judge. They smile and laugh and feed her good lines. In my story, which she appropriates, my sour old man's hump is barely noticeable. She refers to this growth as a *pretty ridge* and speaks of his scarred but ennobled face, his good manners and benevolent attitude. He meets a nice mature woman at a bus stop who turns out to be the daughter separated from him in a train wreck years before. "Why, I thought you were dead!" she remarks. Pathos carries the day: for a decade now the daughter has been placing flowers on the grave thought to be her father's. It is this journey, in fact, which has today been interrupted. "Come home with me," entreats the girl. "Mother could not accept your death. All these years she has faithfully waited." He stops off for a shave; she goes in and buys a new coat she's been eyeing in Eaton's.

I admit her stories make me feel good. I concede that her tales are populated with characters one might willingly invite into one's own home. I am bothered a little by the coincidence of this bus stop meeting, though she waves aside this minor reservation. "A story has got to be true to life," she opines. "Every day I meet someone on the street whom I have not seen in years." Others agree. They give examples.

"All right," I argue. "Even so, you must admit that her version does not sound modern." This observation is met with instant derision. Hands flap in the air, everyone wants to talk at once. Would I be done, then, with Goethe? Are Sophocles, Dante, Shakespeare to be thrown into the incinerator? A hundred names collide in the air. "What about Woody Allen? Sam Shepard? Cecil B. De Mille? Would you throw them out because they do not sound modern?"

I try to edge in my one thin line of defence: that I am speaking only of and for the oral traditionalist.

"Spit!" my wife declares."You think your kind of oral history is an end in itself; I say look where your lies have got us. Abnormality creates more abnormality. You will have people expecting it of themselves and disappointed when it is not achieved. You will not be content until you have us walking about on all fours. You must encourage us to nobility. You must inspire us. *Inspire* us, you fool!"

I don't know. I can't refute the arguments of these people. I despair. How can I go on in the face of such accusations, such hostility, with a story, for instance, about my miserable foot? Why not give up? Retire into a world of pleasant chat. The only pleasure I have left is to look back with a wet nostalgic eye to the good old days. In the old days I was to be found every night down at the Motherlode. Folks would spin off their stools and clap me on the shoulder, saying, "Tell us another one, Deacon!" And they'd spin the other way and punch a neighbour, crying, "This guy is great, his stories will put hair on your chest!" So I'd rock on my heels and launch into the first thing that entered my head. It came easy as breathing. I had only to open my mouth and the magic would fly. "Listen," I would say, "have you heard the one about..." and before you'd know it they'd be doubled up, laughing, wheezing, pounding on the floor and falling against walls, or they'd be sobbing, the tears plopping down their cheeks, their poor hearts bursting. "By God, that was a good one!" they'd say. "By God, Deacon, that was a pip! What a beaut!"

So I don't know now. The heart has gone out of it. Maybe I need the enthusiasm of those good old days, expectant faces lining the bar, urging me on, quiet as snakes while they waited for what was to happen next and always knowing there'd be a good solid snort of another man's liquor at the end. I don't know. Can't tell. Maybe I have begun to lace my tales with too many non-essentials like that rubbish about Gladys or even that my foot was hurting in the first place. Maybe my whole approach is wrong. I've become fancy, gone twisty in the lingo and the mind. I'll have to think about it. Have to lay off the newspaper and TV for a while. Go easy on the booze. Try to recapture what I had at the start. Go back to scratch. Anyway, that's the advice my wife will give, late at night when I roll hurt and trembling into her arms. "Stick to a single incident," she will say. "Make use of chronological time. Keep it simple. You will get your confidence back in time. I'll help you. If you get into trouble, you know you've always got me here to fix it up."

THE BIRTH CONTROL KING ≈ OF THE UPPER VOLTA ≈

The most extraordinary thing happened to me today. I woke up and discovered I had lost yesterday. Amazing! Not a slither, parcel, or dot of it remained. Yes! The sun was dazzling bright, my entire room was lit up like a store-front. I stretched, I yawned, I kicked off my sheets: oh lovely, perfect lovely! — is what I said.

Absolutely. That's how innocent I was.

And here I am forty-seven years old. You'd think I would have had a hint.

Dogs outside my window were having a romp. Squealing, yowling — how I had slept through their hubbub was more than I could imagine. Yet I felt wonderfully excited. Renewed, you might say. "What a dreamy day!" That's exactly what I said to myself — and right away set about performing my exercises. A somersault. Another one. Nothing broke, thank goodness. My room is so small I have to do these flip-flops on a pin-head. But the exhilaration! — I truly felt superb, even while lifting my barbells. Twenty, thirty, this is too easy, I told myself — add more weight! Add a ton. I slid on the ton. Ten, twenty, thirty — no trouble at all. I could have gone on all day pressing these feathers, with barely a pause for breath.

"Oh you're fit," I said laughing, addressing my form in the mirror. "You're in peak condition, Adlai!" I pulled on my pants, scooped back my hair. Washed my face and neck in the little sink, eager to run down to breakfast. "Eat a horse, Adlai," I said, "yes you could. What an appetite you've worked up! Hurry up, now!"

Ah, what a babe. What an innocent. For it was then, hustling through the door, that I made the discovery. The beautiful calendar hanging by the nail drew my eye. And why not, for pictured there was my sweetheart, Greta Gustafsson. I always notice her, entering or leaving. Sultry woman, she'd mope — she'd scratch out my eyes — if I didn't. Everyone needs noticing is what Greta would say. "What a beauty you are," I said, rubbing my cheek against this image. Kissing her bare shoulders. Greta moaned. I moaned also. "Good morning, my darling," I said. "Sleep well, my beauty?" She lowered her eyes. This morning she seemed preoccupied — seemed distant. My heart ached. Greta deserved better than I could give her. She deserved, in the least, a silver frame, a wall with a good view. Yet as it is there is hardly room for myself. For my footlocker and narrow bed. The walls! — stretch out your arms and there you have it. And so ugly! Uneven and fly-specked — filthy! — with immense zigzags cracking all about.

"No, the door," I said, smoothing down her hair, "the door is best for you, beautiful Greta. Don't complain. Don't scold. Things will be looking up for us once I get that job with the Pole. Give me a smile, darling. What would you like for breakfast, my honey? Say the word and I shall get it." I kissed her eyes. Greta likes that. She purred. Oh Greta adores eye-kissing. My perfect Greta.

But wait, for here's the news. Drawing back, I happened to glance at the date. Mercy! "What's this?" I asked myself. Impossible. But yes, there it was. Yesterday had disappeared. Had become, I mean, today. What *do* I mean? I mean at that very second I discovered there had been no August ten in my life. The bold red type was clearly announcing itself: August eleven — anniversary of Blondin's crossing of Niagara Falls on a tightrope wire, so the little historical note informed me. *"God help me!"* I cried, *"I've lost yesterday! What happened to the tenth?"* Greta giggled. Then she saw my stricken face and fell quiet.

Gone, I thought. One whole day! Jesus God!

I stumbled out into the hall. Voices floated up from the dining-room, jibber-jabber, everyone talking at once, the way they always do. Slurp-slurp — you'd think I slept above a hog pen. Jibber-jabber, slurp-slurp — what imps!

"I say," I called, "what's the date down there?"

Silence. Not a word. You'd think I had dropped a giant brickbat on their heads. And out of the stillness came Mergentoire's sprightly reply: "Wednesday! It's Wednesday, you ape!"

Ape? Ape? What had got into sweet Mergentoire?

"Idiot!" I screeched. "Get control of yourself, woman. The *date*, what's the *date*?"

More silence. Utter stealth, you'd have thought. One would have sworn the entire table had fallen asleep. Then Mergentoire's voice again, laughing this time, shrill as a rat: "The eleventh, you rogue! Wednesday the eleventh. The day Blondin went over Niagara on a tightrope!"

Then the clatter of dishes once more, and everyone else shouting up the hideous message too. Chomping away on pancakes, scraping back in their chairs — where's the butter, who's got the milk jug, *oops!* — that sort of thing. All the confusion and turmoil, the belching and bellyaching you get when twenty hard-hat labourers are trying to gulp down their protein before rushing off to their jobs. No shilly-shallying, I mean, quick-quick, sorry old mate, got to run!

What a waste of man and woman's best hour. My old mam and I, we would sit for hours about the breakfast table, munching carrot sticks, dipping our bread into tea, perusing the journals and up-to-date magazines, rattling the tabloids.

— "Ah, son, here's another one."

— "Another one, my mam?"

— "Guinea-Bissau, this one's called. How many does that make, son?"

— "I don't know, my mam. What's your guess?"

— "I count forty-one, son. Forty-one since your old Daddy went into the field."

— "That's a lot of emerging nations, my mam! That's a whole hodgepodge full! Oh, they are really carving it up. What do you think old Daddy would say, my mam?"

— "He'd say 'roll me over, dear. Roll me over in my grave and throw another white right on top of me.' "

— "Tell me about it, my mam."

— "It was the Upper Volta that broke your old Dad's heart. Oh, son, when they let the Upper Volta go they as much as put a dagger through his chest."

— "Cold-blooded murder, my mam?"

— "That's right, son. It was a mean, depraved act and who's to reap the whirlwind now?"

— "Us, my mam?"

— "That's the bite of it, son. But eat your carrots, Adlai, they don't grow on trees and a boy needs to hoard up his strength."

I went back into my room, thinking about poor old mam and all the black African hordes yet to sweep down. Crossing the water on rafts and matchstick canoes, beaming their great white teeth and kicking their great black legs, all to gobble up our jobs and steal our women and make a garbage hole of our neighbourhoods. "Not yet, my mam," I wanted to tell her. "Adlai is holding on. Old Adlai's got the biceps and the brawn, he's got the will-power: you won't find him kissing no woolly hair."

I could see old mam nodding her approval even as I stared with remorse and disbelief at my calendar's lost date. Where was yesterday? Old mam would say the blacks had got it, just as they'd take away anything else I'd be foolish enough to leave lying about.

— "That's right, son, they got it. They'll take the shoes off your feet if you don't tie them up tight!"

Greta Gustafsson gave me her alluring smile. I swayed in close, putting the kiss of sin into her smouldering eyes.

"*I vunt to be alone*," she whispered, turning away.

My heart skipped; it always puts me in a torture, seeing Greta in her moods.

"But Greta!" I whined.

"*Yoo lust a day*," she murmured, resentful and hurt. "*They are my days too and I hold yoo responsible*."

I dropped down on my narrow bed. Scrunching up my toes, for there was not enough room for my feet between it and the wall. Something fishy going on here is what I thought. Adlai, you've got to use your wits if you intend to figure this one out.

Days, I thought — as you would have yourself — just don't disappear.

I consulted my diary, lying open on the footlocker table. Lying open to August ten. To the day that had never been.

7:00 — Wake up, lazy-bones! Exercise. Wash. 7:30 — Pancakes with the gang, mmmmm! 8-6:00 P.M. — Job, uggg (but don't complain!). 7:00 P.M. — Talk To The Pole. 8:00 — Home. Dust room. Wipe sink. Exercise. Bedtime snack. Shut-eye (And no messing about with Greta.)

"Oh there's monkey-business afoot here, Adlai," I said — for it looked to me as if I'd a very busy day. And why not? — a thousand irons in the fire, things to get done, people to see! Life to *live*! My old mam, looking at my diary, would have patted my head. She would have said, "That's dreamy, son. That's top marks. How you get it all done is beyond me. Oh yes, you're a chop off the old block."

So.

So I'd say myself.

Yet I was blotto. I had not even the fumes, not even the ashes, of my past day. Zero.

Greta was sulking, giving me first one cold shoulder and then the next. Drop dead, is what Greta was saying. What a disappointment you are. What a rathead. "You expect too much of me, Greta," I told her. "I do the best I can." But she flounced her hair and thrust out her chin and drew the cloak of gloom over herself.

A *hard* woman. A *tough* woman. Just, I thought, like old mam.

So I forgave her. I decided she was right to be mad. I had let her down. I had promised her she would be safe with me. That I had what it took to keep a good woman happy.

A newshawker was shouting his headlines out on the street, and I rushed to the window. "You!" I yelled, "what's the date?"

His startled black face sought to find mine.

"August 11, boss," he said.

The dogs were still fighting in the dirt, squealing and yowling and spinning in a fury.

"Are those mongrels yours, boy?" I asked.

"Not mine, boss."

The dogs momentarily ceased their yowling to blink up at me. Then they went back to it with renewed ferocity.

"Well then," I asked the boy, "what's the news today?" And he held up his grim headlines to me:

SUMMIT TALKS COLLAPSE

+

AUTO-MAKERS LAY OFF ANOTHER 30,000

+

INFLATION HITS NEW HIGH

My world, I thought, and still there.

"That all, boss?" asked the black face.

And when I didn't answer immediately, he did a little soft-shoe.

It seemed to me I'd seen him before — him or his twin — standing in the line-up to receive his dole, wearing butter-yellow shoes, a red eye patch, a watch-chain long as his arm — and streaming off in his big Rolls-Royce with three boisterous women white as white eggs and laughing like mud-flaps.

But was this true or was it my old Daddy sending his vision across the licking water?

"Listen, kid," I called, "did I buy a paper off you yesterday?"

His black face grinned up at me over his watermelon. "Not off me, boss. I'm fresh brand-new in the country, first day on the job." He danced a swift jig along the pavement, playing a mean tune with his harmonica comb. "I aims to make my fortune, boss," he chirped. "Me and my fourteen brothers looking no way but up. We got a toehold on progress. Gonna git our relatives in. From here on out de sky is de limit!"

I slammed my window down on this strapping young grinner, and proceeded to do one hundred push-ups — a few headstands — to work the vitriol out of my system. It had been the vitriol that had slammed down my old Daddy and made his gums bleed. That had turned him boots up.

— "What killed him, my mam?"

— "Vitriol, son. When the blacks painted up their bodies and screamed their heebie-jeebies he was filled up with vitriol and flung himself into the first river."

— "What was he doing there, my mam, in the distant Upper Volta?"

— "Selling birth control to the Roman Catholics, son. No easy job."

Greta was breathing hard. Clenching her fists as she strode this way and that. Hissing. Stopping me cold with her hot fury. I knew what was on her mind. She wanted me stepping up in the world. Wanted me out of my red suspenders and into top hats. She wanted me to call up the Pole, find out about that job. I stole a look at her, wondering. Trying to figure out what it is about women. Why they drive their men so hard. Why they can't be satisfied. It crossed my mind that I wasn't cut out for a go-getter like Greta. That I'd be better off with some redhead lounging back in a bikini on a leopard-skin rug, selling fertilizer to farmers. With someone all bosom and legs who would say, "I'm for my man, right or wrong. My man is a macho-doctor, good for what ails me." But I didn't think this long. Greta was my heart's need, my solace, my joy. Without her I'd be swinging on vines.

So I stepped out into the hall to make my call.

Mergentoire, I noticed, had put up a new sign: DON'T HOG THE PHONE. This was tacked up beside another one that said NO CALLS AFTER 8 P.M. And another one, dripping blood, that said THIS MEANS YOU.

"The Pole here," the Pole's voice shrieked in my ear. "Speak up!"

But there was thunder overhead. Then the thunder was rumbling down from the third floor, down the stairs, driving towards me. "Out of my way, fat man!" came the nasty cry. Wong, the slant-eye. I shrunk back, hugging the wall. His yellow face whirled past, bumping me — hurling himself off to his job. Late again. This Chinaman, one more of the numberless hordes. "Fat men!" he screeched. "Always fat men! Never looking where they're going! Always hogging the phone!" He clattered on down, flinging back more abuse.

A big country like that, you'd think they'd stay in their rice fields.

The Pole was shouting, too. "Who is it? Speak up! I haven't got all day!"

I gave him my name.

"Oh," he said. "Oh, it's you! The nincompoop! What's on your mind, nincompoop? Why are you bothering me?"

Hold on here, I said to myself. Why is the Pole addressing me in this unseemly fashion? What gives? It had been my impression that the Pole, more than most, held me in high regard. Respected my talents. Why otherwise would he have been trying to give me a job?

"If it's about that job," he now was saying, "you can blow it out of your stove-pipe. I told you yesterday. I've hired someone else. I got some foreign bird at half the pay. Strong! Eight feet tall! Can't speak a word of English. But I'll work the stink off him, don't worry about that!"

And before I could get my wits raked clean the rascal had hung up.

Poles, I thought: what can you say about Poles?

I thought: what a relief! Changing jobs, what a nuisance that would have been! I mopped my brow, thinking: what a close call!

Anyway, I told myself, I like the job I've got. I'm happy. Greta's happy, what's the worry?

I slouched back into my room, feeling pretty good.

"It's the Pole's bad luck," I told Greta. "He missed a good bet. Hiring me was his golden opportunity."

Greta wasn't talking to me. She had put on one of her hats, the one with feathers. Plumed like a cavalier. Scooped low, the brim shading one eye. String of pearls at her throat, as if she intended going some place.

Well, I didn't mind. I liked to see Greta all dressed up.

But she had fire in her eyes — a torrid spitball.

"*Rats!*" she hissed — or something like that.

Her shoulders arched back as she paced, pivoting her hips. I watched those hips, those eyes, stole glances at her flat chest. She looked so luscious, so mysterious — so magnificent and sure of herself.

I wanted to hug and hold her, to weep in her thighs.

But I put the brave face on. "That Pole," I said, "he must have been out of his mind to think I wanted his soft job. Me, at a desk! What a laugh. None of that white-collar malarkey for me. I like being outside breathing in the fresh air. Hauling those rocks. Working in rain, wind, snow. Working up a good sweat in the hard freeze. A man's work, that's what I'm cut out for."

Greta's cruel veil of derision fluttered down.

— "It keeps a body fit, my mam. In tune with nature. It's nice being out there where only the fittest survive. It's educational, old mam. Not a day goes by I don't tip my hat to old Darwin the theorizer."

I could swear my old mam had walked right into the room. She stood not a foot away, shaking her finger.

— "So long as you don't get the heebie-jeebies, son. That's what done in your Daddy. That and the vitriol."

— "I've heard it said he was a drinker too, my mam."

— "Envy, son. The envy and malice of small minds. It was the envy of him that spread that story."

— "And womanizing, my mam? Was he a womanizer, as I've heard?"

She sat down on my bed, spreading her hands palms-up on her lap. She had a spot of soot on her chin, and watery eyes. I reached over and brushed away the soot. Her hair had a singed odour, as if she'd fallen head-first into a smoker's flame.

— "Womanizing won't kill a person, son. There are some as would say it's what keeps a body going. But your Daddy wasn't like that. And if he had been, it isn't likely he would ever have touched black. Now listen to me, Adlai. You listen good. Three thousand nautical miles separated your Daddy in the Upper Volta from us where we were, not to mention umpteen years — but your Daddy's eyes were always looking back home. He kept his heart and his eyes dead set on us. On me and you. He put love first, but he knew he had that. Had our love and our trust. But he was a committed man. An obsessed man. I've told you a thousand times: your Daddy had a mission to protect us, and others like us. Our very way of life. And he went with my blessings. I remember the very day he left I said to him, "Go and do it, Humpter, and do it well, and always know you have me here thumping my feet for every success you have." Humpter, that was my secret pet-name for him. Everytime I would call him Humpter he would blush. Yes, and I would too, for we were just newlyweds, you see. We still had the rice in our hair. But I knew my duty. And he knew his. So he pecked his mouth to my cheek and said to me, "You're the one woman every man dreams of! You know a man's duty comes first!" — and then he shook my shoulder, and left. It was so beautiful, so beautiful the way he said it that I broke down and cried."

— "Did I cry too, my mam?" I asked. But old mam was gazing off into the blue, as if she were back there with him, and didn't answer me straight-out.

— "What's that son? What did you say?"

She had a clump of mud down on her knee, and I brushed this off. Her old skin was leathery and brown and there seemed to be mites running in her hair. This, or some trickery in the air.

She was giving my walls and the room the hard-eye.

— "Is this the best you can do, son? Why this room is hardly bigger than a burying hole. And look there! You've tracked dirt all over the floor. Don't you ever clean up?"

— "Down on my knees, mam, every evening. Down with soap and rag, just like you."

For old mam always had; she'd liked a place clean.

— "Not *last* evening, son."

— "No, old mam. Something must have come up."

— "Excuses won't get you into paradise, Adlai. I'm only glad your Daddy isn't here to see it. And that!" she said, pointing — "Who is that? That smoky-looking temptress up on your door?"

I made way to introduce my sweetheart Greta, but old mam was having none of it. "*Shame, baby, shame!*" she was saying. She stretched back groaning on the bed, letting her feet flop over the edge. She still wore the same ankle-high work boots that had mesmerized me in my childhood. They had the rot of thirty years messing about with turnips and spuds, a lifetime of kicking at grass and dandelion. The laces were covered with mold. The socks on her thin bones were both shoved down.

Old mam closed her eyes.

— "Are you going to take a nap, my mam?"

Greta was hissing at me to get that woman — "that *voh-mahn*" — out of here.

— "I never shut my eyes in the daytime," mam sadly replied. "No, nor sleep in the night-time either, if you want to know the truth."

— "Why not, my mam?"

She reached up — as though dreaming — and with a small sob stroked bent fingers across my cheek.

— "From worrying about you, son, the way I never had to worry about your Daddy, though I'm pained to say it."

— "Why's that, my mam?"

I crouched down, my face only inches from her bird-tracked skin. I was pained, too, and jumping with nerves. My mam looked a thousand years old, all helpless and withery and done-in. I wanted to fling myself down across her bosom, and moan. To say, *Old mam, what's happened to us?* For I had lost a day and my life was going nowhere — but where had hers gone? She smelled musty and — well, *moldy*, — as if she'd been put away in some high cupboard and left there a long time, and now had come down all wizened and crusty.

But I stayed still. I couldn't bring myself to hurt or confuse or embarrass old mam.

— "There are moments, son, when I think you don't care about your old mam. Moments when I wonder if you don't think I brought you up wrong. Times when I think you are holding me responsible for so much that goes on in this mean world."

— "I'd never think that," I said, half-horrified.

— "Or that you don't revere your Daddy, that you don't uphold his cause."

— "No mam!" I cried, "how could you think that?"

She was gripping my hand tightly, her mouth twitching. Her eyes boring up into mine. Yet she looked so ancient, so feeble, so ahead of or behind her times. Her brow as wrinkled as a scrub-board. The flesh so speckled. It was as though a flock of perky chickens had got loose to scratch at her skin, which sagged down over her bones — but all so thin it was practically translucent.

— "Oh don't look at my face!" she suddenly cried out. "Don't stare at me like that! I know what you're thinking! Know how you've turned against me! How you've come to hate your own flesh and blood!"

This speech utterly amazed me.

— "*Me?*" I said. "*Me*, my mam!"

For I'd always thought of us as close. As tight, I'd thought, as nectar and honey.

Mam sobbed. She rolled over, burying her head in the pillow. I eased down on my footlocker, shivering for her. Slowly stroking my hand up and down her backside. Saying, There, there, mam. There, there, good lady.

A fine little weave of bones was about all I could feel.

Her body felt cold. Cold and *icy*. And moist, too. And there arose again that smell, all earthy and wormy, as if she'd washed up from some foul pit or tomb, some ill and dank un-resting place.

— "Don't worry," I soothed her. "Don't trouble yourself, old mam. It was us together through thick and thin for all of those years. For *so many* years. And I tell you the truth, I never knew one from the other, never knew thick *from* thin, that was how much I knew I could count on your love. True, old mam. And it's how much you can count on mine now."

— "Do you mean it, Adlai?"

— "I do, mam. I sure-as-shooting do."

She clawed at my hand. Grappled my fingers up to her lips, and kissed them. "My man," she sobbed. "My little man. My comfort in this sick old age."

We had us a good cry.

And I think old mam might have dozed, for I saw her breath slacken, felt her bones soften and smooth out underneath my stroking hand. I might have dozed or day-dreamed myself — dappled off on beams of sunlight — for at any rate when I next blinked my eyes back to it the aura in the room seemed to have changed. It seemed as if not just minutes but hours, days, whole weeks, had tumbled by.

The dogs were setting up a din outside my window, snarling and yowling.

I could hear Mergentoire at the foot of the stairs, shouting up at me. Get off the pot! Quit slacking! Get a move on! Saying she wasn't holding breakfast all day. Not for the likes of me. Then growling at her son Hedgepolt. Telling him too to shake a leg.

Women. You'd think they were shot from the womb to ferret out wrongdoers and hobnail them to a pristine trail.

What a nag.

Greta was in a huff, down on her knees on the floor, going at the dry mud-tracks with a scrunched-up hat. At *my* mud-tracks, or so it appeared. For they had my hoof-print. But who? How come? Greta throwing up insults at me: *ape* this and *ape* that. She is such a puzzle, Greta is. Aloof much of the time, yet now ready to scratch out my eyes because I had let my own sweet mam walk in and take a moment's rest on my unmade bed.

Isn't Greta funny? I thought. Oh how I wish I knew what makes Greta tick!

But my stomach was growling; I needed my pancakes fast.

— "Mam? You feeling okay?"

Mam sat up, wiping her wet cheeks with the backside of one frail hand.

— "Oh," she said with a brave smile, "it was just like in the old days, us having that good cry. It has done my heart good."

— "Mine too, my mam."

She patted my head — "That's a good lamb!" — then hopped up spiry as a cat with four legs to catch herself and knowing she would. "Time's a battlefield, son," she gaily observed, "but thems that's got the backbone will whack through it to the other side."

— "I'm whacking, mam," I said. "I'm whacking hard."

Her eyes lit up; the old colour came back to her cheeks. "Yes, you got the backbone, the same as your Daddy did. I only hope you got his grit. That you're willing to stand up for what's-what."

— "I will, mam. You can count on me."

She came in for a big hug, and I could swear she lifted me right off the floor.

— "Don't get me wrong, son, what I was saying earlier. I'm not renouncing any of the ways you were raised. I don't apologize for swat. Right is right, and a mother has got to stick to that. No, it was just your Daddy's ghost preying on my mind. Me feeling low, wishing I could be with him. They broke the mold, you know, when they made him."

— "He stood tall, that he did."

She stared off, all misty-eyed. Her hands up to her temples, looking back to those days. "Poor man, it was the birth control that sapped him. Think of the pressure he lived under. Imagine the Upper Volta as it was the day he set foot there. Two hundred thousand Roman Catholics reproducing all over the place. They're like dogs, where two drop down ten more will pop up. So that was the RC's. And that's not to mention three million Mossis with the soles of their feet white as yours or mine and every bit as busy. Or half a million Lobis, another half-million Bobis, plus the thousands of itchy Gurunsis. Not one ever having heard of birth control until he came. And everyone black, black, black! The brightest sunshine makes no difference to a continent like that. Daytime or night-time, you'd never know it. That's what so many blacks can do to a country. Your Daddy had to walk about with a good Eveready just to tell one black hole from another, and hope he didn't fall in. A woman wanting a baby she'd fall down in a ditch and let the men poke at her. That's all there was to it, so your Daddy said. It makes you sick, don't it? Just thinking about it. It does me. But your Daddy was no cry-baby. He was not the man to tuck tail under his britches and run. No, he kept plugging. Kept singing the glories of birth control. He knew it was *us*, our very way of life, our very freedoms, that he was defending. He knew all about their matchstick canoes; knew they'd soon be finding their way across the water. That they'd take our jobs, gut our neighbourhoods, throw down and have their mean pleasure with our women!"

She stood trembling, radiant with his memory, yet sickened by the reality of that other vision.

— "I know it, my mam. I take my hat off to him the same as I take it off to you."

— "So I thumped my foot and said 'Go to it, Humpter. It's your job and you do it well.' "

— "He did it too, mam. He sure did."

Mam vacantly nodded, still trapped back there in time with him. I saw her little foot tapping; saw the worship flare in her eyes.

— "You were tops too, mam," I said. "You kept the home fires burning."

Mam smiled, in a drowsy, far-off way. Her voice went all wispy:

— "Now and then I'd get a sweet letter from him. 'Chalk up another one,' he'd say — and I'd know he'd saved another white child his rightful spot in the world. Another white boy his freedom. His job, his sweetheart, his neighbourhood. And I'd go down on my knees, saying: 'Bless him, bless him, bless Humpter, for that spot he's saved could be my Adlai's!' "

— "He did it too, my mam! He saved my spot! Except for him I bet this very minute some black man would be standing right here where I'm standing. That bed would be his, and the footlocker would be his, my barbells, and probably he'd even have Greta!"

But old mam had switched off. She was beginning to have that tuckered-out look again. She seemed to be fading.

— "It was always my hope," she said wanly, "that one day you'd take up your Daddy's mighty cudgel."

My head sagged down. I looked dumbly at my shoes.

— "I did, Adlai."

I had been dreading this remark since first she entered. I looked miserably at my dirty thumb-nails. Whimpering:

— "I'm sorry, my mam."

Mam stared right through me. Her tongue slashed like a lizard's:

— "As it is, you haven't even married. You don't even have children."

I saw Greta suck in her breath. Saw her face go scarlet.

— "Nary a one," continued mam. "No, you've let your spot, and your children's spots, go to some gang of unruly, howling blacks! You've let the blacks take charge!"

Old mam, I knew, did not mean to hurt. She was only expressing her disappointment in me. Telling me how my Daddy would hang his head.

— "But remember I'm whacking, mam! I'm whacking away. I've got Greta! I've got that Pole I was telling you about!"

But Mam wasn't listening. She was simply smiling her sad understanding at me. Smiling her sad, abandoned hope; letting me see how her dreams and my Daddy's dreams had got splattered by the whirlwind. She laughed, trying to lighten both our loads. "Thick and thin," she said, "It doesn't rain but it pours."

— "I'll shape up," I moaned. "I'll shape up yet!"

Mam was slowly buttoning up her coat. Her fingers were gnarled and spotted. The colour of oatmeal. Nothing but bones. Somehow the soot had got back on her nose. Her hair was like wires. Even as I looked, her finger-nails seemed to be growing. Her cheeks were sunken. She had on her favourite coat. The coat was faded and tatty and hung unevenly at her heels. I remembered that coat. She'd got it off some hook at the Bingo Parlour. She had the little gold locket around her neck. Heart-shaped. My Daddy's image would be on one side; I would be on the other. If unbeknownst to us, some black face hadn't jumped in.

She backed, groaning, out into the hall. Her finger beckoned to me. "Our kind is no more than a spit in the bucket," she said. "You remember that. It's all one big tub out there and what part isn't filled with blacks is stacked up to the brim with Chinese. It's overflowing with Poles and A-rabs and Indians and even Huguenots. That's another bunch your Daddy didn't like, them Huguenots. And the whirlwind's coming. But that don't mean we toss in the towel, does it, son?"

— "You bet!" I said. "You bet, my wonderful old mam!"

She was already vanishing. Holding up her old Victory fist.

— "One more thing, son. Get that tarty woman off your door."

Folding back into the wall, becoming the wall. Stumbling once or twice and then…gone. Yes, gone.

Yet I hung in the doorway, hoping for one final glimpse.

— "Mam?" I whispered. "Mam, are you still there?"

I ran over and kissed the wall. Put my cheek where her visage had been.

— "Mam?" I said. "Will I see you again?"

But she *was* gone. Wall or world, it had swallowed her up. And I stood trembling, pining for a sweet farewell. Longing for one unsullied word of love. Wanting total forgiveness — full recognition — from her.

Afraid — shivering with fear! — that my Daddy next would walk in.

Sighing. Unable to admit that what I wanted most was what I never could have. This: that *both* would leave me alone.

And Christ, which way *now* could I turn? For I wasn't out of these woods yet. I made out Mergentoire at the foot of the stairs, stomping the floor, shaking a spoon.

"I've told you!" she shouted. "Told you and told you! Breakfast this minute or you go hungry!" And spun off.

Hedgepolt, hidden away, was banging on pots and pans.

The dogs were nipping and yowling.

Inside my room Greta was heaping up rage. Barking out her scorn. Quite furious.

"*Kooom* here!" she ordered.

Defiant, sullen, raving Greta. My angry beloved. She'd come down out of her calendar to wipe up mud and listen to the prattle of old mam. To stride the cramped room, to whirl contemptuously about and with guttural, raking voice — dramatic as a blizzard — declare that she had never been so insulted, so humiliated. So violated and abused. *"Like dirt I am treated! Yes? No?"* To ask what kind of flea or toad was I, what creature, what snivelling worm, what formless, horrible, gamboling idiot? *Yes? No?* To ask how *"dot vohmahn"* could dare invade our privacy, rumple our sheets, question the way we conducted our lives. *"Who is dot death-hag to tell me I shood marry, I shood haf children! How dare she? Und did yoo see dot coat? Dose shoes? It's lunacy, sheer lunacy, und I, Greta Gustafsson, I moost put up with theece!"* To rail at the callousness, the bigotry, the inanity, the perversity — at the dim-witted nature of mankind in its totality and my blood-line in its particulars.

"Vy do I stay with yoo?" she shouted. "Vy do I make myself preet-tee? Vy did I ev-vair koom to theece half mahn, to theece child, theece mental deficient! Vot a place your room izz! Vot a stinkhole! I haf seen shoeboxes big-gair. Me, Greta, who has lived in palaces, who kood half kings with the krook of my fing-gair!"

"Oh!" she cried, galloping about, thumping her fists against my head, wrenching up and down. "O-O-O-Oh! De an-sair is only one. *Une!* Me, I am craze-eee too! Greta is birdbrain!"

This Stockholm beauty, what a flame-thrower! What acid! And how beautiful. How divine. How my heart soared to see her in this mood. Sultry. Passionate. Maddeningly dramatic. I had seen her a hundred times this way on the shimmering screen: breathing this fierce energy, this mystery, this power. A dynamo of unrelenting love. Yielding only *to* love, no matter how fatal. Love came first, above her very life. Her every performance insisting that love *was* life. That every risk was worth the taking. *Mata Hari. Camille. Ninotchka. Wild Orchids. The Blue Sea. The Yellow Bed. Anna Karenina.* — Garbo. My very own Garbo. The great Greta Lovisa Gustafsson. Yet never so in my little room. Always the cold shoulder, the blank stare, the senseless smouldering — elusive, self-absorbed, afraid of her shadow! *Above* life.

"Liar!" she now screeched. *"Yoo haf not loved me enough! I haf not vunted your idolization! I haf vunted to be loved as I am! As you haf loved your lunatic old mam! Greta does not vunt to be alone! She does not vunt alvays to be on de vall. Hold me, darling!"*

Oh Greta, Greta, Greta. This much I now knew of Greta, as I was coming to know it of myself: every encounter, including those only imagined, is an affair of the soul. Is cut-throat war. The soul is at vigil; it is in last-ditch battle. It is in armed conflict against the grinning dark, the waiting terror, the foul abyss. It holds off the stinking Hereafter. The soul would defend and preserve our tenuous and fleeting bones. This pitiful, slime-sinking body. Soul is heroic! It goes on warring despite impossible odds of stone and brick-bat and the immense conflagration, the high flames that ever sweep around it.

This I find remarkable.

Nothing else in life is so beautiful.

And Greta now accepted this, too. Greta was willing. *"Any-zing!"* she now wept. *"I vill do any-zing to hold your love! Even theece ugliest of rooms, theece flea-box, theece hole, theece dot! Let it be ours! Hold me, Adlai. Hold and kiss and save your demented Greta!"*

Oh, what a speech! My flesh tingled. Bells clanged in a thousand towers. For we were saving ourselves. We were discovering again that one body alone cannot hold back, cannot assuage, bend, or diffuse the wicked dark. The vile, thunderous, rampaging dark. One's frame falls apart, bones scatter, flesh flies apart like birds over water, but true love, true life, charges on. The bones explode, they mix with air and water, with air and flower, and when they come down they come down rearranged. Love, dreadful love, slouches in.

And so her lips plunged down on mine. The famous Garbo mouth burned, burned and parted. Our tongues slithered and slid like a hundred snakes uncoiling in a single wet hole. A wet, luscious, heavenly bog. We moaned — exultant! What a picnic! What a dreamy, wondrous, spine-tingling dark! What ecstasy! For mouth was nice, but mouth wasn't all. We locked limbs, we licked and scratched, we yowled and bit and spun. Howl, spit, and claw. What a whimpering, roaring, blood-boiling feast love is! The floor scraped at our elbows. Knees cooked. But our singing flesh went on multiplying. Steel replaced backbone. Fire replaced lips. Hands tugged and stroked, tongues slurped, our hips hummed. *Hmmmmmmmmmm!* Our hearts clanged like a Cyclops' thunderbolts. We crashed against the footlocker, kicked against wall, and came grappling — breathless! — up over it. We slithered as one onto the crumbling bed. The mattress sizzled. Smoke shot from my ears. The roof lifted right out of my skull. And still our tongues went on working. For mouth was nice but mouth wasn't all. Matters got deadly. The hum quickened. EEEEEEEEEEEE!!!

"I want you, Garbo!" I thundered.

"Dun't talk, idiot!"

We romped past passion, past love's fury, and settled in for holy worship of piquant — exquisite — lust. And I thought, as I have always thought: What a treasure woman is! What a world! What a dream-time! Oh, wow, Adlai, how lucky you are!

The first time.

The first time ever.

My baptism.

Soul's immersion.

Thus when it was over I still couldn't believe it. Impossible. Greta had wanted *me*? Pitiful me? I studied her sleeping body, amazed. Her little feet! What extraordinary toes! — like the curved white petals of flower. Her bent knees and the fingers so softy folded. How fragile she seemed. The chin tucked so childishly into her bosom. Her breath so faint, so sweet, so...*not there*...that I wanted to convey it into heaven on a quivering rainbow.

This dream had wanted me? Uncanny. No, it was beyond truth. Reality couldn't touch this.

But I touched her — one finger along the ribs — and knew that it had.

"All the news you want!" shouted the black vender. *"Get it here, boss!"*

I went at last down to breakfast.

Mergentoire and her son Hedgepolt sat at the massive table, alone but for each other and a sea of soiled dishes. The steaming atmosphere of daily exhaustion and a mother's eternal, despairing vigilance. What wreckage! Oh the appetite, the furnace-stoking, gut-storming wizardry of twenty hard-hat labourers at their meal! Reaching, sweating, chomping — packing in the fuel. My brusque, unroped companions from the mines, the factories, from field, ditch, and stable; our century's dogly warriors. Our last heroes.

Mergentoire was slumped low, brooding in half-doze, raking a hand idly up and down Hedgepolt's spine. The boy didn't hear me enter; he stayed limp as a rag. Mergentoire's eyes shifted grievously to me. "Here he is," she moaned. "The man who doesn't know what day it is. Who doesn't know today from tomorrow or yesterday from a mile of cotton candy." She looked away dreamily, scratching away at some itch under her bra strap. "How was the funeral?" she asked softly.

My eyebrows went up.

I sat down.

Mergentoire's mood underwent another subtle shifting. She glowered, hoisting a heavy arm in the direction of my room: "I could shoot you," she said, "for what you do up there."

I grinned sheepishly into my lap. My body was still humming: the hum was silent, but I yet had it. *Ummmmmmm.* Like ripples on a lake when the sky is becalmed.

Mergentoire sighed heavily. "Well," she said, "if there's anything left, feel free to gobble it up."

The bread dish was empty. The fruit dish was too. No eggs, no porridge. The coffee pot had six drops left in it.

I didn't mind. My stomach was motor-boating away but my head was off in dreamland. My thighs still had the quiver.

Mergentoire's voice softened again. "The old lady," she said, "I hope she went happy. I hope she'd made her peace with God."

I was studying Hedgepolt, who had a fly trapped in his hand. He opened his fingers slowly, but the fly remained as found. In his palm's centre, faintly buzzing, mindlessly grooming its ugly head.

Mergentoire and I stared at the fly. We stared at Hedgepolt as well, though it was the fly we kept returning to.

Hedgepolt poked a finger at the fly. The fly flipped over and lay on its back, unmoving.

"The old lady," murmured Mergentoire. "How did it go?"

But I hardly heard her. What about that? I was thinking: Hedgepolt has a pet fly.

"The funeral, you ape!" growled Mergentoire. "How did it go?"

The fly lifted, banking away.

"Did anyone come? Did she have flowers?"

Whoa, I thought. *Whoa*, Mergentoire. What gives here? For I knew not at all what she was talking about.

Yet, as I blinked at her my confusion, something tapped at my eyelids. A dim, grey shadow lifted on the previous day. The littered table gave way to rain-soaked ground.

Leaning headstones.

A black, snarling sky.

Rain thundering down.

My shoes sloshing through muck.

Wind whistling past my ears like shrieks from a shut-up thing.

Hedgepolt's sticky hand in mine.

Mergentoire saw something too. And looked to see if she could find evidence of it in my trembling hand. In my besotted eyes.

Whoa, I thought. Whoa, Mergentoire. Let's not go too fast.

— “I was up all night cleaning his shoes,” she said. “Lucky for you he didn't catch cold.” She eyed me shrewdly, raking a coil of hair back behind one ear. Tugging her housecoat up to her throat. “Well, I'm not the one to say it, and God forgive me, but what I say is you can count your blessings she's gone.”

Whoa, Mergentoire.

“I mean, she was *old*. I mean, she's out of her misery now.”

Hedgepolt, I noticed, was now studying me. His mouth opened a little wider. His eyes too. Drool coagulated around his chin.

“Hello, Hedgepolt,” I said.

He closed up his hand. The fly had returned.

I can't understand Hedgepolt and here's why: he looks to be every bit of thirty, yet he's still in grammar school. Still wears his trousers rolled to his knees, still has a runny nose. Can usually be found sucking on a filthy dishrag. I call it so; Mergentoire calls it his security cloth.

This morning he didn't have the cloth. His great head was slung out over the table like an ironing board. Studying me, when he should have been training his fly.

“Say good morning, Hedgepolt,” Mergentoire told him.

Hedgepolt blinked. His tongue slipped out. Slowly he dipped his head and began licking at a clear spot on the table.

I laughed, though his behaviour made me uneasy. This was regressive conditioning, it was backsliding. It went against the pact I had with him. Even so, I went on laughing. “Hey, Hedgepolt,” I said, “who's your mam?”

His eyes jiggled, he straightened rigidly in his seat — then his arm flopped up to point directly at me.

“Good old Hedgepolt,” I warmly murmured. Touched, as I always was, by this odd familial display. Such a good-hearted, agreeable lad, I thought. I leaned over and roughed his hair.

Mergentoire glared.

I ignored her crossness. We all have such days.

“It won't work,” she snapped. “It's time you faced up to things. The old lady — ”

But I cut her off. “The boy needs a haircut, “ I said. “He needs to give more attention to his appearance. One of these days old Hedgepolt is going to start thinking of girls.”

Mergentoire's face went red. She caught her breath. Her fists bunched up and her close little eyes stared angrily into mine. “Not under my roof he won't,” she said heatedly. “Not while I live and breathe!”

Hedgepolt was nodding excitedly, a grand smile on his face.

We had had talks, him and me. I'd set him straight on the birds and the bees.

"Look at him," I said. "He's ready right now. You do want a girlfriend, don't you, Hedgepolt?"

He was nodding as Mergentoire's fist slammed down. She was genuinely fed up now. "Stop saying that," she cried. "Stop dreaming dreams for my Hedgepolt! Quit giving him expectations!"

I thought: *Ah, that Mergentoire, what a case!* I thought: *Dream the dreams, Hedgepolt. Dare to be God!*

And Mergentoire's face drained. She rose up, clutching a fork, clutching the folds of her loose gown — fit to be tied. You'd think she had stepped right into my head: "So it's God now, is it?" she raged. "It's God you want him to be? When he can't even go to the bathroom by himself."

I thought: *Small stuff, Mergentoire*. Thought: *Poor Mergentoire*.

For Mergentoire disliked the interest I took in her boy. Hated the care I had taken in grooming this boy for a normal life. It alarmed her, our walks in the moonlight, our talking of birds and bees. The way he hung onto my every word. Nor could she admit to herself the long way he'd come, under my wing. *A sea of expectations*, I thought. *A sea for everyone*.

"God!" she shouted. "When he can't even tie his shoes? When he doesn't even know what shoes are for?"

Hedgepolt was crying. His wide thick shoulders shook and actual tears were splashing down. One quivering hand reached for the table-cloth. He tried stuffing that into his mouth. Terrible. Oh, what sounds. I knew he was suffering. I knew the hurt he felt. I ached with him. But a mere six months before this he'd been docile as a turnip patch. Empty. A vacuum. His face had never revealed the faintest expression, beyond a stony watching. He had never cried.

It hurt. But this was progress.

Mergentoire whimpered, embracing him, tugging his head to her bosom. "Don't cry," she whispered, sobbing herself. "Oh, don't cry. Mam's sorry. Mam got out on the wrong side of the bed this morning. Mam's sorry she raised her voice. Forgive your Mam? Forgive me, Hedgepolt? Mam would never hurt her Hedgepolt. Mam loves Hedgepolt."

Beautiful. I loved Mergentoire at her mothering.

"Let's see your fly again. Let Mam and Adlai see your nice fly."

They went on blubbering. And, yes, I did too. For I was remembering my own old mam. I was back there with her, my head on her bosom. Sobbing. Getting charlie horses in my gut from all the ache I was carrying.

— "There, there," she'd say. "You're thinking of him, aren't you, son? Of the good Daddy you've never seen? But don't cry. Don't blubber. You know your Daddy has got his work to do. Just as one day you'll have yours."

— "Will I, mam?"

— "Sure you will. Your spot is saved. It's waiting for you."

— "Mam? My mam? Did he ever try it out on you?"

— "Try what, my boy?"

— "His birth control."

— "Oh gracious. Goodness gracious. Oh course he did. I was the first."

— "But mam!"

— "It didn't take, son. Otherwise, would I have had you?"

— "I'm here, am I not, my mam? I'm *real*?"

— "Oh you're real, son."

— "Are you sorry, my mam? That I'm here?"

— "Now, son, don't cry! Don't blubber. Hold those shoulders back. Don't you want your Daddy to be proud of you?"

— "Will he be? Will I grow up to fill his fine shoes?"

— "Oh I doubt that. There can be only one of him. And there's this to think about: long before you've come of age the black tide will have swept over all of us."

— "But my *spot*, my mam!"

— "I've upset you, haven't I? There, there. Mam's sorry. Give a kiss to your potty, unthinking old mam. Mam got up on the wrong side of the bed today. That's it — give a smile to your old mam."

Dear wonderful mam. Dear comforting mam. She was aged then herself, and her back stiff from weeding spuds. From keeping together house and home. Between my Daddy and the bingo I was all she lived for.

— "Is that true, mam? Am I your pudding and pie?"

— "You're it, Adlai. The apple of my eye."

— "I wasn't dropped off on your doorstep? By some man on a black horse?"

Mam would get cross when I'd ask that. She'd get out what she said was my Daddy's old walking stick, and switch my behind.

— "Who's been telling you them stories? Putting these tales in your head."

For it was a fact I'd been hearing things. There was talk that mam wasn't all she said she was. That mam had never wed, for one, and that I'd come down the chimney like a chimney-black.

— "Lies! Lies! Don't listen to them."

But I'd been wondering. Not all I'd heard was going out of both ears.

— "They hint that I'm tar-brushed, old mam. That there's a tar-brush somewhere! That there's not smoke without fire!"

— "Hush! Hush! Don't even whisper it, child. Your Daddy is away yonder in the Upper Volta doing his work. You're making his ears burn."

But I'd find myself looking and wondering. For something else was occurring. Putting the heebie-jeebies on me. I'd look at mam's elbows and her knees. I'd look at her hands and feet. I'd examine her skin. I'd catch her with her housecoat undone and I'd think: *that's* strange. For it seemed to me mam's skin was changing. That her flesh was darkening with every day that went by.

— "What's happening, my mam?" I'd say. "What's happening to you?"

And mam would cover up her face, she'd shiver and shake.

— "It's old age!" she'd moan. "It's my…my Change! It…it's from thinking all the dark thoughts of a lifetime! It's…from having you!"

And I'd laugh. Old mam, what a joker.

But later I'd be looking in mirrors. In bed at night I'd be feeling my hair. A bit *stiff*, I'd think. A bit *wiry*. A bit on the black side.

And next day I'd nag at old mam. I'd say, Mam, don't you have a photo of my Daddy? Don't you have *one* picture of him?

Mam would thump her chest. "In here," she'd say. "In my heart, that's where your Daddy's photo is. And in yours, too, if you had any decency left."

Sweet, dear old mam. Her stick was hard on the behind, but she was ever straight with me.

The dogs' yowling, and not Hedgepolt's weeping, broke up my reverie. They'd come yowling three times around the house and twice up the nettle tree, and now had parked under the dining-room window to kick up dust and yowl all the harder. It was blood-curdling murder out there, with maybe a cat or two mixed in.

I nibbled on a toast scrap from the neighbouring plate. I licked on bacon rind found under the chair.

It didn't matter. Appetite was the last thing I had.

I was remembering a letter I'd received. *Dear Son. My spot's about used up. I'm slipping. Not long left now. Will you come? Can you do that for me?*

I hadn't gone. No, I'd let her dot fade right out.

August 11: anniversary of Blondin's crossing Niagara on a tightrope wire. And mam stretched out in a box on the rain-soaked ground.

"Do you love me, Hedgepolt?" Mergentoire was asking. "Do you love Mergentoire most in the world?" She had his head on her shoulder, was stroking his hair. Her voice soothing, even to me. "Your mam loves *you*," she said. "Adlai loves you too. We are all one big family." Her foot nudged mine under the table. "Tell him, Adlai. Tell him how happy we are."

For Hedgepolt's sake I managed a smile. A nice little nod of the head. "You bet," I said. "She's said a mouthful, son."

Hedgepolt's robe-chewing slackened. His eyes widened. His look swam from her to me. "Brace up, Hedgepolt," I said. "Life has its little monkey-wrenches, but you can follow my example."

And I sat erect, my shoulders back, my expression firm. Pretending I was looking intelligence at him. Happiness, too.

We sat a long time that way.

Strangely, his face shook loose of its idiocy until at last it became one radiant angel's smile.

"*Dad-dee*," he said.

Our jaws dropped. Hedgepolt had never been known to speak before.

"*Dad-dee*," he said again. And his arm flopped towards me. Then with more grace than I could believe he swung it around to point at Mergentoire. "*Mam-mee!*" He patted her head.

Mergentoire's lips quivered. Her eyes glazed over, then moistened. With a deep moan, half-sob, half-joy, she swooped her arms around him. But Hedgepolt's own arm kept on rising. His face was flushed, his heart pounding; I could see he was getting the hang on speech. "*Gret-ta*," he said. "*Gret-ta Gus*-TAFS-son!" He wheeled about, beaming. Dashing to the window. "*Dogs!*" he cried. "*Brutish, snarling dogs!*"

Mergentoire bolted up. We were both dazed. For a moment we shared an uncomprehending look. Then bliss streamed out of her pores. "*You're cured!*" shouted Mergentoire. "*Oh, Adlai, he's cured! My son is cured!*" She embraced him, lifted him off his feet, swirled him around. "*My baby! My baby's no baby no more!*" And she — and both of them — broke off into riotous laughter. They danced and hugged and jumped on the floor. But Hedgepolt was still wanting to talk. He was stammering in excitement, wanting to get it all out:

"Shoes!" he crowed. *"Adlai and Hedgepolt get shoes wet? Walk in muck? See old Mother? Throw flower in grave? Kiss old Mother goodby? Walk home in rain? Adlai hold Hedgepolt's hand?..."*

He spoke on, radiant. And joy, pure joy, in that moment seemed to serenade my bones. It seemed to seep up through my chair and to surge through me like light through a door. And it went on blazing. It went on rising. It shot up through the long table, rattling the dishes; it pulsed over our heads, and spun; it crashed up into the ceiling and went on rising; it crashed through our very walls and went on splashing and tumbling, whirling like a fireball through the atmosphere. Even the dogs, vicious that second before, fell silent. Joy rolled on, flooding the universe. And even then it swept on, shining and beautiful.

We were all in rapture.

"Adlai happy!" screeched Hedgepolt. *"Adlai happy for his old mother? He happy for Hedgepolt? He happy with world?"*

Hold on, I thought. Adlai, hold on.

For it wasn't mam I saw, or Hedgepolt's glee, or the two of us reeling over mam's sorrowful grave, or mud on our shoes. These were but a flick at the eyelids. Joy, purest joy, was shunting these aside. What I was seeing was deep water and over the mammoth face of that water legion upon legion of matchstick canoes and in those canoes a thousand black faces and those faces whooping delight at me the same as I was whooping it back at them. And nothing poor mam could do about it. One by one they were crying out, *I'm coming, I'm coming, make way for me! I'm going no place but* UP UP UP! Oh look at the Devil running! Flags I saw waving by the hundreds. There were the Upper Volta colours and beside it little Benin and Guinea-Bissau. Over there were Gabon and Cameroon, Ghana and the Ivory Coast. Here came Somalia and Djibouti and Botswana, Nigeria and Malawi and Kenya. And a great chorus was riding the waves: *We coming! We are coming, brother!*

Hold on, I thought. Hold on.

For I could hear myself shouting back, as if from a planet a breath's space removed: *Come on, you polecats! There are spots for all of us!* The Upper Volta ears picked up. Their eyes did a double-take. *Is that you, boss?* they asked. *Is that you? Is that the king?* And I gave them my biggest wave: *Come on! Come on! Git the lead out!* At this, the Mossis, the Lobis, even the itchy Gurunsis, scooped their hands into the water, rode the crests of waves, and came crashing forward. *We coming, boss!*

Crashing on past me as I sat rocking in my chair — in my chair or wherever my spot was — delirious in the face of this vision, wondering which was vision and which was real life and finally where it, or they, or even myself, had gone.

Something wet was licking my hand.

My scalp felt tingly.

This day, too, I thought, was slipping away from me. The light seemed eerie. Had I slipped forward into some future year? Adlai, where are you? Adlai is on his tightrope out over the swirling water, balanced between rope and sky, wavering and floundering with his balancing pole. Adlai steering for the river's other shore. Adlai saying Mam, are you there? Mam, will you forgive me? Adlai falling. Adlai crying. Then only the quivering rope and the crashing water there.

"You've done it, Adlai! Hooray for you!"

What's this, I thought. What's happening now? For Mergentoire was hugging me. Hedgepolt was hugging me. And I was hugging myself, too. I was trembling inside a rapture totally new and strange. What a mystery! Sweat dripped from my nose. Is this happiness? I asked.

I could hear Greta upstairs gaily chirping. Calling to me. "Adlai, come draw my bath. Come up and scrub my back and sit with me."

Mergentoire and Hedgepolt were silent. Their eyes rapt.

The dogs beneath the window were silent. Or gone. I thought I could see them racing as a pack down the long street to another place. Soon, perhaps, to splay off into green countryside.

I closed my eyes.

Peace.

Soul's ascension.

And mam's watchful eye splayed off, too. It went whirling away into the dark.

"Adlai, are you coming?" Greta called.

I had the strangest desire. I wanted to say to Greta: "Go home, honey. There are people at home who have need of you."

But I said nothing. I stayed on. Stayed, I say, as if bolted to my chair, as Hedgepolt's head lay warmly in my lap, and Mergentoire leaned against my knees, emptied of her joyful weeping. I sat on, thinking: So many people in the world depend on you. So many. Even if you're nothing — even if you're no one and you don't know which way to turn or whether turning is a thing you're capable of — even then they do.

Oh, mam, they do.

Commentary by
Leon Rooke

≈

Leon Rooke's writing excites us with its spirit and abundance. The following commentary is taken from an essay, "is you is or is you ain't my baby: canadian fiction against the headwinds", published in Brick: A Journal of Reviews 33 *(1988). Rooke invokes a host of purposes that literature may fulfil but emphasizes that none of these can be realized unless literature — like jazz, like life itself — retains the quality of improvisation.*

When I was a young reader/writer I wanted in literature encapsulation, directions, conclusions, findings, examples, aphorism, cutting observation, the vivid pie, syngenetic codes, insights capable of drawing blood, spears of meaning that could startle the secret plumbing and ravage the squatter heart. What *is* life about? This arrangement of nations divided by water and mountain, by barbed wire, as, above, the tumbling heavens give approving serenade. What justice through flight of blind stork, birth's accident, geography's giggle? ("How come these weird myths to our shore?") Love, hatred, it is up to what? I'm dumb, dumb, I said, I admit it, but you're the big cheese: there is nothing you don't know, no skin you cannot inhabit, no fiefdom or planet you cannot explore. If the world is round, if knowledge can be contained, you, little book, made it so. I wanted alchemy — and do yet. I wanted what I could not get enough of — and never can. The firmament keepers. Furnace stokers. Change my life, little book, I said. Orient me to the ways of woman to man and (wo)man to the universe, and the universe to — what? And don't, don't, I pray, let the historian's fumy cyclic theory obtain.

Acquaint me with night and day. Detail the urgent specifics. Inflame me, rapture me, open my flesh with words ("arranged in their proper sequence"). Reveal the unimpeachable truth. Please, I said, and all the better if you can let it sing.

In the rare and sporting book, ***Talk's Body*** (New York: Alfred A. Knopf, 1979), which excavates a theory of creative behaviour by meditation upon the elected objects within his environment —

life as improvisation (mind and memory navigating and/or assimilating the turning wheel) — jazz pianist David Sudnow gives this analysis of the phenomena of now: "When I listen to a Herbie Hancock piano solo, I listen with my hands. I can feel courses of melodies: my palms almost imperceptibly expand and contract, bursts of rapidity and repose make them tighten and relax; the fingers minutely follow the essential shapes and pacing of his improvisations. Most likely" (he continues) "you do not listen to the jazz piano player that way. There are 'parts of you' that do not participate in his movements. If you and I listen to a psychologist or a physiologist talk about hearing, where hearing is reduced to properties of the ear and decoding mechanisms of the brain, the difference between us is ignored. Either scientist might contrast us by saying that memory traces are present in my brain that do not exist in yours, or that habitual skills in pattern recognition are stored somehow in my nervous system but absent in yours, or that perhaps I have an internalized syntax which affords me a greater predictive capacity to hear likely forthcoming notes. In the reduction of the jazz solo to various typical sound-wave sequences and internal coding capabilities, a real communication between Herbie Hancock's hands and my hands goes unnoticed. But this is because the psychologist is not a piano player." I would risk contemptuousness if I drew attention to the parallels between this and the astute reader with a text. Sudnow defines language as "improvisationally choreographed courses of movements". Astute readers are aware that a piece of writing may be revised, and revised again a hundred times; they are largely unaware that, unless it has the air of improvisation — a thing rendered for the first time — it is apt to ring inauthentic and dull; it will have the familiarity of table salt.

SELECTED WORKS BY LEON ROOKE

Last One Home Sleeps in the Yellow Bed. Baton Rouge: Louisiana State University Press, 1968.

Vault: A Story in Three Parts. Northwood Narrows, NH: Lillabulero Press, 1973.

The Love Parlour: Stories. Ottawa: Oberon Press, 1977.

The Broad Back of the Angel. New York: Fiction Collective, 1977.

Cry Evil. Ottawa: Oberon Press, 1980.

Death Suite. Downsview, ON: ECW Press, 1981.

The Birth Control King of the Upper Volta. Downsview, ON: ECW Press, 1982.

Sing Me No Love Songs I'll Say You No Prayers: Selected Stories. New York: The Ecco Press, 1984.

A Bolt of White Cloth. Don Mills, ON: Stoddart Publishing, 1984. New York: The Ecco Press, 1985.

How I Saved The Province. Lantzville, BC: Oolichan Books, 1989.

The Happiness of Others. Erin, ON: The Porcupine's Quill, 1991.

Who Do You Love?: Stories. Toronto: McClelland & Stewart, 1992.

Audrey Thomas

≈

In the introduction to the Audrey Thomas issue of *Room of One's Own* published in 1986, Eleanor Wachtel wrote about Audrey Thomas's subject matter: "Audrey Thomas has become a sophisticated chronicler of the failure of modern relationships, without overlooking the fall-out from these exploded marriages, the children — the apex of contemporary triangles. Connection between men and women fails because the ties between individuals are unequal. Increasingly, as women seize power, or come to subtly assume it from vain, weak men, the relationships dissolve, or last only as long as the women maintain a charade of male dominance."

About Audrey Thomas's style, she wrote: "Increasingly, the work reflects a relaxed Audrey Thomas, leaning over the kitchen table: a raconteur who seems to ramble until the strands suddenly draw together like a net. A carefully crafted casualness enlivened by a fascination with language, dialogue, foreign words and their origins, an acuity of observation."

Both of these quotations raise matter for debate about Audrey Thomas's writing. In the question of her portrayal of modern relationships, is she "a sophisticated chronicler" or is she a propagandist? In the question of her style, is it "carefully crafted casualness" or is it loose rambling? And are the stories "enlivened" by discussions on etymology or might these discussions be seen as discursive intrusions?

Lorraine M. York in an essay entitled "Audrey Thomas" in *Profiles in Canadian Literature*, vol. 8 summarizes poet Dorothy Livesay's comments in an interview "that writers like Thomas, who were exploring women's issues, especially that of women's powerlessness in society, were somehow singing a one-note song, and that they should really be writing about all human beings". Lorraine York continues: "This notion is a familiar one, popping up in readers' responses to writers like Thomas, Margaret Atwood, and Marian Engel; in the minds of some readers, at least, to write about women is to write about the marginal, the frivolous or self-indulgent. And when the writer uses the details of her life as ingredients in her fiction, as Thomas does, this objection is compounded: how dare the writer use the novel or short story to thrash out her own problems?"

In "An Open Letter to Dorothy Livesay", published in *Room of One's Own* in 1980, Audrey Thomas addressed Dorothy Livesay's charges: "But I am a part of the political and economic events of my time, just as Virginia Woolf was (*Mrs. Dalloway*) or Jane Austen or Mrs. Humphrey Ward or Susanah [sic] Moodie or whoever. They are reflected in my work *of necessity*. ... I do not march in marches or wave banners but I have raised/am raising three daughters and I have taught and in both instances I have tried to express openly, verbally, and by example, how I feel about the world we live in."

She has also written in the introduction to *Goodbye Harold, Good Luck* (1986): "Recently I heard the South African writer André Brink speak at Edinburgh University. He said, 'The writer who writes to promote a cause would do better to embrace politics openly.' I believe this wholeheartedly. ... I consider myself a feminist but I do not, consciously, think about feminism when I am making a story."

Obviously, a feminist viewpoint itself is not the issue here; to varying degrees, Margaret Atwood, Alice Munro, and Mavis Gallant also write from a feminist viewpoint. The issue is one of didacticism, of axe-grinding. Does Audrey Thomas chronicle in a sophisticated way or does she propagandize? Does she paint or does she illustrate?

Painting or illustration?

It would be instructive to read a few stories with this question in mind: the title story of *Goodbye Harold, Good Luck*, say, along with "Crossing the Rubicon" and "Natural History" from *Real Mothers* (1981).

Carefully crafted casualness or loose rambling?

Consider such stories as "Natural History" from *Real Mothers*, "Initram" from *Ladies & Escorts* (1977), and "The Dance" from *Goodbye Harold, Good Luck*.

From her very first collection, *Ten Green Bottles* (1967), Audrey Thomas has veered between conventionally shaped stories and stories which push at the conventions. I've never been comfortable with such early experiments as "If One Green Bottle...", finding the fragmented style too irritating to read; I've always preferred the much more conventionally shaped stories in the same collection, like "Xanadu". But her impulse to escape the conventional shapes was undoubtedly the right impulse — though I still prefer her work when it is under tight formal control and therefore charged with greater emotional power, as it is in the two stories included here: "The More Little Mummy in the World" from *Ladies & Escorts* and "Local Customs" from *Goodbye Harold, Good Luck*.

Characteristically, the shape to which Audrey Thomas seems to have escaped is the collage. Why, I wonder, is it that collage seems so suited to her talent?

≈

Barbara Godard in her monograph *Audrey Thomas and Her Works* (Toronto: ECW Press, 1989) and Lorraine M. York in her article "Audrey Thomas" in *Profiles in Canadian Literature*, vol. 8 (Toronto: Dundurn Press, 1991) offer useful commentaries. George Bowering has published an essay, "Snow Red: The Short Stories of Audrey Thomas", in *Open Letter* 3rd ser. 5 (1976); he has also published "Songs & Wisdom: an interview with Audrey Thomas" in *Open Letter* 4th ser. 3 (1979). *Room of One's Own* 10.3–4 (1986) is devoted entirely to Audrey Thomas's work and includes a variety of responses to it along with an important interview by Eleanor Wachtel.

THE MORE LITTLE MUMMY ≈ IN THE WORLD ≈

Oscar A. Lempe
Denver, Color U.S.   14-V-1876
23-XI-1958
Guanauato, Gto.
Recuerdo de Su Esposa
Chijas
Perpetuidad

Louis Montgomery Allen Sr.
New York City   Dec. 6-1887
Feb. 12-1957
Guanauato, Gto.
Perpetuidad

Handprints on this one — of whom? *Su esposa? Su hermosa?* A passing, naughty, unrelated child?

Elisabeth Carnes Allen, D.A.R.

She wandered through the cemetery looking at every stone, imagining the people, what had brought them there, what the town had been like nearly a hundred years before. The lure of what riches? The silver mines perhaps.

Everywhere there were flowers stuck in tins — Mobil Oil tins, paint tins, tomatoes, green chillies:

Chiles Jalapenos, En Escapbeche

She took out her pocket dictionary.

The wind blowing through the cypress trees rattled the tins like bones.

To My Beloved Wife
Maria Concepcion Buchnan

Although there had been a long line-up to see the mummies there were very few people in the Pantheon itself. A young couple with their arms around one another, laughing, exchanging kisses, some old women in black, a gardener. And the dead of course, the multitude of dead stacked six or seven high. The soft brown hills beyond and El Pipla, the boy hero, alone on a hill above the Jardin de la Union, his arm upraised.

Ayer (yesterday). *Hoy* (today).
Manana

Mother
Lily Mast McBride
Born Sept. 19-1882
Died July 22-1926

A pretty blue-grey stone, this one, beautifully incised.

It was very peaceful here with the wreaths, the plastic flowers and the real — gladioli, lilies — the white ones she saw everywhere here, Easter lilies back home — geraniums, carnations. The flowers dead too of course, or dying, sucking up the last dregs of rusty water from the tins. Still, she liked this place better than the churches with their bleeding Christs, their oppressive smell of hot wax, their plaster damned pleading to her for one last chance at salvation.

Some stones were casually propped against still-occupied cabinets. (They couldn't be called tombs and she couldn't think of a better word than "cabinet" — cabin, verb, to confine in a small space, cramp). She turned one over.

Naci Inocente!...
Muero Ignorante
Freyre Jose E.
V-7-1925
Perpetuidad

So much for *perpetuidad*!

She had been thinking of failures and suicides and had gone to mass on Palm Sunday in the hopes of finding something positive — if only for a second, if only for an instant, if only, even, an aura or a whiff of hope for her salvation.

Buenos dias. Adios.

She straightened a tin of gladioli which had fallen over in the wind.

Outside the Parroquia women and men were braiding palms into elaborate patterns. She bought a small crucifix and went in, covering her head, but the Mass was a disappointment. She stood up. She sat down. She prayed. The priest was way way way up in the chancel. Little bells rang. There was no pageantry, no music, nothing to draw her spirit up and away from the deep well of despair into which it seemed to have fallen. Over the words of the priest a poem of Yeats' kept running through her mind:

> That is no country for old men. The young
> In one another's arms, birds in the trees
> — Those dying generations — at their song,
> The salmon-falls, the mackerel-crowded seas,
> Fish, flesh, or fowl, commend all summer long
> Whatever is begotten, born, and dies.

They had been going to come down here together. Had maps, dreams, destinations. Even a tape:

> *Siento molestarle!*
> *No es ninguna molestia!*
> *Salud!*

How much too much please thank you don't mention it.

Instead he took her out (at her request) the night before she left. To a Greek restaurant (again at her request). She drank a lot of wine, and crumbling a bit of bread between her fingers, told him it was she all along whom he really loved.

"Do you think so?" he said and smiled at her over his wine glass. Then in an offhand manner he asked her if she'd ever been in any of the other Greek restaurants along the street, places where you just walked in and took whatever was going, places where the Greeks themselves went, cheaper places than this. (And he, who never went into a restaurant alone, whom had he lingered with in a small café full of the smell of lamb and garlic and the whine of recorded music. Who? Don't ask, or, as he would have put it, "why humiliate yourself?") He had always been Machiavellian; had always known how to put her in her place.

Once they had been at the house of his best friend and contemporary, Peter:

"I was coming in on the bus from the island," her lover said, "toward sunset — a beautiful evening. Suddenly I looked up and there was this incredible cloud formation — incredible! I said to the fellow next to me, without really thinking about it, you know, 'My God, that looks just like the Mushroom Cloud!' I saw the guy look at me and give a little frown and then I realized with a start that he was younger, younger than the Bomb — that he didn't even know what I was talking about. The only mushroom cloud he knew was psilocybin!"

Peter had laughed appreciatively. He was 35.

"It's true. People talk about the generation gap — as a metaphor I mean — but it seems to me there's a real gap — I almost see it as a physical space — between those born before or during the war and those born after it."

"Yes. There's a point at which Rachel and I just can't communicate; we were born into two different worlds." He had turned to her. "When I talk about Marlene Dietrich I don't know if you even know who I mean."

She was immediately defensive. He had wanted her to be, had set her up.

"Of course I know who Marlene Dietrich is."

"Ah yes — you know her name. But is your Marlene Dietrich the same as mine — I doubt it." Peter nodded and began singing "Lili Marlene." Her lover sat back and lit his pipe.

That night at the Greek restaurant he had given her a handsome present — a shoulderbag with three sections, or pouches, like a saddlebag.

"Now you will have three places to put all your clutter," he said, "instead of just one." ("It's not that she doesn't have a place for everything," he said once, at a party, "it's that she has several places." He was very tidy and they fought about the missing cap to the toothpaste.)

Buenos dias. Adios. No comprendo.

In one place there were freshly-dug graves, four in a row, an accident perhaps. This in a courtyard which led to a view of the city. Bougainvillaea had been splashed against the walls, the original purple and the scarlet, blood-coloured. In the distance she could hear the sound of children's voices.

Estoy esperando un paquete.
Lo tiene usted aqui?

When he came to get her at the hospital he was very brusque and efficient, annoyed that she was still in bed and crying. His sons were in the car — they were going camping. Yet still she wanted to buy him gifts — an onyx chess set, a heavy silver ring, a blanket for his bed. Things of beauty and whimsy, things that would make him think of her, remember her and want her.

Donde este? Where is?

He had told her there was nothing wrong, that maybe she should see a shrink. The gifts would only embarrass him. When she began to cry at the bus station, he kissed her quickly on the forehead and then walked away. She hated him; no, she loved him.

She had read in the guidebook that if the rent was not kept up on the crypts (yes, that was the word she had been searching for), the bodies were removed after five years and the bones thrown into a common bone-house to make room for new arrivals. But the region was very dry and some of the bodies would be mummified. When they were, they were put into the museum. Directly outside the cemetery were souvenir stands — skeletons, on horseback or playing fiddles or dancing, with springy arms and legs. Postcards of the mummies, earthenware, bone letter-openers and crochet hooks (human bone?). There were mummies of pale beige toffee with raisin eyes. These were wrapped in red or yellow cellophane. As she approached a man had offered her two large ones in one packet, "*Momias Matrimonias,*" and laughed at her discomfort. Now she was trying to get up enough courage to go into the mummy museum itself.

Death and disease were accepted here. Death was even made fun of, made into toffee to chew or chocolate to lick or tiny plaster figures to decorate, along with gilded pictures of miraculous virgins, the windows and mirrors of buses and cars. She knew now that almost certainly, whenever she saw a street musician, either he was blind or lame or leprous or there was a terribly deformed creature, just out of sight, on behalf of whom he was playing his music.

Her operation had been therapeutic and therefore covered by her insurance. No back streets or borrowed money — things were easier now.

Ayer (yesterday). *Hoy* (today).
Manana

This was a very strange town to walk around in and easy to get lost. The main road ran underneath the town in places, reappearing above ground several hundred yards beyond. It was really a stone-arched tunnel and rather frightening. And there were six or seven main squares, not just one. She had already, in spite of her map, been lost several times. The night before, wandering steep alleys full of wrought-iron balconies, she had stumbled upon a strange religious ceremony in one of the smaller lamplit squares. There were bleachers set out and many of the people were already seated, men, women and children, facing an old church. The church bell began to ring and then a priest appeared high up on the church steps, intoning Hail Marys and Our Fathers. And she understood a bit of it, the history of the week leading up to the arrest of Jesus. Below the steps stood men in purple sackcloth and black hoods, very mediaeval and frightening. A lifesized statue of Christ (looking not unlike the "Jesu Christo Superstare" she had seen in Mexico City) was brought out of the church by more hooded men, carried down the steep steps and put on a flower-decked platform. There was a rope around his neck and it hung down his back, binding his hands behind him. A child-angel and one of the masked men climbed up and sat on either side of him. Torches were lit and as the rest of the masked men shouldered their burden the crowd gave a deep moan of pity and anticipation. The statue had real hair and jointed, movable arms. He terrified her, for he hovered somewhere in a strange space between icon and the living god. The wind blew his hair across his gentle, accepting face. His gown was purple like the garments of the men but his was of velvet, not hemp. A workman beat a drum and the entire affair — Christ, angel, masked men, flowers, scaffolding, torches, priest — began to move. A young boy followed behind, playing a simple pipe and the procession slowly moved out from the small square into the larger one beyond. Behind came small children, some on tricycles, the women in black, the men, balloon sellers, a thin brown pariah dog. The bowed, bound figure of Christ rode above them all. It was amateurish in a way but very powerful; she hid herself in the crowd.

Por que? Why? *No se.* I don't know.
Perdone.

It was as though once she had decided she didn't want it he had washed his hands of the whole affair.

"Ruth Barnes"

Just a small stone marker with a dried-up geranium obscuring the date. Presumably to be buried in this small courtyard was more expensive than to be deposited on the shelves. The wind blowing rattled the tins like bones.

If he were here he would have struck up a friendship with the gardener, would try out the little Spanish he knew and supplement it with laughter and broad gestures. His energy was one of the first things that had excited her. And his keen intelligence, his learning, the whole sum of his life experience. He had been married (twice), had children (one as old as her youngest sister), had suffered and taken chances.

"I find it impossible to live alone," he had said to her the first night, "and yet somehow I always seem to fuck it up — my relationships with women." He showed her pictures of his sons and took her home to bed.

Dispenseme. Excuse me.
Muchas gracias.

Everywhere down here men followed her and tried to feel her up — a woman alone deserved to be treated that way. Then they gave their paycheques to their mothers and went to mass on Sunday.

Hail Mary Full of Grace Blessed is
The Fruit of Thy Womb Jesus

On the train from Nuevo Laredo she had met a middle-aged man who lived in San Miguel. He said the happiest day of his life was the day when they nailed his wife's coffin shut. Federales came on the train looking for contraband. They wore their revolvers tucked into the back of their pants, Pancho Villa style.

"Watch for the Mordida," the American said.

She shook her head.

"'The Bite.' To force someone to give you a bribe. It's a game between the Federales and the people coming back."

Was that what she had done by getting pregnant? Put the bite on him?

The boy-hero stood unconcerned on the distant hill, his arm upraised forever. Her first day in the town she had followed the crude signs and climbed steep stairs and back alleys until she reached the top of that hill. She had taken some bread and fruit with her and sat in a little summer house just below the enormous figure, eating slices of pineapple and writing in her journal. The boy had set fire to the granary in which the Royalists had barricaded themselves. At his feet it said, in Spanish,

"There are still other castles to burn."

She felt quite happy there, after her climb, the whole town at her feet. But in the evening, at a band concert in the Jardin de la Union, she sat on a wrought-iron bench and longed to have him with her, next to her, observing, commenting, loving. Canaries mocked her from the laurel trees around the square.

Where is? *No comprendo.*

She retraced her steps, back through the main courtyard with all its stacked and silent dead, back through the black iron gate with its simple cross on top. There were very few people in line now so there was no reason not to wait.

He had been quite calm when she told him. Just said, "Well, what do you want to do about it?" He left it entirely up to her. Had she wanted him to be otherwise? Had she wanted to bear his child? She wanted to be a writer, a poet — had he not encouraged her, sung her praises? In Chapultapec Park in Mexico City she sat on the grass one Sunday and watched the fathers spoil their children. They were immaculate — it was the mothers, of course, who saw to that. There were funny animal heads on the trash cans in the children's playground. The children laughed and squealed when they stuck their little hands in.

She paid her five pesos and went into the mummy museum.

In Chapultapec Park she had sat on the grass and wept. She wanted to be six years old in a white dress and riding on her father's shoulders, her small hands tugging at his curly hair. She wanted to be held and to be forgiven. She wanted a red balloon.

Her mother was at home making a delicious Sunday dinner.

Ayer. (yesterday). *Hoy* (today).
Manana.

The mummy museum was really a long artificially-lit corridor with the mummies displayed in glass cases along one side. The corridor was hot and very crowded, so that for a moment she experienced a wave of claustrophobia and almost turned around and ran.

Some of the names and dates on the stones had simply been scrawled in the wet plaster.

Aristo Perez
Manuel Torres M.
Maria de los Angeles Rodriguez

So there were the mummies, in glass cases like curios — which of course they were. Most were without clothes, jaundice-coloured and hideously wrinkled. A few had on mouldy shoes and there was one man who had on a complete suit of tattered black clothes. Very few had hair and this surprised her. Was it just an old wives' tale that the hair would keep on growing?

He read her, one night, from John Donne's "The Funerall"

Who ever comes to shroud me, do not harme
        Nor question much
That subtile wreath of haire, which crowns my arme;

and from "A Feaver"

Oh doe not die, for I shall hate
  All women so, when thou art gone,
That thee I shall not celebrate,
  When I remember, thou wast one.

She got up and cut off a lock of her hair and gave it to him; he kissed her neck and put the lock in the back of his grandfather's gold watch.

Donde este? Where is?

The mummies' faces were full of anger and terror. Shrinkage had pulled their mouths open and their hands were clutched across their empty bellies. Her Spanish was not quick enough to understand everything the guides were saying, but there were abnormalities and tumours and other curious things being pointed out as they moved along. The mummies were tall or short, male and female, the men's papery genitals still visible, the women's wrinkled breasts.

She wrote him letter after letter and tore them all up.

Quiero comprar una postal. I wish to buy a postcard.

As she crossed the street to his car and his waiting sons, she stumbled, still drugged and swollen-eyed, against the curb, and turned her ankle. Suddenly she had to sit down on the grass and put her head between her knees. She knew the boys, his sons, were watching her. What had he said to them? Why had he brought them to the hospital? What was he trying to say?

People with limps, people with no legs, blind people, lepers, pariah dogs. The country swarmed with outcasts and with cripples. The tourists bought silver rings and onyx chess sets and turned their heads away. After all, it was not their problem. Charity begins....

"They hate us," the American man had said. "They want our money but they hate us. They would prefer if we just mailed it down."

Almost at the end of the corridor was a display case full of child mummies — some in christening gowns and bonnets, some naked or wrapped in tiny shrouds. In front of the smallest of these a cardboard sign was propped. She pushed closer, in order to read it, then tugged at the guide's elbow.

"Please. *Por favor.* What does the sign say? *Que quiere decir?*"

"*La Momia Mas Pequena del mundo.*" He smiled at her, showing perfect teeth.

"*Si. Si.* In English. *Habla Usted Inglis?*"

"*Ah. Inglis.*"

He smiled again.

"The more little mummy in the world."

It sat there, no bigger than the rubber babies she had played with as a child.

Where were the parents? Why had these children been removed to this terrible glass limbo? She looked at la momia mas Pequena but it refused to answer.

The American had asked her to come and spend a few days with him in San Miguel.

She pushed her way through the tourists and out the exit door. The sun struck her like a slap. She half-ran, half-walked toward the souvenir stands, rummaged quickly through the cards until she found the one she was looking for, the one she knew was certain to be there.

Back at the apartment he had said, "D'you think you could rustle us up some dinner — we'd like to get away before dark." The boys were looking at her curiously. She went into the bedroom and began to pack, tears running down her face, the little plastic hospital bracelet still locked around her wrist.

Go. Come. Are you ready?

Don't forget.

She fumbled in her bag for the change purse, then headed back down the hill. Tonight, drinking her cho-ko-la-tay in that little restaurant near the Plazuela where she had seen the Christ, she would get out the card and address it.

"Having a wonderful time," she would write.

"Wish you were here."

≈ LOCAL CUSTOMS ≈

Years from now will he say to himself, "the breasts of that American girl had a bloom on them, like grapes." A combination of sun oil and the blowing sand, of course, but magic then, magic and terrifying to the twelve-year-old boy who was trying to look and not to look, both at the same time. Years from now will he perhaps rub his thumb and two fingers together and smile? As though he had actually touched them instead of merely staring across at her from his usual observation post under the dusty tamarisk tree. She and her friend are talking to the blind man, who lies propped on one elbow, on his suncot, not looking at either girl but somewhere off to one side. This has nothing to do with modesty; the blind man never looks at the people to whom he is talking. The wind and the fifteen yards between them keep Edward from hearing the conversation, but every so often he hears the blind man laugh and say "We Churmans, ha ha ha, we Churmans." His second day on the beach, Edward chased a newspaper which was blowing away in the wind. He brought the runaway pages to a middle-aged man, very tanned, who was sitting under one of the beach umbrellas. The paper was in German but Edward knew that most Germans spoke English. "Is this your paper?" he said, embarrassed by his high, thin, schoolboy voice. The man frowned in his direction.

"Bitte?"

"Your paper." Edward thrust it at the man.

"Ah, the newspaper. My wife's newspaper, I am afraid. I am blind."

Edward could just make out the shape of the man's eyes behind the thick dark glasses.

That day at lunch Anna said, "I wonder what's the matter with that man? It looks as though there's something wrong with his legs." Edward's father was reading a book, reaching absently for a forkful of salad from time to time. Edward took after his father; they were both long and thin and had the kind of skin that did not tan. Anna was his father's girlfriend.

"Who?" said Edward's father, not looking up.

"The German man over there, with the wife who is always smiling. She holds onto him — or rather, he holds onto her — wherever they go. She pretty well has to stand him up and sit him down."

"He's blind," Edward said. "He told me so this morning."

"Ah, so." Anna nodded her head at him and smiled. She had big white even teeth and was very pretty. Edward liked her in spite of himself. She was almost always willing to play cards or backgammon with him and she never called him Teddy, the way his mother did. ("Teddy's being so difficult lately," he heard her say, talking on the telephone to one of her friends. And then, "like father, like son.") And he knew Anna had nightmares. The walls between the rooms were thin and he had heard her crying out and moaning in the night. Edward knew a lot about bad dreams.

"His wife is Greek," Edward said, "but they've lived in Germany for years and years. She inherited a house in one of the villages, so they come here in the summer. They also have a house in Munich and a chalet in the Austrian alps."

"You are very good at finding things out," Anna said.

"Not really. He likes to talk."

And it was true — the blind man liked to talk. In English, in German, in bad Greek. From the time they arrived in the morning, his wife driving the white Mercedes, until they left in the late afternoon, the blind man lay on his suncot and talked to anyone who would listen. His wife, in a black bathing suit, her dark hair pulled into a low knot at the back of her neck, made trips across the beach and up to the café-bar for bottles of cold water and glasses of iced coffee. It was hard to tell how old she was, with her smooth brown skin and calm, untroubled face. She seemed to smile at everyone and had a special smile and greeting for Edward ever since he had rescued her newspaper. Twice a day she took her husband's hand and led him into the blue water, where they stood side by side up to their necks, facing the open sea for perhaps ten minutes. Then they turned and walked slowly back to their place under the beach umbrella. She handed him his towel and got him settled and went back for a swim on her own. She was a very strong swimmer and one day Edward had a strange thought. What if she got fed up looking after her husband and simply swam away?

In the last few days the wind has gotten worse. The umbrella man has stopped renting out umbrellas because the wind just knocks them out of their stands. "*Oxi*," he said, "no," shaking his head this morning at Edward, who likes to help with the umbrellas and cots, lining them up very early and then collecting the money from the people who want to rent them. One hundred drachmas for an umbrella, fifty drachmas each for a cot.

"*Kaputt*," the umbrella man says, "*verstehen?*"

"I'm *not German*," Edward insists, but the umbrella man ignores this and always addresses him as though he were. Although Edward knows perfectly well that there were good Germans and bad

Germans during the Second World War it upsets him to actually be mistaken for one. Anna said once that she couldn't understand how the Greeks could bear to see a German without wanting to put a bullet through his head.

For three days now the wind has howled all night, rattling the louvred doors and windows in the hotel bedrooms, blowing sand into all the corners. A forest fire is raging in the north. All the young men from the northern villages have been conscripted to fight the fire. Big-bellied water bombers fly back and forth all day. Dmitri, Edward's friend who owns the hotel and café-bar, tells him that some of the islanders are saying it was the tourists who caused the fire but that this isn't true. Last year's fire was started by an old man burning brush in his field and this year's was probably caused by lightning.

"Or maybe the government starts it, who knows?"

Edward does not understand. Dmitri likes him because he collects all the empty bottles from the beach and generally makes himself useful. Dmitri doesn't mind Edward asking him questions.

"Why would the government start a fire?"

"Take people's mind from politics, from troubles." Edward still doesn't understand. It is a small island; sometimes, in the evenings, you can smell the forests burning in the north. The sunsets are spectacular.

Empty containers for Manhattan Ice-Cream, Tartuffo Gelato Italiano, Coke bottles, Sprite bottles, Pizz lemonade, beer, water bottles, Marlboro packets: during the night the wind sweeps all the rubbish into heaps against the low stone wall which separates the beach from the café and the parking lot in front of the small hotel. By 7:00 A.M. Edward has had his first swim of the day and is sorting through the rubbish. If he finds bits of broken glass, or bottle caps, he places them carefully in a plastic bag.

"You good boy," Dmitri says, "maybe you no go back to England. You stay here with me."

Dmitri isn't married. Everybody thinks, at first, that his sister Fotula is his wife. It is really Fotula who owns the place; property here is passed on to the daughters, not the sons. Dmmi, as his friends and family call him, spent five years working in restaurants in New Jersey and Montreal, living in cheap boarding houses and sending money back so that Fotula could build the thirteen-room hotel. In return she sent him photographs of how the work was coming on. Anna has the pink card which advertises the hotel pasted in her diary:

NEAR BEACH RESTAURANT
PERA AMMOS
IF YOU ENJOY SWIMMING AND PINETREES
SURROUNDING IS NO BETTER PLACE

Dmmi and Fotula wear T-shirts made for them by a satisfied client. PERA AMMOS they say, GOLDEN SANDS BEACH RESORT. On the glass case in front of the bar are a lot of pictures of Dmmi in his T-shirt, with his arm around various pretty girls. He says to Edward, "You think I should make new T-shirt? 'Fotula is no my wife'?" He is a handsome dark-haired man of about forty-five. At least Anna says he is handsome; Edward notices he is getting a fat belly.

The whole family works at one job or another about the place. No matter how early Edward arrives with his sack of bottles, the old granny, the *yia yia*, is already sitting on a straight chair on one side of the door to the kitchen, stuffing tomatoes or green peppers, stringing beans. The old grandpa sits on the other side peeling an enormous pan of potatoes. Dmitri and Fotula's older brother, who is a bit simple, sweeps up and waits on tables. A handsome nephew runs the gift shop and even the umbrella man is some sort of relation. The older brother and his wife, who is the chambermaid, have two naughty children who are alternately kissed and slapped. They hold up the wet sheets for their mother to hang on the line, and fall asleep, in the evenings, on their granny's lap.

Edward is an only child. Since the divorce, his parents never speak to one another except over the telephone, and his grandparents live in distant cities. He has already been a boarder at school for three years.

"You think I should get a wife?" Dmitri says to Edward one day. "Maybe nice English womans?" They are busy setting out chairs and wiping down tables. Edward smiles but doesn't answer. If he had thought Dmitri was Fotula's husband, Dmitri had thought Anna was Edward's older sister. He had shown them to the same room. Anna had thought this was very funny.

On the beach an Englishman walks by; he is big and boisterous and wears a black T-shirt with CATS printed on one side, two green cat's eyes on the other. "I say," he calls to no one in particular, certainly not to the boy, for Edward has seen this man has no time for children, "crossing the beach in this wind is like crossing the Gobi Desert!" He is a stupid man with a stupid wife and two stupid daughters. The girls parade around in just their bikini bottoms and are dreadful show-offs. Their breasts have just begun to swell. One has nipples the colour of field mushrooms; the other's are dusty pink, like pencil rubbers. They play frisbee and a game involving two large plastic bats and a tennis ball; they stand at the water's edge each afternoon, squealing and hoping everybody is looking at them, flinging their arms around and missing perfectly easy throws. Edward watches them from the shade of the tamarisk tree. One day they asked him to play and when he shook his head and hurried away they laughed.

"We Churmans," the blind man says, "ha ha ha." He is passing around photographs of his houses.

It is hard to know where to look. Although there is a sign in Greek, English, German and Italian which says NUDITY IS FORBIDDEN many women are barebreasted. And some of the Greek women are very fat. They look terrible in their two-piece suits, their stomachs spilling over in yellowish rolls. Some have dreadful scars and he doesn't see how they can expose themselves like that, talking away to one another, shouting at their children, passing out food. The little Greek boys fill empty Pizz bottles with sea-water and run along the shore, pouring out the water in long streams, shouting "Pizz, pizz" and laughing.

But the other beach is much worse. On the other beach, the beach where Anna and Edward's father go, everyone is stark naked — man, woman and child. Anna knew about the other beach before they came; she has been to this island once before. On their first day, after the business about the rooms had been sorted out and they had unpacked, Anna said, "Come with me and I will show you the most beautiful beach in the world." She led them up a path along the steep cliffs beyond the bay. They walked for about ten minutes and then she started down towards the water. They followed, slipping and sliding behind her, not always sure where to put their feet, until they came out on a small beach covered in smooth grey pebbles, as though they had stumbled upon a gigantic nest of stone eggs. A hundred yards from shore two men, completely naked, were diving from a large rock. "And now," Anna said, spreading her towel over the smooth, round pebbles, "now we take off our clothes and let the sun shine all over us." She was unbuttoning her skirt as she spoke. Soon she and his father had shed all their clothes, their bodies very pale compared to the few other people lying on the beach or swimming in the blue-green water.

"Come on Teddy," his father said, "it's all right. Anna says we're allowed to swim nude over here. Off with your clothes. You look as though you could do with a bit of sunshine."

Nude. It rhymed with rude. What an ugly word.

Anna stood smiling at him. "It feels so nice; why don't you give it a try?"

"In a minute," he said. He spread out his towel and carefully anchored it at the corners with large grey stones.

Anna and his father lay down side by side, faces to the sun, holding hands.

"Aren't you glad we came?" she asked. She leaned over and kissed his father on the belly. His father's cock stirred and thickened. Edward went quickly to the water's edge, pulled off his shorts and ran into the water. The rocks were slippery here and he fell once or twice but was quickly over his head.

When Anna had stood there smiling at him she was wearing only the necklace of blue beads his father had bought her in Athens. For their "anniversary" he had said. The man in the shop swore they were genuine mummy beads and now Edward, swimming, remembered the Mummy Room at the British Museum and one mummy in particular. The brownish bandages covering the body were covered in turn by a broken net of blue beads. Where did the jeweller in Athens get his? From men who robbed tombs? It seemed strange to him, as he floated on his back in the cool water, the sun so hot against his closed eyes, that Anna would want to wear something like that, something that had been shut up in a tomb for hundreds and hundreds of years, maybe something that had a curse on it.

Edward had been on a school tour of the museum and the guide had told them all about the curses connected with the tombs. When they were going through from one hall to another there had been a marble statue of a girl, a goddess maybe, lying on her stomach, asleep. One of the boys pretended to stick his finger up her bum when the guard wasn't looking.

When Edward came out of the water he quickly wrapped himself in his towel and moved away from Anna and his father.

He went one more time to the pebble beach and sat in the shade of the cliff. A French couple came to share the shade and the woman showed him an angry red circle on her arm. *"La méduse,"* she said, *"attention!"* Edward was surprised that anyone would think he was French. Her husband was wearing only the top of his wetsuit and had been spearing fish. When Edward looked puzzled (what was a *méduse*?) he said, "jelay-fish" then turned his back and began talking to his wife in rapid French.

After that Edward said he preferred the sandy beach by the hotel. For a moment he thought his father was angry. Then he shrugged. "It's up to you. We can join you at lunchtime. If you need anything, just put it on the bill." And so their routine was quickly established. Edward stayed on the sandy beach; he helped Dmitri and the umbrella man; he swam; he watched. Sometimes he ate lunch with his father and Anna. Sometimes he helped Dmitri and his brother wait on tables. Lunch was their busiest time, for the buses had arrived from the town by then, and the people in cars and young men riding motor scooters or hanging on behind the driver. The beach filled up and everybody wanted beer or Sprite or Pizz, salad, moussaka, fish and chips, ice-cream and iced coffee. One day Dmitri asked him to take an order to the family with the English girls and he refused. Dmitri laughed.

"What's the matter? They your girlfriends?"

Edward shook his head, furious. He went back to his room and lay on his bed until lunchtime was almost over. Anna, worried that he'd had too much sun, brought him a big plate of watermelon and played Snap with him until the sun was lower in the sky. His father sat on the adjoining balcony reading a book and when he suggested they all go to the other taverna, about ten minutes away and in the opposite direction to the pebbly beach, Edward, who had always refused before out of loyalty to Dmitri, agreed at once. Anna and his father liked the other taverna better in the evenings. It was lively and cooler and often had local musicians. The evening was pleasant and they stayed late, walking back along the cliffs. A girl had fallen from the path and onto the rocks a few weeks before. She had been drunk and there was no moon. A German girl. Edward thought of her lying there in the darkness, her head split open like a watermelon, and watched very carefully where he put his feet.

And the next day Dmitri offered to show him some card tricks so they were friends again.

"So how you like this ice-land," Dmitri said, shuffling the cards. Edward shook his head, puzzled. "Karpathos, how you like it?"

"Eye-land," Edward corrected him, "this eye-land."

On the beach Greek-American women changed from one language to another in the middle of a sentence. "Okay, *pethi mou*, now you're really going to get it!" Switching the backs of their children's legs with narrow bamboo fishing poles. Edward was learning, slowly, but the air was full of words he didn't understand. He tried to imagine Dmmi learning English in Elizabeth, New Jersey.

One morning when Edward went down to arrange his things in his favourite spot under the tamarisk tree, a young man was there, curled up in a cotton sleeping bag. Edward wasn't sure what to do. He felt that this was his spot, although he knew that it wasn't, not really. He also knew that if he didn't arrange his things now, before he had breakfast, somebody else would come along and claim it. The tree provided shade all day and you didn't have to pay for an umbrella. And the whole beach was there in front of him, like a continuous film. As he stood there, undecided, the young man turned over and opened his eyes.

"Good morning," he said. He was German. "I am taking your place?"

Edward shrugged. "Not really. But I like it here under the tree. I don't tan very well," he confessed.

The young man sat up and the sleeping bag fell back around his waist. He laughed.

"I also. I do not tan very well." He showed Edward his back. "Yesterday I fall asleep in the sun. Now I am all burned up." When he stepped out of the sleeping bag, the backs of his legs were bright red.

"You could get sunstroke," Edward said, "You should be careful."

The man nodded. "Yah. I drank some beer and I fall asleep. Very dumb."

"Where were you?"

"On the other beach, mit the rocks."

"Where are you staying?"

"I have a little tent," he said. "I am staying on the beaches mostly. But the wind is too strong and pulls it down, my tent. And the sun is very hot."

"You should stay out of the sun today," Edward said, "or you will get sick." He offered him one side of the shade from the tree.

The man went to shave and wash up in the public washroom and Edward went for his breakfast. Anna and his father were still asleep. The only people in the café were Dmitri and the old granny and grandpa and the couple Anna called "the newly-weds," although the girl didn't wear a wedding ring. She was taking a picture of her boyfriend eating yoghurt and honey. She was always taking pictures of her boyfriend or he of her. "James Hooper," he said to her now, posing, "this is your life."

The young German asked if he could join Edward for breakfast. Edward said yes, but added he had to hurry and help the umbrella man set out the cots and umbrellas. The man nodded and smiled. Edward liked the way he looked right at you.

"Kalli-mara," Dmitri said to Edward, *"Tee-kanees?"*

"Kalla," Edward replied.

"You speak Greek?" the young man said to Edward.

"A little."

They spent the day together, under the tamarisk tree. The young man's name was Karl. He was tall and thin, with reddish hair and pale blue eyes. He seemed always to be wearing a slight frown but he had a nice smile. He had a degree in psychology, he said, but couldn't get a job, so he was selling potatoes in a shop in Berlin.

"I am very bad. Some ladies come in and they want very cheap potatoes, not much money, and some are wanting very expensive potatoes, high class, and I always forget what lady wants what potatoes. I am not a very good potato-seller."

Edward told him a little about his school and where he lived in Sussex and a little about his father and Anna, although he said "my father and stepmother" which was what she was, really, and it sounded nicer.

"Are you married?" he said.

"Me? I am too shy. Someday maybe."

The German was travelling alone. He was very well organized and had only his small rucksack and tent and cotton sleeping bag. Edward's father and Anna made fun of the Americans with their enormous packs. "Life-support systems," they called them. They would approve of the way this man travelled so lightly.

"I bring only — what you call them — necessaries," he said. "But a book of course. One book. However, even with one book I am not very far." It was a very fat paperback, *Gravity's Rainbow*.

"What's it about?" Edward asked.

"The wars," the young man said.

Edward thought he said "divorce."

"But I am not in the mood for reading. I like to watch. For example," he said smiling, "you notice how the women lie when they lie on the beach. Always with one leg up, only one, like so," and he bent his right leg into a triangle. "And the mothers, they are always calling so loudly to their children, do this, don't do that. And the young girls are always rubbing each other with oil." He showed Edward a small black notebook in which he wrote down what he saw. Edward told him about the "newly-weds" who were always taking pictures and about all the Greeks from New Jersey.

"Yah. On this island most all the men go away to make money. They send money back. They come back to visit, to die. They fix up the villages."

They were going to a village that night, Edward said, to a festival. They were being picked up by a taxi. He wanted to invite his new friend to come with them but wasn't sure how Anna and his father would feel about that. Dmitri's handsome nephew was supposed to be minding the gift shop but instead was showing off with a friend of his, a young man in a white panama hat, for some Greek-American girls. They had a tape-recorder going full blast.

" 'Beat it'," the young German said, laughing. " 'Beat it'. You like Michael Jackson? You like to dance?"

Edward shrugged. The blind man's wife came across the beach in her black bathing suit. She smiled her special smile.

"And how are you today?" she said.

"Everybody knows you," his new friend said, admiringly. It made Edward feel good to hear him say it.

That evening they arrived early at the mountain village because Anna wanted to be up there when the sun set. Edward had sat in front with the taxi driver, whose name was Adonis. He had a horn that played "My Old Kentucky Home." The air was very cool and they sat on a stone wall, outside the church, waiting for the procession to begin. Anna wore an embroidered shawl over her sundress and looked very beautiful. But Edward's father became impatient when he discovered the procession wouldn't start for some time and suggested they go for a walk. So they walked away from the village, past grape-vines and terraces of olive trees, past a house where two small children were being coached in the dancing by a mama and a proud grandpa. And further along a very new, very black baby goat showed off for them while its mother calmly ate her dinner. Anna and Edward's father walked with their arms around one another; Edward dropped a little behind. The sunset turned the stone terraces, the fields, their faces, the whole sky golden, then rose, then a deep orangey-red. Somewhere a group of musicians were playing the strange, mournful, repetitive music they had heard before at the other taverna on the beach. Edward said it reminded him of bees and his father smiled at him. "That's a very interesting perception."

Walking back to the main village they came upon the musicians entering a house. "They will go from house to house tonight and make up songs to honour the people," Anna said. She had been reading the guidebook. A little further on, through an open doorway, Edward saw a man in a brown suit, humming to himself, select a gaudy tie from an open chest of drawers.

The taverna, which was famous for its home-made sausages, was jammed with people. The proprietor's son, not much older than Edward, was very busy laying plastic tablecloths, bringing baskets of bread, bottles of retsina and beer, plates of the famous sausages. The blind man and his wife were sitting with a large group. When she saw Edward, the blind man's wife, in a full red skirt and red blouse, her hair braided into a crown on top of her head, got up from the table and came across the room. She gave Edward and his father and Anna each a sprig of wild thyme.

"It is the custom here," she said, "on feast days."

"If there were some instrument to measure happiness," Anna said, "I'm sure that mine, tonight, would break it."

"Anna," Edward's father said, "will you do me the honour of marrying me?"

Edward saw his friend, the young German, over in a corner reading his book. They smiled and waved.

"Another new friend?" Edward's father said.

"He has a degree in clinical psychology," Edward said, "but has to sell potatoes in Berlin."

"Isn't he wonderful?" Anna said. "Edward, would you do me the honour of marrying me?"

One morning very early Edward and Karl walked over the cliffs and all the way into the town. Karl showed him how to find the path even when it didn't look as though there was one and how there were small heaps of stone every so often, "little stone men" Karl called them, when the path made a sudden turn, and splashes of red paint. Karl needed to find out when boats were leaving for Crete. He had to be in Athens on a certain day to get his flight back to Berlin. He really wanted to take an old boat that went all the way to Piraeus but nobody knew exactly when it would arrive and nobody knew where he could get a ticket. "Dmmi says it is a very funny boat," Karl told Edward, "but when I say how funny he just laughs." Instead of his usual singlet or khaki shirt Karl was wearing a blue shirt covered in bright flowers. It made him look quite different. "You like it?" Karl said. "I wear it for the very first time."

Edward imagined himself, in a few years, travelling from place to place with his rucksack on his back.

The walk along the cliffs took just over an hour and they watched the sun rise as they walked along. The air smelled of wild thyme and oregano. They passed a field of oats, golden in the morning light.

"So sometimes I am thinking we are in the Bible," Karl said.

In town they had a Nescafé at the port and then visited the bank, the travel agent, the post office, a vegetable shop where they bought round yellow melons and grapes, a shop that sold yoghurt, one that sold nuts and spirits. Everything fit neatly into Karl's rucksack.

Anna had asked Edward to try and match some embroidery silk. They found a shop with hundreds of boxes of silks and cottons, and with the aid of the proprietor, a very old man, they were able to match the sample exactly. The shop had a painted fish on a sign outside the door and it also sold fishing equipment — fishing line and sinkers, fishnet, flippers, masks. Karl, who had a snorkelling outfit, offered to buy one for Edward. That afternoon they took their gear to the pebble beach and went snorkelling in the deep water. Edward was amazed to find that he could see through the bodies of some of the fish. Sometimes they brushed against his mask; sometimes they brushed against his body or swam between his legs. Karl, who was swimming alongside him, warned him away from a group of what looked like pale purple bubbles. Back on the beach, drying off, he told Edward they were jellyfish. Edward remembered the French woman and her warning about the *méduse*.

Anna came over to where they were sitting and asked to borrow the mask and snorkel. Edward's flippers were too small; Karl's were too big. She stood there, smiling, swinging the mask and talking to the young man. She was a soft brown all over and wore nothing but the blue and silver necklace.

Edward noticed how, when the water ran over the shingle as it flowed back into the sea, it made a hissing sound.

The blind man lies on his suncot and laughs — "Ha ha ha, we Churmans, ha ha ha." Edward, tired of sitting still, wishing Anna were there so he could show her his latest card trick, gets up, picks up his snorkelling equipment and goes down to the water.

Edward sees the octopus first. As the crowd gathers, he keeps repeating it: "I'm the one that found it!" He wishes Anna and his father would come back.

He had been snorkelling for about an hour and as he came in towards the beach he kept his face down in the water until the last minute, until he was almost lying on the sand. That was when a clump of something swam between his mask and the edge of the shore. Whatever it was had brushed against his cheek and he stood up in a panic. It was a small octopus, the tips of its tentacles curling and uncurling, just under the surface of the water. Perhaps it had hurt itself when it collided with his mask. Edward knelt down in the water to have a better look. The young man in the panama hat was walking by. His green-and-white striped swimming trunks were much too tight and now he stood above Edward, smiling.

"What you got?"

Edward didn't like the young man but he was too excited to keep quiet and ignore him.

"It's an octopus! It crashed right into my mask! Do you think it's hurt?"

"Otopothi," the young man said, squatting down. "Very nice to eat." He gave it a poke with his finger and the tentacles curled in upon themselves like strange warty fingers, like the tips of young ferns. Its eyes were shut tight. The young man laughed. He wore a large gold cross on a gold chain. His chest, his belly, his legs were covered in whorls of coarse black hair.

"Very nice to eat. I show you." He reached down quickly and picked up the creature. Now the tentacles twisted around the young man's hand. He offered the octopus to Edward.

"You like? I show you how to fix. Dmmi cook it for you." The tentacles curled, uncurled (*"la méduse, attention!"*). Edward put his hands behind his back.

The man in the panama hat laughed, showing glints of gold among his strong white teeth.

"You no like?"

Edward hesitated. A small crowd had gathered. The young man laughed again and called to two of his friends. He said something in Greek and they laughed and came forward. Edward wondered what it would be like to grab the octopus and run with it, drop it in the blind man's lap. Would the blind man's wife stop smiling, then?

The three young men moved out a bit into the water, forming a loose triangle. The man in the hat let the octopus go and they began to play with it, scooting it through the water towards one another, standing up to their knees in water, laughing. Edward stood near but not too near, watching. The octopus was frantic now; it turned an ugly red and squirted its ink at the young men. Their legs were covered in it and this made them laugh even harder. The man in the panama hat called something to two pretty Greek girls and rubbed the black stuff into the skin of his thighs. The girls giggled.

As more and more people joined the crowd Edward called out, "I'm the one that found it! It crashed right into my mask!" But still he stood at the edge of the game, in his flippers, holding the mask and snorkel. He wanted to touch the octopus, to hold it, maybe get somebody to take a photograph. He could see the "newly-weds" in the crowd; the girl, as usual, had her camera on a cord around her wrist. He could see the English girls, who had left off making an elaborate sandcastle and stood there, shameless, their little titties sticking out for everybody to see. But the idea of really holding the thing made him feel sick. The way it would twist and turn, curl and uncurl against his hand. It was horrible to think about, horrible to look at, boneless, like a wrinkled purse made of skin. Big ones could kill a man. What if there were big ones out there, under the cliffs where he'd been swimming? The afternoon sun beat down on the back of his neck.

The man in the panama hat was tired of the game. He scooped up the octopus and looked around for Edward.

"You sure you no like? Very nice to eat." (Surprising his father and Anna at dinner that night. "Dmmi cooked something special. I caught it.") He shook his head.

"Okay. Thank you for my supper." The man in the hat began to walk to the far side of the beach, where the rocks were. The crowd broke up. Edward took his flippers off and followed at a distance, walking just at the edge of the water.

When the man got to the rocks he began slapping the octopus against the rocks, very hard. The first blow must have killed it. Slap, slap — it sounded like wet wash against a rock, like wet towels. In the showers at school, sometimes the prefects would slap the younger boys with towels. Slap. Slap. It was horrible, beastly. Why hadn't he swum back out with it and let it go? Edward knew what he was doing; he'd seen the fishermen sometimes, early in the morning, slapping octopus against the rocks and his German friend had explained why they did this. "We are pounding the veal," he said, "they are pounding the octopus." He had given Edward his address in Berlin. "Maybe someday you will come and see me." Edward wished Karl was there right now. He'd know what to do.

The man in the panama hat walked back along the beach, the dead octopus draped over his arm, the tentacles hanging down, not twisting now, limp, harmless.

One of the pretty Greek girls called to him and he stopped. While Edward watched the young man tore off a tentacle and threw it to the girl. She caught it, ("bravo, bravo" called the man in the panama hat), wound it around her wrist like some horrible bracelet, smiled and went on talking to her friend.

The two stupid English girls had gone up to the café for ice-cream or drinks. Their mother and father were asleep in their sun-cots farther along the beach. Edward, who was now very familiar with the kitchen of Dmitri and Fotula, thought that the mother's skin was turning the colour of a cockroach. He put on his flippers and glancing around to make sure no one was looking, he quickly stamped the sandcastle into the ground. Served them right. Then he turned and walked backwards, went into the sea. He wet his mask, spit on it, rubbed the spit around. He put the mask on, bit the mouthpiece of the snorkel, turned away from the beach and began to swim. He tried not to think about the dead octopus, about the tentacle torn off and draped over the girl's arm or the possibility of others out there somewhere, waiting.

And that night he has a strange dream. He is on one of the turquoise and cream buses, going into the port. There is a young man on the bus and perhaps an older man who isn't feeling very well. He turns around in his seat and in the seat behind Edward sees a Greek girl holding an octopus in her lap. He thinks, "now I will get to see the colour of its eyes." He suggests to the girl that she tickle it so that its eyes will open. She does this and it looks right at him — its eyes are bright, bright blue. Then it begins to turn into a baby, quite a pretty round-faced baby, and it smiles. But as it opens its mouth wider Edward can see that as well as having a mouth and lips it has a hole, like a large siphon, at the back of its throat. It is very round, this hole, and fleshy, and the edges are moving slightly in and out.

Edward wakes up to the sound of Anna crying out in the other room.

Commentary by
Audrey Thomas

≈

Audrey Thomas seeks to convey the often quirky nature of reality by exploiting the unlimited possibilities of language, technique, and form. The following commentary is taken from "Basmati Rice: An Essay about Words", published in Canadian Literature *100 (1984). Here Thomas likens the playfulness and the inventiveness of words to the sparkle and the suggestiveness found in both photography and stained glass.*

I am a dilettante (related to the Italian for "delight"). I never learn any language properly but love to dabble in them. I have studied, at one time or another, Latin, Anglo-Saxon, Middle English, Old Norse, French, Italian and, most recently, Greek. I spent a winter in Athens a few years ago and saw, every day, little green vans scurrying around the city with ΜΕΤΑΦΟΡΗ posted on a card in the front windshield. "Metaphors." When I enquired I discovered that these vans are for hire and they *transfer* goods from one section of the city to another. Now I long to write an essay called "A Metaphor is not a Truck".

Last year I took two terms of sign language at night school. I was amused by the fact that in ASL (American Sign Language) the sign for "woman" has to do with the tying of bonnet strings and the sign for "man" with the tipping of a hat. These are charming archaisms, like "horsepower" in English. (I am also interested in mirrors, mirror images, going into and through mirrors, so signing, which one does to someone facing you, is fascinating — and very difficult. I often came home with an aching hand.) I would like to take more sign language; I would like to become, as an African man once said to me, about English, "absolutely fluid in that language".

Words words words. Sometimes it all gets on top of me and I feel like the monster made out of words in *The Faerie Queene*. I can't leave them alone; I am obsessed. I move through the city watching for signs with letters missing ("Beef live with onions" advertises a cheap café near Granville and Broadway, " ELF SERVE" says a gas station out on Hastings) and I am always on the lookout for messages within words: can you see the harm in pharmacy, the dent in accident, the over in lover? In short, I play.

There is a phenomenon, most commonly observed in photography but also talked about by people who make stained glass. It is called "halation" and it refers to the spreading of light beyond its proper boundary. (With stained glass it happens when two colours are next to one another.) I think words can do that too, or perhaps I should say that I would like to think that there is no "proper boundary" for words. Let them spill over from one language to another, let them leap out at us like kittens at play. "Wit", said Mark Van Doren, "is the only wall between us and the dark." If a writer, if an artist of *any* sort, stops approaching his materials with wit, with laughter, then he is lost. The other day I was making a curry and listening to some old Beatles songs on the radio. John or Paul was yelling "Can't Buy Me Love" and I was thinking about Basmati rice. Suddenly I realized "Basmati rice" had the same number of syllables as "Can't Buy Me Love", so every time John or Paul or whoever got to the chorus I yelled out "Basmati rice!" and did a little soft-shoe shuffle while I stirred the curry sauce. (Everybody had a good time.)

SELECTED WORKS BY AUDREY THOMAS

Ten Green Bottles: Short Stories. Indianapolis, IN: Bobbs-Merrill, 1967. Rpt. as *Ten Green Bottles.* Ottawa: Oberon Press, 1977.

Munchmeyer and Prospero on The Island. Indianapolis, IN: Bobbs-Merrill, 1971.

Ladies & Escorts. Ottawa: Oberon Press, 1977.

Real Mothers: Short Stories. Vancouver: Talonbooks, 1981.

Two in the Bush and Other Stories. New Canadian Library 163. Toronto: McClelland and Stewart, [1981].

Goodbye Harold, Good Luck. Introd. Audrey Thomas. Markham, ON: Viking/Penguin Books, 1986. [Paperback ed.] Markham, ON: Penguin Books, 1987.

The Wild Blue Yonder. Markham, ON: Viking/Penguin Books, 1990. [Paperback ed.] Toronto: Penguin Books, 1991.

John Metcalf

≈

I can't even pretend to objectivity in writing about my own work but I think that Tim Struthers chose well in the two stories he selected: "Gentle as Flowers Make the Stones" from *The Teeth of My Father* (1975) and "The Nipples of Venus" from *Adult Entertainment* (1986). I certainly wouldn't have chosen any of my early stories as I find them too florid now, 'fine writing' raising its head here and there. I might have argued for including "Single Gents Only" or "The Eastmill Reception Centre" — from *Adult Entertainment* — instead of "Gentle as Flowers Make the Stones" but I always tend to prefer my more recent work. Is that because it's better?

In regard to reputation and 'classic' status, an attempt at objectivity compels me to admit that even with several books of stories and novellas to my credit since 1970, my work has been excluded from every Canadian trade anthology of national scope for the last fifteen years. What does this mean? I choose to believe that this exclusion does not mean my writing is inadequate but is because the anthologists dislike the stand that I have taken in *Kicking Against the Pricks* (1982; 2nd ed., 1986), *What Is A Canadian Literature?* (1988), *Volleys* (1990), and elsewhere against what I perceive as their undiscriminating cultural nationalism. Time will undoubtedly tell.

I still enjoy the compression in "Gentle as Flowers Make the Stones", the experimentation with italic and sentence fragments in the scenes at Bernice's house. Ray Smith once said that he thought the story was one of the most 'perfect' stories in Canadian literature but it's probably that very compression and control in the writing which puts off some readers. Leon Rooke has often said to me that he finds my stories so over-controlled as to be clenched, while I criticize his sometimes for being overly loose — differences of temperament perhaps.

I've written about "Gentle as Flowers Make the Stones" in an essay called "Building Castles" in the anthology *Making It New: Contemporary Canadian Stories* (Toronto: Methuen, 1982). I concluded that essay with a description of the way I believe readers have to learn to read:

"Writing is very hard work but at the same time it is delightful play. When I think about the act of writing, I often think it's like the play of small children on the beach absorbed in building sandcastles and towns with roads and tunnels all decorated with flags made from popsicle sticks and bits of cigarette packets.

"And then the wonderful application of water.

"Writing stories has something about it of that tranced pleasure, and I'm convinced that if readers are to share fully in the delight of writing they must be prepared to play *with* writers; they must launch a car through the tunnel to judge the banking and texture of the sand. Does it need more water? They must pat and stroke and probe. They must roll up trousers, tuck skirts into knickers, get down on hands and knees, and muck about."

In an interview by Tim Struthers published in the University of Guelph's literary magazine *Carousel* 8 (1992), I was asked about "The Nipples of Venus":

"The middle-aged couple in the story's first two sections are done in a highly stylized manner. I wanted to absolutely *pack* those two small pieces, wanted them pregnant with information and implication, wanted them to be a *poetry* of weariness. They're supposed to suggest so much about the couple — age, weariness, affection, irritation, separation, accommodation to each other and to their shared history. Hugh Hood said he thought they were over-stylized, *mannered* and I agree they're mannered but they *work*. Splendidly. It's shorthand but it's poetic shorthand. It's still emotionally moving.

"In the third section, the husband finds a garden café and sits there drinking beer while his wife sleeps off the discomfort of her lunch. He watches two male lizards competing for the charms of a female. The lizard which is the challenger has a stump instead of a tail. It is a wounded creature. Gradually, we realize that the husband is identifying with this stump-tailed and rather ineffectual suitor.

"The next section of the story details a gruesome daytrip on a tourist bus where people discuss the various horrors that have happened to them in Italy. Among the tourists are a son and his ancient mother who together offer us a vision of aging and debility — the things which inexorably face the middle-aged couple in the story...."

I was then asked how I thought the ending of "The Nipples of Venus" should be read:

"This ending is odd and unresolved. It's possible it didn't happen at all. Who is this strange, dignified girl? Is she a real girl? Or might she be a goddess? I *do* give her the attributes of Venus in Renaissance painting and literature — sparrows and doves.... I wanted the scene to be a little ambiguous. And I still do. I don't want to peg it down too much. There's the violence. The man has hit the girl quite hard. There is the suggestion in the story that both of them are sexually aroused by the violence. What do we make of that as good liberals? What would feminists think? Don't ask. It's uncomfortable. Even the narrator is uncomfortable with it. But it has broken the ice in him. There was something in the experience that was sexually and spiritually liberating. I want the reader to have to deal with that possibility.

"But what finally does the liberation achieve? It doesn't result in action. It leads only to reverie and daydream.

"There's a huge sadness intended in the story. In the last two paragraphs in Reardon's restaurant. The Businessman's Luncheon Special with the ginger-coloured gravy...."

≈

Robert Lecker made an important contribution to studies in the short story with *On the Line: Readings in the Short Fiction of Clark Blaise John Metcalf and Hugh Hood* (Downsview, ON: ECW Press, 1982). Douglas Rollins has written a very useful monograph, *John Metcalf and His Works* (Toronto: ECW Press, 1985). Articles by Kent Thompson and Barry Cameron are collected in *The Montreal Story Tellers: Memoirs, Photographs, Critical Essays* (Montreal: Véhicule Press, 1985). *The Malahat Review* 70 (1985) contains tributes by Alice Munro and Keath Fraser in addition to various critical essays such as Simone Vauthier's "Rambling Through John Metcalf's 'The Estuary'". Barry Cameron has written a book, *John Metcalf* (Boston: Twayne, 1986). Michael Darling contributed an interesting essay, "The Use of Language in Metcalf's 'Single Gents Only'", to *Writers in Aspic* (Montreal: Véhicule Press, 1988). Louis K. MacKendrick gives detailed readings of "Keys and Watercress" and "The Years in Exile" in his article "John Metcalf" in *Profiles in Canadian Literature*, vol. 8 (Toronto: Dundurn Press, 1991). W. J. Keith has included an essay, "'Criticism in Practice': John Metcalf's Private Part", in *An Independent Stance: Essays on English-Canadian Criticism and*

Fiction (Erin, ON: The Porcupine's Quill, 1991). A number of issues concerning the short story are discussed in John Metcalf, *Kicking Against the Pricks* (Downsview, ON: ECW Press, 1982; 2nd ed., Guelph, ON: Red Kite Press, 1986), in John Metcalf, *What Is A Canadian Literature?* (Guelph, ON: Red Kite Press, 1988), and in Sam Solecki, John Metcalf, and W. J. Keith, *Volleys* (Erin, ON: The Porcupine's Quill, 1990). Interviews by Barry Cameron, Geoff Hancock, and J. R. (Tim) Struthers appear, respectively, in *Queen's Quarterly* 82 (1975), *Canadian Fiction Magazine* 39 (1981), and *Carousel* [University of Guelph] 8 (1992).

GENTLE AS FLOWERS ≈ MAKE THE STONES ≈

Fists, teeth clenched, Jim Haine stood naked and shivering staring at the lighted rectangle. He must have slept through the first knocks, the calling. Even the buzzing of the doorbell had made them nervous; he'd had to wad it up with paper days before. The pounding and shouting continued. The male was beginning to dart through the trails between the *Aponogeton crispus* and the blades of the *Echinodorus martii*.

Above the pounding, words: 'pass-key,' 'furniture,' 'bailiffs.'

Lackey!

Lickspittle!

The female was losing colour rapidly. She'd shaken off the feeding fry and was diving and pancaking through the weed-trails.

Hour after hour he had watched the two fish cleaning one of the blades of a Sword plant, watched their ritual procession, watched the female dotting the pearly eggs in rows up the length of the leaf, the milt-shedding male following; slow, solemn, seeming to move without motion, like carved galleons or bright painted rocking-horses.

The first eggs had turned grey, broken down to flocculent slime; the second hatch, despite copper sulphate and the addition of peat extracts, had simply died.

"I know you're in there, Mr. Haine!"

A renewed burst of door-knob rattling.

He had watched the parents fanning the eggs; watched them stand guard. Nightly, during the hatch, he had watched the parents transport the jelly blobs to new hiding places, watched them spitting the blobs onto the underside of leaves to hang glued and wriggling. He had watched the fry become free-swimming, discover the flat sides of their parents, wriggle and feed there from the mucous secretions.

"Tomorrow…hands of our lawyers!"

The shouting and vibration stopped too late.

The frenzied Discus had turned on the fry, snapping, engulfing, beaking through their brood.

A sheet of paper slid beneath the door.

He did not stay to watch the carnage; the flash of the turning fish, the litter floating across the surface of the tank, the tiny commas drifting towards the suction of the filter's mouth.

He went back into his bedroom and worked himself into the sleeping-bag. Four more weeks and they would have lost their tadpole look, growing towards their maturity, becoming disc-shaped.

He studied the All-Island Realties notice. Nasty print. Two months rent: $72.50 per month; $145.00. And two more months before he could apply for the last third of his Arts Bursary. He reached for the largest butt and, staring into the flame of the match, considered his position. A change of abode was indicated. And preferably by evening.

Taking his night-pencil, his Granby Zoo pencil with animal-head pictures, he wrote on the back of the notice *God Rend You, All-Island Realties*. And then doodled. And then found himself writing out again from memory what he had completed the day before.

Into your hands, my father and my mother, I commend
My darling and delight, my little girl,
Lest she be frightened by the sudden dark
Or the terrible teeth of the dog who guards your world.

"Your world" was exactly right. No use in fucking about with "Hades" or "Tartarus."

Parvula ne nigras horrescat Erotion umbras
Oraque Tartarei prodigiosa canis.

"Sudden dark" wasn't bad either.

There was a sense of rightness, too, in dividing the sentences of the original into stanzas.

The night had produced no advances on stanza two.

She would have been but six cold winters old if she had lived
Even those few days more;

That could stand. But

Inter tam veteres ludat lasciva patronos

"Patronos," that was the bugger. "Protectors" was impossible; "guardians" too custodial. Something grave was needed, grave yet tender.

"veteres patronos"

His pencil worked loops and curlicues on the paper.

The muffled phone in the kitchen rang twice, stopped, rang again. Pulling on his jeans, he went to answer it.

"Jim? It's Jackie, man."

Jackie's voice dropped to a whisper.

"The Desert Express Is In."

"Good shit?" said Jim.

"Up a tree — you know? A read mindfuck, man."

"Far out," said Jim.

"Hey, and that Gold, man. What a taste! Two tokes and you're wasted!"

"Tonight, man," said Jim.

He hung up the phone and sighed.

"veteres patronos"

veteres patronos

His possessions, by design, fitted into two large cardboard cartons. Kettle and mug. Sleeping-bag and inflatable mattress. Clothes. One picture. Writing materials. An alarm clock. The few books he had not sold.

He stirred the coffee and Coffeemate together and wandered into the front room. On the table there lay the medium felt pen, the fine, and the fountain pen. Beside them, the three pads of paper, white, yellow, and pale blue, the porcelain ashtray, the square of blotting paper, the Edwardian silver matchbox.

He sat at the table drinking the coffee. He tried to visualize the three stanzas of the completed poem on the page. He'd have to supply a title; and at the end, in brackets, "The poet commends the soul of a pet slave girl to his parents who are already in the lower world. Adapted from Martial. *Epigrams. Book V. 34.*" Less distracting than under the title.

"veteres patronos"

He stared at the aquarium; had only a half of the fry survived — a little half of all his pretty ones — growing to the size of a dime, a quarter, a silver dollar, he could have sold them through Réal to Ideal Import Aquariums for twelve to fifteen dollars each.

With the medium felt pen on white paper he wrote:

Sixty *Symphysodon discus* at a conservative \$12.00 = \$720.00
Minus \$25.00 for the tank
\$10.00 for the pump and filter
\$30.00 for the breeding fish
\$15.00 for weed, tubifex worm, whiteworm, brine shrimp, and *daphnia*.
An inevitable profit of \$640.00.

Work was impossible.

He needed money; he needed a place to live.

He began packing his belongings into the two cartons. The \$3,500 of his Canada Council grant eroded by child-support payments, eroded by the cling of old habits. He would have to abandon the aquarium and hope that Réal could get it out.

The last of the air from the mattress.

Pevensey!

Pevensey might be good for a \$30.00 review. Maybe even \$60.00 for a round-up. If he could be trapped. He rolled the mattress and sleeping-bag brooding about the toadish Pevensey. Who had promised to review *The Distance Travelled* and lied.

Lack of space, old boy. Hands were tied.

In his Toad-of-Toad's-Hall tweeds and deerstalker.

In his moustache.

Who weekly reviewed *English Formal Gardens of the Eighteenth Century* or *The Rose Grower's Vade Mecum*, toadish Memoirs of endless toadish Generals.

Opening the freezer compartment of the fridge, he took out the perspex map-case which contained his completed poems and work sheets and wiped off the condensation; he kept them there in case of fire.

The kipper and the cardboard cup of Bar-B-Q Sauce he would leave to All-Island Realties as quit claim and compensation.

"*Montreal Herald*," said the girl. "Entertainments."

"Charles Pevensey, please."

"I'm sorry. He is not in this morning."

"Oh. That's strange. I'd understood he's been trying to contact me. Something about the length of my review."

"Oh," said the girl. "I see. Well, he might be in later. If you could call back at about eleven?"

Could one, he wondered, "beard" a toad?

Hefting his Air Canada bag, he stood looking around the bare white room. He'd shift the cartons after nightfall. The picture. The sleeping-bag would protect it.

A potato-shape in black crayon. A single red eye near the top. Seven orange sprouts. He'd typed underneath:

"Daddy" by Anna Haine
(Age 2½)

The newsprint was yellowing, the expensive non-glare glass dusty; the top edge of the frame was furred. He wiped it clean with his forefinger.

Orange arms and legs of course, silly Jim.

He tried to recall the name of the girl who'd got it framed for him. A painter sort of girl. Black hair, he remembered.

Frances?

Sonia?

But it was gone.

The *Montreal Herald* building reared concrete and glass. As he walked along towards the main entrance, past the emporia of used office-furniture, the pawn shops, the slum side streets, he wondered, as he often wondered, why he always had a compulsion to lie about his occupation to the people who gave him lifts; why he claimed to be a professor at McGill, a male nurse, a pest-control officer, a journalist.

The escalator conveyed him to the potted palms of Third Floor Reception, the elevator to the Fourth. Below him on the first and second floors, the giant drums and rollers of the *Herald* presses. He smiled at the memory of a wrench-brandishing Charlie Chaplin swimming through the cogs. He turned down the corridor to Entertainments and pushing through the swing doors, walked up the aisle between the desks to Pevensey's corner. The desk was piled with review copies, a hundred more stacked in the window embrasure behind.

He stood irresolute for a few moments and then went into the pen and sat in Pevensey's chair. The clattering typewriters paid no attention. Opposite, on the other side of the room, he noticed another set of swing doors. Glass port holes. He glanced at the top copy-sheet in the folder; a review of *Heraldry and You*. He took three cigarettes from the open package on the desk.

A tall blonde girl was walking up the aisle, looked about twenty, shoulder bag, shades. Legs too thin. She went into the next pen and dropped her bag on the desk. A plaque on the desk said *Youth Beat*. Her typewriter cover was dotted with stick-on flowers and butterflies. He felt her staring at him.

"Excuse me, sir."

"Umm?"

"Are you looking for someone?"

"What an attractive pendant!" he said, staring at her breasts.

"Oh, thank you."

He turned back to the file of copy.

"Excuse me…"

He did his blank look.

"If you're waiting for Mr. Pevensey, I'm afraid…"

"Mr. Pevensey!" called Jim.

A tactical blunder.

Pevensey, what looked like a teapot in his hand, glanced, pushed back through the swing doors, disappeared. Jim hurried after him.

"Mr. Pevensey!" he shouted to the echo of the footsteps on the concrete stairs. He ran down and found himself in an empty corridor facing two doors.

"PEV-EN-SEY."

One door led to the cafeteria, the other to the library. The cafeteria was nearly empty; the library girl claimed not to know who

Pevensey was. He walked back up the corridor, past the foot of the stairs, found a washroom. Locking himself into a cubicle, he took the Magic Marker from his Air Canada bag and wrote on the wall:

Charles Pevensey has a PERSONAL subscription to the *Reader's Digest*.

He lowered his trousers and sat.
He needed money.
He needed breakfast.
He needed a place to live.

A downtown breakfast would be more expensive than the Budapest where he usually ate; he liked the Budapest because George, the owner, had gold teeth and always said, "For you, gentlemans?" Today, he decided, would have to be a toast day.

Toast reminded him that it was Monday. He added a note to his list:

Cantor's Bakery 11:30 p.m. (if poss.)

The woman there sold him Friday's Kaiser rolls for two cents each. He also needed more tins of Brunswick sardines. Holding steady at twenty-nine cents a tin.

Moving upset him. And he was fond of the Victoria Manor Apartments. He would miss the conversations with Mrs. McGregor who gave him milk and who, on the day he'd moved in six months or so ago, had slipped a note under his door which read:

They are all FLQ in this building.
Signed:
The Lady Next Door.
(Scottish)

And Bernie who ran the FCI Detective Agency on the first floor. He'd miss the stairways which were always jammed with struggling furniture; the conversations with the basement owner of the Harold Quinn School of Music; the showcase outside the Starkman Orthopedic Shoe Company next door which was full of plaster casts of deformed feet.

The rest of the list read:

Call Réal.
Call McCready.
Night of the Jewish Ladies.

Staying with Myrna would be impossible; she'd want to screw all the time which was wasteful and irritating when he was nearing a possible form. Alan was still shacked up with the Bell Telephone girl.

Carol?

He remembered the last time he'd been forced to use her place. No. Not even for a few days could he live in the maelstrom of *her* emotional life. He remembered how, at her last gasp, she'd sobbed a stanza of Sylvia Plath. Nor, come to think of it, could he stomach her brown rice with bits in, wheat germ salad, and other organic filth. And he definitely wasn't inclined to endure lectures on the power of Sisterhood and the glories of multiple clitoral orgasm.

Remembering a glimpse of her naked in the bathroom, one foot on the rim of the tub, thigh, hip, the creases of her waist suffused in morning sunlight. Pure Bonnard stuff. Painter's work. He wondered if she still brushed her teeth with twigs, still washed her hair with honey.

He strained and grunted.

veteres patronos

He was being too literal. Again. He needed to get further from the text. To preserve. Intact. The main line of. Intent. But let. The.

The outer door banged shut; the bolt of the next cubicle slotted home. Checkered trousers rumpled over a pair of brown shoes.

Inter tam veteres ludat lasciva patronos
Et nomen blaeso garriat ore meum.

"Care!" said Jim.

The brown shoes cleared his throat.

Yes.

Expand it.

She would have been but six cold winters old if she had lived
Even those few days more; so let her walk
And run a child still in your elder care

"You beautiful, *inevitable* bastard!" said Jim.

"Are you O.K.?" said the brown shoes.

"What?"

Breakfasted on toast and coffee (twenty-five cents) now 12:35 and his guts hollow. Used the counter phone. Professor McCready was teaching; would he care to leave a message. The white globes above the length of the counter reminded him of a night scene. A café. A woman singing. Degas? Renoir?

Just beyond, in that place between night and twilight, not to be pried at, not to be forced, the words were moving in his head.

He walked up towards Dorchester and the Queen Elizabeth Hotel weighing his chances in the lottery of grant renewal. His other two references were certain to be good. He'd sent McCready a Xerox of the central poems of *Marriage Suite* now nine days ago along with the Letter of Reference form. Sixteen days to the deadline.

He strolled into the foyer of the Queen Elizabeth and wandered round looking for the notice board. Conventions, Annual Meetings, Associations of. Sometimes, wearing shirt and tie, under buffet conditions, it was possible to lunch or dine with Travel Agents, Furniture Retailers, Pharmaceutical Sales.

In the hardcover Classics Book Store on St. Catherine Street, he checked the number of copies of *The Distance Travelled*, arranged them more advantageously. He was classified under Canadiana and surrounded by Esquimaux and whales.

He strolled back on the other side of the street to the paperback store and browsed through the literary magazines, off-set and mimeo, looking for work by his contemporaries. *Edifice, Now, Ssip,* another new thing from Vancouver called *Up Yours.*

He walked up to the Sheraton and consulted the notice board; looked in at Mansfield Book Mart; checked the Sonesta Hotel.

The same girl answered the phone again. Professor McCready had just left for the day; would he care to leave a message.

Ten cents.

He copied down McCready's home number from the directory.

Academe — Intercede for us

Standing closed in the phone booth, he stared out at the flow of cars along Sherbrooke.

Jury of Experts — Compassionately Adjudicate us

Significance of Past Contribution — Justify us

Selling the drugs for Jackie would probably bring him $40.00 or $50.00 but he resented the waste of time, the endless phone calls.

The Desert Express Is In.

Poor glazed bastard.

He wondered what peyote looked like; what one *did* with it? Smoked it? Made an infusion? Ate it? He went back towards Classics to find out. For all he cared, they could stuff it up their collective fundament. As he walked along, he constructed arguments:

Look, man. You've dropped acid. You've done chemicals. O.K. But this is pure, it's like ORGANIC.

Or, for the carriage trade,

It's like acid, but SMOOTH. It's the difference between a bottle of Brights and a bottle of wine.

In Classics he gleaned the necessary sales information.

You ate it.

Devotees of the cactus cult are said to be "following the Peyote Road" — he copied the expression into his notebook. The practice had spread from Mexico to the Kiowa, Comanche, and Apache Indians. Ingestion put one in touch with *mana* — the LIFE FORCE. Introspection resulted. Visions of God, Jesus, and those on the Other Side were vouchsafed.

The prospect of being forced to stay with Jackie was depressing. In the gloom of obligatory candles he would have to listen to the latest fragment of Jackie's novel — the action of which all took place in Jackie's head during a seven-hour freak-out on top of Mount Royal and involved him in varieties of Cosmic Union with stars, planets, and a bi-sexual Cree Guide called Big Bear.

And he, in turn, would have to pay tribute by giving Jackie a copy of his latest verse. He'd already chopped *Howl* into tiny sections. He considered Gerard Manley Hopkins.

O the mind
                MIND
has mountains
                    cliffs
                    of
                    fall
                    SHEER
nomanfathomed.

It's like a lyric, man. They write themselves.

He resolved to call Carol.

For an hour or more, he stood watching the work on a construction site on Dorchester. He watched the tamping of the dynamite in the rock, watched the crane swing the coir nets and matting into place, waited for the dull *crump* and the heave of the matting and then the buckets grubbing out the boulders and scree. He could feel the words edging closer. He watched until he no longer saw the yellow helmets, the clanking bulldozers, the trucks churning up the muddy slope, until his eyes unfocused.

The end of the afternoon was growing cold. The words hurried him across the approach of the Place du Canada where the wind was clacking the wire halyards against the aluminum flagpoles.

He found an empty table at the back of the Steerarama and sat warming his hands on the coffee cup. Shapes of figures passing beyond the net-curtained windows. Light on the chrome of the cash register. A sheen of light across the polished lino below the cash register, a green square, a red square, part of a green square before the carpet edge.

Et nomen blaeso garriat ore meum.

The horns were long, buffed and lacquered, the colours running from grey through beige to jet at the points. From the astrakhan middle where the horns were joined hung a card which read:

Our "Famous" Steerburger
(6 oz. of Prime Beef)

As he tilted his head, the light ran the horns' curved length.

blaeso garriat demanded "lisping," "stammering."

The gloss had given him,

And lisp my name with stammering tongue.

Which made the child sound like a cross between a half-wit and Shirley Temple.

"lisping"

"prattle"

"babble"

He stared at the cinnamon Danish in the glass case on the counter. But the Night of the Jewish Ladies had promised refreshments.

Although a bending of the text, a real distortion of meaning even, and swaying on a tightrope over sentimentality, "baby talk" might.

Might.

If it was somehow balanced off.

He smoothed the paper placemat with the edge of his hand and sat staring at the drawing of the smiling waitress.

Bienvenue

He gave her spectacles, a moustache, gaps in her teeth.

Suddenly he started to write.

She would have been but six cold winters old if she had lived
Even those few days more; so let her walk
And run a child still in your elder care
And safely play, and tease you with my name in baby talk.

Nodding at what he'd written, he stretched and leaned back. Everything depended now on the resolution of the final stanza. Blondin poised over Niagara had little on this. Lips working, he read the lines through again and again.

Precarious.

The *ands* repetition wasn't bad, wasn't *too* obtrusive in its suggestion of the child. But it was the tension in "tease"; it was only "tease" and its implications that were keeping him aloft.

He found that he was gazing at the cinnamon Danish; he wanted the cinnamon Danish very much. He could feel the pressure of the final stanza, the bulge and push of it in his head. The hunger had turned to hollow pain. Half an hour to his meeting Mrs. Wise on the mezzanine in her russet linen pant suit and carrying a copy of the

Montreal Herald. A group of young wives, she'd said, meeting in each other's houses, quite informally, to discuss, to listen to speakers, to be stimulated, to broaden horizons.

Now you mustn't be modest, Mr. Haine. Quite a few of the girls saw your photograph and the piece about you in the Gazette.

He hoped they'd pay him the $25.00 after the reading and not at some polite interval; he hoped it was sandwiches and not cakes. Sandwiches with meat in.

Or egg.

Or cheese.

He felt an urge to delete the inverted commas on the *Our "Famous" Steerburger* sign with his Magic Marker.

He hoped that payment would be made in cash.

The last time had been cakes.

Seventeen members of the Canadian Authors Association gathered in a salon of the Laurentian Hotel. The president had asked everyone to stand one after another to announce their names. Most were hyphenated ladies.

Against their rising conversation, he had read from *The Distance Travelled*. During the last two poems a waiter had wheeled in a trolley of iced cakes and an urn of coffee.

The president, a large lady, had called the meeting to order.

When he'd finished reading, sudden silence ensued.

Answering the president's call for questions, a lady with aggressive orange hair had said,

"Am I right in assuming you've had your work published?"

"Ah, yes."

"And you didn't pay for it?"

"Pay for it?"

"To have it published."

"Oh. No."

"Well, my question is — who do you know?"

"Know?"

"In Toronto."

Alone in the cream and gold sitting room, he examined the mantelpiece with its tiny fluted columns, shelves, alcoves, its three inset oval mirrors. He examined the silver-framed bride and groom. He examined the Royal Doulton lady in her windblown crinolines, the knicknacks, the small copper frying-pan-looking thing that said *A Gift from Jerusalem*, the Royal reclining Doulton lady. Glancing round at the open door, he turned back and peered into the centre mirror to see if hairs were sticking out of his nose.

He sank for a few minutes into the gold plush settee.

The doorbell kept ringing; the litany continued.

Bernice! It's beautiful!

We only finished moving in three weeks ago.

The pair of brass lamps which flanked the settee were in the form of huge pineapples. He touched the prickly brass leaves. The lamp-shades were covered in plastic. On the long table at the far end of the room, a white tablecloth covered food; he stared at the stacked plates and cups and saucers, at the tablecloth's mysterious humps and hollows. He took a cigarette from the silver box. Which of the little things on the occasional tables, he wondered, were ashtrays? Each time the front door opened, the chandelier above him tinkled.

Oh, Bernice! And quarry-tile in the kitchen too!

Would you like the tour?

And as the tramplings went upstairs, faintly:

master-bedroom...

cedar-lined...

A plump woman wandered in. He nodded and smiled at her. She hesitated in the doorway staring at him. The green Chinese lady gazed from her gilt frame. The plump woman went around the other end of the settee and stood fingering the drapes. He tried to remember the painter's name; Tetchi, Tretchisomething — a name that sounded vaguely like a disease.

"Are you the poet?" said the plump woman.

"Yes, that's right."

He smiled.

"We had a nudist last week," she said.

Panty-hose. Stocking-top. The whites of their thighs.

Seated in the centre of the room on the footstool provided, he read to the assembled ladies. He read from his first Ryerson chapbook.

He read his Dylan orotundities,

In a once more summer time than this.

His Auden atrocities,

Love, now, like light.

He read for forty minutes, giving them Nature, Time, and Love.

The pièce de résistance proved to be lox.

With rye bread. And cream cheese. Salami. Half-sours. Palma ham. Lima bean salad with mint. Devilled eggs and sculptured radishes. The cheese-board afforded Limburger, Gouda, Cheddar, Danish Blue, Feta, and Gruyère.

Are poets different than other people?

Salami.

...or do you wait for inspiration?

Potato salad.

"No, of course not. It's my pleasure. For...?"

"Bernice."

Jenny. Helen. Shirley. Joan. Ruby.

WITH BEST WISHES.

Nine Distance Travelled *at $6.00 (Author's Discount $2.00 = $18.00 Profit).*

"Well, I don't want to sound pompous, but I suppose you'd call it vision."

Radish.

"Pardon?"

"...was wondering if Bernice had arranged a lift downtown for you? Because I'm leaving soon if you'd like a ride?"

"Over there," she said as they crunched across the gravel. "What my dear husband calls 'the Kraut bucket'."

He wondered how old she was. Thirty-five. Expensively styled black hair. A year or two more maybe. Her strained skirt rode higher as they slammed the doors. He glanced at the nylon gleam of her thighs. She seemed unconcerned.

"Cigarette?" she said.

He leaned towards the flame. Her perfume was heavy in the car.

She blew out smoke in a long sigh.

"I liked your poems," she said.

"Thank you."

"I'm not just saying that. I thought they were really good."

"I really appreciate that."

"You're very polite — a very polite person, aren't you?"

She turned the key and roared the motor.

"What makes you say that?" he said.

She shrugged.

"Nothing."

As they turned out of the drive, she said, "How do you stand it?"

"Stand what?"

"Oh, for Christ's sake!" she said.

He stared at her profile.

"Why do you go then?" he said.

"*Stand what!*" she said.

"What the hell did you expect me to say?"

She shrugged and then crushed the cigarette into the ashtray.

"Are you married?"

"No," he said. "Why?"

She turned onto the access road to the Trans-Canada.

"Kids," she said. "My dear husband's dinners. Even Bernice Wise is a vacation."

She snapped on the radio.

They settled into the drive back from Pointe Claire. She drove with angry concentration. The nylon sheen of her thighs green in the glow from the radio dial. The winding and unwinding notes of a harpsichord, the intricate figurings, absolved him from conversation. Mesmeric the rise and fall of headlights, the steady bore of the engine, the weaving patterns of the lanes of traffic; mesmeric the play of light and shadow, the approach and fall of overpasses, the rush of the concrete void. The heater was making him drowsy. The words were drifting. Her gloved hand moved on the gear-shift.

Trying to break free, the swell of the words lifting and stirring like pan ice.

Mollia non rigidus caespes tegat ossa, nec illi,
Terra, gravis fueris: non fuit illa tibi.

The final movement of the poem, dear ladies, changing direction, *terra*, changing direction, *terra* in the vocative.

All, all, dear ladies, a question of balance.

"rigidus caespes"

"Sod" was ludicrous; he toyed with "rock," "turf," and "stones." He was being trapped into the literal again; the morning at the *Montreal Herald* was repeating itself.

"Charles Pevensey has a PERSONAL subscription to the *Reader's Digest*."

Pleasing.

There was something about the toadlike Pevensey that had been working on his mind all day. An echo of the name's sound. *Epitaph on Salomon Pavy*. Because it was an echo too, he knew, of Ben Jonson. *Epitaph on Elizabeth, L. H.*

Pevensey. Pevensey.

Penshurst.

COUPLETS.

It needed couplets. *That* was the connection. The bastard needed couplets. He sat up and patted his pockets, finding a pencil stub in his shirt. His pad was in the Air Canada bag on the back seat. Removing the cigarettes from his package, wrapping them in the silver paper.

"Yes, please," she said.

"What? Oh, sorry."

"Will you light me one?"

As she took it from him, she said, "I'm sorry I was bitchy before."

"That's O.K."

"Just one of those days," she said.

He spread the inner part of the packet on his knee and started to write, then scribbled over the words.

The car stopping and starting now. Neon signs. *Salada Tea*. Traffic lights. *Uniroyal Tire*. They turned south onto Decarie heading downtown. Past the first of the restaurants.

"Mr. Haine?"

She glanced in the rear mirror and then smiled at him.

"If you want to write it down," she said.

"What?"

"It's 743-6981."

Gentle as flowers...he wrote.

"And if a man answers?"

She laughed.

Gentle as flowers make the stones

She pulled into the right-hand lane and took the exit to Queen Mary Road.

"You know something?" she said.

He grunted enquiry, crossing through a word he'd written.

"You've got a cruel mouth. I bet a lot of women have told you that."

"Me, cruel? I'm nice," he said.

"James Haine," she said. "Does anyone call you 'James'?"

"No. Nor Jimmy."

Dare he use "comfort"?

"Actually," she said, "my name isn't Rena. Well, it *is*, but my friends call me Midge."

"Midge?"

"Short for Midgicovsky — from school."

"That's a nice name," he said. "I like that."

"And you *have* got a cruel mouth."

"Oh, Grandmama!"

"What's that meant to mean?"

A girl's name — two syllables.

"You're making me sound like the Big Bad Wolf."

"What?"

"You know. All the better to bite you with sort of stuff."

She laughed.

"Well, you *have*," she said. "And anyway, you don't hear me screaming for help."

That comfort...

"Anyway, I like it," she said. "You're different."

He glanced at the Duc de Lorraine bakery as they turned onto Côte des Neiges. He used to buy warm croissants there in his richer days. Surprise her with coffee, cognac, croissants. After writing all night, waking up in the early morning with the dog before she was awake.

Two syllables.

She braked and changed lanes.

Gentle as flowers make the stones
That comfort Liza's tender bones.

Turning off Côte des Neiges, she took the road leading up to the Mountain.

"It's so beautiful up here at night," she said. "You don't mind, do you? I always come this way on the way home."

On the left, the cemetery spreading up the slope for acres behind the black railings; mausoleums, statues, crosses, the dull glimmer of the endless rows of polished marble headstones.

Past Beaver Lake. On to the summit.

She parked the car at the Mount Royal Lookout, silence settling as they gazed over the lights of the city. A ghostly wedge from the revolving sweep of the searchlight on top of Place Ville Marie shone against the cloudbank to their left, shone, disappeared, shone.

"I never get tired of this view," she said.

He nodded.

She sighed.

"Jim?"

As he turned, she stretched across, her arms reaching out for him. She kissed his chin, the corner of his mouth, found his lips. Twisting towards her in the awkwardness of the seat, the gear-shift, he put his arms round her, one hand on a breast.

"Hold me," she whispered.

His back was hurting.

Her mouth was hot and open. Squirming, she reached up and unhooked her brassiere. After a few moments, she pushed her face into his neck.

"That's the sad thing about getting old," she said, her breath hot and moist on his flesh, "having your breasts fall."

"Not old," he mumbled.

She kissed him open-mouthed, then biting gently at his lower lip. She was breathing heavily.

"Get in the back," she whispered.

As they kissed again, her legs were stirring restlessly. His hand moved over nylon. She lifted herself, pulling up her skirt. She stretched out one leg and drew the other up, gasped as his fingers found her.

"We can't," she whispered. "We mustn't."

Her breathing was throaty.

"I'm off the pill and I haven't got anything with me."

His fingers were moving.

"You don't mind?"

She moved her bottom further off the edge of the seat; she was gripping his other arm and making noises.

The side of his face was sweaty against the shiny plastic upholstery.

She was arching, arching herself towards him.

Suddenly her body went rigid and she clamped his hand still. They lay quiet, the rate of her breathing slowing. Her eyes were closed; her face slack. He watched the sweep of the searchlight against the cloudbank.

Lie lightly, Earth…

No.

After a minute or so, she moved her legs, easing herself up.

"Mmmm," she sighed.

She pushed him towards the other side. Her hands undoing his belt buckle, she whispered, "Go on, lie back." She was pushing up his shirt. She lay with her cheek against his stomach and then he felt the heat of her mouth on him. Her hand moving too.

Her hair was stiff, lacquered.

He grunted and she moved her head; sperm pumped onto his stomach.

They lay in silence.

He could feel the sperm getting cold, running down his side, cold on his hip.

"There's some Kleenex in my purse," she said.

She wiped his thigh and stomach, and pulling down his shirt, snuggled up against him, kissing his mouth, his chin, his neck. He stroked her shoulders, back, running his hand down to her buttocks and up again. She pulled herself higher until her cheek was against his.

"Was it good for you, too?" she whispered.

"Mmm."

He felt a mounting excitement.

All, all, dear ladies, a question of balance.

And he'd found it.

His balancing pole, as it were, commas.

COMMAS

No risk of falling now; no staggering run up the incline of a sagging rope.

Earth COMMA *lie lightly on her* COMMA *who* COMMA
Living COMMA *scarcely burdened you.*

Tears were welling in his half-shut eyes, the lights of the city lancing gold and silver along his wet lashes, the poem perfect.

Gentle as flowers make the stones
That comfort Liza's tender bones.
Earth, lie lightly on her, who,
Living, scarcely burdened you.

Feeling his hot tears on her cheek, she lifted her head to look at him.

"You're crying," she whispered. "Don't cry."

She brushed the backs of her fingers against his cheek.

"Jim?"

He stirred, shifting himself of some of her weight.

"Jim?"

She nestled against him.

"You know something?" she said. "You're very sweet."

≈ THE NIPPLES OF VENUS ≈

Rome stank of exhaust fumes and below our hotel room on the Via Sistina motor bikes and scooters snarled and ripped past late into the night rattling the window and the plywood wardrobe. The bathroom, a boxed-in corner, was the size of two upright coffins. It was impossible to sit on the toilet without jamming your knees against the wash-basin. In the chest of drawers, Helen discovered crackers, crumbs, and Pan Am cheese.

I'd reserved the room by phone from Florence, choosing the hotel from a guidebook from a list headed: Moderate. We would only have to put up with it for Saturday and Sunday and would then fly home on Monday. After nearly three weeks spent mainly in Florence and Venice, I had no real interest in looking at things Roman. I felt…not tired, exactly. Couldn't take in any more. I'd had enough. 'Surfeited' was the word, perhaps. I was sick of cameras and photographs and tourists and tourism and disliking myself for being part of the problem. I felt burdened by history, ashamed of my ignorance, numbed by the succession of *ponte, porta, piazza*, and *palazzo*. I was beginning to feel like…who was it? Twain, I think, Mark Twain, who when asked what he'd thought of Rome said to his wife:

Was that the place we saw the yellow dog?

Helen was bulged and bloated and the elastic of her underpants and pantyhose had left red weals and ribbing on the flesh of her stomach. She'd been constipated for nearly two weeks.

I'd told her to stop eating pasta, to relax, to stop worrying about whether the children would leave the iron switched on, about aviation disasters, devaluation of the lira, cancer of the colon, but at night I heard her sighing, grinding her teeth, restless under the sheets, gnawing on the bones of her worries.

That waiter in — where was it? Milan? No. Definitely not in Milan. Bologna? — a waiter who'd worked for some years in Soho in the family restaurant — he'd told us that the tortellini, the tiny stuffed shells of pasta in our soup, were commonly called 'the nipples of Venus'.

Fettuccine, tuffolini, capelletti, manicotti, gnocchi…

Mia moglie è malata.

Dov'è una farmacia?

Aspirina?

Bicarbonato di soda?

...polenta, rigatoni, tortellini...
Praaaaaaaaap...
Scooters on the Via Sistina.
Praaaaaaaaap...
Helen passing gas.

The Spanish Steps were just at the top of the street anyway and at the very least, Helen said, we had to see the Trevi Fountain and St. Peter's and the Pantheon.

They all looked much as they looked in photographs. Not as attractive, really. The Spanish Steps were littered with American college students. The sweep of St. Peter's Square was ruined even at that early hour by parked coaches from Luton, Belgrade, Brussels, and Brighton. Knowing that St. Peter's itself would be hung with acres of martyrdom and suchlike, I refused to set foot in it. The Trevi Fountain was rimmed with people taking its photograph and was magnificient but disappointing.

Places of historical interest often make me feel as if I'm eight again and the sermon will never end. I enjoyed the *doors* of the Pantheon — I always seem drawn to bronze — but the hushed interior struck me as lugubrious. Helen, on the other hand, is an inveterate reader of every notice, explication, plaque, and advisement.

Straightening up and taking off her reading glasses, she says, "This is the tomb of Raphael."

"How about a coffee?"

"Born 1483."

"Espresso. You like that. In the square."

"Died in 1520."

"Nice coffee."

And then it was back to the Spanish Steps because she wanted to go jostling up and down the Via Condotti looking in the windows — Ferragamo, Gabrielli, Bulgari, Valentino, Gucci. And then in search of even more pairs of shoes, purses, scarves, gloves, and sweaters, it was down to the stores and boutiques on the Via del Tritone.

For lunch I ate *funghi arrosto alla Romana*. Helen ordered *risotto alla parmigiana* and had to go back to the hotel. She said she'd just lie there for a bit and if the pains went away she'd have a little nap. She asked me if I thought it was cancer, so I said that people with cancer *lost* weight and that it was *risotto*, *manifestly* risotto, *risotto first and last*.

"There's no need to shout at me."

"I am *not* shouting. I am speaking emphatically."

"You don't mind?" she said. "Really?"

"I'll go for a stroll around," I said.
"You won't feel I'm deserting you?"
"Just rest."

I strolled up the Via Sistina and stood looking down the sweep of the Spanish Steps. Then sauntered on. Some seventy-five yards to the right of the Steps, seventy-five yards or so past the Trinità dei Monti along the stretch of gravel road which leads into the grounds of the Villa Borghese, tucked away behind a thick hedge and shaded by trees, was an outdoor café hidden in a narrow garden. The garden was just a strip between the road and the edge of the steep hill which fell away down towards the Via Condotti or whatever was beneath. The Piazza di Spagna, perhaps. Houses must have been built almost flush with the face of the hill because through the screening pampas grass I could glimpse below the leaning rusty fence at the garden's edge the warm ripple of terra cotta roof tiles.

The garden was paved with stone flagstones. Shrubs and flowers grew in low-walled beds and urns. In the centre of the garden was a small rectangular pond with reeds growing in it, the flash of fish red and gold. The tall hedge which hid the garden from the road was dark, evergreen yew trees.

It was quiet there, the traffic noises muted to a murmur. Round white metal tables shaded by gay umbrellas, white folding chairs. Two old waiters were bringing food and drinks from the hut at the garden's entrance. There were only three couples and a family at the tables. The yew hedge was straggly and needed cutting back. The shrubs and flowers in the stone-walled beds were gone a little to seed, unweeded.

I sat at the only table without an umbrella, a table set into a corner formed by the hedge and a low stone wall. The wall screened the inner garden a little from the openness of the entrance and from the shingled hut-like place the food came from. All along the top of the wall stood pots of geraniums and jutting out from the wall near my corner table was the basin of a fountain. The basin was in the form of a scallop shell. The stone shell looked much older than the wall. It looked as if it had come down in the world, ending up here in this garden café after gracing for two hundred years or more some ducal garden or palazzo courtyard. The stone was softer than the stone of the wall, grainy, the sharpness of cuts and flutes blurred and weathered.

I sat enjoying the warmth of the sun. The Becks beer bottle and my glass were beaded with condensation. Sparrows were hopping between tables pecking crumbs. Water was trickling down the wall and falling into the stone scallop shell from a narrow copper pipe which led away down behind the wall and towards the hut at the garden's entrance. Where the pipe crossed the central path feet had squashed it almost flat. The small sound of the water was starting to take over my mind. The glint and sparkle of the sunlight on the water, the tinkling sound of it, the changes in the sound of it as it rose and deepened around the domed bronze grate before draining — it all held me in deepening relaxation.

Somewhere just below me were famous guidebook attractions — the Baraccia Fountain, the Antico Caffe Greco, the rooms where John Keats died now preserved as a museum and containing memorabilia of Byron and Shelley — but all I wanted of Rome was to sit on in the sunshine drinking cold beer and listening to the loveliness of water running, the trill and spirtle, the rill and trickle of it.

Watching the sparrow, the small cockings of its head, watching the little boy in the white shirt and red bow-tie balancing face-down over his father's thigh, I was aware suddenly at the corner of my eye of flickering movement. I turned my head and there, reared up on its front legs on the rim of the stone scallop shell, was a lizard. It stood motionless. I turned more towards it. Its back was a matte black but its throat and neck and sides were touched with a green so brilliant it looked almost metallic, as if it had been dusted with metallic powder.

Set on the stone surround of the scallop shell were two pots of geraniums and from the shadow of these now appeared another lizard, smaller than the first, not as dark in colouring, dun rather than black and with not a trace of the shimmering peacock green — compared with the male a scrawny creature drab and dowdy.

This lizard waddled down into the curve of the stone basin where she stopped and raised her head as if watching or listening. Or was she perhaps scenting what was on the air? I'd read somewhere that snakes 'smelled' with their tongues. Were lizards, I wondered, like snakes in that? Would they go into water? Was she going to drink?

I was startled by loud rustlings in the hedge near my chair. A bird? A bird rootling about in dead leaves. But it wasn't that kind of noise quite. Not as loud. And, I realized, it was more continuous than the noise a bird would have made — rustling, twig-snapping, pushing, scuffling. The noise was travelling along *inside* the hedge. Slowly, cautiously, not wanting to frighten away the lizards on the stone scallop shell, I bent and parted branches, peering.

And then the noise stopped.

As I sat up, I saw that the stone bowl was empty, the brown lizard disappeared behind the geranium pots again. The green lizard was still motionless where he'd been before. Every few seconds his neck pulsed. Suddenly I saw on the wall level with my knee a lizard climbing. Every two or three inches it stopped, clinging, seeming to listen. It too was green but it had no tail. Where its tail should have been was a glossy rounded stump.

Lacking the tail's long grace, the lizard looked unbalanced, clumsy. About half the tail was gone. It was broken off just below the place where the body tapered. The stump was a scaleless wound, shiny, slightly bulbous, in colour a very dark red mixed with black. The end of the stump bulged out like a blob of smoke-swirled sealing-wax.

Just as its head was sticking up over the edge of the stone shell, the other lizard ran at it. The mutilated lizard turned and flashed halfway down the wall but then stopped, head-down, clinging. The pursuing lizard stopped too and cocked its head at an angle as if hearing something commanding to its right.

Seconds later, the stubby lizard skittered down the rest of the wall, but then stopped again on the flagstones. The pursuing lizard pursued but himself stopped poised above the wall's last course of stones. It was like watching the flurry of a silent movie with the action frozen every few seconds. And then the damaged lizard was negotiating in dreamy slow motion dead twigs and blown leaves on his way back into the hedge. He *clambered* over them as if they were thick boughs, back legs cocked up at funny angles like a cartoon animal, crawling, ludicrous. His pursuer faced in the opposite direction intently, fiercely.

Peculiar little creatures.

I signalled to the waiter for another beer.

I sat on in the sunshine, drifting, smelling the smell on my fingers of crushed geranium leaves, listening to the sounds the water made.

And then the noises in the hedge started again.

And again the lizard with the stump was climbing the wall.

And again the lizard on the top was rushing at it, driving it down.

By the time I was finishing my third beer, the attacks and retreats were almost continuous. The stubby lizard always climbed the wall at exactly the same place. The defending lizard always returned to the exact spot on the stone surround of the scallop shell where the attacking lizard would appear. The stop-frame chases flowed and halted down the wall, across the flagstones, halted, round an urn, into the hedge.

But with each sortie the damaged lizard was being driven further and further away. Finally, the pursuing lizard hauled his length into the hedge and I listened to their blundering progress over the litter of twigs and rusty needles in the hedge-bottom, the rustlings and cracklings, the scrabblings travelling further and further away from my chair until there was silence.

The sun had moved around the crown of the tree and was now full on me. I could feel the sweat starting on my chest, in the hollow of my throat, the damp prickle of sweat in my groin. I glanced at my watch to see how long she'd been sleeping. I thought of strolling back to the hotel and having a shower, but the thought of showering in the boxed-in bathroom inside the glass device with its folding glass doors like a compressed telephone booth — the thought of touching with every movement cold, soap-slimy glass…

I lifted the empty Becks bottle and nodded at the waiter as he passed.

A dragon-fly hovered over the pond, its wings at certain angles a blue iridescence.

I wondered about my chances of finding a Roman restaurant or trattoria serving *Abbracchio alla Romana*, a dish I'd read about with interest. And while I was thinking about restaurants and roast lamb flavoured with rosemary and anchovies and about poor Helen's *risotto* and about how long I'd been sitting in the garden and Helen worrying there in that plywood room heavy with exhaust fumes…

you might have been killed…you know I only nap for an hour…I got so scared…

…while I was thinking about this and these and listening to the water's trickle and looking at the white, heavy plumes of the pampas grass, there on top of the wall, my eye caught by the movement, was the lizard with the stump.

I studied the face of the wall, scanned the bottom of the hedge, looked as far around the base of the urn as I could see without moving, but there was no sign of the other lizard, no sound of pursuit.

He stood motionless on top of the wall just above the scallop shell where the scrawny brown female still basked. The stump looked as if blood and flesh had oozed from the wound and then hardened into this glossy, bulging scab.

The coast's clear, Charlie!

Come on!

Come on!

He was clinging head-down to the wall inches above the stone shell.

The female had raised her head.

Now he seemed to be studying a pale wedge of crumbling mortar.

Come on!

And then he waddled down onto the stone surround and seized the female lizard firmly about the middle in his jaws.

They lay at right angles to each other as if catatonic. The female's front right leg dangled in the air.

Come on, you gimpy retard! Let go! You're biting the wrong one. It's the GREEN ones we bite. The brown ones are the ones we…

The waiter's voice startled me.

I smiled, shook my head, picked up the four cash-register slips, leaned over to one side to get at my wallet in my back pocket. When he'd gone and I turned back to the stone scallop shell, the female had already vanished and the end of the stump, somewhere between the colour of a ripening blackberry and a blood blister, was just disappearing into the shadows behind one of the pots of geraniums.

I got up slowly and quietly. I was careful not to scrape my chair on the flagstones. I set it down silently. I looked down to make sure my shoe wasn't going to knock against one of the table's tubular legs. One by one, I placed the coins on the saucer.

No, I told Helen on Sunday morning, not the Forum, not the Colosseum, not the Capitoline, the Palatine, or the Quirinal. I wanted to be lazy. I wanted to be taken somewhere. But not to monuments. Trees and fields. But not *walking*. I didn't want to *do* anything. I wanted to see farmhouses and outbuildings. What I wanted — yes, that was it exactly — a coach tour! I wanted to gaze out of the window at red and orange roof tiles, at ochre walls, poppies growing wild on the roadsides, vines.

At 10 a.m. we were waiting in a small office in a side street for the arrival of the coach. The brochure in the hotel lobby had described the outing as Extended Alban Hills Tours — Castelli Romani. Our coach was apparently now touring some of the larger hotels picking up other passengers. The whole operation seemed a bit makeshift and fly-by-night. The two young men running it seemed to do nothing but shout denials on the phone and hustle out into the street screaming at drivers as coach after coach checked in at the office before setting out to tour whatever they were advertised as touring. Commands and queries were hysterical. Tickets were counted and recounted. And then recounted. Coaches were finally dispatched with operatic gesture as if they were full of troops going up to some heroic Front.

As each coach pulled up, we looked inquiry at one or other of the young men. 'This is not yours,' said their hands. 'Patience.' 'Do not fear. When your conveyance arrives, we will inform you,' said their gestures.

We were both startled by the entry of a large, stout man with a shaved head who barged into the tiny office saying something that sounded challenging or jeering. His voice was harsh. He limped, throwing out one leg stiffly. Helen sat up in the plastic chair and drew her legs in. Something about his appearance suggested that he'd survived a bad car-crash. He leaned on an aluminum stick which ended in a large rubber bulb. He was wearing rimless blue-tinted glasses. His lip was permanently drawn up a little at one side. There was a lot of visible metal in his teeth. He stumped about in the confined space shouting and growling.

The young man with the mauve leather shoes shouted 'no' a lot and 'never' and slapped the counter with a plastic ruler. The other young man picked up a glossy brochure and, gazing fixedly at the ceiling, twisted it as if wringing a neck. The shaven-headed man pushed a pile of pamphlets off the counter with the rubber tip of his aluminum stick.

A coach pulled up and a young woman in a yellow dress got down from it and clattered on heels into the office. They all shouted at her. She spat — *teh* — and made a coarse gesture.

The young man with the mauve leather shoes went outside to shout up at the coach driver. Through the window, we watched him counting, pulling each finger down in turn.

...five, six, *seven*.

Further heart-rending pantomime followed.

Still in full flow, he burst back into the office brandishing the tickets in an accusatory way. Peering and pouting into the mirror of a compact, the girl in the yellow dress continued applying lipstick. They all shouted questions at her, possibly rhetorical. The horrible shaven-headed man shook the handle of his aluminum cane in her face.

She spat again — *teh*.

The bus driver sounded his horn.

The other young man spoke beseechingly to the potted azalea.

"Is that," said Helen, "the Castelli Romani coach? Or isn't it the Castelli Romani coach?"

There was silence as everyone stared at her.

"It *is*, dear madam, it *is*," said the horribly bald man.

"Good," said Helen.

And I followed her out.

We nodded to the other seven passengers as we climbed aboard and seated ourselves behind them near the front of the coach. They sounded American. There were two middle-aged couples, a middle-aged man on his own, rather melancholy-looking, and a middle-aged man with an old woman.

"Here he comes goosewalking," said Helen.

"*Stepping*," I said.

The shaven-headed man, leg lifting up and then swinging to the side, was stumping across the road leaning on the aluminum cane. His jacket was a flapping black-and-white plaid.

"Oh, *no*!" I said. "You don't think *he's*..."

"I told you," said Helen. "I told you this was going to be awful."

The shaven-headed man climbed up into the bus, hooked his aluminum cane over the handrail above the steps, and unclipped the microphone. Holding it in front of his mouth, he surveyed us.

"Today," he said with strange, metallic sibilance, "today you are my children."

Helen nudged.

"Today I am taking you into the Alban Hills. I will show you many wonders. I will show you extinct volcanoes. I will show you the lake of the famous Caligula. I will show you the headquarters of the German Army in World War II. Together we will visit Castel Gandolfo, Albano, Genzano, Frascati, and Rocca di Papa. We will leave ancient Rome by going past the Colosseum and out onto the Via Appia Antica completed by Appius Claudius in 312 before Christ."

He nodded slowly.

"Oh yes, my children."

Still nodding.

"*Before Christ.*"

He looked from face to face.

"You will know this famous road as the Appian Way and you will have seen it in the movie *Spartacus* with the star Kirk Douglas."

"Oh, God!" said Helen.

"Well, my children," he said, tapping the bus driver on the shoulder, "are you ready? But you are curious about me. Who *is* this man, you are saying."

He inclined his shaved head in a bow.

"*Who* am I?"

He chuckled into the microphone.

"They call me Kojak."

Cypresses standing guard along the Appian Way over sepulchres and sarcophagi, umbrella pines shading fragments of statuary. Tombs B.C. Tombs A.D. Statuary contemporaneous with Julius Caesar, of whom we would have read in the play of that name by William Shakespeare. It was impossible to ignore or block out his voice, and after a few minutes we'd come to dread the clicking on of the microphone and the harsh, metallic commentary.

You will pay attention to your left and you will see...

A sarcophagus.

You will pay attention opposite and you will see...

"Opposite what?"

"He means straight ahead."

"Oh."

...to your right and in one minute you will see a famous school for women drivers...

Into view hove a scrap-metal dealer's yard mountainous with wrecked cars.

You will pay attention...

But despite the irritation of the rasping voice, I found the expedition soothing and the motion of the coach restful. The landscape as it passed was pleasing. Fields. Hedges. Garden plots. The warmth of terra cotta tiles. Hills. White clouds in a sky of blue.

The Pope's summer residence at Castel Gandolfo was a glimpse through open ornate gates up a drive to a house, then the high encircling stone wall around the park.

Beech trees.

In the narrow, steep streets of the small town, the coach's length negotiated the sharp turns, eased around corners, trundled past the elaborate façade of the church and through the piazza with its fountain by Bernini.

The famous Peach Festival took place in June.

At Lake Albano we were to stop for half an hour.

No less, my children, and no more.

The coach pulled into the restaurant parking lot and backed into line with more than a dozen others. The restaurant, a cafeteria sort of place, was built on the very edge of the lake. It was jammed with tourists. Washrooms were at the bottom of a central staircase and children ran up and down the stairs, shouting. There was a faint smell of disinfectant. Lost children cried.

In the plastic display cases were sandwiches with dubious fillings, tired-looking panini, and slices of soggy pizza that were being reheated in microwave ovens until greasy.

The man from our coach who was travelling with the old woman sat staring out of the plate-glass window which overlooked the lake. The old woman was spooning in with trembling speed what looked like a huge English trifle, mounds of whipped cream, maraschino cherries, custard, cake.

Helen and I bought an ice cream we didn't really want. We stood on the wooden dock beside the restaurant and looked at the lake which was unnaturally blue. There was a strong breeze. White sails were swooping over the water. I felt cold and wished we could get back in the coach.

"So this was a volcano," said Helen.

"I guess so."

"The top blew off and then it filled up with water."

"I suppose that's it."

The man from our coach who was on his own, the melancholy-looking man, wandered onto the other side of the dock. He stood holding an ice-cream cone and looking across the lake. He looked a bit like Stan Laurel. We nodded to him. He nodded to us and made a sort of gesture at the lake with his ice cream as if to convey approval.

We smiled and nodded.

The engine of the coach was throbbing as we sat waiting for the man and the old woman to shuffle across the parking lot. The stiff breeze suddenly blew the man's hair down, revealing him as bald. From one side of his head hung a long hank which had been trained up and over his bald pate. He looked naked and bizarre as he stood there, the length of hair hanging from the side of his head and fluttering below his shoulder. It looked as if he'd been scalped. The attached hair looked like a dead thing, like a pelt.

Seemingly unembarrassed, he lifted the hair back, settling it as if it were a beret, patting it into place. The old woman stood perhaps two feet from the side of the coach smiling at it with a little smile.

And so, my children, we head now for Genzano and for Frascati, the Queen of the Castelli…

We did not stop in Genzano which also had Baroque fountains possibly by Bernini in the piazzas and a palazzo of some sort. Down below the town was the Lake of Nemi from which two of Caligula's warships had been recovered only to be burned by the retreating Adolf Hitler.

The famous Feast of Flowers took place in May.

"Why do I know the name Frascati?" said Helen.

"Because of the wine?"

"Have I had it?"

I shrugged.

"I had some *years* ago," I said. "Must be thirty years ago now — at a wedding. We drank it with strawberries."

"Whose wedding?"

"And I don't think I've had it since. Um? Oh…a friend from college. I haven't heard from him — Tony Cranbrook…oh, it's been *years*."

"There," said Helen, "what kind of tree is that?"

I shook my head.

Frascati.

The wine was dry and golden.

Gold in candlelight.

The marriage of Tony Cranbrook had been celebrated in the village church, frayed purple hassocks, that special Anglican smell of damp and dust and stone, marble memorials let into the wall:

…departed this life June 11th 1795 in the sure and certain hope of the resurrection and of the life everlasting…

Afterwards, the younger people had strolled back through deep lanes to the family house for the reception. I'd walked with a girl called Susan who turned out to be the sister of one of the bridesmaids. She'd picked a buttercup and lodged it behind her ear. She'd said:

Do you know what this means in Tahiti?

Late in the evening they'd been wandering about the house calling to us to come and eat strawberries, calling out that I had to make another speech.

Jack?

We know you're there!

Susan?

Jack and Su-san!

The larger drawing-room was warm and quick with candlelight. In the centre of the dark polished refectory table stood a gleaming silver épergne piled with tiny wild strawberries. By the side of it stood octagonal silver sugar casters. The candelabra on the table glossed the wood's dark grain. Reflected in the épergne's curves and facets, points of flame quivered.

You will pay attention to your right…

Traffic was thickening.

Fisher!

The bus was slowing.

Susan Fisher!

…above the piazza. The Villa is still owned by the Aldobrandini family. You will notice the central avenue of box trees. The park is noted for its grottos and Baroque fountains.

"Doubtless by Bernini," I said.

"Is that a *palm* tree?" said Helen.

The Villa is open to tourists only in the morning and upon application to the officials of the Frascati Tourist Office. If you will con-

sult your watches, you will see that it is now afternoon so we will proceed immediately to the largest of the Frascati wine cellars.

The aluminum cane with its rubber bulb thumping down, the leg swinging up and to the side, Kojak led the straggling procession towards a large grey stone building at the bottom end of the sloping piazza. A steep flight of steps led down to a terrace and the main entrance. Kojak, teeth bared with the exertion, started to stump and crab his way down.

"Oh, look at the poor old thing, Jack," said Helen. "He'll never manage her on his own down here."

I went back across the road to where they were still waiting to cross and put my arm under the old woman's. She seemed almost weightless.

"I appreciate this," he said, nodding vigorously on the other side of her. "Nelson Morrison. We're from Trenton, New Jersey."

"Not at all," I said. "Not at all. It's a pleasure."

The old woman did not look at either of us.

"That's the way," I said. "That's it."

"She's not a big talker. She doesn't speak very often, do you, Mother?"

Step by step we edged her down.

"But she enjoys it, don't you, Mother? You can tell she enjoys it. She likes to go out. We went on a boat, didn't we, Mother?"

"Nearly there," I said.

"Do you remember the boat in Venice, Mother? Do you? I think it's a naughty day today, isn't it? You're only hearing what you want to hear."

"One more," I said.

"But she did enjoy it. Every year you'll find us somewhere, won't he, Mother?"

Inside, the others were sitting at a refectory table in a vaulted cellar. It was lit by bare bulbs. It was cool, almost cold, after coming in out of the sunshine. In places, the brickwork glistened with moisture. Kojak, a cigarette held up between thumb and forefinger, was holding forth.

The cellars apparently extended under the building for more than a mile of natural caves and caverns. In the tunnels and corridors were more than a million bottles of wine. Today, however, there was nothing to see as the wine-making did not take place until September. But famous and authentic food was available at the café and counter just a bit further down the tunnel and bottles of the finest Frascati were advantageously for sale. If we desired to buy wine, it would be his pleasure to negotiate for us.

He paused.

He surveyed us through the blue-tinted spectacles.

Slowly, he shook his head.

The five bottles of wine on the table were provided free of charge for us to drink on its own or as an accompaniment to food we might purchase. While he was talking, a girl with a sacking apron round her waist and with broken-backed men's shoes on her feet scuffed in with a tray of tumblers. Kojak started pouring the wine. It looked as if it had been drawn from a barrel minutes before. It was greenish and cloudy. It was thin and vile and tasted like tin. I decided to drink it quickly.

I didn't actually see it happen because I was leaning over saying something to Helen. I heard the melancholy man, the man who was travelling alone, say, "No thank you. I don't drink."

Glass chinking against glass.

"No thank you."

A chair scraping.

And there was Kojak mopping at his trouser leg with a handkerchief and grinding out what sounded like imprecations which were getting louder and louder. The melancholy man had somehow moved his glass away while Kojak was pouring or had tried to cover it or pushed away the neck of the bottle. Raised fist quivering, Kojak was addressing the vaulted roof.

Grabbing a bottle-neck in his meaty hand, he upended the bottle over the little man's glass, wine glugging and splashing onto the table.

"Doesn't drink!" snarled Kojak.

He slammed the bottle down on the table.

"Doesn't drink!"

He flicked drops of wine onto the table off the back of his splashed hand.

"Mama mia! Doesn't drink!"

Grinding and growling he stumped off towards the café.

He left behind him a silence.

Into the silence, one of the women said,

"Perhaps it's a custom you're supposed to drink it? If you don't it's insulting?"

"Now wait a minute," said her husband.

"Like covering your head?" she added.

"Maybe I'm out of line," said the other man, "but in my book that was inappropriate behaviour."

"I never did much like the taste of alcohol," said the melancholy man.

His accent was British and glumly northern.

"They seem to sup it with everything here," he said, shaking his head in gloomy disapproval.

"Where are you folks from?" said the man in the turquoise shirt.

"Canada," said Helen.

"You hear that, June? Ottawa? Did we visit Ottawa, June?"

"Maybe," said June, "being that he's European, and..."

"It's nothing to do with being European," said Helen. "It's to do with being rude and a bully. And he's not getting a tip from *us*."

"Yeah," said June's husband, "and what's with all these jokes about women drivers? I'll tell you something, okay? *My wife drives better than I drive*. Okay?"

He looked around the table.

"Okay?"

"I've seen them," said the melancholy man, "in those little places where they eat their breakfasts standing up, I've seen them in there first thing in the morning — imagine — taking raw spirits."

The old woman sat hunched within a tweed coat, little eyes watching. She made me think of a fledgling that had fallen from the nest. Her tumbler was empty. She was looking at me. Then she seemed to be looking at the nearest bottle. I raised my eyebrows. Her eyes seemed to grow wider. I poured her more and her hand crept out to secure the glass.

"*Jack*!" whispered Helen.

"What the hell difference does it make?"

I poured more of the stuff for myself.

June and Chuck were from North Dakota. Norm and Joanne were from California. Chuck was in construction. Norm was on a disability pension and sold patio furniture. Joanne was a nurse. George Robinson was from Bradford and did something to do with textile machinery. Nelson and his mother travelled every summer and last summer had visited Yugoslavia but had suffered from the food.

I explained to June that it was quite possible that I sounded very like the guy on a PBS series because the series had been made by the BBC and I had been born in the UK but was now Canadian. She told me my accent was cute. I told her I thought her accent cute too. We toasted each other's accents. Helen began giving me looks.

June had bought a purse in Rome. Joanne had bought a purse in Florence. Florence was noted for purses. June and Chuck were going to Florence after Rome. Helen had bought a purse in Florence — the best area of Florence for purses being on the far side of the Ponte Vecchio. In Venice there were far fewer stores selling purses. Shoes, on the other hand, shoe stores were everywhere. Norm said he'd observed more shoe stores in Italy than in any other country in the world.

Nelson disliked olive oil.

George could not abide eggplants. Doris, George's wife who had died of cancer the year before, had never fancied tomatoes.

Nelson was flushed and becoming loquacious.

Chuck said he'd had better pizza in Grand Forks, North Dakota, where at least they put cheese on it and it wasn't runny.

George said the look of eggplants made him think of native women.

Joanne said a little pasta went a long way.

Milan?

After Venice, Norm and Joanne were booked into Milan. What was Milan like? Had anyone been there?

"Don't speak to me about Milan!" said Helen.

"Not a favourite subject with us," I said.

"We got mugged there," said Helen, "and they stole a gold bracelet I'd had since I was twenty-one."

"'They'," I said, "being three girls."

"We were walking along on the sidewalk just outside that monstrous railway station…"

"Three *girls*, for Christ's sake!"

"They came running up to us," said Helen.

"Two of them not more than thirteen years old," I said, "and the other about eighteen or nineteen."

"One of them had a newspaper sort of folded to show columns of figures and another had a bundle of tickets of some sort and they were waving these in our faces..."

"And talking at us very loudly and quickly…"

"…and, well, *brandishing* these…"

"…and sort of grabbing at you, pulling your sleeve…"

"*Touching* you," said Helen.

"*Right*!" said Norm. "Okay."

"*Exactly*," said Joanne. "That's *exactly*…"

"And then," I said, "I felt the tallest girl's hand going inside my jacket — you know — to your inside pocket…"

"We were so *distracted*, you see," said Helen, "what with all the talking and them pointing at the paper and waving things under your nose and being *touched*…"

"So anyway," I said, "when I felt *that* I realized what was happening and I hit this girl's arm away and…"

"Oh, it was *awful*!" said Helen. "Because *I* thought they were just beggars, you see, or kids trying to sell lottery tickets or something, and I was really horrible to Jack for hitting this girl…I mean, he hit her *really hard* and I thought they were just begging so I couldn't believe he'd…"

"But the best part," I said, "was that I probably wasn't the main target in the first place because we walked on into the station and we were buying tickets — we were in the line — and Helen…"

"I'd suddenly felt the weight," said Helen. "The difference, I mean, and I looked down at my wrist and the bracelet was gone. I hadn't felt a thing when they'd grabbed it. Not with all that other touching. They must have pulled and broken the safety chain and…"

"Of course," I said, "I ran back to the entrance but..."

I spread my hands.

"Long gone."

"With us," said Joanne, "it was postcards and guidebooks they were waving about."

"Where?"

"Here. In Rome."

"Girls? The same?"

"Gypsies," said Norm.

"Did they get anything?" said Helen.

"A Leica," said Joanne.

"Misdirection of attention," said Norm.

"Were they girl-gypsies?" I said.

"Misdirecting," said Norm. "It's the basic principle of illusionism."

"I was robbed right at the airport," said Nelson.

"It must be a national *industry*," said George.

"They had a baby in a shawl and I was just standing there with Mother and they pushed this baby against my chest and well, naturally, you…"

"I don't *believe* this!" said Norm. "This I do not *believe*!"

"And while I was holding it, the other two women were shouting at me in Italian and they had a magazine they were showing me…"

"What did they steal?"

"Airplane ticket. Passport. Traveller's cheques. But I had some American bills in the top pocket of my blazer so they didn't get that."

"Did you feel it?" said Joanne.

He shook his head.

"No. They just took the baby and walked away and I only realized when I was going to change a traveller's cheque at the cambio office because we were going to get on the bus, weren't we, Mother?"

"A baby!" said June.

"But a few minutes later," said Nelson, "one of the women came up to me on her own with the ticket and my passport."

"Why would she give them back?" said Helen. "Don't they sell them to spies or something?"

"I paid her for them," said Nelson.

"Paid her?" said June.

"*Paid her*!" said Norm.

"*PAID*!" said Chuck.

"Ten dollars," said Nelson.

"They must have seen you coming!" said George.

"They must have seen *all* of you coming," said Chuck.

Nelson poured himself another murky tumbler of Frascati.

"It wasn't much," he said. "Ten dollars. She got what she wanted. I got what I wanted."

He shrugged. Raising the glass, he said,

"A short life but a merry one!"

We stared at him.

"I got what I wanted, didn't I, Mother? And then we went on the green and red bus, didn't we? Do you remember? On the green and red bus?"

The old woman started making loud squeak noises in her throat.

It was the first sound we'd heard her make.

She sounded like a guinea pig.

"It's time for tinkles!" sang Nelson. "It's tinkle time."

And raising her up and half carrying her to the door of the women's malodorous toilet, he turned with her, almost as if waltzing, and backed his way in.

✲

...not entirely without incident.

Don't mention Milan to us!

...except for Helen's getting mugged.

It all made a good story, a story with which we regaled our friends and neighbours. We became quite practised in the telling of it. We told it at parties and over dinners, feeding each other lines.

But the story we told was a story different in one particular from what really happened — though Helen doesn't know that.

The scene often comes to mind. I see it when the pages blur. I see it in my desk-top in the wood's repetitive grain. I see it when I gaze unseeing out of the window of the restaurant after lunch, the sun hot on my shoulder and sleeve. I see it when I'm lying in bed in the morning in those drowsy minutes after being awakened by the clink and chink of Helen's bottles as she applies moisturizing cream, foundation, blush, and shadow.

Chuck from Grand Forks, North Dakota, had been right. They *had* seen all of us coming. Easy pickings. Meek and nearing middle age, ready to be fleeced, lambs to the slaughter.

She'd been the first female I'd hit since childhood. I hadn't intended to hit her hard. I'd moved instinctively. Her eyes had widened with the pain of it.

I'd noticed her even before she'd run towards us. Good legs, high breasts pushing at the tight grey cotton dress, long light-brown hair. She was wearing bright yellow plastic sandals. She had no make-up on and looked a bit grubby, looked the young gamin she probably was.

I'd been carrying a suitcase and felt sweaty even though it was early in the morning. Her hand as it touched the side of my chest, my breast, was cool against my heat.

When I struck her arm, there was no panic in her eyes, just a widening. There was a hauteur in her expression. Our eyes held each other's for what seemed long seconds.

When Helen discovered her bracelet gone, I hurried out of the vast ticket hall but under the colonnade and out of sight I slowed to a walk. There is no rational, sensible explanation for what followed.

I stood in the archway of the entrance. The two small girls had gone. She stood facing me across the width of the curving road. It was as if she'd been waiting for me.

We stood staring at each other.

Behind her was a sidewalk café. The white metal chairs and tables were screened by square white tubs containing small, bushy bay trees. The bays were dark and glossy. Dozens of sparrows hopped about on the edges of the tubs. Pigeons were pecking along the sidewalk near her feet. Among them was a reddish-brown pigeon and two white ones. In the strong morning light I could see the lines of her body under the grey cotton dress. She was gently rubbing at her arm.

Sitting there in Reardon's restaurant, drowsy in the sunshine after eating the Businessman's Luncheon Special ($4.95), the cream of celery soup, the minced-beef pie with ginger-coloured gravy, the french fries, the sliced string beans, waiting for the waitress to bring coffee, sitting there with the winter sun warm through the window on my shoulder and sleeve, I walk out of the shadow of the arch and stand waiting on the edge of the sidewalk. She nods to me. It is a nod which is casually intimate, a nod of acknowledgement and greeting. I wait for a gap in the sweeping traffic.

She watches me approaching.

Commentary by John Metcalf

≈

John Metcalf's writing reveals an exquisite preciseness of detail and an extraordinary power of suggestion. The following commentary is taken from an essay, "The Curate's Egg", published in Essays on Canadian Writing *30 (1984-85). In it Metcalf argues that only by careful attention to the techniques necessary for depicting the particulars of a story's world can a writer — or a reader — discover the story's centre and implications.*

What did I *mean* by the story as "performance", by the story as "thing to be experienced"?

I am going to be entirely presumptuous now and speak for other writers too. Good writers would refuse to allow that that beloved CanLit abstraction "theme" was an element which was in any way abstractable. To be plonkingly boring, *how* something is written *is* what is written. The quest for "theme" — what the story is "about" — is arid and doomed to failure. The American poet John Ciardi puts this succinctly when he advised readers of poetry not to ask "What does this poem mean?" but rather "*How* does this poem mean?"

This sounds simple but is not.

Although writers usually know what a story is "about" before they start writing, stories for them are a process of discovery. A story's general "theme" is so basic — and uninteresting — that it's taken for granted. What does *that* mean? As Degas grew older, he no longer had much interest in painting in facial detail; heads became shapes. Was he painting and drawing dancers and nudes in bathtubs or was he drawing *lines*?

It means something like that.

What is being discovered as the writing and rewriting progresses is the fascination of the theme's ramifications, variations, and *embodiment*. The writer is fascinated by the embodiment of the theme in the physical world of the story (texture) and fascinated by the literary and rhetorical devices necessary to capture and suggest that world.

Sometimes writers do *not* know what a story is "about"; the language itself reveals to them new directions, new dimensions as it unfolds. This is true for all writers to some degree or another;

language is alive under their hands as clay is for a potter. Sometimes it has its own shape and insistence.

I chose the word "embodiment" carefully but it is, I realize, quite the *wrong* word. It seems to imply that a preconceived idea is given concrete form. I mean exactly the reverse. Stories do not begin with an idea; usually they begin with a detail, a sound, a voice.

The writer's special kind of attention is first caught by, let us say, a woman's dress. This image stays in his mind. He does not know why. Later, he might find himself seeing this woman in this dress standing in a particular room. In this room on the mantelpiece is a large ormolu clock. The process of accretion continues. Soon the writer knows that here is the world of a story. By the time that this world is ready to be written about, the accumulation of details and images in the writer's mind will have suggested the nature they have in common; the general thematic aspect of the story will have emerged and clarified itself through particularities.

Yes, *yes*.

But what grips the writer is that marvellous *clock*. Victorian. Black. Cold to the touch. Its ornamental pillars. Its architrave and pediment. Its massive weight. The remorseless swing of its brass pendulum visible through its glass door. It is a clock like a house.

SELECTED WORKS BY JOHN METCALF

"The Geography of Time." *Prism international* 4.1 (1964): 6-30; and *Prism international* 4.2 (1964): 28-43.

New Canadian Writing, 1969: Stories by John Metcalf, D. O. Spettigue and C. J. Newman. Toronto: Clarke, Irwin, 1969. 3-63.

The Lady Who Sold Furniture. Toronto: Clarke, Irwin, 1970.

The Teeth of My Father. Ottawa: Oberon Press, 1975.

Girl in Gingham. Ottawa: Oberon Press, 1978. Rpt. as *Private Parts: A Memoir*. Scarborough, ON: New American Library, 1980.

Selected Stories. New Canadian Library 168. Toronto: McClelland and Stewart, 1982.

Adult Entertainment: Short Fiction. Toronto: Macmillan, 1986. Rpt. as *Adult Entertainment*. Vintage Contemporaries. Toronto: Vintage/Random House, 1990.

Margaret Atwood

≈

Whenever I read Margaret Atwood's work, I am struck more than anything else by her intelligence; that is to say, her intellect often seems to dominate her work. She is unlike most of the other writers in this anthology in that she is an openly political writer; she has axes to grind. Mavis Gallant's stories are also often concerned with politics — with the turmoil of Europe, the German past, Fascism — but she explores these political concerns by concentrating on the way they have shaped or influenced families or individuals. These families or individuals do not *stand for* 'society' or some such abstraction, but are people who are entirely and absolutely themselves. If we as readers wish to draw any larger or more abstract significance, she leaves that up to us. Margaret Atwood's intention and approach is, in contrast, often openly didactic.

In an essay called "An End to Audience?" in her *Second Words: Selected Critical Prose*, Margaret Atwood wrote: "I believe that fiction writing is the guardian of the moral and ethical sense of the community. Especially now that organized religion is scattered and in disarray, and politicians have, Lord knows, lost their credibility, fiction is one of the few forms left through which we may examine our society not in its particular but in its typical aspects; through which we can see ourselves and the ways in which we behave towards each other, through which we can see others and judge them and ourselves." She goes on: "Writing is a craft, true, and discussions of the position of colons and the rhyming of *plastic* and *spastic* have some place in it...."

Her statement in the first quoted passage that fiction enables us to examine our society "not in its particular but in its typical aspects", and the implication in the second that the craft of writing is separable from and subsidiary to the 'message' of the writing, fundamentally differentiates Margaret Atwood from the other writers in this anthology. Characteristically, Margaret Atwood is committed to presenting ideas and political positions. The central problem with writing which advances ideas is that we can take issue with the ideas advanced *as ideas*; we can disagree intellectually with particular moral and ethical positions or with the political ideas of left, right, and centre. But it is impossible to 'disagree' with our experience of the particularities of a Mavis Gallant story.

As will be obvious by now, I have reservations about Margaret Atwood's theory and practice. The stories by Margaret Atwood included here, however, exhibit the strengths for which she has been widely appreciated. Her best stories reverberate with memorable comic or tragic effects. She can be very funny indeed and the story "Hurricane Hazel" — reprinted from her collection *Bluebeard's Egg* (1983) — is an almost perfect comic performance. The feminist position which is inherent in the story is not advanced as an argument; the young male, Buddy, is seen through the grave eyes of the narrator as something as alien as a being from Mars, and the rituals of teen courtship are described almost as by an anthropologist observing savage rites.

"Hurricane Hazel" has for me only one flaw and it is that place in the story where Margaret Atwood intrudes on the comic texture to hammer home unnecessarily a point that was being made delicately by the whole shape of the scene. I draw attention to this because it illustrates my reservations about her editorializing and because it provides an example for discussion. In the section of the story where the narrator and Buddy go with Charlie and Trish to the beach and Buddy confers upon the narrator his "identity bracelet" — a scene wittily set with refuse and, essentially Atwoodian detail, a decaying weiner — the scene is undercut and weakened by the passage which discusses the significance of the bestowing of the bracelet: "Another interpretation has since become possible: that Buddy was putting his name on me, like a *Reserved* sign or an ownership label, or a tattoo on a cow's ear, or a brand. But at the time nobody thought that way."

Sometimes I feel that Margaret Atwood is, paradoxically, most emotionally powerful when she is at her most intellectual. When we were discussing the choice of stories for this book, I advanced the rather heretical notion that I thought Margaret Atwood's best and most moving prose was to be found in her relatively little-known book *Murder in the Dark: Short Fictions and Prose Poems* (1983). Among the pieces in that book, I particularly admire "Women's Novels", "Happy Endings", and "Liking Men". Have they a place in an anthology of stories? Are they stories? Do labels really matter? We decided against these pieces — choosing instead the ominously prophetic story "The Age of Lead" from her collection *Wilderness Tips* (1991) — but I wonder if that was the right decision. Hemingway, of course, published the very brief descriptive 'inter-story' pieces in *In Our Time* as a separate and earlier book called *in our time* — and look at the impact and importance of *those* pieces. It's interesting that Margaret Atwood has continued exploring this form in a variety of pieces collected in *Good Bones* (1992).

≈

There is a considerable body of critical work on Margaret Atwood. Highly recommended are two identically entitled monographs: one on her poetry, Jean Mallinson's *Margaret Atwood and Her Works* (Toronto: ECW Press, 1985); the other on her fiction, Ildikó de Papp Carrington's *Margaret Atwood and Her Works* (Toronto: ECW Press, 1987). Russell Brown's article "Atwood's Sacred Wells" in *Essays on Canadian Writing* 17 (1980) discusses a number of her early stories in the context of some of her other works. Lee Briscoe Thompson contributes an interesting survey of Margaret Atwood's story collection *Dancing Girls and Other Stories* in *The Art of Margaret Atwood: Essays in Criticism,* edited by Arnold E. Davidson and Cathy N. Davidson (Toronto: House of Anansi, 1981). W. J. Keith presents a careful evaluation of more and less rewarding ways of reading the title story of Margaret Atwood's story collection *Bluebeard's Egg* in *An Independent Stance: Essays on English-Canadian Criticism and Fiction* (Erin, ON: The Porcupine's Quill, 1991). Margaret Atwood offers a number of comments on the short story form in her introduction, "Reading Blind", to *The Best American Short Stories 1989* (Boston: Houghton Mifflin, 1989). *Margaret Atwood: Conversations,* edited by Earl G. Ingersoll (Willowdale, ON: Firefly Books, 1990), provides a range of insights into the author and her work.

≈ HURRICANE HAZEL ≈

The summer I was fourteen, we lived in a one-room cabin, on a hundred acres of back-concession scrub farmland. The cabin was surrounded by a stand of tall old maples, which had been left there when the land was cut over, and the light sifted down in shafts, like those in pictures I had seen in Sunday school, much earlier, of knights looking for the Holy Grail, helmets off, eyes rolled up purely. Probably these trees were the reason my parents had bought the land: if they hadn't, someone else would have bought it and sold off the maples. This was the kind of thing my parents were in the habit of doing.

The cabin was of squared timber. It hadn't been built there originally, but had been moved from some other location by the people who had owned it before us, two high-school teachers who were interested in antiques. The logs had been numbered, then dismantled and put back together in the original order, and the cracks had been re-chinked with white cement, which was already beginning to fall out in places; so was the putty on the small panes of the windows. I knew this because one of my first jobs had been to wash them. I did this grudgingly, as I did most jobs around the house at the time.

We slept on one side of the room. The sleeping areas were divided off by parachutes, which my father had bought at the war-surplus store, where he often bought things: khaki-coloured pants with pockets on the knees, knife, fork, and spoon sets which locked together and snapped apart and were impossible to eat with, rain capes with camouflage markings on them, a jungle hammock with mosquito-netting sides that smelled like the inside of a work sock and gave you a kink in the back, despite which my brother and I used to compete for the privilege of sleeping in it. The parachutes had been cut open and were hung like curtains from lengths of thick wire strung from wall to wall. The parachutes inside the house were dark green, but there was a smaller orange one set up outside, like a tent, for my three-year-old sister to play in.

I had the cubicle in the southeast corner. I slept there on a narrow bed with wire coil springs that squeaked whenever I turned over. On the other side of the cabin, the living side, there was a table coated with ruined varnish and a couple of much-painted chairs, the paint now cracked like a dried mud flat so that you could see what colours had been used before. There was a dresser with plates in it, which smelled even mustier than the rest of the things in the cabin, and a couple of rocking chairs, which didn't work too well on the uneven boards of the floor. All this furniture had been in the cabin when we bought it; perhaps it was the schoolteachers' idea of pioneer décor.

There was also a sort of counter where my mother washed the dishes and kept the primus stove she cooked on when it was raining. The rest of the time she cooked outdoors, on a fireplace with a grate of iron rods. When we ate outside we didn't use chairs: instead we sat on rounds of logs, because the ground itself was damp. The cabin was in a river valley; at night there was heavy dew, and the heat of the morning sunlight made an almost visible steam.

My father had moved us into the cabin early in the summer. Then he'd taken off for the forests on the north shore of the St. Lawrence, where he was doing some exploration for a pulp-and-paper company. All the time we were going through our daily routine, which revolved mainly around mealtimes and what we would eat at them, he was flying in bush planes into valleys with sides so steep the pilot had to cut the engine to get down into them, or trudging over portages past great rocky out-crops, or almost upsetting in rapids. For two weeks he was trapped by a forest fire which encircled him on all sides, and was saved only by torrential rains, during which he sat in his tent and toasted his extra socks at the fire, like weiners, to get them dry. These were the kinds of stories we heard after he came back.

My father made sure before he went that we had a supply of split and stacked wood and enough staples and tinned goods to keep us going. When we needed other things, such as milk and butter, I was sent on foot to the nearest store, which was a mile and a half away, at the top of an almost perpendicular hill which, much later, got turned into a ski resort. At that time there was only a dirt road, in the middle of what I thought of as nowhere, which let loose clouds of dust every time a car went past. Sometimes the cars would honk, and I would pretend not to notice.

The woman at the store, who was fat and always damp, was curious about us; she would ask how my mother was getting along. Didn't she mind it, all alone in that tumbledown place with no proper stove and no man around? She put the two things on the same level. I resented that kind of prying, but I was at the age when anybody's opinion mattered to me, and I could see that she thought my mother was strange.

If my mother had any reservations about being left alone on a remote farm with a three-year-old, no telephone, no car, no electricity, and only me for help, she didn't state them. She had been in such situations before, and by that time she must have been used to them. Whatever was going on she treated as normal; in the middle of crises, such as cars stuck up to their axles in mud, she would suggest we sing a song.

That summer she probably missed my father, though she would never say so; conversations in our family were not about feelings. Sometimes, in the evenings, she would write letters, though she claimed she could never think of what to say. During the days, when she wasn't cooking or washing the dishes, she did small tasks which could be interrupted at any time. She would cut the grass, even though the irregular plot in front of the house was overgrown with weeds and nothing would make it look any more like a lawn; or she would pick up the fallen branches under the maple trees.

I looked after my little sister for part of the mornings: that was one of my jobs. At these times my mother would sometimes drag a rocking chair out onto the bumpy grass and read books, novels of historical times or accounts of archaeological expeditions. If I came up behind her and spoke to her while she was reading, she would scream. When it was sunny she would put on shorts, which she would never wear when other people were around. She thought she had bony knees; this was the only thing about her personal appearance that she showed much awareness about. For the most part she was indifferent to clothes. She wanted them to cover what they were supposed to cover and to stay in one piece, and that was all she expected from them.

When I wasn't taking care of my sister, I would go off by myself. I would climb one of the maples, which was out of sight of the house and had a comfortable fork in it, and read *Wuthering Heights*; or I would walk along the old logging road, now grown up in saplings. I knew my way around in the weedy and brambly jungle back there, and I'd been across the river to the open field on the other side, where the next-door farmer was allowed to graze his cows, to keep down the thistles and burdock. This was where I'd found what I thought was the pioneers' house, the real one, though it was nothing now but a square depression surrounded by grass-covered ridges. The first year, this man had planted a bushel of peas, and he'd harvested a bushel. We knew this from the schoolteachers, who looked up records.

If my brother had made this discovery, he would have drawn a map of it. He would have drawn a map of the whole area, with everything neatly labelled. I didn't even attempt this; instead, I merely wandered around, picking raspberries and thimbleberries, or sunning myself in the tall weeds, surrounded by the smell of milk-weed and daisies and crushed leaves, made dizzy by the sun and the light reflected from the white pages of my book, with grasshoppers landing on me and leaving traces of their brown spit.

Towards my mother I was surly, though by myself I was lazy and aimless. It was hard even to walk through the grass, and lifting my hand to brush away the grasshoppers was an effort. I seemed always to be half asleep. I told myself that I wanted to be doing something; by that I meant something that would earn money, elsewhere. I wanted a summer job, but I was too young for one.

My brother had a job. He was two years older than I was, and now he was a Junior Ranger, cutting brush by the sides of highways somewhere in northern Ontario, living in tents with a batch of other sixteen-year-old boys. This was his first summer away. I resented his absence and envied him, but I also looked for his letters every day. The mail was delivered by a woman who lived on a nearby farm; she drove it around in her own car. When there was something for us she would toot her horn, and I would walk out to the dusty galva-nized mailbox that stood on a post beside our gate.

My brother wrote letters to my mother as well as to me. Those to her were informative, descriptive, factual. He said what he was doing, what they ate, where they did their laundry. He said that the town near their camp had a main street that was held up only by the telephone wires. My mother was pleased by these letters, and read them out loud to me.

I did not read my brother's letters out loud to her. They were pri-vate, and filled with the sort of hilarious and vulgar commentary that we often indulged in when we were alone. To other people we seemed grave and attentive, but by ourselves we made fun of things relentlessly, outdoing each other with what we considered to be revolting details. My brother's letters were illustrated with drawings of his tent-mates, showing them with many-legged bugs jumping around on their heads, with spots on their faces, with wavy lines indicating smelliness radiating from their feet, with apple cores in the beards they were all attempting to grow. He included unsavoury details of their personal habits, such as snoring. I took these letters straight from the mailbox to the maple tree, where I read them over several times. Then I smuggled them into the cabin under my T-shirt and hid them under my bed.

I got other letters too, from my boyfriend, whose name was Buddy. My brother used a fountain pen; Buddy's letters were in blue ball-point, the kind that splotched, leaving greasy blobs that came off on my fingers. They contained ponderous compliments, like those made by other people's uncles. Many words were enclosed by quotation marks; others were underlined. There were no pictures.

I liked getting these letters from Buddy, but also they embarrassed me. The trouble was that I knew what my brother would say about Buddy, partly because he had already said some of it. He spoke as if both he and I took it for granted that I would soon be getting rid of Buddy, as if Buddy were a stray dog it would be my duty to send to the Humane Society if the owner could not be found. Even Buddy's name, my brother said, was like a dog's. He said I should call Buddy "Pal" or "Sport" and teach him to fetch.

I found my brother's way of speaking about Buddy both funny and cruel: funny because it was in some ways accurate, cruel for the same reason. It was true that there was something dog-like about Buddy: the affability, the dumb faithfulness about the eyes, the dutiful way he plodded through the rituals of dating. He was the kind of boy (though I never knew this with certainty, because I never saw it) who would help his mother carry in the groceries without being asked, not because he felt like it but simply because it was prescribed. He said things like, "That's the way the cookie crumbles," and when he said this I had the feeling he would still be saying it forty years later.

Buddy was a lot older than I was. He was eighteen, almost nineteen, and he'd quit school long ago to work at a garage. He had his own car, a third-hand Dodge, which he kept spotlessly clean and shining. He smoked and drank beer, though he drank the beer only when he wasn't out with me but was with other boys his own age. He would mention how many bottles he had drunk in an offhand way, as if disclaiming praise.

He made me anxious, because I didn't know how to talk to him. Our phone conversations consisted mostly of pauses and monosyllables, though they went on a long time; which was infuriating to my father, who would walk past me in the hall, snapping his first two fingers together like a pair of scissors, meaning I was to cut it short. But cutting short a conversation with Buddy was like trying to divide water, because Buddy's conversations had no shape, and I couldn't give them a shape myself. I hadn't yet learned any of those stratagems girls were supposed to use on men. I didn't know how to ask leading questions, or how to lie about certain kinds of things, which I was later to call being tactful. So mostly I said nothing, which didn't seem to bother Buddy at all.

I knew enough to realize, however, that it was a bad tactic to appear too smart. But if I had chosen to show off, Buddy might not have minded: he was the kind of boy for whom cleverness was female. Maybe he would have liked a controlled display of it, as if it were a special kind of pie or a piece of well-done embroidery. But I never figured out what Buddy really wanted; I never figured out why Buddy was going out with me in the first place. Possibly it was because I was there. Buddy's world, I gradually discovered, was much less alterable than mine: it contained a long list of things that could never be changed or fixed.

All of this started at the beginning of May, when I was in grade ten. I was two or three years younger than most of the others in my class, because at that time they still believed in skipping you ahead if you could do the work. The year before, when I'd entered high school, I had been twelve, which was a liability when other people were fifteen. I rode my bicycle to school when other girls in my class were walking, slowly, languorously, holding their notebooks up against their bodies to protect and display their breasts. I had no breasts; I could still wear things I'd worn when I was eleven. I took to sewing my own clothes, out of patterns I bought at Eaton's. The clothes never came out looking like the pictures on the pattern envelopes; also they were too big. I must have been making them the size I wanted to be. My mother told me these clothes looked very nice on me, which was untrue and no help at all. I felt like a flat-chested midget, surrounded as I was by girls who were already oily and glandular, who shaved their legs and put pink medicated make-up on their pimples and fainted interestingly during gym, whose flesh was sleek and plumped-out and faintly shining, as if it had been injected under the skin with cream.

The boys were even more alarming. Some of them, the ones who were doing grade nine for the second time, wore leather jackets and were thought to have bicycle chains in their lockers. A few of them were high-voiced and spindly, but these of course I ignored. I knew the difference between someone who was a drip or a pill, on the one hand, and cute or a dream on the other. Buddy wasn't a dream, but he was cute, and that counted for a lot. Once I started going out with Buddy, I found I could pass for normal. I was now included in the kinds of conversations girls had in the washroom while they were putting on their lipstick. I was now teased.

Despite this, I knew that Buddy was a kind of accident: I hadn't come by him honestly. He had been handed over to me by Trish, who had come up to me out of nowhere and asked me to go out with her and her boyfriend Charlie and Charlie's cousin. Trish had a large mouth and prominent teeth and long sandy hair, which she tied back in a pony tail. She wore fuzzy pink sweaters and was a cheerleader, though not the best one. If she hadn't been going steady with Charlie, she would have had a reputation, because of the way she laughed and wiggled; as it was, she was safe enough for the time being. Trish told me I would like Buddy because he was so cute. She also mentioned that he had a car; Charlie didn't have a car. It's likely that I was put into Buddy's life by Trish so that Trish and Charlie could neck in the back seat of Buddy's car at drive-in movies, but I doubt that Buddy knew this. Neither did I, at the time.

We always had to go to the early show — a source of grumbling from Trish and Charlie — because I wasn't allowed to stay out past eleven. My father didn't object to my having boyfriends, as such, but he wanted them to be prompt in their pick-up and delivery. He didn't see why they had to moon around outside the front door when they were dropping me off. Buddy wasn't as bad in this respect as some of the later ones, in my father's opinion. With those, I got into the habit of coming in after the deadline, and my father would sit me down and explain very patiently that if I was on my way to catch a train and I was late for it, the train would go without me, and that was why I should always be in on time. This cut no ice with me at all, since, as I would point out, our house wasn't a train. It must have been then that I began to lose faith in reasonable argument as the sole measure of truth. My mother's rationale for promptness was more understandable: if I wasn't home on time, she would think I had been in a car accident. We knew without admitting it that sex was the hidden agenda at these discussions, more hidden for my father than for my mother: she knew about cars and accidents.

At the drive-in Buddy and Charlie would buy popcorn and Cokes, and we would all munch in unison as the pale shadowy figures materialized on the screen, bluish in the diminishing light. By the time the popcorn was gone it would be dark. There would be rustlings, creakings, suppressed moans from the back seat, which Buddy and I would pretend to ignore. Buddy would smoke a few cigarettes, one arm around my shoulders. After that we would neck, decorously enough compared with what was going on behind us.

Buddy's mouth was soft, his body large and comforting. I didn't know what I was supposed to feel during these sessions. Whatever I did feel was not very erotic, though it wasn't unpleasant either. It was more like being hugged by a friendly Newfoundland dog or an animated quilt than anything else. I kept my knees pressed together and my arms around his back. Sooner or later Buddy would attempt to move his hands around to the front, but I knew I was supposed to stop him, so I did. Judging from his reaction, which was resigned but good-natured, this was the correct thing to do, though he would always try again the next week.

It occurred to me very much later that Trish had selected me, not despite the fact that I was younger and less experienced than she was, but because of it. She needed a chaperone. Charlie was thinner than Buddy, better-looking, more intense; he got drunk sometimes, said Trish, with an already matronly shake of her head. Buddy was seen as solid, dependable, and a little slow, and so perhaps was I.

After I had been going out with Buddy for a month or so, my brother decided it would be in my own best interests to learn Greek. By that he meant he would teach it to me whether I liked it or not. In the past he had taught me many things, some of which I had wanted to know: how to read, how to shoot with a bow, how to skip flat rocks, how to swim, how to play chess, how to aim a rifle, how to paddle a canoe and scale and gut a fish. I hadn't learned many of them very well, except the reading. He had also taught me how to swear, sneak out of bedroom windows at night, make horrible smells with chemicals, and burp at will. His manner, whatever the subject, was always benignly but somewhat distantly pedagogical, as if I were a whole classroom by myself.

The Greek was something he himself was learning; he was two grades ahead of me and was at a different high school, one that was only for boys. He started me with the alphabet. As usual, I didn't learn fast enough for him, so he began leaving notes about the house, with Greek letters substituted for the letters of the English words. I would find one in the bathtub when I was about to take a bath before going out with Buddy, set it aside for later, turn on the tap and find myself drenched by the shower. (*Turn off the shower*, the note would read when translated.) Or there would be a message taped to the closed door of my room, which would turn out to be a warning about what would fall on me — a wet towel, a clump of cooked spaghetti — when I opened it. Or one on my dresser would announce a Frenched bed or inform me that my alarm clock was set to go off at 3 A.M. I didn't ever learn much real Greek, but I did learn to transpose quickly. It was by such ruses, perhaps, that my brother was seeking to head me off, delay my departure from the world he still inhabited, a world in which hydrogen sulphide and chess gambits were still more interesting than sex, and Buddy, and the Buddies to come, were still safely and merely ridiculous.

My brother and Buddy existed on different layers altogether. My brother, for instance, was neither cute nor a pill. Instead he had the preternatural good looks associated with English schoolboys, the kind who turned out to be pyromaniacs in films of the sixties, or with posters of soldiers painted at the time of World War One; he looked as if he ought to have green skin and slightly pointed ears, as if his name should have been Nemo, or something like it; as if he could see through you. All of these things I thought later; at the time he was just my brother, and I didn't have any ideas about how he looked. He had a maroon sweater with holes in the elbows, which my mother kept trying to replace or throw out, but she was never successful. He took her lack of interest in clothes one step further.

Whenever I started to talk like what he thought of as a teenager, whenever I mentioned sock hops or the hit parade, or anything remotely similar, my brother would quote passages out of the black-head-remover ads in his old comic books, the ones he'd collected when he was ten or eleven: "Mary never knew why she was not POPULAR, until.... Someone should tell her! Mary, NOW there's something you can do about those UGLY BLACKHEADS! *Later*.... Mary, I'd like to ask you to the dance. (*Thinks*: Now that Mary's got rid of those UGLY BLACKHEADS, she's the most POPULAR girl in the class.)" I knew that if I ever became the most popular girl in the class, which was not likely, I would get no points at all from my brother.

When I told Buddy I would be away for the summer, he thought I was "going to the cottage," which was what a lot of people in Toronto did; those who had cottages, that is. What he had in mind was something like Lake Simcoe, where you could ride around in fast motorboats and maybe go water-skiing, and where there would be a drive-in. He thought there would be other boys around; he said I would go out with them and forget all about him, but he said it as a joke.

I was vague about where I was actually going. Buddy and I hadn't talked about our families much; it wouldn't be easy to explain to him my parents' preferences for solitude and outhouses and other odd things. When he said he would come up and visit me, I told him it was too far away, too difficult to find. But I couldn't refuse to give him the address, and his letters arrived faithfully every week, smeared and blobby, the handwriting round and laborious and child-like. Buddy pressed so hard the pen sometimes went through, and if I closed my eyes and ran my fingers over the paper I could feel the letters engraved on the page like braille.

I answered Buddy's first letter sitting at the uneven table with its cracked geological surface. The air was damp and warm; the pad of lined paper I was writing on was sticking to the tacky varnish. My mother was doing the dishes, in the enamel dishpan, by the light of one of the oil lamps. Usually I helped her, but ever since Buddy had appeared on the scene she'd been letting me off more frequently, as if she felt I needed the energy for other things. I had the second oil lamp, turned up as high as it would go without smoking. From behind the green parachute curtain I could hear the light breathing of my sister.

Dear Buddy, I wrote, and stopped. Writing his name embarrassed me. When you saw it on a blank sheet of paper like that, it seemed a strange thing to call someone. Buddy's name bore no relation to what I could really remember of him, which was mostly the smell of his freshly washed T-shirts, mixed with the smell of cigarette smoke and Old Spice aftershave. *Buddy*. As a word, it reminded me of *pudding*. I could feel under my hand the little roll of fat at the back of his neck, hardly noticeable now, but it would get larger, later, when he was not even that much older.

My mother's back was towards me but I felt as if she were watching me anyway; or listening, perhaps, to the absence of sound, because I wasn't writing. I couldn't think of what to say to Buddy. I could describe what I'd been doing, but as soon as I began I saw how hopeless this would be.

In the morning I'd made a village out of sand, down on the one small available sandbar, to amuse my sister. I was good at these villages. Each house had stone windows; the roads were paved with stone also, and trees and flowers grew in the gardens, which were surrounded by hedges of moss. When the villages were finished, my sister would play with them, running her toy cars along the roads and moving the stick people I'd made for her, in effect ruining them, which annoyed me.

When I could get away, I'd waded down the river by myself, to be out of range. There was a seam of clay I already knew about, and I'd gouged a chunk out of it and spent some time making it into beads, leaving them on a stump in the sun to harden. Some of them were in the shape of skulls, and I intended to paint these later and string them into a necklace. I had some notion that they would form part of a costume for Hallowe'en, though at the same time I knew I was already too old for this.

Then I'd walked back along the river bank, climbing over the tangles of fallen trees that blocked the way, scratching my bare legs on the brambles. I'd picked a few flowers, as a peace offering to my mother, who must have known I'd deserted her on purpose. These were now wilting in a jam jar on the dresser: bladder campion, jewelweed, Queen Anne's Lace. In our family you were supposed to know the names of things you picked and put in jars.

Nothing I did seemed normal in the light of Buddy; spelled out, my activities looked childish or absurd. What did other girls the age people thought I was do when they weren't with boys? They talked on the telephone, they listened to records; wasn't that it? They went to movies, they washed their hair. But they didn't wash their hair by standing up to their knees in an ice-cold river and pouring water over their heads from an enamel basin. I didn't wish to appear eccentric to Buddy; I wished to disguise myself. This had been easier in the city, where we lived in a more ordinary way: such things as my parents' refusal to buy a television set and sit in front of it eating their dinners off fold-up trays, and their failure to acquire an indoor clothes dryer, were minor digressions that took place behind the scenes.

In the end I wrote Buddy about the weather, and said I missed him and hoped I would see him soon. After studying the blotchy X's and O's, much underlined, which came after Buddy's signature, I imitated them. I sealed this forgery and addressed it, and the next morning I walked out to the main road and put it in our loaf-shaped mailbox, raising the little flag to show there was a letter.

Buddy arrived unannounced on Sunday morning in August, after we had done the dishes. I don't know how he found out where we lived. He must have asked at the crossroads where there were a few houses, a gas station, and a general store with Coca-Cola ads on the screen door and a post office at the back. The people there would have been able to help Buddy decipher the rural-route number; probably they knew anyway exactly where we were.

My mother was in her shorts, in front of the house, cutting the grass and weeds with a small scythe. I was carrying a pail of water up the slippery and decaying wooden steps from the river. I knew that when I got to the top of the steps my mother would ask me what I wanted for lunch, which would drive me mad with irritation. I never knew what I wanted for lunch, and if I did know there was never any of it. It didn't occur to me then that my mother was even more bored with mealtimes than I was, since she had to do the actual cooking, or that her question might have been a request for help.

Then we heard a noise, a roaring motor noise, exaggerated but muffled too, like a gas lawnmower inside a tin garage. We both stopped dead in our tracks and looked at one another; we had a way of doing that whenever we heard any machine-made sound out on the main road. We believed, I think, that nobody knew we were there. The good part of this was that nobody would come in, but the bad part was that somebody might, thinking our place uninhabited, and the sort of people who would try it would be the sort we would least want to see.

The noise stopped for a few minutes; then it started up again, louder this time. It was coming in, along our road. My mother dropped her scythe and ran into the house. I knew she was going to change out of her shorts. I continued stolidly up the steps, carrying the pail of water. If I'd known it was Buddy I would have brushed my hair and put on lipstick.

When I saw Buddy's car, I was surprised and almost horrified. I felt I had been caught out. What would Buddy think of the decaying cabin, the parachute curtains, the decrepit furniture, the jam jar with its drooping flowers? My first idea was to keep him out of the house, at least. I went to meet the car, which was floundering over the road towards me. I was conscious of the dead leaves and dirt sticking to my wet bare feet.

Buddy got out of the car and looked up at the trees. Charlie and Trish, who were in the back seat, got out too. They gazed around, but after one quick look they gave no indication that they thought this place where I was living was hardly what they had expected; except that they talked too loudly. I knew though that I was on the defensive.

Buddy's car had a big hole in the muffler, which he hadn't had time to fix yet, and Charlie and Trish were full of stories about the annoyed looks people in the backroads villages had given them as they'd roared through. Buddy was more reserved, almost shy. "You got my letter, eh?" he said, but I hadn't, not the one that announced this visit. That letter arrived several days later, filled with a wistful loneliness it would have been handy to have known about in advance.

Charlie and Trish and Buddy wanted to go on a picnic. It was their idea that we would drive over to Pike Lake, about fifteen miles away, where there was a public beach. They thought we could go swimming. My mother had come out by this time. Now that she had her slacks on she was behaving as if everything was under control. She agreed to this plan; she knew there was nothing for them to do around our place. She didn't seem to mind my going off with Buddy for a whole day, because we would be back before dark.

The three of them stood around the car; my mother tried to make conversation with them while I ran to the cabin to get my swimsuit and a towel. Trish already had her swimsuit on; I'd seen the top of it under her shirt. Maybe there would be no place to change. This was the kind of thing you couldn't ask about without feeling like a fool, so I changed in my cubicle of parachute silk. My suit was left over from last year; it was red, and a little too small.

My mother, who didn't usually give instructions, told Buddy to drive carefully; probably because the noise made his car sound a lot more dangerous than it was. When he started up it was like a rocket taking off, and it was even worse inside. I sat in the front seat beside Buddy. All the windows were rolled down, and when we reached the paved highway Buddy stuck his left elbow out the window. He held the steering wheel with one hand, and with the other he reached across the seat and took hold of my hand. He wanted me to move over so I was next to him and he could put his arm around me, but I was nervous about the driving. He gave me a reproachful look and put his hand back on the wheel.

I had seen road signs pointing to Pike Lake before but I had never actually been there. It turned out to be small and round, with flattish countryside around it. The public beach was crowded, because it was a weekend: teenagers in groups and young couples with children mostly. Some people had portable radios. Trish and I changed behind the car, even though we were only taking off our outer clothes to reveal our bathing suits, which everybody was going to see anyway. While we were doing this, Trish told me that she and Charlie were now secretly engaged. They were going to get married as soon as she was old enough. No one was supposed to know, except Buddy of course, and me. She said her parents would have kittens if they found out. I promised not to tell; at the same time, I felt a cold finger travelling down my spine. When we came out from behind the car, Buddy and Charlie were already standing up to their ankles in the water, the sun reflecting from their white backs.

The beach was dusty and hot, with trash from picnickers left here and there about it: paper plates showing half-moons above the sand, dented paper cups, bottles. Part of a hot-dog weiner floated near where we waded in, pallid, greyish-pink, lost-looking. The lake was shallow and weedy, the water the temperature of cooling soup. The bottom was of sand so fine-grained it was almost mud; I expected leeches in it, and clams, which would probably be dead, because of the warmth. I swam out into it anyway. Trish was screaming because she had walked into some water weeds; then she was splashing Charlie. I felt that I ought to be doing these things too, and that Buddy would note the omission. But instead I floated on my back in the lukewarm water, squinting up at the cloudless sky, which was depthless and hot blue and had things like microbes drifting across it, which I knew were the rods and cones in my eyeballs. I had skipped ahead in the health book; I even knew what a zygote was. In a while Buddy swam out to join me and spurted water at me out of his mouth, grinning.

After that we swam back to the beach and lay down on Trish's over-sized pink beach towel, which had a picture of a mermaid tossing a bubble on it. I felt sticky, as if the water had left a film on me. Trish and Charlie were nowhere to be seen; at last I spotted them, walking hand in hand near the water at the far end of the beach. Buddy wanted me to rub some suntan lotion onto him. He wasn't tanned at all, except for his face and his hands and forearms, and I remembered that he worked all week and didn't have time to lie around in the sun the way I did. The skin of his back was soft and slightly loose over the muscles, like a sweater or a puppy's neck.

When I lay back down beside him, Buddy took hold of my hand, even though it was greasy with the suntan lotion. "How about Charlie, eh?" he said, shaking his head in mock disapproval, as if Charlie had been naughty or stupid. He didn't say Charlie and Trish. He put his arm over me and started to kiss me, right on the beach, in the full sunlight, in front of everyone. I pulled back.

"There's people watching," I said.

"Want me to put the towel over your head?" he said.

I sat up, brushing sand off me and tugging up the front of my bathing suit. I brushed some sand off Buddy too: his stuck worse because of the lotion. My back felt parched and I was dizzy from the heat and brightness. Later, I knew, I would get a headache.

"Where's the lunch?" I said.

"Who's hungry?" he said. "Not for food, anyways." But he didn't seem annoyed. Maybe this was the way I was supposed to behave.

I walked to the car and got out the lunch, which was in a brown paper bag, and we sat on Trish's towel and ate egg-salad sandwiches and drank warm fizzy Coke, in silence. When we had finished, I said I wanted to go and sit under a tree. Buddy came with me, bringing the towel. He shook it before we sat down.

"You don't want ants in your pants," he said. He lit a cigarette and smoked half of it, leaning against the tree trunk — an elm, I noticed — and looking at me in an odd way, as if he was making up his mind about something. Then he said, "I want you to have something." His voice was offhand, affable, the way it usually was; his eyes weren't. On the whole he looked frightened. He undid the silver bracelet from his wrist. It had always been there, and I knew what was written on it: *Buddy*, engraved in flowing script. It was an imitation army I.D. tag; a lot of the boys wore them.

"My identity bracelet," he said.

"Oh," I said as he slid it over my hand, which now, I could tell, smelled of onions. I ran my fingers over Buddy's silver name as if admiring it. I had no thought of refusing it; that would have been impossible, because I would never have been able to explain what was wrong with taking it. Also I felt that Buddy had something on me: that, now he had accidentally seen something about me that was real, he knew too much about my deviations from the norm. I felt I had to correct that somehow. It occurred to me, years later, that many women probably had become engaged and even married this way.

It was years later too that I realized Buddy had used the wrong word: it wasn't an identity bracelet, it was an identification bracelet. The difference escaped me at the time. But maybe it was the right word after all, and what Buddy was handing over to me was his identity, some key part of himself that I was expected to keep for him and watch over.

Another interpretation has since become possible: that Buddy was putting his name on me, like a *Reserved* sign or an ownership label, or a tattoo on a cow's ear, or a brand. But at the time nobody thought that way. Everyone knew that getting a boy's I.D. bracelet was a privilege, not a degradation, and this is how Trish greeted it when she came back from her walk with Charlie. She spotted the transfer instantly.

"Let's *see*," she said, as if she hadn't seen this ornament of Buddy's many times before, and I had to hold out my wrist for her to admire, while Buddy looked sheepishly on.

When I was back at the log house, I took off Buddy's identification bracelet and hid it under the bed. I was embarrassed by it, though the reason I gave myself was that I didn't want it to get lost. I put it on again in September though, when I went back to the city and back to school. It was the equivalent of a white fur sweater-collar, the kind with pom-poms. Buddy, among other things, was something to wear.

I was in grade eleven now, and studying Ancient Egypt and *The Mill on the Floss*. I was on the volleyball team; I sang in the choir. Buddy was still working at the garage, and shortly after school began he got a hernia, from lifting something too heavy. I didn't know what a hernia was. I thought it might be something sexual, but at the same time it had the sound of something that happened to old men, not to someone as young as Buddy. I looked it up in our medical book. When my brother heard about Buddy's hernia, he sniggered in an irritating way and said it was the kind of thing you could expect from Buddy.

Buddy was in a hospital for a couple of days. After that I went to visit him at home, because he wanted me to. I felt I should take him something; not flowers though. So I took him some peanut-butter cookies, baked by my mother. I knew, if the subject came up, that I would lie and say I had made them myself.

This was the first time I had ever been to Buddy's house. I hadn't even known where he lived; I hadn't thought of him as having a house at all or living anywhere in particular. I had to get there by bus and streetcar, since of course Buddy couldn't drive me.

It was Indian summer; the air was thick and damp, though there was a breeze that helped some. I walked along the street, which was lined with narrow, two-storey row houses, the kind that would much later be renovated and become fashionable, though at that time they were considered merely old-fashioned and inconvenient. It was a Saturday afternoon, and a couple of the men were mowing their cramped lawns, one of them in his undershirt.

The front door of Buddy's house was wide open; only the screen door was closed. I rang the doorbell; when nothing happened, I went in. There was a note, in Buddy's blotchy blue ball-point writing, lying on the floor: COME ON UP, it said. It must have fallen down from where it had been taped to the inside of the door.

The hallway had faded pink rose-trellis paper; the house smelled faintly of humid wood, polish, rugs in summer. I peered into the living room as I went towards the stairs: there was too much furniture in it and the curtains were drawn, but it was immaculately clean. I could tell that Buddy's mother had different ideas about housework than my mother had. Nobody seemed to be home, and I wondered if Buddy had arranged it this way on purpose, so I wouldn't run into his mother.

I climbed the stairs; in the mirror at the top I was coming to meet myself. In the dim light I seemed older, my flesh plumped and flushed by the heat, my eyes in shadow.

"Is that you?" Buddy called to me. He was in the front bedroom, lying propped up in a bed that was much too large for the room. The bed was of chocolate-coloured varnished wood, the head and foot carved; it was this bed, huge, outmoded, ceremonial, that made me more nervous than anything else in the room, including Buddy. The window was open, and the white lace-edged curtains — of a kind my mother never would have considered, because of the way they would have to be bleached, starched, and ironed — shifted a little in the air. The sound of the lawn-mowers came in through the window.

I hesitated in the doorway, smiled, went in. Buddy was wearing a white T-shirt, and had just the sheet over him, pulled up to his waist. He looked softer, shorter, a little shrunken. He smiled back at me and held out his hand.

"I brought you some cookies," I said. We were both shy, because of the silence and emptiness. I took hold of his hand and he pulled me gently towards him. The bed was so high that I had to climb half onto it. I set the bag of cookies down beside him and put my arms around his neck. His skin smelled of cigarette smoke and soap, and his hair was neatly combed and still a little wet. His mouth tasted of toothpaste. I thought of him hobbling around, in pain maybe, getting ready for me. I had never thought a great deal about boys getting themselves ready for girls, cleaning themselves, looking at themselves in bathroom mirrors, waiting, being anxious, wanting to please. I realized now that they did this, that it wasn't only the other way around. I opened my eyes and looked at Buddy as I was kissing him. I had never done this before, either. Buddy with his eyes closed was different, and stranger, than Buddy with his eyes open. He looked asleep, and as if he was having a troublesome dream.

This was the most I had ever kissed him. It was safe enough: he was wounded. When he groaned a little I thought it was because I was hurting him. "Careful," he said, moving me to one side.

I stopped kissing him and put my face down on his shoulder, against his neck. I could see the dresser, which matched the bed; it had a white crocheted runner on it, and some baby pictures in silver stands. Over it was a mirror, in a sombre frame with a carved festoon of roses, and inside the frame there was Buddy, with me lying beside him. I thought this must be the bedroom of Buddy's parents, and their bed. There was something sad about lying there with Buddy in the cramped formal room with its heavy prettiness, its gaiety which was both ornate and dark. This room was almost foreign to me; it was a celebration of something I could not identify with and would never be able to share. It would not take very much to make Buddy happy, ever; only something like this. This was what he was expecting of me, this not very much, and it was a lot more than I had. This was the most afraid I ever got, of Buddy.

"Hey," said Buddy. "Cheer up, eh? Everything still works okay." He thought I was worried about his injury.

After that we found that I had rolled on the bag of cookies, and crushed them into bits, and that made everything safer, because we could laugh. But when it was time for me to go, Buddy became wistful. He held onto my hand. "What if I won't let you go?" he said.

When I was walking back towards the streetcar stop, I saw a woman coming towards me, carrying a big brown leather purse and a paper bag. She had a muscular and determined face, the face of a woman who has had to fight, something or other, in some way or another, for a long time. She looked at me as if she thought I was up to no good, and I became conscious of the creases in my cotton dress, from where I had been lying on the bed with Buddy. I thought she might be Buddy's mother.

Buddy got better quite soon. In the weeks after that, he ceased to be an indulgence or even a joke, and became instead an obligation. We continued to go out, on the same nights as we always had, but there was an edginess about Buddy that hadn't been there before. Sometimes Trish and Charlie went with us, but they no longer necked extravagantly in the back seat. Instead they held hands and talked together in low voices about things that sounded serious and even gloomy, such as the prices of apartments. Trish had started to collect china. But Charlie had his own car now, and more and more frequently Buddy and I were alone, no longer protected. Buddy's breathing became heavier and he no longer smiled good-naturedly when I took hold of his hands to stop him. He was tired of me being fourteen.

I began to forget about Buddy when I wasn't with him. The forgetting was deliberate: it was the same as remembering, only in reverse. Instead of talking to Buddy for hours on the phone, I spent a lot of time making dolls' clothes for my little sister's dolls. When I wasn't doing that, I read through my brother's collection of comic books, long since discarded by him, lying on the floor of my room with my feet up on the bed. My brother was no longer teaching me Greek. He had gone right off the deep end, into trigonometry, which we both knew I would never learn no matter what.

Buddy ended on a night in October, suddenly, like a light being switched off. I was supposed to be going out with him, but at the dinner table my father said that I should reconsider: Toronto was about to be hit by a major storm, a hurricane, with torrential rain and gale-force winds, and he didn't think I should be out in it, especially in a car like Buddy's. It was already dark: the rain was pelting against the windows behind our drawn curtains, and the wind was up and roaring like breakers in the ash trees outside. I could feel our house growing smaller. My mother said she would get out some candles, in case the electricity failed. Luckily, she said, we were on high ground. My father said that it was my decision, of course, but anyone who would go out on a night like this would have to be crazy.

Buddy phoned to see when he should pick me up. I said that the weather was getting bad, and maybe we should go out the next night. Buddy said why be afraid of a little rain? He wanted to see me. I said I wanted to see him, too, but maybe it was too dangerous. Buddy said I was just making excuses. I said I wasn't.

My father walked past me along the hall, snapping his fingers together like a pair of scissors. I said anyone who would go out on a night like this would have to be crazy, Buddy could turn on the radio and hear for himself, we were having a hurricane, but Buddy sounded as if he didn't really know what that meant. He said if I wouldn't go out with him during a hurricane I didn't love him enough. I was shocked: this was the first time he had ever used the word *love,* out loud and not just at the ends of letters, to describe what we were supposed to be doing. When I told him he was being stupid he hung up on me, which made me angry. But he was right, of course. I didn't love him enough.

Instead of going out with Buddy, I stayed home and played a game of chess with my brother, who won, as he always did. I was never a very good chess player: I couldn't stand the silent waiting. There was a feeling of reunion about this game, which would not, however, last long. Buddy was gone, but he had been a symptom.

This was the first of a long series of atmospherically supercharged break-ups with men, though I didn't realize it at the time. Blizzards, thunderstorms, heat waves, hailstorms: I later broke up in all of them. I'm not sure what it was. Possibly it had something to do with positive ions, which were not to be discovered for many years; but I came to believe that there was something about me that inspired extreme gestures, though I could never pinpoint what it was. After one such rupture, during a downpour of freezing rain, my ex-boyfriend gave me a valentine consisting of a real cow's heart with an actual arrow stuck through it. He'd been meaning to do it anyway, he said, and he couldn't think of any other girl who would appreciate it. For weeks I wondered whether or not this was a compliment.

Buddy was not this friendly. After the break-up, he never spoke to me again. Through Trish, he asked for his identification bracelet back, and I handed it over to her in the girls' washroom at lunch hour. There was someone else he wanted to give it to, Trish told me, a girl named Mary Jo who took typing instead of French, a sure sign in those days that you would leave school early and get a job or something. Mary Jo had a round, good-natured face, bangs down over her forehead like a sheepdog's, and heavy breasts, and she did in fact leave school early. Meanwhile she wore Buddy's name in silver upon her wrist. Trish switched allegiances, though not all at once. Somewhat later, I heard she had been telling stories about how I'd lived in a cowshed all summer.

It would be wrong to say that I didn't miss Buddy. In this respect too he was the first in a series. Later, I always missed men when they were gone, even when they meant what is usually called absolutely nothing to me. For me, I was to discover, there was no such category as absolutely nothing.

But all that was in the future. The morning after the hurricane, I had only the sensation of having come unscathed through a major calamity. After we had listened to the news, cars overturned with their drivers in them, demolished houses, all that rampaging water and disaster and washed-away money, my brother and I put on our rubber boots and walked down the old, pot-holed and now pitted and raddled Pottery Road to witness the destruction first-hand.

There wasn't as much as we had hoped. Trees and branches were down, but not that many of them. The Don River was flooded and muddy, but it was hard to tell whether the parts of cars half sunk in it and the mangled truck tires, heaps of sticks, planks, and assorted debris washing along or strewn on land where the water had already begun to recede were new or just more of the junk we were used to seeing in it. The sky was still overcast; our boots squelched in the mud, out of which no hands were poking up. I had wanted something more like tragedy. Two people had actually been drowned there during the night, but we did not learn that until later. This is what I have remembered most clearly about Buddy: the ordinary-looking wreckage, the flatness of the water, the melancholy light.

≈ THE AGE OF LEAD ≈

The man has been buried for a hundred and fifty years. They dug a hole in the frozen gravel, deep into the permafrost, and put him down there so the wolves couldn't get to him. Or that is the speculation.

When they dug the hole the permafrost was exposed to the air, which was warmer. This made the permafrost melt. But it froze again after the man was covered up, so that when he was brought to the surface he was completely enclosed in ice. They took the lid off the coffin and it was like those maraschino cherries you used to freeze in ice-cube trays for fancy tropical drinks: a vague shape, looming through a solid cloud.

They they melted the ice and he came to light. He is almost the same as when he was buried. The freezing water has pushed his lips away from his teeth into an astonished snarl, and he's a beige colour, like a gravy stain on linen, instead of pink, but everything is still there. He even has eyeballs, except that they aren't white but the light brown of milky tea. With these tea-stained eyes he regards Jane: an indecipherable gaze, innocent, ferocious, amazed, but contemplative, like a werewolf meditating, caught in a flash of lightning at the exact split second of his tumultuous change.

Jane doesn't watch very much television. She used to watch it more. She used to watch comedy series, in the evenings, and when she was a student at university she would watch afternoon soaps about hospitals and rich people, as a way of procrastinating. For a while, not so long ago, she would watch the evening news, taking in the disasters with her feet tucked up on the chesterfield, a throw rug over her legs, drinking a hot milk and rum to relax before bed. It was all a form of escape.

But what you can see on television, at whatever time of day, is edging too close to her own life; though in her life, nothing stays put in those tidy compartments, comedy here, seedy romance and sentimental tears there, accidents and violent deaths in thirty-second clips they call *bites,* as if they were chocolate bars. In her life, everything is mixed together. *Laugh, I thought I'd die*, Vincent used to say, a very long time ago, in a voice imitating the banality of mothers; and that's how it's getting to be. So when she flicks on the television these days, she flicks it off again soon enough. Even the commercials, with their surreal dailiness, are beginning to look sinister, to suggest meanings behind themselves, behind their façade of cleanliness, lusciousness, health, power, and speed.

Tonight she leaves the television on, because what she is seeing is so unlike what she usually sees. There is nothing sinister behind this image of the frozen man. It is entirely itself. *What you sees is what you gets*, as Vincent also used to say, crossing his eyes, baring his teeth at one side, pushing his nose into a horror-movie snout. Although it never was, with him.

The man they've dug up and melted was a young man. Or still is: it's difficult to know what tense should be applied to him, he is so insistently present. Despite the distortions caused by the ice and the emaciation of his illness, you can see his youthfulness, the absence of toughening, of wear. According to the dates painted carefully onto his nameplate, he was only twenty years old. His name was John Torrington. He was, or is, a sailor, a seaman. He wasn't an able-bodied seaman though; he was a petty officer, one of those marginally in command. Being in command has little to do with the ableness of the body.

He was one of the first to die. This is why he got a coffin and a metal nameplate, and a deep hole in the permafrost — because they still had the energy, and the piety, for such things, that early. There would have been a burial service read over him, and prayers. As time went on and became nebulous and things did not get better, they must have kept the energy for themselves; and also the prayers. The prayers would have ceased to be routine and become desperate, and then hopeless. The later dead ones got cairns of piled stones, and the much later ones not even that. They ended up as bones, and as the soles of boots and the occasional button, sprinkled over the frozen stony treeless relentless ground in a trail heading south. It was like the trails in fairy tales, of bread crumbs or seeds or white stones. But in this case nothing had sprouted or lit up in the moonlight, forming a miraculous pathway to life; no rescuers had followed. It took ten years before anyone knew even the barest beginnings of what had been happening to them.

All of them together were the Franklin Expedition. Jane has seldom paid much attention to history except when it has overlapped with her knowledge of antique furniture and real estate — "19th C. pine harvest table," or "Prime location Georgian centre hall, impeccable reno" — but she knows what the Franklin Expedition was. The two ships with their bad-luck names have been on stamps — the *Terror*, the *Erebus*. Also she took it in school, along with a lot of other doomed expeditions. Not many of those explorers seemed to have come out of it very well. They were always getting scurvy, or lost.

What the Franklin Expedition was looking for was the Northwest Passage, an open seaway across the top of the Arctic, so people, merchants, could get to India from England without going all the way around South America. They wanted to go that way because it would cost less and increase their profits. This was much less exotic than Marco Polo or the headwaters of the Nile; nevertheless, the idea of exploration appealed to her then: to get onto a boat and just go somewhere, somewhere mapless, off into the unknown. To launch yourself into fright; to find things out. There was something daring and noble about it, despite all of the losses and failures, or perhaps because of them. It was like having sex, in high school, in those days before the Pill, even if you took precautions. If you were a girl, that is. If you were a boy, for whom such a risk was fairly minimal, you had to do other things: things with weapons or large amounts of alcohol, or high-speed vehicles, which at her suburban Toronto high school, back then at the beginning of the sixties, meant switchblades, beer, and drag races down the main streets on Saturday nights.

Now, gazing at the television as the lozenge of ice gradually melts and the outline of the young sailor's body clears and sharpens, Jane remembers Vincent, sixteen and with more hair then, quirking one eyebrow and lifting his lip in a mock sneer and saying, "Franklin, my dear, I don't give a damn." He said it loud enough to be heard, but the history teacher ignored him, not knowing what else to do. It was hard for the teachers to keep Vincent in line, because he never seemed to be afraid of anything that might happen to him.

He was hollow-eyed even then; he frequently looked as if he'd been up all night. Even then he resembled a very young old man, or else a dissipated child. The dark circles under his eyes were the ancient part, but when he smiled he had lovely white teeth, like the magazine ads for baby foods. He made fun of everything, and was adored. He wasn't adored the way other boys were adored, those boys with surly lower lips and greased hair and a studied air of smouldering menace. He was adored like a pet. Not a dog, but a cat. He went where he liked, and nobody owned him. Nobody called him Vince.

Strangely enough, Jane's mother approved of him. She didn't usually approve of the boys Jane went out with. Maybe she approved of him because it was obvious to her that no bad results would follow from Jane's going out with him: no heartaches, no heaviness, nothing burdensome. None of what she called *consequences*. Consequences: the weightiness of the body, the growing flesh hauled around like a bundle, the tiny frill-framed goblin head in the carriage. Babies and marriage, in that order. This was how she understood men and their furtive, fumbling, threatening desires, because Jane herself had been a consequence. She had been a mistake, she had been a war baby. She had been a crime that had needed to be paid for, over and over.

By the time she was sixteen, Jane had heard enough about this to last her several lifetimes. In her mother's account of the way things were, you were young briefly and then you fell. You plummeted downwards like an overripe apple and hit the ground with a squash; you fell, and everything about you fell too. You got fallen arches and a fallen womb, and your hair and teeth fell out. That's what having a baby did to you. It subjected you to the force of gravity.

This is how she remembers her mother, still: in terms of a pendulous, drooping, wilting motion. Her sagging breasts, the downturned lines around her mouth. Jane conjures her up: there she is, as usual, sitting at the kitchen table with a cup of cooling tea, exhausted after her job clerking at Eaton's department store, standing all day behind the jewellery counter with her bum stuffed into a girdle and her swelling feet crammed into the mandatory medium-heeled shoes, smiling her envious, disapproving smile at the spoiled customers who turned up their noses at pieces of glittering junk she herself could never afford to buy. Jane's mother sighs, picks at the canned spaghetti Jane has heated up for her. Silent words waft out of her like stale talcum powder: *What can you expect*, always a statement, never a question. Jane tries at this distance for pity, but comes up with none.

As for Jane's father, he'd run away from home when Jane was five, leaving her mother in the lurch. That's what her mother called it — "running away from home" — as if he'd been an irresponsible child. Money arrived from time to time, but that was the total sum of his contribution to family life. Jane resented him for it, but she didn't blame him. Her mother inspired in almost everyone who encountered her a vicious desire for escape.

Jane and Vincent would sit out in the cramped backyard of Jane's house, which was one of the squinty-windowed little stuccoed wartime bungalows at the bottom of the hill. At the top of the hill were the richer houses, and the richer people: the girls who owned cashmere sweaters, at least one of them, instead of the Orlon and lambswool so familiar to Jane. Vincent lived about halfway up the hill. He still had a father, in theory.

They would sit against the back fence, near the spindly cosmos flowers that passed for a garden, as far away from the house itself as they could get. They would drink gin, decanted by Vincent from his father's liquor hoard and smuggled in an old military pocket flask he'd picked up somewhere. They would imitate their mothers.

"I pinch and I scrape and I work my fingers to the bone, and what thanks do I get?" Vincent would say peevishly. "No help from you, Sonny Boy. You're just like your father. Free as the birds, out all night, do as you like and you don't care one pin about anyone else's feelings. Now take out that garbage."

"It's love that does it to you," Jane would reply, in the resigned, ponderous voice of her mother. "You wait and see, my girl. One of these days you'll come down off your devil-may-care high horse." As Jane said this, and even though she was making fun, she could picture love, with a capital L, descending out of the sky towards her like a huge foot. Her mother's life had been a disaster, but in her own view an inevitable disaster, as in songs and movies. It was Love that was responsible, and in the face of Love, what could be done? Love was like a steamroller. There was no avoiding it, it went over you and you came out flat.

Jane's mother waited, fearfully and uttering warnings, but with a sort of gloating relish, for the same thing to happen to Jane. Every time Jane went out with a new boy her mother inspected him as a potential agent of downfall. She distrusted most of these boys; she distrusted their sulky, pulpy mouths, their eyes half-closed in the up-drifting smoke of their cigarettes, their slow, sauntering manner of walking, their clothing that was too tight, too full: too full of their bodies. They looked this way even when they weren't putting on the sulks and swaggers, when they were trying to appear bright-eyed and industrious and polite for Jane's mother's benefit, saying goodbye at the front door, dressed in their shirts and ties and their pressed heavy-date suits. They couldn't help the way they looked, the way they were. They were helpless; one kiss in a dark corner would reduce them to speechlessness; they were sleepwalkers in their own liquid bodies. Jane, on the other hand, was wide awake.

Jane and Vincent did not exactly go out together. Instead they made fun of going out. When the coast was clear and Jane's mother wasn't home, Vincent would appear at the door with his face painted bright yellow, and Jane would put her bathrobe on back to front and they would order Chinese food and alarm the delivery boy and eat sitting cross-legged on the floor, clumsily, with chopsticks. Or Vincent would turn up in a threadbare thirty-year-old suit and a bowler hat and a cane, and Jane would rummage around in the cupboard for a discarded church-going hat of her mother's, with smashed cloth violets and a veil, and they would go downtown and walk around, making loud remarks about the passers-by, pretending to be old, or poor, or crazy. It was thoughtless and in bad taste, which was what they both liked about it.

Vincent took Jane to the graduation formal, and they picked out her dress together at one of the second-hand clothing shops Vincent frequented, giggling at the shock and admiration they hoped to cause. They hesitated between a flame-red with falling-off sequins and a backless hip-hugging black with a plunge front, and chose the black, to go with Jane's hair. Vincent sent a poisonous-looking lime-green orchid, the colour of her eyes, he said, and Jane painted her eyelids and fingernails to match. Vincent wore white tie and tails, and a top hat, all frayed Sally-Ann issue and ludicrously too large for him. They tangoed around the gymnasium, even though the music was not a tango, under the tissue-paper flowers, cutting a black swath through the sea of pastel tulle, unsmiling, projecting a corny sexual menace, Vincent with Jane's long pearl necklace clenched between his teeth.

The applause was mostly for him, because of the way he was adored. Though mostly by the girls, thinks Jane. But he seemed to be popular enough among the boys as well. Probably he told them dirty jokes, in the proverbial locker room. He knew enough of them.

As he dipped Jane backwards, he dropped the pearls and whispered into her ear, "No belts, no pins, no pads, no chafing." It was from an ad for tampons, but it was also their leitmotif. It was what they both wanted; freedom from the world of mothers, the world of precautions, the world of burdens and fate and heavy female constraints upon the flesh. They wanted a life without consequences. Until recently, they'd managed it.

The scientists have melted the entire length of the young sailor now, at least the upper layer of him. They've been pouring warm water over him, gently and patiently; they don't want to thaw him too abruptly. It's as if John Torrington is asleep and they don't want to startle him.

Now his feet have been revealed. They're bare, and white rather than beige; they look like the feet of someone who's been walking on a cold floor, on a winter day. That is the quality of the light that they reflect: winter sunlight, in early morning. There is something intensely painful to Jane about the absence of socks. They could have left him his socks. But maybe the others needed them. His big toes are tied together with a strip of cloth; the man talking says this was to keep the body tidily packaged for burial, but Jane is not convinced. His arms are tied to his body, his ankles are tied together. You do that when you don't want a person walking around.

This part is almost too much for Jane; it is too reminiscent. She reaches for the channel switcher, but luckily the show (it is only a show, it's only another show) changes to two of the historical experts, analyzing the clothing. There's a close-up of John Torrington's shirt, a simple, high-collared, pin-striped white-and-blue cotton, with mother-of-pearl buttons. The stripes are a printed pattern, rather than a woven one; woven would have been more expensive. The trousers are grey linen. Ah, thinks Jane. Wardrobe. She feels better: this is something she knows about. She loves the solemnity, the reverence, with which the stripes and buttons are discussed. An interest in the clothing of the present is frivolity, an interest in the clothing of the past is archaeology; a point Vincent would have appreciated.

After high school, Jane and Vincent both got scholarships to university, although Vincent had appeared to study less, and did better. That summer they did everything together. They got summer jobs at the same hamburger heaven, they went to movies together after work, although Vincent never paid for Jane. They still occasionally dressed up in old clothes and pretended to be a weird couple, but it no longer felt careless and filled with absurd invention. It was beginning to occur to them that they might conceivably end up looking like that.

In her first year at university Jane stopped going out with other boys; she needed a part-time job to help pay her way, and that and the schoolwork and Vincent took up all her time. She thought she might be in love with Vincent. She thought that maybe they should make love, to find out. She had never done such a thing, entirely; she had been too afraid of the untrustworthiness of men, of the gravity of love, too afraid of consequences. She thought, however, that she might trust Vincent.

But things didn't go that way. They held hands, but they didn't hug. they hugged, but they didn't pet; they kissed, but they didn't neck. Vincent liked looking at her, but he liked it so much he would never close his eyes. She would close hers and then open them, and there would be Vincent, his own eyes shining in the light from the streetlamp or the moon, peering at her inquisitively as if waiting to see what odd female thing she would do next, for his delighted amusement. Making love with Vincent did not seem altogether possible.

(Later, after she had flung herself into the current of opinion that had swollen to a river by the late sixties, she no longer said "making love"; she said "having sex." But it amounted to the same thing. You had sex, and love got made out of it whether you liked it or not. You woke up in a bed or more likely on a mattress, with an arm around you, and found yourself wondering what it might be like to keep on doing it. At that point Jane would start looking at her watch. She had no intention of being left in any lurches. She would do the leaving herself. And she did.)

Jane and Vincent wandered off to different cities. They wrote each other postcards. Jane did this and that. She ran a co-op food store in Vancouver, did the financial stuff for a diminutive theatre in Montreal, acted as managing editor for a small publisher, ran the publicity for a dance company. She had a head for details and for adding up small sums — having to scrape her way through university had been instructive — and such jobs were often available if you didn't demand much money for doing them. Jane could see no reason to tie herself down, to make any sort of soul-stunting commitment, to anything or anyone. It was the early seventies; the old heavy women's world of girdles and precautions and consequences had been swept away. There were a lot of windows opening, a lot of doors: you could look in, then you could go in, then you could come out again.

She lived with several men, but in each of the apartments there were always cardboard boxes, belonging to her, that she never got around to unpacking; just as well, because it was that much easier to move out. When she got past thirty she decided it might be nice to have a child, some time, later. She tried to figure out a way of doing this without becoming a mother. Her own mother had moved to Florida, and sent rambling, grumbling letters, to which Jane did not often reply.

Jane moved back to Toronto, and found it ten times more interesting than when she'd left it. Vincent was already there. He'd come back from Europe, where he'd been studying film; he'd opened a design studio. He and Jane met for lunch, and it was the same: the same air of conspiracy between them, the same sense of their own potential for outrageousness. They might still have been sitting in

Jane's garden, beside the cosmos flowers, drinking forbidden gin and making fun.

Jane found herself moving in Vincent's circles, or were they orbits? Vincent knew a great many people, people of all kinds; some were artists and some wanted to be, and some wanted to know the ones who were. Some had money to begin with, some made money; they all spent it. There was a lot more talk about money, these days, or among these people. Few of them knew how to manage it, and Jane found herself helping them out. She developed a small business among them, handling their money. She would gather it in, put it away safely for them, tell them what they could spend, dole out an allowance. She would note with interest the things they bought, filing their receipted bills: what furniture, what clothing, which *objets*. They were delighted with their money, enchanted with it. It was like milk and cookies for them, after school. Watching them play with their money, Jane felt responsible and indulgent, and a little matronly. She stored her own money carefully away, and eventually bought a townhouse with it.

All this time she was with Vincent, more or less. They'd tried being lovers but had not made a success of it. Vincent had gone along with this scheme because Jane had wanted it, but he was elusive, he would not make declarations. What worked with other men did not work with him: appeals to his protective instincts, pretences at jealousy, requests to remove stuck lids from jars. Sex with him was more like a musical workout. He couldn't take it seriously, and accused her of being too solemn about it. She thought he might be gay, but was afraid to ask him; she dreaded feeling irrelevant to him, excluded. It took them months to get back to normal.

He was older now, they both were. He had thinning temples and a widow's peak, and his bright inquisitive eyes had receded even further into his head. What went on between them continued to look like a courtship, but was not one. He was always bringing her things: a new, peculiar food to eat, a new grotesquerie to see, a new piece of gossip, which he would present to her with a sense of occasion, like a flower. She in her turn appreciated him. It was like a yogic exercise, appreciating Vincent; it was like appreciating an anchovy, or a tone. He was not everyone's taste.

There's a black-and-white print on the television, then another: the nineteenth century's version of itself, in etchings. Sir John Franklin, older and fatter than Jane had supposed; the *Terror* and the *Erebus*, locked fast in the crush of the ice. In the high Arctic, a hundred and fifty years ago, it's the dead of winter. There is no sun at all, no moon; only the rustling northern lights, like electronic music, and the hard little stars.

What did they do for love, on such a ship, at such a time? Furtive solitary gropings, confused and mournful dreams, the sublimation of novels. The usual, among those who have become solitary.

Down in the hold, surrounded by the creaking of the wooden hull and the stale odours of men far too long enclosed, John Torrington lies dying. He must have known it; you can see it on his face. He turns towards Jane his tea-coloured look of puzzled reproach.

Who held his hand, who read to him, who brought him water? Who, if anyone, loved him? And what did they tell him about whatever it was that was killing him? Consumption, brain fever, Original Sin. All those Victorian reasons, which meant nothing and were the wrong ones. But they must have been comforting. If you are dying, you want to know why.

In the eighties, things started to slide. Toronto was not so much fun any more. There were too many people, too many poor people. You could see them begging on the streets, which were clogged with fumes and cars. The cheap artists' studios were torn down or converted to coy and upscale office space; the artists had migrated elsewhere. Whole streets were torn up or knocked down. The air was full of windblown grit.

People were dying. They were dying too early. One of Jane's clients, a man who owned an antique store, died almost overnight of bone cancer. Another, a woman who was an entertainment lawyer, was trying on a dress in a boutique and had a heart attack. She fell over and they called the ambulance, and she was dead on arrival. A theatrical producer died of AIDS, and a photographer; the lover of the photographer shot himself, either out of grief or because he knew he was next. A friend of a friend died of emphysema, another of viral pneumonia, another of hepatitis picked up on a tropical vacation, another of spinal meningitis. It was as if they had been weakened by some mysterious agent, a thing like a colourless gas, scentless and invisible, so that any germ that happened along could invade their bodies, take them over.

Jane began to notice news items of the kind she'd once skimmed over. Maple groves dying of acid rain, hormones in the beef, mercury in the fish, pesticides in the vegetables, poison sprayed on the fruit, God knows what in the drinking water. She subscribed to a bottled spring-water service and felt better for a few weeks, then read in the paper that it wouldn't do her much good, because whatever it was had been seeping into everything. Each time you took a breath, you breathed some of it in. She thought about moving out of the city, then read about toxic dumps, radioactive waste, concealed here and there in the countryside and masked by the lush, deceitful green of waving trees.

Vincent has been dead for less than a year. He was not put into the permafrost or frozen in ice. He went into the Necropolis, the only Toronto cemetery of whose general ambience he approved; he got flower bulbs planted on top of him, by Jane and others. Mostly by Jane. Right now John Torrington, recently thawed after a hundred and fifty years, probably looks better than Vincent.

A week before Vincent's forty-third birthday, Jane went to see him in the hospital. He was in for tests. Like fun he was. He was in for the unspeakable, the unknown. He was in for a mutated virus that didn't even have a name yet. It was creeping up his spine, and when it reached his brain it would kill him. It was not, as they said, responding to treatment. He was in for the duration.

It was white in his room, wintry. He lay packed in ice, for the pain. A white sheet wrapped him, his white thin feet poked out the bottom of it. They were so pale and cold. Jane took one look at him, laid out on ice like a salmon, and began to cry.

"Oh Vincent," she said. "What will I do without you?" This sounded awful. It sounded like Jane and Vincent making fun, of obsolete books, obsolete movies, their obsolete mothers. It also sounded selfish: here she was, worrying about herself and her future, when Vincent was the one who was sick. But it was true. There would be a lot less to do, altogether, without Vincent.

Vincent gazed up at her; the shadows under his eyes were cavernous. "Lighten up," he said, not very loudly, because he could not speak very loudly now. By this time she was sitting down, leaning forward; she was holding one of his hands. It was thin as the claw of a bird. "Who says I'm going to die?" He spent a moment considering this, revised it. "You're right," he said. "They got me. It was the Pod People from outer space. They said, 'All I want is your poddy.' "

Jane cried more. It was worse because he was trying to be funny. "But what *is* it?" she said. "Have they found out yet?"

Vincent smiled his ancient, jaunty smile, his smile of detachment, of amusement. There were his beautiful teeth, juvenile as ever. "Who knows?" he said. "It must have been something I ate."

Jane sat with the tears running down her face. She felt desolate: left behind, stranded. Their mothers had finally caught up to them and been proven right. There were consequences after all; but they were the consequences to things you didn't even know you'd done.

The scientists are back on the screen. They are excited, their earnest mouths are twitching, you could almost call them joyful. They know why John Torrington died; they know, at last, why the Franklin Expedition went so terribly wrong. They've snipped off pieces of John Torrington, a fingernail, a lock of hair, they've run them through machines and come out with the answers.

There is a shot of an old tin can, pulled open to show the seam. It looks like a bomb casing. A finger points: it was the tin cans that did it, a new invention back then, a new technology, the ultimate defence against starvation and scurvy. The Franklin Expedition was excellently provisioned with tin cans, stuffed full of meat and soup and soldered together with lead. The whole expedition got lead-poisoning. Nobody knew it. Nobody could taste it. It invaded their bones, their lungs, their brains, weakening them and confusing their thinking, so that at the end those that had not yet died in the ships set out in an idiotic trek across the stony, icy ground, pulling a lifeboat laden down with toothbrushes, soap, handkerchiefs, and slippers, useless pieces of junk. When they were found ten years later, they were skeletons in tattered coats, lying where they'd collapsed. They'd been heading back towards the ships. It was what they'd been eating that had killed them.

Jane switches off the television and goes into her kitchen — all white, done over the year before last, the outmoded butcher-block, counters from the seventies torn out and carted away — to make herself some hot milk and rum. Then she decides against it; she won't sleep anyway. Everything in here looks ownerless. Her toaster oven, so perfect for solo dining, her microwave for the vegetables, her espresso maker — they're sitting around waiting for her departure, for this evening or forever, in order to assume their final, real appearances of purposeless objects adrift in the physical world. They might as well be pieces of an exploded spaceship orbiting the moon.

She thinks about Vincent's apartment, so carefully arranged, filled with the beautiful or deliberately ugly possessions he once loved. She thinks about his closet, with its quirky particular outfits, empty now of his arms and legs. It has all been broken up now, sold, given away.

Increasingly the sidewalk that runs past her house is cluttered with plastic drinking cups, crumpled soft-drink cans, used take-out plates. She picks them up, clears them away, but they appear again overnight, like a trail left by an army on the march or by the fleeing residents of a city under bombardment, discarding the objects that were once thought essential but are now too heavy to carry.

Commentary by
Margaret Atwood

≈

Margaret Atwood's writing is characterized by strikingly individual and archetypal images of human existence. The following commentary is taken from an essay, "An End to Audience?", first published in Dalhousie Review *60 (1980) and republished in Atwood's* Second Words: Selected Critical Prose *(Toronto: House of Anansi, 1982). Here Atwood reflects on the urgent and eternal role of literature in bearing witness to human experience.*

Writing can also be an art, and one of the reasons that so many writers dodge this on television talk shows is that art is hard to define or describe. Money is easier to talk about, so we talk about money. Nevertheless, art happens. It happens when you have the craft and the vocation and are waiting for something else, something extra, or maybe not waiting; in any case it happens. It's the extra rabbit coming out of the hat, the one you didn't put there. It's Odysseus standing by the blood-filled trench, except that the blood is his own. It is bringing the dead to life and giving voices to those who lack them so that they may speak for themselves. It is not "expressing yourself". It is opening yourself, discarding your *self*, so that the language and the world may be evoked through you. *Evocation* is quite different from *expression*. Because we are so fixated on the latter, we forget that writing also does the former. Maybe the writer *expresses*; but *evocation*, calling up, is what writing does for the reader. Writing is also a kind of sooth-saying, a truth-telling. It is a naming of the world, a reverse incarnation: the flesh becoming word. It's also a witnessing. *Come with me*, the writer is saying to the reader. *There is a story I have to tell you, there is something you need to know*. The writer is both an eye-witness and an I-witness, the one to whom personal experience happens and the one who makes experience personal for others. The writer *bears witness*. Bearing witness is not the same as self-expression.

SELECTED WORKS BY MARGARET ATWOOD

Dancing Girls and Other Stories. Toronto: McClelland and Stewart, 1977. Toronto: Seal Books/McClelland and Stewart-Bantam, 1978.

Bluebeard's Egg. Toronto: McClelland and Stewart, 1983. Toronto: Seal Books/McClelland and Stewart-Bantam, 1984.

Murder in the Dark: Short Fictions and Prose Poems. Toronto: Coach House Press, 1983.

Wilderness Tips. Toronto: McClelland & Stewart, 1991. Toronto: Seal Books/McClelland-Bantam, 1992.

Good Bones. Toronto: Coach House Press, 1992.

Clark Blaise

≈

I've always considered Blaise's first two books, *A North American Education* (1973) and *Tribal Justice* (1974), to be two of the best collections of stories ever published in Canada. The stories are as rich in texture and as compelling now as they were twenty years ago. They are wearing well. The wealth of detail and the gorgeous sensuality in these stories are pleasures which are inexhaustible. Significantly, both books are much admired by other writers but still lack the general readership they deserve. These two collections remain among the most underrated books in Canadian literature.

From Blaise's first two books we have selected the title story of *A North American Education.* We might have chosen something else from these books to represent him. From *A North American Education* I also have a fondness for "Eyes" and "Extractions and Contractions" and "The Salesman's Son Grows Older". From *Tribal Justice* I've always admired "How I Became a Jew" and "The Seizure". Choices among the stories from Blaise's first two books are difficult to make.

In one sense, Blaise's books are one book. Some critics have accused him of doing nothing much more than writing versions of his autobiography over and over again: the fat child, the English-Canadian mother, the French-Canadian father, life as the son of a salesman in Florida, Pittsburgh, Cincinnati... I've never understood the point of this criticism. It is as if such critics believe that the stories are somehow lesser because autobiographical, less imaginative, taking less effort. But the stories are all different in emphasis and detail and each is a wonderfully crafted unique artifact. I suspect that for Blaise there really isn't a clear dividing line between autobiography and fiction; he blurs the idea of genres. We might consider the travel book *Days and Nights in Calcutta* (1977) that he wrote with his wife, Bharati Mukherjee, as fiction, too, because in writing it he uses all the devices of fiction. Read the wonderful section in which he describes attending a lecture on the poetry of Rabindranath Tagore during which the electricity fails; it would require only a nudge for this piece of 'non-fiction' to become 'fiction'. Blaise explores the relationship between autobiography and fiction in his third collection, *Resident Alien* (1986), which includes stories and essays and which is essential reading in any consideration of his work. The story "Identity" from *Resident Alien*, as so often in Blaise, could be regarded as a story or an essay or a memoir. What do these labels really mean or matter? What matters is that, once read, these pieces will never leave your mind.

Blaise has profoundly influenced many younger writers through his fiction, his teaching, and his essays. In *Resident Alien* he describes being a writing student and trying to emulate the cadences of William Faulkner:

"What I *knew*, at the age of twenty, was suburban life in Pittsburgh in the mid-fifties; I knew it cold. I knew the retail trade in furniture, paper routes, baseball, the charms and terrors of women and gobs of facts in astronomy, sports, archaeology and geography. Those were the elements, in fact, of many later stories and my first novel, but if I had tried it as an undergraduate — and probably I did — it would have come out like warm, flat soda water.

"It's alchemy, taking the facts, the common language, the world and characters we know, and transforming them into something never before seen, hitherto unknown and forever fresh."

And that, of course, is the point: alchemy. In Blaise's writing the autobiographical is transformed, *transmuted* by art into stories 'forever fresh'. Dross into gold.

The last paragraph I've been quoting continues: "(Do you know what's wrong with that sentence? the Faulknerite in me asks. It's that last word 'fresh'. Not wrong because of its meaning, but wrong because of its rhythm. 'Never before seen' is a phrase of five syllables, as is 'hitherto unknown', and I now must find a *two*-syllable synonym for 'fresh' to balance the scales of 'forever'. But I also like the alliteration. Fragrant? Or a good Faulknerian 'fecund'?) Forever fertile." Blaise's examination of individual phrases demonstrates his love of the craft of writing.

Like the rest of Blaise's work, "A North American Education" is characterized by a commanding and exquisite use of language. The title of the story is a reference to Flaubert's novel *Sentimental Education* and accompanying the varieties of loss and sadness in the story is the loss for the narrator of Europe and its civilization. Blaise's preoccupation with the decay of culture is also reflected in our other selection, "Meditations on Starch"; this concern is embodied in the image of the narrator's son capering with a street band near the famous office where Freud explored and changed the intellectual underpinnings of the twentieth century. "Meditations on Starch" is reprinted from Blaise's fourth collection, *Man and His World* (1992). Individually and as a group, the stories assembled in that volume daringly extend and complicate his range in subject, technique, style, and mood.

≈

Robert Lecker has written brilliantly on Blaise in *An Other I: The Fictions of Clark Blaise* (Toronto: ECW Press, 1988). This study includes a chapter on the large body of stories collected in *A North American Education* and *Tribal Justice*, a chapter on *Resident Alien*, separate essays on "A North American Education" and "Notes Beyond a History", in addition to a detailed personal chronology written by Blaise. Barry Cameron has also written illuminatingly on Blaise in his monograph *Clark Blaise and His Works* (Toronto: ECW Press, 1985). Michael Darling has written perceptively on the story "The Salesman's Son Grows Older" in *The Montreal Story Tellers: Memoirs, Photographs, Critical Essays* (Montreal: Véhicule Press, 1985). An interview with Blaise from *Journal of Canadian Fiction* 2.4 (1973) and several articles by him on the craft of fiction are gathered in *How Stories Mean* (Erin, ON: The Porcupine's Quill, 1993). Other interviews with Blaise by Geoff Hancock, Barry Cameron, and L. G. Daniels appear, respectively, in *Canadian Fiction Magazine* 34–35 (1980), *Essays on Canadian Writing* 23 (1982), and *New Canadian Review* 1.1 (1987).

A NORTH AMERICAN ≈ EDUCATION ≈

Eleven years after the death of Napoleon, in the presidency of Andrew Jackson, my grandfather, Boniface Thibidault, was born. For most of his life he was a *journalier*, a day laborer, with a few years off for wars and buccaneering. Then at the age of fifty, a father and widower, he left Paris and came alone to the New World and settled in Sorel, a few miles down river from Montreal. He worked in the shipyards for a year or two then married his young housekeeper, an eighteen-year-old named Lise Beaudette. Lise, my grandmother, had that resigned look of a Quebec girl marked early for a nursing order if marriage couldn't catch her, by accident, first. In twenty years she bore fifteen children, eight of them boys, five of whom survived. The final child, a son, was named Jean-Louis and given at birth to the Church. As was the custom with the last boy, he was sent to the monastery as soon as he could walk, and remained with the Brothers for a dozen years, taking his meals and instructions as an apprentice.

It would have been fitting if Boniface Thibidault, then nearly eighty, had earned a fortune in Sorel — but he didn't. Or if a son had survived to pass on his stories — but none were listening. Or if Boniface himself had written something — but he was illiterate. Boniface was cut out for something different. One spring morning in 1912, the man who had seen two child brides through menopause stood in the mud outside his cottage and defied Sorel's first horseless carriage to churn its way through the April muck to his door, and if by the Grace of God it did, to try going on while he, an old man, pushed it back downhill. Money was evenly divided on the man and the driver, whom Boniface also defamed for good measure. The driver was later acquitted of manslaughter in Sorel's first fatality and it was never ascertained if Boniface died of the bumping, the strain, or perhaps the shock of meeting his match. Jean-Louis wasn't there. He left the church a year later by walking out and never looking back. He was my father.

The death of Boniface was in keeping with the life, yet I think of my grandfather as someone special, a character from a well-packed novel who enters once and is never fully forgotten. I think of Flaubert's *Sentimental Education* and the porters who littered the decks of the *Ville-de-Montereau* on the morning of September 15, 1840, when young Frédéric Moreau was about to sail. My grandfather was already eight in 1840, a good age for cabin boys. But while Frédéric was about to meet Arnoux and his grand passion, Boniface was content to pocket a tip and beat it, out of the novel and back into his demimonde.

I have seen one picture of my grandfather, taken on a ferry between Quebec and Levis in 1895. He looks strangely like Sigmund Freud: bearded, straw-hatted, buttoned against the river breezes. It must have been a cold day — the vapor from the nearby horses steams in the background. As a young man he must have been, briefly, extraordinary. I think of him as a face in a Gold Rush shot, the once face that seems both incidental and immortal guarding a claim or watering a horse, the face that seems lifted from the crowd, from history, the face that could be dynastic.

And my father, Jean-Louis Thibidault, who became Gene and T. B. Doe — he too stands out in pictures. A handsome man, a contemporary man (and yet not even a man of this century. His original half-brothers back in France would now be 120 years old; he would be, by now, just seventy); a salesman and businessman. I still have many pictures, those my mother gave me. The earliest is of a strong handsome man with very short legs. He is lounging on an old canvas chaise under a maple tree, long before aluminum furniture, long before I was born. A scene north of Montreal, just after they were married. It is an impressive picture, but for the legs, which barely reach the grass. Later he would grow into his shortness, would learn the vanities of the short and never again stretch out casually, like the tall. In another picture I am standing with him on a Florida beach. I am five, he is forty-two. I am already the man I was destined to be; he is still the youth he always was. My mother must have taken the shot — I can tell, for I occupy the center — and it is one of those embarrassing shots parents often take. I am in my wet transparent underpants and I've just been swimming at Daytona Beach. It is 1946, our first morning in Florida. It isn't a vacation; we've arrived to start again, in the sun. The war is over, the border is open, the old black Packard is parked behind us. I had wanted to swim but had no trunks; my father took me down in my underwear. But in the picture my face is worried, my cupped hands are reaching down to cover myself, but I was late or the picture early — it seems instead that I am pointing to it, a fleshy little spot on my transparent pants. On the back of the picture my father had written:

Thibidault et fils,
Daytona, avr/46

We'd left Montreal four days before, with snow still gray in the tenements' shadow, the trees black and budless over the dingy winter street. Our destination was a town named Hartley where my father had a friend from Montreal who'd started a lawn furniture factory. My father was to become a traveling salesman for Laverdure's Lawn Laddies, and I was to begin my life as a salesman's son. As reader of back issues, as a collector of cancelled stamps (the inkier the better), as student and teacher of languages.

Thibidault et fils; Thibidault and son. After a week in Hartley I developed worms. My feet bled from itching and scratching. The worms were visible; I could prick them with pins. My mother took me to a clinic where the doctor sprayed my foot with a liquid freeze. Going on, the ice was pleasant, for Florida feet are always hot. Out on the bench I scraped my initials in the frost of my foot. It seemed right to me (before the pain of the thaw began); I was from Up North, the freezing was a friendly gesture for a Florida doctor. My mother held my foot between her hands and told me stories of her childhood, ice-skating for miles on the Battleford River in Saskatchewan, then riding home under fur rugs in a horse-drawn sleigh. Though she was the same age as my father, she was the eldest of six — somewhere between them was a missing generation. The next morning the itching was worse and half a dozen new worms radiated from the ball of my foot. My mother then consulted her old *Canadian Doctor's Home Companion* — my grandfather Blankenship had been a doctor, active for years in curling circles, Anglican missions, and crackpot Toryism — and learned that foot-worms, etc., were unknown in Canada but sometimes afflicted Canadian travelers in Tropical Regions. Common to all hot climes, the book went on, due to poor sanitation and the unspeakable habits of the non-white peoples, even in the Gulf Coast and Indian Territories of our southern neighbor. No known cure, but lack of attention can be fatal.

My mother called in a neighbor, our first contact with the slovenly woman who lived downstairs. She came up with a bottle of carbolic acid and another of alcohol and poured the acid over the worms and told me to yell when it got too hot. Then with alcohol she wiped it off. The next morning my foot had peeled and the worms were gone. And I thought, inspecting my peeled, brown foot, that in some small way I had become less northern, less hateful to the kids around me though I still sounded strange and they shouted after me, "Yankee, Yankee!"

My father was already browned and already spoke with a passable southern accent. When he wasn't on the road with Lawn Laddies he walked around barefoot or in shower clogs. But he never got worms, and he was embarrassed that I had.

Thibidault and son: he was a fisherman and I always fished at his side. Fished for what? I wonder now — he was too short and vain a man to really be a fisherman. He dressed too well, couldn't swim, despised the taste of fish, shunned the cold, the heat, the bugs, the rain. And yet we fished every Sunday, wherever we lived. Canada, Florida, the Middle West, heedless as deer of crossing borders. The tackle box (oily childhood smell) creaked at our feet. The fir-lined shores and pink granite beaches of Ontario gleamed behind us. Every cast became a fresh hope, a trout or *doré* or even a muskie. But we never caught a muskie or a trout, just the snake-like fork-boned pike that we let go by cutting the line when the plug was swallowed deep. And in Florida, with my father in his Harry Truman shirts and sharkskin pants, the warm bait-well sloshing with half-dead shiners, we waited for bass and channel cat in Okeechobee, Kissimmee and a dozen other bug-beclouded lakes. Gar fish, those tropical pike, drifted by the boat. Gators churned in a narrow channel and dragonflies lit on my cane pole tip. And as I grew older and we came back North (but not all the way), I remember our Sundays in Cincinnati, standing shoulder-to-shoulder with a few hundred others around a clay-banked tub lit with arc-lamps. Scummy pay-lakes with a hot dog stand behind, a vision of hell for a Canadian or a Floridian, but we paid and we fished and we never caught a thing. Ten hours every Sunday from Memorial Day to Labor Day, an unquestioning ritual that would see me dress in my fishing khakis, race out early and buy the Sunday paper before we left (so I could check the baseball averages — what a normal kid I might have been!), then pack the tacklebox and portable radio (for the Cincinnati doubleheader) in the trunk. Then I would get my father up. He'd have his coffee and a few cigarettes then shout, "Mildred, Frankie and I are going fishing!" She would be upstairs reading or sewing. We were still living in a duplex; a few months later my parents were to start their furniture store and we would never fish again. We walked out, my father and I, nodding to the neighbors (a few kids, younger than I, asked if they could go, a few young fathers would squint and ask, "Not again, Gene?"); and silently we drove, and later, silently, we fished.

Then came a Sunday just before Labor Day when I was thirteen and we didn't go fishing. I was dressed for it and the car was packed as usual, but my father drove to the County Fair instead. Not the Hamilton County Fair in Cincinnati — we drove across the river into Boone County, Kentucky, where things were once again southern and shoddy.

I had known from the books and articles my mother was leaving in the bathroom, that I was supposed to be learning about sex. I'd read the books and figured out the anatomy for myself; I wondered only how to ask a girl for it and what to do once I got there. Sex was something like dancing, I supposed, too intricate and spontaneous for a boy like me. And so we toured the Fair Grounds that morning, saying nothing, reviewing the prize sows and heifers, watching a stock-car race and a miniature rodeo. I could tell from my father's breathing, his coughing, his attempt to put his arm around my shoulder, that this was the day he was going to talk to me about sex, the facts of life, and the thought embarrassed him as much as it did me. I wanted to tell him to never mind; I didn't need it, it was something that selfish people did to one another.

He led me to a remote tent far off the fairway. There was a long male line outside, men with a few boys my age, joking loudly and smelling bad. My father looked away, silent. So this is the place, I thought, where I'm going to see it, going to learn something good and dirty, something they couldn't put on those Britannica Films and show in school. The sign over the entrance said only: *Princess Hi-Yalla. Shows Continuously.*

There was a smell, over the heat, over the hundred men straining for a place, over the fumes of pigsties and stockyards. It was the smell of furtiveness, rural slaughter and unquenchable famine. The smell of boy's rooms in the high school. The smell of sex on the hoof. The "Princess" on the runway wore not a stitch, and she was already lathered like a racehorse from her continuous dance. There was no avoiding the bright pink lower lips that she'd painted; no avoiding the shrinking, smiling, puckering, wrinkled labia. "Kiss, baby?" she called out, and the men went wild. The lips smacked us softly. The Princess was more a dowager, and more black than brown or yellow. She bent forward to watch herself, like a ventriloquist with a dummy. I couldn't turn away as my father had; it seemed less offensive to watch her wide flat breasts instead, and to think of her as another native from the *National Geographic*. She asked a guard for a slice of gum, then held it over the first row. "Who gwina wet it up fo' baby?" And a farmer licked both sides while his friends made appreciative noises, then handed it back. The Princess inserted it slowly, as though it hurt, spreading her legs like the bow-legged rodeo clown I'd seen a few minutes earlier. Her lower mouth chewed, her abdomen heaved, and she doubled forward to watch the process. "Blow a bubble!" the farmer called, his friends screamed with laughter. But a row of boys in overalls, my age, stared at the woman and didn't smile. Nothing would amaze them — they were waiting for a bubble. Then she cupped her hand underneath and gum came slithering out. "Who wants this?" she called, holding it high, and men were whistling and throwing other things on the stage: key rings, handkerchiefs, cigarettes. She threw the gum toward us — I remember ducking as it came my way, but someone caught it. "Now then," she said, and her voice was as loud as a gospel singer's, "baby's fixin' to have herself a cig'rette." She walked to the edge of the stage (I could see her moist footprints in the dust), her toes curled over the side. "Which of you men out there is givin' baby a cig'rette?" Another farmer standing behind his fat adolescent son threw up two cigarettes. The boy, I remember, was in overalls and had the cretinous look of fat boys in overalls: big, sweating, red-cheeked, with eyes like calves' in a roping event. By the time I looked back on stage, the Princess had inserted the cigarette and had thrust baby out over the runway and was asking for matches. She held the match herself. And the cigarette glowed, smoke came out, an ash formed…

I heard moaning, long low moans, and I felt the eyes of a dozen farmers leap to the boy in overalls. He was jumping and whimpering and the men were laughing as he tried to dig into his sealed-up pants. Forgetting the buttons at his shoulders, he was holding his crotch as though it burned. He was running in place, moaning, then screaming, "Daddy!" and I forgot about the Princess. Men cleared a circle around him and began clapping and chanting, "Whip it out!" and the boy was crying, "Daddy, I cain't hold it back no more!"

My father grabbed me then by the elbow, and said, "Well, have you seen enough?" The farm boy had collapsed on the dirt floor, and was twitching on his back as though a live wire were passed through his body. A navy-blue stain that I thought was blood was spreading between his legs. I though he'd managed to pull his penis off. My father led me out and he was mad at me for something — it was *me* who had brought him there, and his duties as my father — and just as we stepped from the tent I yelled, "Wait — it's happening to me too." I wanted to cry with embarrassment for I hadn't felt any urgency before entering the tent. It seemed like a sudden, irresistible need to urinate, something I couldn't hold back. But worse than water;

something was ripping at my crotch. My light-colored fishing khakis would turn brown in water, and the dark stain was already forming.

"Jesus Christ — are you *sick?* That was an old woman — how could *she*...how could *you*..." He jerked me forward by the elbow. "Jesus God," he muttered, pulling me along down the fairway, then letting me go and walking so fast I had to run, both hands trying to cup the mess I had made. Thousands of people passed me, smiling, laughing. "I don't know about you," my father said. *"I think there's something wrong with you,"* and it was the worse thing my father could say about me. We were in the car. I was crying in the back seat. "Don't tell me someone didn't see you — didn't you think of that? Or what if a customer saw *me* — but you didn't think of that either, did you? Here I take you to something I thought you'd like, something any *normal* boy would like, and — "

I'd been afraid to talk. The wetness was drying, a stain remained. "You know Murray Lieberman?" my father asked a few minutes later.

"The salesman?"

"He has a kid your age and so we were talking —"

"Never mind," I said.

"Well, what in the name of God is wrong with two fathers getting together, eh? It was supposed to *show* you what it's like, about women, I mean. It's better than any drawing, isn't it? You want books all the time? You want to *read* about it, or do you want to see it? At least now you *know*, so go ahead and read. Tell your mother we were fishing today, O.K.? And *that* — that was a coke you spilled, all right?"

And no other talk, man-to-man, or father-to-son, had ever taken place.

I think back to Boniface Thibidault — how would he, how *did* he, show his sons what to do and where to do it? He was a Frenchman, not a North American; he learned it in Paris, not in a monastery as my father had. And I am, partially at least, a Frenchman too. My father should have taken me to a *cocotte*, to his own mistress perhaps, for the initiation, *la déniasement*. And I, in my own love-making, would have forever honored him. But this is North America and my father, despite everything, was in his silence a Quebec Catholic of the nineteenth century. Sex, despite my dreams of something better, something nobler, still smells of the circus tent, of something raw and murderous. Other kinds of sex, the adjusted, contented, fulfilling sex of school and manual, seem insubstantial, willfully ignorant of the depths.

At thirteen I was oldest of eighty kids on the block, a thankless distinction, and my parents at fifty had a good twenty years on the next oldest, who, it happened, shared our duplex.

There lived on that street, and I was beginning to notice in that summer before the sideshow at the county fair, several girl brides and one or two maturely youthful wives. The brides, under twenty and with the first or second youngsters, were a sloppy crew who patrolled the street in cut-away shorts and bra-less elasticized halters that had to be pulled up every few steps. They set their hair so tightly in pin curlers that the effect, at a distance, was of the mange. Barefoot they pushed their baby strollers, thighs sloshing as they walked, or sat on porch furniture reading movie magazines or holding tinted plastic baby bottles between their knees. Though they sat in the sun all day they never tanned. They were spreading week by week while their husbands, hard athletic gas-pumpers, played touch football on the street every Sunday.

But there were others; in particular the wife next door, our two floors being mirror images of the other, everything back-to-back but otherwise identical. What was their name? She was a fair woman, about thirty, with hair only lightly bleached and the kind of figure that one first judges slightly too plump until something voluptuous in her, or you, makes you look again and you see that she is merely extraordinary; a full woman who had once been a lanky girl. She had three children, two of them girls who favored the husband, but I can't quite place his name or face. Her name was Annette.

She was French. That had been a point of discussion once. Born in Maine, she would often chat with my father in what French she remembered while her husband played football or read inside. By that time I had forgotten most of my French. And now I remember the husband. His name was Lance — Lance! — and he was dark, square-shouldered, with a severe crewcut that sliced across an ample bald spot. He traveled a lot; I recall him sitting in a lawn chair on summer evenings, reading the paper and drinking a beer till the mosquitoes drove him in.

And that left Annette alone, and Annette had no friends on the block. She gave the impression, justified, of far outdistancing the neighborhood girls. Perhaps she frightened them, being older and by comparison, a goddess. She would sit on a lawn chair in the front yard, on those male-less afternoons of toddling children and cranky mothers and was so stunning in a modest sundress that I would stay inside and peek at her through a hole I had cut in the curtains. Delivery trucks, forced to creep through the litter of kids and abandoned toys, lingered longer than they had to, just to look. At thirteen I could stare for hours, unconscious of peeping, unaware, really, of what I wanted or expected to see. It was almost like fishing, with patience and anticipation keeping me rooted.

My parents were at the new property, cleaning it up for a grand opening. I was given three or four dollars a day for food and I'd spend fifty or sixty cents of it on meaty and starchy grease down at the shopping center. I was getting fat. Every few days I carried a bulging pocketful of wadded bills down to the bank and cashed them for a ten or twenty. And the bills would accumulate in my wallet. I was too young to open an account without my parents' finding out; the question was how to spend it. After a couple of weeks I'd go downtown and spend astounding sums, for a child, on stamps.

While I was in the shopping center I began stealing magazines from the drugstore. The scandal mags, the Hollywood parties, the early *Playboy* and its imitators — I stole because I was too good to be seen buying them. I placed them between the pages of the *Sporting News*, which I also read cover-to-cover, then dropped a wadded five-dollar bill in the newspaper honor box, raced home, and feasted. Never one for risks, I burned the residue or threw them out in the neighbor's garbage can, my conscience clear for a month's more stealing and secret reading. There was never a time in my life when sex had been so palpable; when the very sight of any girl vaguely developed or any woman up to forty and still in trim could make my breath come short, make my crotch tingle under my baggy pants. In the supermarket, when young mothers dipped low to pick a carton of Cokes from the bottom shelf, I dipped with them. When the counter girl at the drugstore plunged her dipper in the ice cream tub, I hung over the counter to catch a glimpse of her lacy bra; when the neighbor women hung out their clothes, I would take the stairs two at a time to watch from above. When those young wives hooked their thumbs under the knitted elastic halters and gave an upward tug, I let out a little whimper. How close it was to madness; how many other fat thirteen- and fourteen-year-olds with a drop more violence, provocation, self-pity or whatever, would plunge a knife sixty times into those bellies, just to run their fingers inside the shorts and peel the halter back, allowing the breasts to ooze aside? And especially living next to Annette whose figure made flimsy styles seem indecent and modest dresses maddening. Her body possessed the clothes too greedily, sucked the material to her flesh. She was the woman, I now realize, that Dostoyevski and Kazantzakis and even Faulkner knew; a Grushenka or the young village widow, a dormant body that kindled violence.

The duplexes were mirror images with only the staircases and bathrooms adjoining. In the summer with Annette at home, her children out playing or taking a nap, her husband away, or just at work, she took many baths. From wherever I sat in our duplex watching television or reading my magazines, I could hear the drop of the drain plug in her bathroom, the splash of water rushing in, the quick expansion of the hot water pipes.

I could imagine the rest, exquisitely. First testing the water with her finger, then drying the finger on her shorts and then letting them drop. Testing the water again before unhooking the bra in a careless sweep and with another swipe, peeling off her panties. The thought of Annette naked, a foot away, made the walls seem paper-thin, made the tiles grow warm. Ear against the tiles I could hear the waves she made as she settled back, the squeaking of her heels on the bottom of the tub as she straightened her legs, the wringing of a face cloth, plunk of soap as it dropped. The scene was as vivid, with my eyes closed and my hot ear on the warm tile, as murders on old radio shows. I thought of the childhood comic character who could shrink himself with magic sand; how for me that had always translated itself into watching the Hollywood starlets from their bathroom heating registers. But Annette was better or at least as good, and so available. If only there were a way, a shaft for midgets. It wasn't right to house strangers so intimately without providing a way to spy. I looked down to the tile floor — a crack? Something a bobby pin could be twisted in, just a modest, modest opening? And I saw the pipes under the sink, two slim swan-necks, one for hot, one for cold, that cut jaggedly through the tile wall — they had to connect! Then on my hands and knees I scraped away the plaster that held the chromium collar around the pipe. As I had hoped, the hole was a good quarter-inch wider than the pipes and all that blocked a straight-on view of the other bathroom were the collars on Annette's pipes. It would be nothing to punch my way through, slide the rings down, and lie on the tile floor in comfort of my own bathroom and watch it all; Annette bathing! Ring level was below the tub, but given the distance the angle might correct itself. But detection would be unbearable; if caught I'd commit suicide. She was already out of the bath (but there'll be other days, I thought). She took ten-minute baths (how much more could a man bear?), the water was draining and now she was running the lavatory faucet which seemed just over my head. How long before she took another bath? It would seem, now that I had a plan, as long as the wait between issues of my favorite magazines.

I rested on the floor under the sink until Annette left her bathroom. Then I walked down to the shopping center and had a Coke to steady myself. I bought a nailfile. When I got back Annette was sitting in her yard, wearing a striped housedress and looking, as usual, fresh from a bath. I said hello and she smiled very kindly. Then I turned my door handle and cried, "Oh, no!"

"What is it, Frankie?" she asked, getting up from her chair.

"I left my key inside."

"Shall I call your father?"

"No," I said, "I think I can get in through the window. But could I use your bathroom first?"

"Of course."

I checked upstairs for kids. Then I locked myself inside and with the new file, scraped away the plaster and pulled one collar down. Careful as always, aware that I would make a good murderer or a good detective, I cleaned up the plaster crumbs. I'd forgotten to leave our own bathroom light on, but it seemed that I could see all the way through. Time would tell. *Take a bath*, I willed her, as I flushed the toilet. It reminded me of fishing as a child, trying to influence the fish to bite. It's very hot, sticky, just right for a nice cool bath... My own flesh was stippled, I shivered as I stepped outside and saw her again. She'd soon be *mine* — something to do for the rest of the summer! My throat was so tense I couldn't even thank her. I climbed inside through the living-room window that I had left open.

I took the stairs two at a time, stretched myself out under the sink to admire the job. I'd forgotten to leave *her* light on, but I thought I could see the white of her tub in the darkened bathroom, and even an empty tub was enough to sustain me.

How obvious was the pipe and collar? It suddenly seemed blatant, that she would enter the bathroom, undress, sit in the tub, turn to the wall, and scream. Do a peeper's eyes shine too brightly? In school I'd often been able to stare a kid into turning around — it was now an unwanted gift.

You're getting warm again, Annette. Very very hot. You want another bath. You're getting up from the chair, coming inside, up the stairs... I kept on for hours till it was dark. I heard the kids taking baths and saw nothing. The white of the bathtub was another skin of plaster, no telling how thick. I'd been cheated.

Another day. There had to be another link — I had faith that the builders of duplexes were men who provided, out of guilt, certain amenities. Fans were in the ceiling. Windows opened on the opposite sides, the heating ducts were useless without a metal drill. Only the medicine cabinets were left. They had to be back-to-back. I opened ours, found the four corner screws, undid them, took out the medicines quietly (even my old Florida carbolic acid), then eased the chest from its plaster nest. It worked. I was facing the metal backing of Annette's medicine chest. The fit was tight and I could never take a chance of tampering with hers — what if I gave it a nudge when Lance was shaving and the whole thing came crashing down, revealing me leaning over my sink in the hole where our medicine chest had been?

The used-razor slot. A little slot in the middle. I popped the paper coating with the nailfile. I darkened our own bathroom. If Annette opened her chest, I'd see her. But would she open it with her clothes off? Was she tall enough to make it count? How many hours would I have to stand there, stretched over the sink, waiting, and could I, every day, put the chest back up and take it down without some loud disaster? What if my father came home to shave, unexpectedly?

I waited all afternoon and all evening and when eight o'clock came I ended the vigil and put the chest back up. With a desire so urgent, there *had* to be a way of penetrating an inch and a half of tile and plaster. When she was in her bath I felt I could have devoured the walls between us. Anything *heard* so clearly had to yield to vision — that was another natural law — just as anything dreamt had to become real, eventually.

I became a baby-sitter, the oldest kid on the block, quiet and responsible. I watched television in nearly every duplex on the street, ignored the whimpers, filled bottles, and my pockets bulged with more unneeded cash. I poked around the young parents' bedrooms and medicine cabinets, only half-repelled by the clutter and unfamiliar odors, the stickiness, the grayness of young married life in a Midwest suburb. I found boxes of prophylactics in top drawers and learned to put one on and to walk around with it on until the lubrication stuck to my underwear. Sex books and nudist magazines showing pubic hair were stuffed in nightstands, and in one or two homes I found piles of home-made snaps of the young wife when she'd been slim and high school young, sitting naked in the sun, in a woods somewhere. She'd been posed in dozens of ways, legs wide apart, fingers on her pubic hair, tongue curled between her teeth. Others of her, and of a neighbor woman, on the same living-room sofa that I was sitting on: fatter now, her breasts now resting on a roll of fat around her middle, her thighs shadowed where the skin had grown soft. *This is the girl I see every day*, pushing that carriage, looking like a fat girl at a high school hang-out. Those bigger girls in my school, in bright blue sweaters, earrings, black curly hair, bad skin, black corduroy jackets, smoking. They become like this; they *are* like this.

These were the weeks in August, when my mother was leaving the articles around. Soon my father would take me to the county fair. There were no answers to the questions I asked, holding those snapshots, looking again (by daylight) at the wife (in ragged shorts and elastic halter) who had consented to the pictures. They were like murder victims, the photos were like police shots in the scandal magazines, the women looked like mistresses of bandits. There was no place in the world for the life I wanted, for the pure woman I would someday, somehow, marry.

I baby-sat for Annette and Lance, then for Annette alone, and I worked again on the lavatory scheme, the used-razor slot, and discovered the slight deficiencies in the architecture that had thrown my calculations off. I could see from their bathroom into ours much better than I could ever see into theirs. Annette kept a neat house and life with her, even I could appreciate, must have been a joy of lust and efficiency, in surroundings as clean and attractive as a *Playboy* studio.

One evening she came over when my parents were working, to ask me to baby-sit for a couple of hours. Lance wasn't in. Her children were never a problem and though it was a week night and school had begun, I agreed. She left me a slice of Lance's birthday cake, and begged me to go to sleep in case she was late.

An hour later, after some reading, I used her bathroom, innocently. If only I lived here, with Annette over there! I opened her medicine chest to learn some more about her: a few interesting pills "for pain," Tampex Super (naturally, I thought), gauze and adhesive, something for piles (for him, I hoped). And then I heard a noise from our bathroom; I heard our light snap on. My parents must have come home early.

I knew from a cough that it wasn't my mother. The Thibidault medicine chest was opened. I peered through the razor slot and saw young fingers among our bottles, blond hair and a tanned forehead: Annette. She picked out a jar, then closed the door. I fell to the floor and put my eye against the pipes. Bare golden legs. Then our light went out.

I looked into our bathroom for the next few seconds then ran to Annette's front bedroom where the youngest girl slept, and pressed over her crib to look out the window. She was just stepping out and walking slowly to the station wagon of Thibidault Furniture, which had been parked. She got in the far side and the car immediately, silently, backed away, with just its parking lights on…

And that was all. For some reason, perhaps the shame of my complicity, I never asked my father why he had come home or why Annette had been in our bathroom. I didn't have to — I'd gotten a glimpse of Annette, which was all I could handle anyway. I didn't understand the rest. *Thibidault et fils*, fishing again.

Jean-Louis Thibidault, twice-divorced, is dead; buried in Venice, Florida. Bridge of Sighs Cemetery. I even asked his widow if I could have him removed to Sorel, Quebec. She didn't mind, but the *prêtre-vicaire* of my father's old parish turned me down. When my father was born, Venice, Florida, was five miles offshore and fifty feet underwater. The thought of him buried there tortures my soul.

There was another Sunday in Florida. A hurricane was a hundred miles offshore and due to strike Fort Lauderdale within the next six hours. We drove from our house down Las Olas to the beach (Fort Lauderdale was still an inland city then), and parked half a mile away, safe from the paint-blasting sand. We could hear the breakers under the shriek of the wind, shaking the wooden bridge we walked on. Then we watched them crash, brown with weeds and suspended sand. And we could see them miles offshore, rolling in forty feet high and flashing their foam like icebergs. A few men in swimming suits and woolen sweaters were standing in the crater pools, pulling out the deep-sea fish that had been stunned by the trip and waves. Other fish littered the beach, their bellies blasted by the change in pressure. My mother's face was raw and her glasses webbed with salt. She went back to the car on her own. My father and I sat on the bench for another hour and I could see behind his crusty sunglasses. His eyes were moist and dancing, his hair stiff and matted. We sat on the bench until we were soaked and the municipal guards rounded us up. Then they barricaded the boulevards and we went back to the car, the best day of fishing we'd ever had, and we walked hand in hand for the last time, talking excitedly, dodging coconuts, power lines, and shattered glass, feeling brave and united in the face of the storm. My father and me. What a day it was, what a once-in-a-lifetime day it was.

≈ MEDITATIONS ON STARCH ≈

POTATOES: Mr. Spud opened at the local mall, and hired my high school boy for his first job. He was saving for a trip to Europe, where he has relatives.

He's been taught to do amazing things with potatoes. They're just a shell of their former selves. No longer prized for snowy yields, for understated contribution to stews, now they're just parka-like pockets waiting to be stuffed. It's the fate of blandness in the mall-managed world, I tell him, to be upscaled into glamour like pita bread and bagels, chicken and veal. Stuffed with yoghurt, sour cream and cottage cheese, spread with peppers, cheese and broccoli, topped with Thousand Island dressing and bacon bits.

What wizard thought this up?

Mother!

I still like mashed potatoes. Even the name is honest and reassuring, after the *gepashke*t concoctions with alfalfa sprouts and garbanzo beans. Butter-topped, cream-coloured bins of heroic self-indulgence, inviting a finger-dip the way a full can of white enamel compels a brush.

Is there a taste explosion in the world finer than the first lick of the Dairy Queen cone, the roughened vanilla from a freshly opened tub, the drowning in concentrated carbohydrate where fats and starches come together in snowy concupiscence?

CORN: My son never knew his grandmother, whose presence comes back to me as I stand at the Mr. Spud toppings bar. She only exists in these sharpened moments, triggered by significant images that otherwise baffle me. "Mother," I murmur, "what do you make of this?" Questions to my mother are questions to history, answers from her are brief parables of the twentieth century.

Don't you know? she tells me. The yearning for a clean, quick, anonymous bite is universal.

My mother found herself in Prague in 1933. Her art school in Germany had just been closed down. One of her professors offered escape with him to Rio. Many went to Paris and Brussels. These weren't the Big-Time Bauhausers; New York and L.A. weren't in the cards. These were commercial designers ("but not designing enough," my mother would joke). Shanghai, Istanbul, Alexandria, Stockholm, with the leaders taking off for Caracas and Rio. One got to Vera Cruz. Maybe eventually some of them made their way to America. My mother got to Montréal.

I was a stamp collector. I knew the tales behind those thick letters with the high-denomination stamps, the elegant handwriting in black ink turning to olive. Cancelled stamps are less valuable than mint, but I treasured them for the urgency of cancellation. My mother had known a time when the germ of genius was clustered in the back streets of Dresden and Weimar and Dessau, before the Big Bang flung it to tin shacks on the shores of Maracaibo.

The poles of her existence can move me to tears, the B. Traven world of artists from the heartland of order and austerity rotting in the rat-invested tropics. She showed me photos of an art college, hand-painted signs on a tin-roofed shack, Herr Professor in jodhpurs and bush shirt, teaching from a canvas deckchair.

"Poor old Dieter," she'd say.

She'd wanted a career in fashion design. Her surviving portfolios from art school feature ice-skaters and ballerinas. She was the Degas of Dresden. But the faces of the skaters and dancers seem grated on, dark and heavy, like hers. The eyes are shadowed, in the movie-fashion of the day. They stop just short of grotesquerie, for those girls will never soar, never leap. She could get the bodies, but not the faces. I can't tell if it's Expressionism, autobiography, or mild incompetence. I don't know if these were the drawings she kept out of fondness, or the ones that didn't sell. Others found their way into magazines. The idea of my mother influencing the Prague Spring Collection of 1934 fills me with wonder.

Or do I read too much into those drawings, too much into everything about her? Had she somehow, secretly, read Kafka? The idea of her Europe, of pre-war Central Europe, tugs at me, the continent I missed by the barest of margins.

There was no concept of Eastern or Western Europe in those days — Warsaw and Prague were as western as Paris. Russia and Spain, of course, didn't count; they were Asian, or African. Budapest and Bucharest had reputations of pervasive dishonesty, deriving perhaps from the perversity of their languages. So the stories I grew up with and passed on to my son were of an *idea* of Europe that hasn't existed in eighty years, a Holy Roman Empire in which a single language and a single passport dominated all others and the rest of the world suffered paroxysms of exclusion for not being European, and specifically, German.

When he was twelve, I asked my boy what he wanted to be when he grew up. "A European," he answered.

In Prague she got a job painting commercial signboards to hang over doorways, like British pub placards. One of the first signs she painted was for something called "Indian Corn". A corn café! Nothing but stubby ears of corn, cut in half, standing in pools of butter. In Prague, in 1933.

She had never eaten corn. Her parents considered it servants' food, part of a cuisine beneath serious cultivation. Nothing that required labour in the eating — and corn on the cob looked like work — was part of their diet. My grandparents, whom I of course never met, favoured pre-nouvelle cuisine French cooking, which meant soft, smothered, simmering things, the mashed potatoes of their day, short on fibre, low on spices, long on labour and quickly digested. Much favoured were compotes and warm puddings, since they detested anything cold as well as anything hot. Worst of all were the still-churning, molten messes that had become chic in Germany with the rise of Mussolini. Upscaling the lowly pasta. My grandfather's response to history is summarized in a single gastronomic grumble. "Why couldn't *il Duce* have been a Frenchman! At least we would have eaten properly." My grandmother, no less patrician, responded, "Be grateful. He could have been Hungarian."

Of all the stories I want to know, of all the things my mother told me of the secret lives of complicated people, I remember only these ridiculous little lines. So she painted her cob — half a cob, and the cobs weren't big in those days — standing up like a stubby candle in its pool of butter. Each kernel was treated like a window in an apartment tower, radiating a buttery light. It wasn't easy, before acrylics, before the conventions of Magic Realism, being a German artist, to devote herself to a humble corncob.

"I didn't know anything at first. Or maybe I discovered it as I worked. It was love for America," is how she put it. "A craving for Indian corn saved my life."

Frank Kafka had been living a few blocks away just a decade earlier. He'd written *Amerika* under the same mysterious craving, though it didn't save his life. Maybe America-worship was in the air, at least among those who professed no longing for Germany. For my mother, Prague was just another provincial German city with an interesting Slavic component to be respected, but faintly pitied. She couldn't imagine civilized discourse in any language but German, with the possible exception of French in well-defined circumstances. French and German divided the dignified world between them, the spheres of pleasure and labour, though her French years were still in the future.

Her boss had a son, named Jürgen Jaeger — a good movie name, and he had dabbled in films like many German-speakers in the '20s. He still thought of himself as a set-designer, a property man ("but not a man of property," he joked, and the joke has survived them all because my mother jotted it down). He also identified strongly with Hitler's Sudeten policy, feeling himself mightily abused by the majority Czechs with their dirty, mongrel ways. I am making him sound unappealing — a Hitler of sorts, another expansionist sign-painter with acting ambitions, born on the rim of Germany — but my mother never did. His attitudes were too common to be evil. I'm sure most Prague-born German-speakers yearned for enosis with the Fatherland, all other implications of Hitler-rule to be put aside, temporarily.

This, then, was my mother's situation in 1933. She was thirty and unmarried, talented, attractive, and stateless. She had an admirer whose rechannelled ambition was to join the political and if necessary military services of the greater German state. I have seen his picture, the suggestive swagger, as I interpret it, of one leg up on the running board, elbow on the windshield, body tight against the touring-car's flank. No monocle, no duelling scars, but a leather coat, a self-regarding little blond moustache, and a short, elegant cigarette that can only be carried in a theatrical gold case. He strikes the pose of a big-game hunter, even on a Carpathian picnic in the summer of 1934. This is the man who must be eliminated before I can be born.

Pictures of my mother show her always smoking, though I never saw her smoke, nor empty an ashtray without a show of disgust.

I came into her papers five years ago. That's when I unwrapped the first of many portfolios she'd been keeping under her bed. I had never seen them, and she had shared everything with me, I'd thought, the only child, the late-born son, the artistic and sensitive man in the family. Some of these I had seen — my grandparents sometime in the late twenties at a resort in the mountains. Taking the Cure. All those faces, relaxing, carefree, getting away from business and the city and the nameless sickness that seemed to stalk them.

I look like my grandfather — her genes won out. The gene for baldness, carried through the mother. The gene for Alzheimer's disease — who carries that? My mother maintained a saving fiction all the years that she was able, that her parents could have left Germany in time, just as she had, there was an uncle in Montréal who would sponsor them all, but her father lost first the will, then the sense of all urgency. It was, in his case, a medical, not political problem.

"Who is this man?" I asked her, and she pretended to look, and to smile. "He's very handsome, mama. Like a movie star." Still no response. The photo is sepia, faded, and extremely small. If only it could be blown up, Jaeger and the touring-car, the mountains and forest in the background, I might understand just a little more. There are other pictures, equally small, taken from upper windows, overlooking city squares. Brno? Bratislava? Carlsbad? Prague, perhaps, or the view from a Carpathian resort hotel. Maybe Jürgen is standing at her side, whispering, "*Sehr schön.*"

"Jürgen Jaeger, mama, does it mean anything?"

She held her hand out to appease me, her fingers now blue-edged tines, but she didn't look.

I can read German, speak it enough. Her old-style handwriting is difficult. *I tell him he must do what he must do. His father has interests in Germany. They have relatives in Leipzig.*

I read it out loud, looking at its author's face, which gives back nothing. She probably jotted down these notes in ten seconds, sixty years ago. Now, the simplest resurrected fact of her life embraces the world. If I don't take these boxes now, they will be lost. She is going away and won't be coming back, and we have decided we must leave Canada.

He says, "Der Führer may be a little crude for your tastes, but he's no fool! He knows who makes money for him. And with this Rosenfeld getting elected in America, well...."

There is another tiny, sepia street scene. It is the most precious picture in the box. For an artist, my mother took terrible pictures. A tram snakes off the top of the frame. Half of a bundled Frau crosses the street. Uniformed men — police, army, Czech, German? — fill the space at the corner, outside a coffee shop. There seems to be an *Apothek* next door. Cold-looking children play a sidewalk game using chalk just outside its door. You would miss it if you weren't looking for it, the sign for *Korn* struggling for attention against much larger and fancier boards.

This is the picture to be enlarged, at any cost. I palm it and slip it away, knowing I am taking her soul, and fearing that something will slice through all the blown cells in her brain and reach out for it, and then destroy it.

Fly! Fly! Go west and don't stop. I tell you this as a friend, as someone who knows.

This on a worn sheet of airmail paper, initialled with what appears to be a double "J" inside a crest, with a swastika hanging below it. So strange to see, as it were, a sincere swastika and not some gangland graffiti.

J.J., Visa Clerk, Leipzig.

RICE: In my wife's culture, Usha is called a "cousin-sister" which means any female relative approximate in age. Actually she is Anu's first cousin, daughter of my father-in-law's oldest brother. In the ancestral long-ago, they had lived in the same Calcutta house, the *jethoo-bari*, part of a joint family numbering forty.

She is married to Pramod, and both are physicists. But instead of staying in the university world and settling down on some Big Ten campus, Pramod had taken a position in Holland, setting up a lab, and the Dutch government had recommended him for similar work in Indonesia and Surinam and before too many years, he had found himself side-tracked into sophisticated, high-level nuclear management, the protocols of which led, inevitably, to international agencies. He is now with the UN's nuclear-monitoring agency in Vienna, and Usha works as a researcher in physics for the University. They have been in Vienna for fifteen years, their children are European, they own an apartment in the city and a garden house in Wiener-Neustadt. It's a comfortable life in a country where immigration and assimilation as we know them are impossible.

We are all together this night in Vienna, enjoying a huge Bengali banquet, cooked from locally gathered fish and rice and vegetables, simmered in spices brought back from frequent trips to London and Bombay. My son and I have our Eurail passes, Anu will be with us only three days before going on to India to visit her mother and sister.

It's this life we lead, I silently explain to myself, and to the ghost of my mother. Vienna was another of her cities, briefly. The world has opened for us, no fears of the unknown. My mother shrank from the very idea of India, but tried to disguise it with images of Gandhi and respect for ancient wisdom.

How under-defined I feel, at fifty, compared to Pramod; a father who has written some books, who teaches when he must, who dabbles in cultures that have their hooks in him.

We are talking of Canada. "They've become like the British," Anu says, spooning out rice to our son. "Hateful little people."

The Sens had visited Niagara Falls last summer, and been turned away at the border for an afternoon's visit. For pleasure trips they use their Indian, not UN passports. "He said things to us I wouldn't say to a servant," says Usha Sen. "'How do I know you will leave when you say? How do I know you own a house as you say?' They are very suspicious about Indians, I must say."

"I told him to go to hell," says Jyoti, the Harvard boy. "Who needs the hassle? The Austrians are bad enough, but I always thought Canadians were better."

I remember when it wasn't so, in our cosmopolitan refuge of Montréal, when my mother and I lived like Alexandrians in a large apartment in Outremont after my father's death. We had original paintings on our walls, French-Canadian artists only. My father was an old man even in my earliest memories, a lawyer nearing retirement, then dead two months after achieving it. I remember the visits of his grown-up children from an earlier marriage, of being the same age as his grandchildren, and of wondering what, exactly, to call our relationship. My son and Jyoti are, precisely, second cousins. Usha is his first-cousin-once-removed. He calls her *mashi*, aunt.

"Have more rice, please. There is plenty."

"Mother, this isn't Calcutta," says Tapati, the MIT daughter. Everything this evening is exquisite. There is no cuisine in the world that excites me like Indian, no painting that thrills me like Moghul miniatures, no city for better or worse, like Calcutta. After India, Europe is a bore. I'm staying back for my son's sake, his ancient dream of being European.

Anu is explaining our move to the States. "To be Indian in Canada was to be a second-class citizen no matter how good you were, no matter how Canadian you tried to be. At least if we're second-class in the States we know it's because we're just second-rate." I wish I could sink into the rice, the dimple-topped pyramids of snowy rice scooped out for fish and vegetables. I want to grab handfuls of rice and smear them over my head and rub them in my face. I want to do something vulgar and extravagant in this apartment of excellence, among these diligent and exquisite people, out of my own shame, the accumulated guilt and incomprehensions of my life.

Tapati is asking our son, "Is there anything special you want to see in Vienna? I can take you there."

They are amazed that for who he is and what he represents to them — America, after all, the place and people they most admire — he speaks only English. Usha's children have been raised in Europe, but with Indian ways. Each of them speaks eight languages, but they have no country. Jyoti writes rock lyrics in German, plays in an Austrian band, studies economics at Harvard. Tapati has a Ph.D. and an MBA and now interns at the World Bank. Both are in America, but not of it — too exquisite for the mall-culture America I know.

"Anything," he says. "It doesn't matter."

"No, there must be something."

He looks to me for help. He wants Europe, he wants saturation, a way of entering. He's been studying German in high school, but it's the last thing in the world he'll admit here to his second cousins. He doesn't trust himself to understand a single word. He's heard Bengali all his life, but never thought it part of himself. He spent half his life in a French-speaking city and did his French exercises perfectly, like history. It's the legacy of the New World. Jyoti has already told him, he'd trade it all — the languages, the sophistication that dazzles his Harvard friends — for a simple work permit, for the chance to stay and work the summer at Mr. Spud.

"And what about you, Uncle?"

"Berggasse 19," I say.

"The Freud house?" Usha asks. "Why that — there's nothing there, believe me."

"Wasn't he a coke-head?" my son asks in all seriousness, and the question sails over the heads of all but Jyoti, who smiles and nods. A conspiratorial friendship is starting to grow.

"Berggasse is very near my lab," says Usha. "We can take the tram there tomorrow. But it's not what you think — it's just a couple of rooms with photos on the walls."

"Bor-ring," Jyoti hums, as my boy suppresses a grin.

We're there at eleven o'clock the next morning, my son and I, and Jyoti who's brought his guitar along. He'll do Freud with us, and we'll do the music shops with him. He's promised us a tour of the lowlife dives of Vienna, the coffee shops where the Punkers hang out, the places where he spent his high school years avoiding expectations to be good and dutiful.

The first cousins have gone out for a proper Viennese lunch, *Kaffeeschlag mit Sachertorte.* Nothing that has to do with the man who once compared the ego — rational and altruistic — to Europe, and the libido — rapacious and murderous — to Asia, inspires my wife to sympathy. A foolish little man, racist and chauvinist, with bad science to justify it.

It is a sunny, summer day, cool but bright, sweater weather. Children are playing on the sidewalk of Berggasse, outside the corner *Apothek*. Jyoti says to us, "Watch this — you think the Austrians know anything?" He asks the oldest boy, "Do you know the Freud house?"

"Did they just move in?" he asks.

"Get that?" he laughs, turning to us. My son translates it.

"You could ask anyone on this street. Old, young, it doesn't matter. One group wants to forget, and the other one never knew." We cross over the narrow street, looking for brass plates outside the formal doors. Number 19 is just a flat, as it always was, squeezed between other flats and offices.

Usha was right, it's only an old doctor's office cluttered with photos. The second-cousins browse respectfully, faintly embarrassed by all the fuss. It's all Jyoti can do not to unzip his guitar case and start banging out something scandalous for the Freud Museum. I don't know what I expected to find.

This is the room where all of them came, I want to say. Princess Marie sat there. And the young Viennese Circle — see their pictures! — met here, in this room. In this room, someone challenged the incomprehensible with bad science and bad politics, in the name nevertheless of reason. The smallest facts had the deepest gravity, chance events were all connected, public events were the ritualized form of private projection.

Son! Are you listening?

Someone dared to say our dreams had a pattern, our dysfunctions a cause, our beliefs a pathology. On the walls, the Holy Roman Empire surrenders, and Freud stands on the dais, Vienna's most honoured, most famous citizen, as the Austrian Republic is declared. Here, Freud is welcoming the President of the Republic and his cabinet on the quarter-century anniversary of *The Interpretation of Dreams*. His birth-cottage is decked with bunting.

And it chokes me, suddenly, the realization that science and music and literature can be so advanced, and do nothing to influence a political culture in its infancy. Austrian democracy was younger than Ghana's when the Nazis crushed it. I want to turn to my son and remind him of the great despairing poems I've read to him, of Yeats, of Auden, and the vast literature of the Holocaust that radiates from this room and a thousand others in this city, and echoes off these grey, sunny streets. The tradition, however faintly, I belong to. Poems about the imbalance of what we are capable of feeling and thinking, and what we have inflicted.

They've gone.

"They heard music outside," the ticket-seller tells me. "They said for you to follow the music."

At first I hear nothing. I watch the children across the street, and the old women slogging their way from shop to shop, carrying groceries in string bags.

Berggasse slopes downward, and I follow it a block, half-imagining a rhythm, a few high notes and a beat in the air. Turn right, twist left. People are in the streets now, following something.

Up ahead in a small square at the rim of a fountain I can see them, clowns juggling, and a small crowd clustered. The performers wear top hats and putty noses, their cheeks are reddened, and one of the boys is darker than all the others, in a borrowed top hat, crouched on one knee like Chuck Berry, cutting in front of the clowns and drummers, leading everyone in lyrics I can't understand. And at the edge of the fountain is my boy in a borrowed vest and putty nose, punching a tambourine and doing a snake-dance on the fountain's edge.

Commentary by
Clark Blaise

≈

Clark Blaise's prose haunts us with its exactness, its vividness, and its poetry. The following commentary is taken from an interview recorded at the time of the publication of his first book and published in Journal of Canadian Fiction *2.4 (1973). Here Blaise speaks of the aspects of language and of technique that give fiction pinpoint accuracy, rich sensuality, and indefinable mysteriousness.*

I think the real reason I'm fond of "personal" fiction is that two things move me in fiction — texture and voice.

Texture is detail arranged and selected and enhanced. It is the inclusion of detail from several planes of reference: dialogue, fantasy, direct passive observation ("I am a camera"), allusion, psychic wound, symbol, straight fact, etc. etc. — the sum of all that is *voice*....

Texture implies both vitality and unevenness — it probably rules out most satire. I think the job of fiction is to view life through a microscope so that every grain gets its due and no one can confuse salt with sugar. You hear a lot about cinema being the visual medium — this is false. It *degrades* the visual by its inability to focus. It takes the visual for granted. Only the word — for me — is truly visual. I'm reminded of something from Nabokov's *Speak, Memory* where he speaks of the words learned in his childhood always possessing a *colour*, and in later life he sought the proper word with precisely the sensual involvement of a painter seeking a tone. That's what I mean by language as (for me) a visual experience and only secondarily a musical (poetic) one. It seems that the expressive gift, when it occurs in language, is frequently visual or aural. Otherwise, presumably, it is legalistic or journalistic, an expediency to communicate data.

By *voice* I am referring to the control, what is commonly referred to when we mention the "world" of a certain author; the limits of probability and chance in his construction, the sanctions he leaves us for our own variations, what we sense of his own final concerns and bafflements. Again, my interest in voice is not one of "character". I see the construction of "character" as an honourable but not necessarily compelling occupation.

When I "see" a story it is always in terms of its images and situation, the tone and texture and discovery that seems immanent in that situation — and very rarely do these intimations demand a thirty-eight-year-old spinster or a college drop-out on an acid trip. I try to work out a voice that will allow for a simultaneity of image and action. Sometimes it is "second person", frequently first person, commonly present tense. Sometimes it will have no time-referent beyond the present moment. In my book *A North American Education*, most of the Montreal stories — "Eyes", "Words for the Winter", "Extractions and Contractions", and "Going to India" — follow, at least in part, this pattern. Those are stories of texture and voice — details selected with an eye to their aptness but also to their "vapour trails", their slow dissolve into something more diffuse and nameless.

SELECTED WORKS BY CLARK BLAISE

"Thibidault et fils." M.F.A. Thesis Iowa 1964.

New Canadian Writing, 1968: Stories by David Lewis Stein, Clark Blaise and Dave Godfrey. Toronto: Clarke, Irwin, 1968. 67-134.

A North American Education: A Book of Short Fiction. Toronto: Doubleday, 1973. Rpt. as *A North American Education*. New Press Canadian Classics. Toronto: General Publishing, 1984.

Tribal Justice. Toronto: Doubleday, 1974. New Press Canadian Classics. Toronto: General Publishing, 1984.

Resident Alien. Introd. Clark Blaise. Markham, ON: Penguin Books, 1986.

Man and His World. Erin, ON: The Porcupine's Quill, 1992.

Ray Smith

≈

Ray Smith's first book, the story collection *Cape Breton is the Thought-Control Centre of Canada* (1969), has been reissued in a new edition by The Porcupine's Quill, twenty years after its original publication. Smith contributed a lengthy and fascinating introduction, "The Age of Innocence", to the new edition which explains how he came to write the stories and describes their theoretical underpinnings. Of the collection as a whole, Smith says he "was trying to tear down the edifice of 160 years of prose tradition and build a new one in its place."

Smith's originality and importance lie in the fact that from the very beginning of his career he turned away from the conventions of realism and started to create stories totally unlike those of early twentieth-century masters of the form. For possible models he turned to the imaginative constructs of later writers like Jorge Luis Borges and Vladimir Nabokov as well as to the work of such contemporary Americans as Kurt Vonnegut, Jr., Thomas Pynchon, John Barth, Donald Barthelme, and Richard Brautigan. His achievement has been undervalued in Canada because literary nationalists have preferred realistic stories which, often ploddingly, 'show Canadians who and where they are'. Smith parodies this kind of story in "Symbols in Agony: A Canadian Short Story" published in *Journal of Canadian Fiction* 1.2 (1972).

Not all the stories in *Cape Breton* work for me — "The Galoshes" seems insufficiently invented and "The Dwarf in his Valley Ate Codfish" is flatly incomprehensible — but "Peril", "Smoke", "Colours", and "A Cynical Tale" are remarkable and enduring inventions. Smith has a special fondness for "Smoke", the concluding story in the collection: "Here at last I achieved sufficient dislocation for fruitful insight while operating throughout with surfaces and progresses of blithe and beguiling charm", he notes modestly. I think "Peril", the story from *Cape Breton* which we have included here, is the best piece in the collection. Like all of Smith's stories, "Peril" is almost dandyish in the glitter of its artifice.

In his introduction to the new edition of *Cape Breton is the Thought-Control Centre of Canada,* Smith incorporated a commentary which he wrote in 1971 about his stories "A Cynical Tale" and "Peril". He tips his hat to the writer Joyce Cary, who created an entrancing portrait of an artist, Gulley Jimson, in the novel *The Horse's Mouth.* In "Peril", Smith notes, we see "Three incidents which each contain a hidden peril. Three youngish men, rather similar, rather different, take a walk. They meet a stranger or strangers and converse about one thing and another, then go on. In the graveyard walk, the peril is in the necromancer's sanity along with the slim chance that he may be able to conjure the dead. (His description of his introduction to the art is, incidentally, a loving parody of Gulley Jimson explaining his conversion to painting.) The peril in the park is in the question: Is either of them sane or is this Chesterton's ghost? The peril of the beach is that, if everything is as presented — hidden in the geography is the fact that there is only one landward way off the beach and the couple does not have a boat — then Purlieu has lunched with a god and goddess."

Searchers after theme will be disappointed in Smith's work for his stories exhibit an elegant playfulness and focus on nuances of language and dialect and on arcane historical and cultural reference. He said to me once, "Being a Canadian, of course I have no language." It's possible to look at all his fiction, including his novels *Lord Nelson Tavern* (1974) and *A Night at the Opera* (1992), as exercises in other languages, other dialects, as elaborate parody and pastiche. In essence, then, his work represents a love affair with language — and languages.

For our other selection, we chose "The Princess The Boeing and The Hot Pastrami Sandwich" from Smith's third book, the story collection *Century* (1986). If length had not been a consideration, we could have picked from the same book Smith's story "The Continental". However, "The Princess The Boeing and The Hot Pastrami Sandwich" is a moving and an elegantly performed story. Its sentimentality — with which Smith often flirts — is held firmly in check.

Some readers complain that Smith's stories shy away from strong emotion and are too contrived, too artificial. This is certainly a possible judgement but I would suggest that Smith's stories need to be compared not with stories in the realist tradition but with other stories in what Smith calls The Alternate Tradition, the tradition which stems from Laurence Sterne's late eighteenth-century novel *Tristram Shandy.*

Of his own early stories, Smith said in the 1971 commentary incorporated in the introduction to the new edition of *Cape Breton* that "They are part of a body of work called 'speculative fiction'. Generally ironic in tone. Aesthetic in approach; which means, I suppose, an indirect approach to many social and political problems of the world around us. This is in clear contrast to the other rising body of writing which includes things like revolutionary writings, the new journalism, documentary novels and the like, all of which try to grapple directly with the aforesaid social and political problems. I should emphasize, or repeat, that speculative fiction doesn't ignore the world, but approaches it somewhat indirectly."

≈

The best critical examination of Smith's work yet written is an essay by Lawrence Garber on *Cape Breton is the Thought-Control Centre of Canada* which not only examines the stories in detail but also describes The Alternate Tradition and Smith's place in it. This essay can be found in *The Montreal Story Tellers: Memoirs, Photographs, Critical Essays* (Montreal: Véhicule Press, 1985). For a number of viewpoints on Smith's *Lord Nelson Tavern*, see the articles by Lawrence Garber, Barbara Godard, Douglas Barbour, Arnold E. Davidson and Cathy N. Davidson, and Louis K. MacKendrick which appear, respectively, in *Books in Canada* June–July 1974, *Open Letter* 3rd ser. 2 (1975), *Open Letter* 3rd ser. 5 (1976), *Canadian Literature* 92 (1982), and *The Montreal Story Tellers* (1985). Ray Smith has written a number of important essays describing his approach to reading and writing. In addition to "The Age of Innocence", the introductory essay to the twentieth-anniversary edition of *Cape Breton is the Thought-Control Centre of Canada* (Erin, ON: The Porcupine's Quill, 1989), see "A Refusal To Mourn the Death, by Bullshit, of Literature in the Eighties" in *Carry On Bumping* (Toronto: ECW Press, 1988), "Three Propositions on the Art of Writing" in *Canadian Fiction Magazine* 66 (1989), and "Trust Me — Have I Ever Told You a Fiction Before?" in *How Stories Mean* (Erin, ON: The Porcupine's Quill, 1993).

≈ PERIL ≈

1.

The rain poured down. It poured down upon the bare trees and the dead grass, upon the bushes and the gravestones. It splashed on the top of the coffin, it drummed on the umbrellas the mourners held, it trickled down Passquick's neck and over his forehead and down the sides of his nose. The rain fell cold out of cold clouds through the grey air; a perfect day for a funeral.

That one, said Passquick to himself, is the widow. Over there is the daughter; those will be friends and relations; that one standing off with the beard and sad eyes, that one is the enemy.

The minister said certain cue words. The mechanism was tripped and the coffin sank slowly into the pit. The minister threw a clod of earth in. The widow shredded flowers. Some of the other men threw clods in. Passquick thought he might do the same, but someone was sure to find he had never known the deceased. They would think him morbid. So Passquick moved away.

Then he noticed, off behind a clump of bushes, the gravediggers. They stood under a tree as if for protection, smoking for the same reason, knowing neither did much good. When the widow goes they will sidle over and cover the coffin. Will they pun together? Perhaps he should circle back and meet them. No, that would not do....

At the lane where the cars were parked, Passquick turned and saw the mourners approaching. Near the end of the group was a red-faced man, middle-aged, chubby. That would be an uncle, a travelling salesman of, say, plumbing supplies. "I travel in bathtubs," he would be telling the man beside him. Yes, see, they were chuckling together.

Passquick wandered off through the cemetery, through the rain. Behind him doors slammed and the engines started up. A line of sight through the bushes and gravestones gave him a glimpse of the gravediggers hard at it; they had their work cut out for them.

It was some time later, as he rounded a clump of shrubs, that Passquick ran into the man in the black cape.

"Oh!" cried the man in the cape and leaped up and looked afraid.

Passquick mumbled an apology, bowed slightly (cemeteries bring out the formalities) and turned to go.

"Oh, I'm sorry," said the man. "I thought you were one of the sexton's men. You don't have to... It's ruined anyway...."

Passquick asked what was ruined.

"The spell, it's ruined now. I'll have to start over again tomorrow.... Oh, don't apologize; you couldn't help it. Really, it's my..."

The man in the cape was middle-aged, thin and bony, the blue veins in his cheeks showing as they do sooner or later on people who use blade razors, and a great beak of a nose. He was dressed all in black, and the black cape hanging to his ankles had a hood which was tied tight around his face and came to a dull point at the crown.

"I'm always frightening away mourners and visitors. That's why the sexton is always after me and that's why I came today, there aren't many people here on rainy days. Most people have the sense to come in out of the...oh, sorry, of course you..."

Passquick laughed.

"But so are you; so we're senseless together."

The man in the cape didn't take that one at all well. He coughed meaningfully and began secreting his paraphernalia in a black bag.

"What I meant was, if I say we're both senseless and I know I'm not, then you can't be either...it was meant ironically...."

"Straw for your irony!" said the man with unexpected vehemence. "I've suffered from the irony of the fair-weather friends, of the hail-fellow-well-mets. Cruel, that's what it is, cruel I say, the way you all go on. Why..."

"It wasn't meant to be unkind; it was meant in a friendly way...."

"Yes, I'm sure.... Well..."

They mumbled back and forth until the little man was mollified. Then Passquick asked timidly what the little man did...was... is...err....

"Why, I'm a necromancer, of course."

"A necromancer?"

"I conjure the dead."

"Oh yes, of course."

"I'm a journeyman, though I'm not working with a master these days. Journeymen usually work with one master or another."

"It must be hard for you without a master's experience and wisdom to direct and guide your work...."

"Well, yes...."

The necromancer had all his bones and joss sticks and such in the black bag. As they walked away he explained that you had to be careful, many master necromancers were just frauds.

"Out for a quick buck, shysters, *no faith*. Sometimes you wonder...."

As they strolled along he pointed out various graves he had worked: a good job on this one…this was the first…dropped a brick that night…. He explained that he no longer worked nights because he was afraid of the dark.

"It's silly, I know, but there are bats and owls twittering and hooting…awfully scary…and then you occasionally get graverobbers and bodysnatchers…."

"That right?"

"Oh yes, and they like to work completely in secret. Don't forget your average bodysnatcher is just a common thug; quite fierce when aroused…."

Passquick admitted that necromancy wasn't the simple trade he might have thought it.

"But it isn't a trade," cried the necromancer.

"Well, of course…"

"Trade! How gross! The very idea! Why I'd…" That petulance again.

"I mean, I meant it rather as a euphemism. As one minister would speak to another of their 'trade'; it's…"

"Then you're a necromancer too?"

There was no doubt about it; as dull-witted necromancers went, this one pretty well took the cake. After Passquick had explained it all and got things going again, the necromancer went on:

"No, you see, necromancy's an art. You must have heard it called 'the art of necromancy' or 'one of the black arts'? Yes, well, that's what it is, you see. Those poets and painters, they like to call themselves artists, but what do they create, eh, what, really?"

"Poems and paintings?"

"Yes, of course, any fool can see that. But what is a poem? Dead scratchings on dead paper. And a painting? Dead paint on a dead canvas. Dead: *no life*. But your necromancer, now, he's a different kettle of fish. Give him dead matter and he puts life into it, real guts, spirit…."

Now there was an argument for you; Passquick accepted it as soon as decently possible. The necromancer went on:

"And what does society do? Eh? I'll tell you what society does, it rejects its necromancers. We have to skulk about graveyards, mortuaries and hospitals like…like common thugs. We have no artistic freedom; we are scoffed at, humiliated, hunted down…you just don't realize what it means to be forced to live outside society… most of us are warm human beings who need love, who want to love in return, to be accepted…."

"But instead you have to live underground...."

Fortunately the necromancer missed it and went on to talk about the younger necromancers he had met.

"Perhaps I'm growing older, perhaps I'm getting a bit conservative, but I think their work is pretty hollow. They've got no style, no elegance, no...beauty in their work. Rebels, that's what they are, rebels. And" — he grasped Passquick's sleeve for emphasis — "they don't even know what they're rebelling against, you know what I mean? This new stuff, it's all shallow...so shallow...."

He shook his head to show the weight of his sorrow.

"Terrible," murmured Passquick. "Terrible...."

It was while the necromancer was explaining how he had gone as a clerk with a big brokerage house until one day...that he and Passquick came to the gate of the cemetery and found they had to separate. "...skinned my eyeballs," the necromancer was saying.

"Well," said Passquick, "it's been a pleasure meeting you."

"No, no, the pleasure was all mine. It's so rarely you meet someone who really appreciates the struggle and the sacrifice.... The world should make a place for necromancers...."

And so they trudged down their separate ways through the cold rain. Amid the cars and the people and the buildings, Passquick felt a great joy in his heart; he floated down the street. When he got home he had a bath and sipped hot lemonade as the steam rose about him. There's nothing like a graveyard on a rainy day, he said, to bring it out in people. But he couldn't think of a word for "it".

2.

Period watched the carousel from a distance. Between him and the carousel stretched a green lawn with tree shadows like continents on a map. The lawn was so flat that Period had the impression (as had also many before him) that the lawn could be rolled up on a pole and carried away. (The carpet movers, stout, slow, their cloth caps...) The month was May, a morning. The only people about were the women with their children and the pensioners on their benches.

Ump-tiddly music was piped out of the carousel. Period set off across the park toward a bench which was closer to the carousel but off to the right. A course tangential to a point on the radius....

But really, he thought, why am I thinking about tangents when I am in the midst of this wonderful scene? Oh joyful! Joyful! The mothers and children and pensioners, he saw as he moved slowly along, were arranged most artfully about. The scene was like a painting in its serenity; yet the figures were too small. It was like music in its harmony; but music was too demanding. Light hung everywhere; the shadows were blinding. The little toddlers toddled roly-poly short distances and their cries and laughs came lightly on the breeze, shattered, the sequence jumbled, random, like a volley of arrows shot by little painted soldiers.

So also the ump-tiddly music from the carousel.

The turf sprang underfoot, green and fresh and young. The melted-frost moisture would still be inches from the surface, nourishing, full of rich goodness, plant food, the cycle of water, interlocking with other cycles, cloud, animal and plant remains, compost, smelling words....

Period staggered. He was dizzy, a city man overwhelmed by nature. How can I know, I've never lived on a farm, never grown crops, my lungs dirty from soot and cigarettes, I can't smell the smells true, I can't.... Nature is also cruel...bad years, drought and flood, blight and locusts.... There's too much...I must...humility...

The park had at least the advantage of being well-treed. Of course, one saw the lamp posts, the gravelled walks, flowerbeds and such, but the trees hid the buildings and streets and deadened the noise enough for a city man to call it almost silence.

But really, such a wonderful scene! And anyway, so what if a park is man-made? Think of it, he thought, as a park, a first-hand park, not second-hand countryside. A farmer would never be able to enjoy a park as much as I can. The birds, for example, are not imported, transplanted country birds, but real live original city park birds.

And the carousel! Four hundred and twenty-three thousand bitter-sweet fantasies about Pierrot and Pierrette. That! for your Colin Clout and other such rude goatherds.

The bench Period had chosen sat beside a path and not far from a fountain (from which he took a drink of chlorinated water — well it wards off the bloody plague, doesn't it?) and gave a pleasant view of the carousel with a blooming lilac bush coyly obscuring it. Period sat down and stretched half a dozen limbs, yawned, groaned, hummed and whistled and finally sat still for at least twenty seconds. Then he enmeshed himself on purpose in the actions of smoking a cigarette — and the earth smells be damned — and decided to think about nothing. It was while he was failing at this that G. K. Chesterton came along and sat down beside him.

"I am G. K. Chesterton," announced G. K. Chesterton.

"Are you really? I'm..."

"Of course not. Chesterton has been dead for years."

"That's what I thought. I'm..."

"I'm his ghost."

Period couldn't recall what Chesterton had looked like around the face (a beard?), but he knew he had been fat and that he sat in the park a lot.

"Yes, I ghost wrote all his stories, poems and essays."

"Even Father Brown?"

"Especially Father Brown."

"I didn't know Chesterton wrote essays."

"Neither did I. I expect he did though, don't you. If a man wrote stories and poems, he surely must have written essays, don't you think?... Or do you?"

"It seems probable."

"Yes...that's what I thought."

"Um."

"And who did you almost say you were?"

"Uhh...Pierrot."

"That right? You meet the strangest people around a park in the morning. Pierrot, eh?"

"Yes, I live in that carousel over there."

"That's not a carousel. That's a bandstand. A carousel is a merry-go-round. That's a bandstand."

"I know, but it has the same shape as a carousel and "carousel" has a better sound to it."

"Quite right. Of course. Yes."

G. K. gazed off at the carousel and muttered to himself awhile. Then he undid the neck of his tweed cape and turned to look at Period. There was so much fat about his neck that G. K. had to turn his shoulders too; a very elaborate and dignified movement.

"You're a bit happy for a Pierrot," he said after a time. "I thought Pierrots were supposed to be sad unless there was a Pierrette about. In which case the Pierrot (a) was allowed to be bitter-sweet and (b) would not have the time of day for anyone else. How d'ye explain that?"

"Well, it's true that I've lost my Pierrette, but the fact is, I've been trying to lose her for months."

"That right?"

"Yeah." They nodded at each other for some time. "Not very bright, you know." They nodded some more. "In fact," added Period after a full thirty seconds of nodding, "I would say offhand that when the Pierrettes were lining up outside the brains department my Pierrette was pretty near the end of the line. When she got to the pot…"

"Nothing but bone with the marrow sucked out, eh?"

"In other words, yes, a bonehead."

"That was implied in my metaphor," said G. K. stuffily.

"It was also implied in mine; and mine was before yours."

G. K. Chesterton turned enthusiastically.

"Pierrot, I like you. You stand up for yourself. That's the way, meh boy, put 'em in their places; don't be afraid to swagger. Wave the fist. Shake the…err..."

"Stick?"

"The very word. The...very…word."

Period nodded and grinned and G. K. Chesterton nodded and grinned. Period stared across the park at the carousel and G. K. stared at him. This went on for a while.

"Tell me though," said G. K. at length, "tell me; your Pierrette, was she pretty at all? I mean…"

Period stared.

"Pretty? Pretty, you ask?"

"Uhh…yes, more or less, I guess I did.…"

Period extended his arms to indicate something which would require great imagination.

"My Pierrette was (is, I suppose you could say), was — is…well, even your massive brain cannot (I contend) project an image of a woman possessing half her beauty."

"No shit?"

"Oh yes…yes. I tell you, she had a bust…well, you wouldn't believe it. Numbers alone couldn't express…I mean, I have a certain facility with words, but I'm sorry, I'm afraid I couldn't begin to.…"

"Don't say you're sorry, meh boy. Sign of weakness."

Period shook his head.

"You're right, of course, Mr. Chesterton. I apologize too much."

"A terrible habit," said Chesterton with terrible sincerity. "A habit which you must…*smash!*"

G. K. illustrated this by bringing his fist down with crushing force upon his knee. "Ow!"

"But there's another side to it," said Period, brightening up. "You see, I never mean my apologies."

They went on about this for a while. Then Period went back to gazing at his carousel and G. K. Chesterton took from the folds of his cape a little volume of Hazlitt's essays bound in leather. He began to read one of the essays. Thus they sat for about half an hour.

"Must be off now," said Chesterton at last.

"Going anywhere in particular?"

"Of course not."

"Well, good day. It's been nice meeting you, Mr. Chesterton."

"An honour, I assure you. I might have been Cecil Rhodes and then we'd never have gotten on, I'm sure."

"And I might have been the young Goethe."

"Heaven forbid."

When Chesterton was some distance along the path he turned and called back: "But then meh boy, you aren't such great shakes as a Pierrot."

"No? Why is that? And how would you know anyway?"

"No. Because your feet are too big. And because I say so. Respect your elders and don't be so blasted impudent." He turned and went. The words "young pup" floated back from him inside a balloon as green as your eye.

"It's a carousel," said Period. "And damn the consequences!"

He walked the opposite way along the tangent and not long after that the office workers began to arrive with their sandwiches and their little cartons of milk. Somewhere among them wandered a Pierrette, boneheaded, disconsolate and stacked.

3.

Purlieu came out of the boulders at the south end of the beach and began walking north. The August sun hung high above his left shoulder and the water lapped and swished on his left. On his right, at the top of the beach, a cliff rose and the cliff was topped with twisted pines.

The day was a weekday so the beach was empty. Purlieu went along doing the various things people do while walking on beaches: he ran, he walked, he picked up driftwood, skipped stones, teased waves, etc. When he had gone a bit of a distance he took off his shoes because sand kept getting in them. Some time later he took off his shirt and undershirt so as to let the sun at his shoulders. Later still he rolled up his pantlegs so as to tease the waves without getting the cuffs wet. Purlieu was doing his usual mediocre job of relaxing.

When he had gone a mile, Purlieu was halfway along the beach. Here the cliff turned away and ran inland as far as the eye could see. Now, at the top of the beach, was a sand ridge as high as a man. This ridge marked a waterline of some sort (high water of storms, perhaps) and was topped with eel-grass. Behind the ridge (Purlieu scrambled up to see) lay a wasteland of sand dunes covered with waving eel-grass. The dunes rolled away for a mile or so until they stopped at the edge of a harbour. The cliff formed the southern edge of the dune waste and of the harbour. The highest of the dunes was in the middle. It rose about twenty feet and had the appearance of a castlekeep. Purlieu thought he would like to climb it; he considered this and kept considering it until at last he did not climb it, but slid back down and continued along the beach.

Purlieu had not gone much further when he became aware of the weight of clothing he was carrying. He had his shirt and undershirt, his shoes and socks in his hands. That was obviously pointless, he decided after five minutes' thought; I will put them down on a driftwood log. This he did; and went on toward the north.

The north end of the beach was marked by two man-made structures. Shiny, black, low in the ocean lay the line of a breakwater. The breakwater ran through the surf and on up the beach and in past the ridge at the top of the beach. It kept the beach from sliding into the harbour mouth which flowed just beyond it. Some distance in from the top of the beach (and astride the breakwater) stood a little lighthouse to mark the harbour. On the far side of the harbour mouth rose a high treeless hill with grass of the peculiar grey-green which grass takes on when it has been blasted by gales and kissed by the fog.

It was when Purlieu was halfway along the north half of the beach that he decided to tease the waves again. With his cuffs rolled up and no excess baggage in his arms he became quite daring. So he fell; a wave had teased back.

After much complex deliberation Purlieu came to a decision about his situation: he would take off his wet pants and wet underpants and go for a swim while they dried. The point was that if anyone came onto the beach, Purlieu would have time to get out of the water and into his clothes. Purlieu put the things on a driftwood log and raced into the water.

Well known are the felicitations of a swim in the ocean: Purlieu had a whale of a time.

The first thing Purlieu felt when he came out of the water was the immensity about him. The beach swung off to the south in a crescent, one of those sumptuous curves only nature has the patience to bother with. The cliff, which had seemed so high at the time, was a pencil line. Then the sheer waste of dunes, wide as an epoch, and the pretty lighthouse, the hill, the sky and the sea....

So, inadequately, the great landscape: Purlieu leaped for joy!

The second thing he felt when he came out of the water was that he was not alone. This for good reason, for he wasn't.

Not far from the pants and undershorts sat an old man in a wheelchair. Over the man's knees was draped a blanket; in his knobby right hand he held a cane and the cane was stuck in the sand. The old man wore a sleeveless grey pullover over a long-sleeved shirt. On his head he wore a tweed workman's cap. His lower lip jutted out, sunglasses covered his eyes and his head nodded forward and back slightly and continually. The old man did not seem to be looking at Purlieu; he seemed to be looking at the sea. But, of course, the sunglasses…

About ten feet to the old man's right and back a bit stood a table. The table was of wood and Purlieu could see that the legs would fold and the top come down and it would thus be portable and like a small suitcase. It had been constructed, Purlieu guessed, in *fin de siècle* England for those elaborate picnics one reads about. Behind the table, preparing an elaborate picnic lunch, stood a young girl, naked.

Of course Purlieu felt certain things upon seeing the naked girl. But she seemed quite unconcerned with her nakedness, with his nakedness, with everything but preparing the lunch. She smiled at Purlieu and gestured did he want any. Of course he gestured yes.

"Wet," said the old man to Purlieu without turning his head to look at him.

"Wet, sir?"

"Yes, sir, wet, sir."

"Yes, sir, I've been in the water."

"The ocean."

"The sea," said the girl and looked up and smiled.

"How was the water?"

"Fine…just right."

The old man's head kept nodding. He did not turn it at all to look at Purlieu and he said nothing else, so Purlieu, rather at a loss for words, turned and looked out to sea. He wished he had a towel to dry himself with. The sun had moved so that it was shining in almost straight across the water at the beach and Purlieu also wished he had sunglasses. He didn't have sunglasses and he didn't have a towel and he was still too wet to put his clothes on (which he probably wouldn't have done anyway because of the girl being naked), so he just stood looking out to sea.

"Did you see any eels, jellyfish, or other marine life whilst you were swimming?"

Purlieu, who hadn't, said he hadn't.

"Perhaps it's the wrong time of year," said the girl.

"Poppycock," said the old man.

Purlieu shifted his feet uncomfortably.

"I used to swim myself," said the old man in a tough voice, as if he were angry at remembering something he could no longer enjoy. "I won races at it. We did a different stroke in those days. I think it was different; I don't suppose we thought much about the type of stroke we did."

Purlieu went through the elaborate motions of sitting down on the log beside his clothes.

"Do you race, meh boy?"

"Err…no…no, I don't…race."

"Hunhh."

"Neither do I," added the girl.

And that was that for a while. The old man sat there nodding and staring at the sea; the girl took from little drawers in the picnic box sandwiches, radishes, hard-boiled eggs and the like and went on preparing the lunch; and Purlieu went on in his usual way, looking and thinking and sooner or later ending up in much the same place he had started.

At last the girl asked if they would like the lemonade now.

"Why yes, thank you," said Purlieu. "Lemonade would be lovely just now." The old man grunted a grunt which clearly articulated an affirmative answer. The girl brought them each a glass of lemonade with ice cubes tinkling.

"Thank you very much," said Purlieu.

The old man grunted ditto.

"The air," Purlieu ventured, "is very bright, isn't it?" It was a brave venture; he realized this. But it worked out well enough:

"Yes," replied the old man. "It is very clean air, clear in a way, yet very full. That is a paradox: clean (or empty) yet full."

"It's the light," said the girl.

"Yes, the light."

At this point the girl began to serve the picnic food. She carried a little tray each to the old man and to Purlieu. The old man's wheelchair had some ingenuity to hold the tray. The girl took a tray for herself and sat on a log on her side of the old man and as far forward as Purlieu so that the three formed an isosceles triangle, broad-based upon the sea.

They all ate with relish.

The little waves lapped and swished against the beach. Purlieu squinted at the blinding sun fragments splashed upon the water. Near to shore the water was a light blue (and light in weight, he remarked to himself) and darker blue farther out. But bright everywhere: the sea! the sea!

During the meal the old man gave a bit of a monologue starting with the smoked oysters the girl had served:

"The molluscs are fascinating creatures and little understood by man," he began. "I have made a particular study of the molluscs and have found out some very interesting things about them...."

Purlieu noticed when he next turned to the sea that the sun was now obscured somewhat by high thin clouds which had come out of the west, quite suddenly, as clouds will do upon the ocean. The water darkened and a bit of a breeze sprang up.

"The tide is on the flow," said the old man. "The wind is freshening for the evening."

"It looks like a storm this evening."

"There's gold upon the sea," said the girl.

"No. The storm won't begin till after midnight. But I grant you the sea *looks* like storm in an hour or so."

"Peace," whispered the girl. "Peace."

It was about this time that some combination of the senses suggested to Purlieu that if he looked back over the dunes he would see something that hadn't been there the last time he looked. So he looked.

Apart from a band of light along the ridge at the top of the beach where the light gathered, the tops of the highest dunes with the castlekeep off to the south rising high and stolid and the sky above, the dunes seemed much darker than they really were. At first Purlieu could see nothing that had not been there before; but very soon he saw the horseman.

"Why there's a horseman," he said.

"Where...oh, there!" said the girl.

"Going to light the light in the lighthouse," said the old man.

"Comes from over beyond," and he gestured vaguely to over beyond.

"You can't hear the hooves," said the girl.

"No you can't."

And you couldn't. The sound was perhaps lost bouncing about the dunes. Neither were the horse's hooves visible, for the crest at the top of the beach hid them.

Purlieu and the girl stood and watched the silent horseman ride by. One or twice he disappeared from view beyond high dunes. For a while he turned as he went to look at them and the light struck his face. After a time he disappeared beyond a dune far off toward the lighthouse and did not reappear on the other side.

Purlieu noticed suddenly that he was cold. But still the girl did not seem to want to get dressed; in fact, she seemed not to have any clothes about. So Purlieu stayed naked.

"Sailors," said the old man, "have a great feeling for lighthouses. Imagine what they feel. It is deep twilight and you are on watch on the starboard bridge wing. There is light in the wheel room but it is low enough to leave you with the dark. Overhead there has been a mackerel sky at sunset and now clouds are gathering in the southwest. It is chilly; the wind is stiffening; you shiver and you think about the rain that will be coming. You look down into the sea which is coursing by: the sea. Here I pause to let you imagine what the sailor feels about the sea."

The old man paused. Purlieu and the girl glanced at one another, then out to sea. Purlieu felt uncomfortable and felt sure the girl did too. He felt certain things about the sea, but as he was not on a ship he felt he probably did not feel as the sailor would have felt.

"And then you look up and there, off the starboard bow, a pinpoint for a moment in the darkness is the light of the lighthouse you've been steering for all week. And now comes a great surge. You remember the peculiar sensation of stepping onto land after a week...of the warmth of your favourite waterfront bar...of the contrast between the enclosed spaces of land where you can walk for miles and the open spaces of the sea where you live in cramped tension...of land and home and love...."

For a long time Purlieu and the girl stared at the sea and the sun darkened until at last it slid down into the thin band of clear sky just above the horizon leaving the clouds black and throwing a yellow path over the sea toward them, the yellow deepening to richest gold on the tops of the waves that lapped and swished against the shore.

"The sea...the sea..." whispered the girl.

"Yes, the sea," grunted the old man.

Then the same feeling came and Purlieu (and this time the girl) turned and saw the horseman riding back between the dunes. In the direct gold light of the sun, the horseman was gold now and he gleamed against the dark sky beyond. When he went briefly behind a dune his disappearances were sudden and surprising; and so his reappearances. And still the horse could not be heard, nor the horse's hooves be seen.

So the three waited; the old man in his wheelchair nodding his head at the sea and Purlieu and the girl, naked, watching the horseman ride by. When the horseman was near the cliff, he turned out of the dunes and continued down the beach to the boulders at the south end. Then the horseman was gone and Purlieu said he thought he would be getting on too.

"It's been a pleasure meeting you," he said.

"And you too, meh boy."

"You don't meet many people on the beach," said the girl.

After other pleasantries, Purlieu began to walk off south. Then he paused and asked if he could help with the picnic box.

"No, thank you," replied the girl. "It's very easy. It all fits together and folds up. There's a place for it on the wheelchair."

"Very cunning appurtenance," added the old man. "Made to give pleasure."

"Well…" and Purlieu walked on a way before turning to ask if perhaps they'd like him to wait and walk with them.

"No, that's all right. But thank you," said the girl.

"We go the other way, you see."

"Oh."

He left them like that, the old man staring at the sea and nodding from his wheelchair and the lovely naked girl packing the picnic box. As he walked along he picked up the clothes he had dropped and when he reached the far end of the beach he put them on. It was only then that he turned and looked back.

The light from the lighthouse swung about. It swept the dunes and the beach; it disappeared over the sea, flashed across the hill. But Purlieu could not see the old man and the girl. It did not occur to him until much later to wonder what had been the other way.

THE PRINCESS THE BOEING AND ≈ THE HOT PASTRAMI SANDWICH ≈

Ian knew he was perhaps sentimental, even silly, but he was moved by landscape and the air in it. I live in the world and this is the world, he thought, as he broke down out of the cloud into the clear air and floated to a stop in the powder snow just below the avalanche platform. This Austrian valley stretching off to the right and left was deep — he could not see the valley floor from here — and steep-walled, the sides dark with rock faces and precarious evergreens picked out by the snow: a dramatic and gloomy scene. But what moved him most was the mist clinging to the mountains across and below, the mist woven through the trees, seeming still. He thought that the people who, over the centuries, lived in these valleys and who spent the long winters looking up at such mist, who climbed up through the dark woods and into the mist, would naturally come to believe in strange beings dwelling here: werewolves, goblins, trolls. Yet I don't feel gloomy because of the mist; rather, I feel...peaceful, mildly exhilarated, privileged to see the mist, because...because it is below me. And he turned and skied down into the forest, the mist.

Stephanie did not share this interest in landscape: hers was a social bent. At midday, eating wurst and dark rye in the mid-mountain restaurant, she talked of the people around them.

"You'd think the British Government had imposed currency controls," she remarked. "This is the third day in a row that couple has been brown-bagging it."

She knew they were English because their outfits were at least fifteen years out of date and the woman had watery blue eyes. "And only an English woman could have that color hair; I think it's some sort of old-fashioned rinse they buy at Boots or Marks and Spencer where it is stocked not for profit but as a tradition."

Stephanie could go on for hours like this: acute, perhaps cutting, but rarely cruel and never nasty. She was entranced by the hand movements of the English woman, the precise, almost prissy way she would select a triangle of sandwich from its waxed paper wrapper and insert it between her teeth with her lips withdrawn slightly so as not to get soiled; how, nevertheless, after chewing each piece of sandwich, the English woman cleansed her lips with a paper napkin, making sure the few crumbs were carried back to the wax paper. Sometimes a crumb fell to the table; methodically she plucked it up and placed it with the others while lifting her watery blue eyes and sweeping her gaze across the windows.

"It's absolutely, quintessentially middle-class English. I bet they're chewing each mouthful a set number of times. And contrast her with either of the Stuttgart women over there..." They had parked next to the two German couples at the lift base and had noted the Stuttgart licence plates.

Ian looked and followed the argument: she was right, of course. But he was more interested in the window beside their table, the two walls of windows and the mid-mountain view of the valley and of the wisps of mist which suddenly evoked in his mind a passage played on the oboe, something, he thought, by Schubert.

"...while the hair on *his* hands is...inappropriate: it seems almost obscene..."

Stephanie was talking now about the English man's hands, neat, plump and offensive.

The oboe line took a turn which caused a wave of melancholy to surge through him; with difficulty Ian controlled the tears, turning away from the streamers of mist and examining the fall of Stephanie's hair, straight and brown with a henna tint; beautiful hair. And the glint and vivacity of her blue eyes, how lively; he loved the sparkle of her life, like the sun on the blue waters of Penobscot Bay last summer. They had been in Maine visiting Stephanie's Aunt Ethel and Uncle Edgar who had a house on the water in Searsport. Every day Ian stole an hour or two of reading on the lawn but read little, for the light on the water, the light glistening in the clear air above the bay, ravished him.

How clear-headed must people be who live with this light before them, with this air around them. Twenty or thirty miles away, the cumulus-humilis clouds floated white and benign over the ocean, clearly visible; overhead, on its weathered pole, the Stars and Stripes snapped in the breeze. Every spring Uncle Edgar retired the old flag and raised a new one, the red, white and blue strong and assertive, the new cloth heavy as sailcloth. Once New England had been powerful among the United States because of clear-headed, vigorous people; but it was powerful no longer. He must read some American history to find out what had happened: had the clarity failed, or had a different Texan or Californian clarity bested it, made it irrelevant?

But the clear air was most like Stephanie's mind and he loved her for the clarity, the vigor and the agility of her mind sparkling before him. She was the business manager of their union, paid the bills, reorganized the mortgage from time to time, booked their hotels and flights, wheedled window seats for Ian. From a Qantas window seat, while she slept beside him, Ian watched moonlight shining on towering clouds over the South Pacific, stared down into the depths between the clouds and pondered the immensity of the Pacific, wondered at the idea of lazy happiness the Pacific evoked in him, so different from the brutal menace of the North Atlantic. He remembered a line in a book, something like: "The *USS Bashful* chugged slowly between the islands of Apathy and Tedium with an occasional side-trip to Monotony." The names suggested the boredom of the sailors in an irrelevant backwater of World War II, but for Ian the important thing was the immensity of the ocean under the hot blue sky decorated with towering but harmless clouds. He thought of a television series about the war in which the Pacific had seemed so, and the goings-on across the Gilberts, Marshalls, Carolines and Marianas seemed, however gigantic in human terms, somehow small and insignificant in oceanic terms. Surely more important was that Gauguin and Stevenson had come here seeking peace rather than adventure. Was there something about these skies that granted a comforting humility? Not a humility which suggested the vanity of human desires, the futility of action, but the proper scale of man's state in the universe. And just as the North Atlantic could be peaceful in reality (as on Penobscot Bay) so the Pacific could be brutal; and somehow this was all connected with the *Enola Gay* in a sky of towering clouds; and the fireball and the towering cloud that sunny Sunday morning.

And presently Ian was able to watch the glow of dawn grow over the Tasman Sea, lighting the depths between the clouds, dispelling the moonlight mystery and revealing, at last, the blue waters, green growing luxuriance and red tiled roofs of Sydney under the sun.

Ian and Stephanie had one child, Elizabeth, who shared qualities from both of them. Her hair, blond in infancy like Ian's, darkened like Stephanie's and she had Stephanie's quick, chatty sanity. Yet she could lie quiet in her father's lap while he read to her about the princess with the golden cup and the silver cup and the tin cup and the wicked stepmother who tried to steal them.

"Am I a princess, Daddy?"

"You're my princess, Lisa."

"But maybe you're not my real father and Mummy's not my real mother and my real Mummy and Daddy are a king and queen in a faraway land and they're hiding me from the wicked stepmother. Couldn't that be, Daddy?"

"It *could* be, I suppose, but then someday a herald from the king and queen would come and take you back to be a princess and you wouldn't see Mummy and Daddy anymore."

"Oh yes I would, because I would be a princess and I would give commands and you and Mummy would get on a Boeing 747 and fly to the faraway land and visit me in the palace all 'spenses paid."

She was six years old when the herald came to her disguised as a drunk in a late model car; as far as is known, she did not become a princess in a faraway land; nor were commands given in regard to Boeing 747 flights; and her light faded from their lives ever so gradually, like the fading light of a northern summer sunset; and all their lives her memory glowed like the sun on the horizon.

Sunsets, though, were too easy, too obvious, like the beauty of Rio de Janeiro: Ian had decided that cityscapes were a form of landscape, and took a perverse pleasure in strolling about Edinburgh in the chill drizzles of January.

"By the Water of Leith, we sat down and wept," he murmured. Stephanie, with a more sensible attitude toward gestures, hustled him off to a talky pub on Rose Street and a pint of Leith Heavy for each of them, pun intended. She did not mention Elizabeth — what was the point? — but talked instead of the bright Celtic humor in the Scottish eyes, the languid curl of humor in the voices which caressed and piqued the words. "There is a generosity about the Scots which is most appealing. The Irish have sharper tongues, I think, they're more interested in pinching you into a reaction. It's easy to see why the Irish have a greater reputation for charm and laughter than the Scots, because they make jokes for an audience, they always have one eye on the listeners, looking for reaction, approval, a conspiracy of wit. The Scots, on the other hand, make a joke just for the friend and give it privately as a gift; theirs is a domestic friendship, warm and cosy. The Irish are performers on public display, and are therefore like actors, always a bit false and a bit disreputable. Now look at the group of three by the window, the girl with the green scarf and the two men. For some reason which I can't guess, although she is with the tall guy, she is trying to flatter the one in the blue sweater. Why she is doing it is not important — perhaps he's had a fight with his girlfriend; anyway, I don't mean she's trying to promote an affair with him — but she is definitely making up to him, but is doing it without making anyone, especially the tall one, uncomfortable. That touch on the sleeve, see, and the way she leans forward slightly when she laughs: those are inclusive gestures when we see that her other elbow is always near the tall one and her eyes go to the tall one quickly and without change *during* the laugh. She is flirting, of course, but openly and innocently, to promote the unity and warmth of friendship, not the division and... guile of an affair."

But while she went shopping along Princes Street, he walked in the drizzle through the squares and crescents of New Town, a section of cityscape remarkable, perhaps unique in the world, for its civilized unity and warmth, its lack of division and guile. In the late afternoon gloom, he stood in Charlotte Square swept by winds and sheets of rain and considered the admirable Adams' proportions about him. Here one could well imagine Hume's clarity, sanity and especially his good cheer (even though Hume had surely been dead before the square was built); here one could accept the notion of a semi-barbaric people bootstrapping themselves into a moral, intellectual and scientific force in the world; here one could look from the deepening darkness at the warmth of the windows of gold light and the people within, warm and chatty. He stood in Charlotte Square for some time gazing at the windows while the wet wind harried him; and so he mourned his daughter.

Stephanie had always been alert to his moods, but had thought it wise to leave him to "moon on his own." His suggestions about a trip to Greenland enraged her, for Elizabeth had been her daughter too. She took him instead to Cortina where, yes, he was entranced by the Dolomites changing color through the day, a shimmer of colors: rose, rose pink, pink, dark pink, red, red gold, gold, pale gold, ochre, buff, sand, pale orange, salmon, salmon pink, and so to pink again; a useless list of words, he said to Stephanie, because the colors of the mountains were too delicate, too evanescent for words.

Too evanescent indeed, said Stephanie to herself, and tried to interest him in people; though Cortina is an international resort, everyone becomes Italian to a degree, enamored of display, of pose, of excess, of opera.

"Italians are, of course, the most transparent and the most opaque of Europeans, for their motivations are all operatic: simple and childishly obvious. At the same time, however, we have to suspect that behind all the shouting and laughter and waving of hands there might be real human beings who think and feel just as we do; who, could they be cornered and somehow forced to stop acting, would admit to the ordinary muddle of ambiguous and obscure emotions. 'Yes, it is true, we Italians are basically human beings like the rest of you. Heavens, I suppose we're no different from the Swiss. Imagine! But I think perhaps our centuries of political instability — an accident of history more than an expression of character — have forced us in upon our families and the privacy of our own souls. When public life is always false, when it always means something other than what it pretends, then we adapt by becoming performers: actors and singers. Our deep affinity for opera is, as you have pointed out, Signora Stephanie, obvious enough to the point of cliché, but it is nonetheless real. But inside, yes, we Italians are just like everyone else, even the Swiss.' "

"He didn't say that to you."

"He did."

"I wish I'd been here to hear it. He certainly didn't look very reflective."

Ian had, on a pretext, snuck out to look at the mountains under the moonlight to see if they changed color (they did) and Stephanie had filled in the time talking at the bar with Emilio whom they had met when he and his rather plain young wife had been seated with them at dinner. Emilio, as Ian had suggested, was handsome, even beautiful, the classic tall, dark Italian with delicate yet masculine features, a voice like the caress of true love (heartbreakingly beautiful with an undertone of poignant sadness) and gestures which displayed, with pellucid clarity, a remarkable range of simple, obvious, direct emotions utterly devoid of obscurity or ambiguity. Or, as Stephanie had put it, "Pretty but boring."

Now she said: "Ah, but he *was* reflective."

"What do you mean, 'was'?"

"Well, as soon as he said Italians were like the Swiss — said it the second time, I mean, at the conclusion — his face began to change, rather as if he had choked on his drink, which he may well have done. His eyes began to bulge out, his cheeks took on a red flush and his lips began to tremble. He staggered to his feet and had to hold on to the bar with one hand while the other rested, palm outwards, on his brow. His eyes looked up to heaven in supplication, his eyelids fluttered, then gradually he seemed to regain control. When his legs were steady, he let go of the bar, held one hand to his heart, flourished the other in the air and began to sing some aria by, I think, Donizetti. But before he was two lines into it his body was wracked by spasms and he began another one, this time sad, so that he went down on one knee, clasped his hands before him in prayer and began to weep. Two lines into that one his body froze for a few seconds, then he leapt to his feet and gave a scornful 'Ha!' and began a derisive song of a young hero defying tyranny. He went through half a dozen of these changes, the variety remarkable, the clarity perfect, but they began to come faster, one beginning before the other was quite over. Gradually he was moving toward the balcony door over there. By this time, of course, he had the attention of the room. With the door open, he grabbed the red cape of the woman — you remember, the one in black who was sitting on the beige couch — wrapped himself in it, paused, then vaulted out, up to the railing, turned to sing snatches from ten arias, then leaped off."

"But it's thirty feet to the ground there!"

"Not to worry: he disappeared in a flash of light and a puff of smoke. Opera, you must remember, is an essentially harmless entertainment."

But while Ian enjoyed the felicity of her wit, he was thinking of the white wastes of Greenland and less than a year later, in storms of argument, they separated, he not to Greenland but to Arabia; she, after considering London and Paris, to New York. Of course, he was seeking some sort of cleansing purity under the sun, craving the simplicity of a stark land under blue sky; but he found government regulations about travel, he found jovial and sharklike businessmen in his hotel: a computer programmer, a construction engineer, a stock consultant, a hotel architect, a highway contractor, a perfume manufacturer, a pipeline surveyor, a salesman of executive jets; and he found money; and air conditioning. Thus, when Stephanie called and suggested he visit her in New York, he accepted with rather more enthusiasm than he let on.

They were both beaten by the frustration of their grief for Elizabeth and by their separation and wanted a way back, not so much to what had been, but to something like it, something they could live through together. Ian recognized that she was the wiser of the two and put himself in her hands. Indeed, by coming to New York he was admitting he could not live without her and she was right. He worried that perhaps she would talk to him endlessly about people and how people must get on and talk and deal with one another and he was prepared to endure this, but she did not do it. Instead, after a certain amount of hesitation — a day or two while he talked of the loathsome hotel life of Riyadh — she came to a decision and showed him:

a one-armed man who smiled,
an aged, reclusive actress buying oranges,

Berman the tailor who joked as he smoked and coughed his lungs out,

three child prostitutes joking with a cop,

an off-duty cop who bought them many drinks and, in the small hours, wept for all the lost people of his city,

a little old lady from Dubuque,

a struggling actress from Sandusky,

Berman the deli owner who claimed he made the best hot pastrami sandwich in New York ("by which, of course, I mean the woild"), and who certainly made a great one,

the body of a heroin addict, black, about fourteen,

three fat ladies squinching up their eyes with delight as they bit into pastries,

a famous writer-actor-director playing clarinet rather warily in a club,

two chess players in the park, both from one of the Baltic republics, one small, neat and quiet, the other large, dishevelled and talkative,

a man who danced with his wife, repeatedly, and obviously loved it,

a young woman on a street corner who seemed not to have enough hands for her briefcase, portfolio, shopping bag, suit jacket, wallet and lunchbag, and who smiled with all her teeth when a truck driver whistled at her, but did not whistle back,

a young woman studying viola at a famous music school who laughed brightly but nevertheless committed suicide a few weeks later,

a flight attendant who said, "Memphis? No, we don't have a base in Memphis, but I wish we did: no more Memphis layovers!"

an insurance executive who wrote fine poetry,

a well-known movie actor, a specialist in villains, who bowed graciously as he held open the door of a shop for a young woman he did not know and who did not recognize him,

a pickpocket getting caught and shrugging,

a man in a business suit standing in the middle of traffic with tears running down his cheeks,

a man whose clothes were held together with safety pins and who claimed the earth is crystalline and will shatter if we all get together and hum the right note,

a man who said, "The fish import business? What I don't know about the fish import business you could roll into a ball and stuff up a mosquito's nose and still have room for my wife's left bazoom and let me tell you, my wife is built, ya know what I mean?"

a roomful of people having sexual intercourse with strangers, two smashing transvestites who, for two and a half hours, explained Monteverdi's place in the history of Western music, nay, of Western civilization,

ten lords aleaping,

eleven pipers piping,

twelve drummers (one the leader of his own band) drumming,

and old Uncle Tom Cobbleigh and all,

and Ian had to admit to Stephanie's victory so that, although she loved him more than ever and conceded that their next trip should be down the storybook, castellated Rhine from Mainz to Cologne, he had to concede that it should be on a boat filled with people drinking and singing and dancing,

and so it was,

and they lived fairly happily for quite a while afterwards.

Commentary by
Ray Smith

≈

Ray Smith's fiction tantalizes and captivates us through a style that is by turns evanescent, frank, and animated. The following commentary is taken from an essay, "A Refusal To Mourn the Death, by Bullshit, of Literature in the Eighties", published in Carry On Bumping *(Toronto: ECW Press, 1988). Here Smith defends the power of artistic play, if it is engaged in honestly, to create a fanciful yet penetrating vision of the world.*

Perhaps this suggests a name for the cluster of my irritation: games. Heaven knows, I'm the last writer in Canada with the right to bitch about game playing in fiction. But efficiency is all: a writer plays games only to breach his own stupidity, to slough off the drag of cliché; to grope out some fresh handle on the intractable material; to tease, con, coax, shock the reader out of complacency. Less is usually best here, but some writers do it more and better than others. Borges came to his game and word play honestly: out of Cervantes, his own several languages, his voracious reading, his librarianship, his bad eyes: it's all the real stuff of the man's life, and his work breathes it. You can sense the same about Nabokov: he didn't just dream butterflies, he went out and caught them and killed them and mounted them with pins. *Pale Fire* is a deadly serious joke; or not all reality is kitchen sinks, beer halls, and the labour movement. But to the second-rate mind, game playing looks like an easy, fun way to baffle the opposition: Look Ma, No Hands! And because I'm at times a game playing writer, this sort of sham irks me most, is the most insulting to the art: Goddammit, this is my life and the agony and delight of the world around me that I'm trying to crunch onto the paper and if you want to play games, go frazzle your lobes in the video arcade.

SELECTED WORKS BY RAY SMITH

Cape Breton is the Thought Control Center of Canada. Toronto: House of Anansi, 1969. Rpt. as *Cape Breton is the Thought-Control Centre of Canada*. Sherbrooke Street 2. Introd. Ray Smith. Erin, ON: The Porcupine's Quill, 1989.

Lord Nelson Tavern: A Novel. Toronto: McClelland and Stewart, 1974. Rpt. as *Lord Nelson Tavern*. New Canadian Library 158. Toronto: McClelland and Stewart, [1981].

Century. Toronto: Stoddart Publishing, 1986.

A Night at the Opera. Erin, ON: The Porcupine's Quill, 1992.

Credits

≈

"An Autobiography", page 4.
Copyright © 1963, 1964, 1969, 1972, 1973 by Mavis Gallant. First published in *The New Yorker*. By permission of Macmillan Canada.

"Irina", page 23.
Copyright © 1973, 1974, 1975, 1976, 1977, 1978, 1979 by Mavis Gallant. First appeared in *The New Yorker*. By permission of Georges Borchart, Inc. Literary Agency, New York.

"A Small Piece of Blue", page 46.
From *One Way Ticket*, first published by Secker & Warburg (UK) and McClelland & Stewart. Copyright © 1961 and 1971 by Norman Levine. Reprinted by permission of the author.

"Something Happened Here", page 57.
From *Something Happened Here*, first published by Viking/Penguin 1991. Copyright © 1991 by Norman Levine. Reprinted by permission of the author.

"Getting to Williamstown", page 76.
Copyright, Hugh Hood. By permission of author.

"Going Out as a Ghost", page 86.
Copyright, Hugh Hood. By permission of author.

"Royal Beatings", page 104.
From *Who Do You Think You Are?* by Alice Munro. Reprinted by permission of Macmillan Canada.

"Meneseteung", page 124.
From *Friend of My Youth* by Alice Munro. Used by permission of the Canadian Publishers, McClelland & Stewart, Toronto.

"The Deacon's Tale", page 150.
From *The Happiness of Others* by Leon Rooke. Copyright © 1980, 1991 (renewed) by Leon Rooke. Reprinted by permission of The Porcupine's Quill and the author.

"The Birth Control King of the Upper Volta," page 164.
From *The Birth Control King of the Upper Volta* by Leon Rooke. Copyright © 1982 by Leon Rooke. Reprinted by permission of the author.

"The More Little Mummy in the World", page 196.
From *Ladies & Escorts* by Audrey Thomas. Published in Canada by Oberon Press, 1977. Included with permission of Audrey A. Thomas. Copyright © 1975 by Audrey A. Thomas.

"Local Customs", page 206.
From *Goodbye Harold, Good Luck* by Audrey Thomas. Copyright © 1986 by Audrey Thomas. Reprinted by permission of Penguin Books Canada Limited.

"Gentle as Flowers Make the Stones", page 229.
Copyright John Metcalf. By permission of the author.

"The Nipples of Venus", page 247.
Copyright John Metcalf. By permission of the author.

"Hurricane Hazel", page 274.
From *Bluebeard's Egg* by Margaret Atwood. Used by permission of the Canadian Publishers, McClelland & Stewart, Toronto.

"The Age of Lead", page 294.
From *Wilderness Tips* by Margaret Atwood. Used by permission of the Canadian Publishers, McClelland & Stewart, Toronto.

"A North American Education", page 314.
From *A North American Education* by Clark Blaise, 1973. Published by Doubleday Canada Ltd. By permission of Elaine Markson Literary Agency, Inc. and author.

"Meditations on Starch", page 328.
From *Man and His World* by Clark Blaise. Published by The Porcupine's Quill, 1992. By permission.

"Peril", page 344.
From *Cape Breton is the Thought-Control Centre of Canada* by Ray Smith. Published by The Porcupine's Quill, 1989. By permission.

"The Princess The Boeing and The Hot Pastrami Sandwich", page 358.
From *Century* by Ray Smith. Published by Stoddart Publishing, 1986. Reprinted by permission.